The Pauper of Park Lane

by

William Le Queux

The Pauper of Park Lane
by William Le Queux

Copyright © 2023

All Rights reserved.

ISBN: 978-93-59951-86-7

Published by

DOUBLE 9 BOOKS

2/13-B, Ansari Road
Daryaganj, New Delhi – 110002
info@double9books.com
www.double9books.com
Tel. 011-40042856

ABOUT THE AUTHOR

Anglo-French journalist and author William Tufnell Le Queux was born on July 2, 1864, and died on October 13, 1927. He was also a diplomat (honorary consul for San Marino), a traveler (in Europe, the Balkans, and North Africa), a fan of flying (he presided over the first British air meeting at Doncaster in 1909), and a wireless pioneer who played music on his own station long before radio was widely available. However, he often exaggerated his own skills and accomplishments. The Great War in England in 1897 (1894), a fantasy about an invasion by France and Russia, and The Invasion of 1910 (1906), a fantasy about an invasion by Germany, are his best-known works. Le Queux was born in the city. The man who raised him was English, and his father was French. He went to school in Europe and learned art in Paris from Ignazio (or Ignace) Spiridon. As a young man, he walked across Europe and then made a living by writing for French newspapers. He moved back to London in the late 1880s and managed the magazines Gossip and Piccadilly. In 1891, he became a parliamentary reporter for The Globe. He stopped working as a reporter in 1893 to focus on writing and traveling.

CONTENTS

Chapter One
Introduces a Man and a Mystery 9

Chapter Two
Concerns a Silent Secret.. 15

Chapter Three
Tells of a Woman's Love 21

Chapter Four
Which is Distinctly Mysterious 27

Chapter Five
What a Constable Saw 33

Chapter Six
Mentions a Curious Confession 38

Chapter Seven
Contains Several Revelations.. 44

Chapter Eight
The Pauper of Park Lane 50

Chapter Nine
In which Levi Gives Advice.. 55

Chapter Ten
Shows a Woman's Peril 61

Chapter Eleven
Samuel Statham Makes Confession 67

Chapter Twelve

In which a Woman's Honour is at Stake 73

Chapter Thirteen

Describes the Man from Nowhere 79

Chapter Fourteen

Reveals a Clever Conspiracy 84

Chapter Fifteen

More about Marion 91

Chapter Sixteen

On Dangerous Ground 97

Chapter Seventeen

In which a Scot Becomes Anxious 103

Chapter Eighteen

The Outsider 110

Chapter Nineteen

The Man who Loved 117

Chapter Twenty

Explains Jean Adam's Suggestion 123

Chapter Twenty One

Shows Mr Statham at Home 130

Chapter Twenty Two

Tells of the Three 137

Chapter Twenty Three

London Lovers 143

Chapter Twenty Four

Truth or Untruth 150

Chapter Twenty Five

Two Men and a Woman 156

Chapter Twenty Six

Which Puts a Serious Question 162

Chapter Twenty Seven

In the Web 168

Chapter Twenty Eight

Old Sam has a Visitor 174

Chapter Twenty Nine

In which Marion is Indiscreet.. 180

Chapter Thirty

The Spider's Parlour 186

Chapter Thirty One

"His Name!"... 192

Chapter Thirty Two

Man's Broken Promises 198

Chapter Thirty Three

Against the Rules... 204

Chapter Thirty Four

The Mysterious Mademoiselle 210

Chapter Thirty Five

In which there is another Mystery 216

Chapter Thirty Six

The Locked Door in Park Lane.. 223

Chapter Thirty Seven

Max Barclay is Inquisitive... 228

Chapter Thirty Eight

Friend or Foe? 233

Chapter Thirty Nine

The City of Unrest... 239

Chapter Forty

Gives a Clue 245

Chapter Forty One

The Gateway of the East.. 250

Chapter Forty Two

Advances a Theory 255

Chapter Forty Three

The Lost Beloved 260

Chapter Forty Four

Tells of a Determination 265

Chapter Forty Five

The Impending Blow 270

Chapter Forty Six

To Learn the Truth 276

Chapter Forty Seven

Contains More Mystery 281

Chapter Forty Eight

Not Counting the Cost 286

Chapter Forty Nine

What Lay behind the Door 291

Chapter Fifty

Face to Face 297

Chapter Fifty One

Describes Another Surprise 302

Chapter Fifty Two

Contains a Complete Revelation 308

Chapter One
Introduces a Man and a Mystery

"There's some mystery about that girl—I'm certain of it."

"What makes you suspect that?"

"Well, first, she's evidently a lady—the daughter of a man who has come down in the world most probably: and secondly—"

"Ah! You mean the secret lover—the man who was here yesterday and bought a twenty-guinea evening gown of her to send to his sister—eh?" exclaimed Mr Warner, "buyer" of the costume department of the great drapery house of Cunnington's, in Oxford Street, that huge store which, as everybody knows, competes with Whiteley's and Harrod's for the premier place of the middle-class trade in London.

"Yes," laughed Miss Thomas, the rather stout middle-aged woman who was head saleswoman of the department, as she stood in the small, glass-partitioned office of the buyer, a pleasant-faced man of forty-five who was an expert in ladies' costumes, and twice yearly bought his stock personally in Paris and in Berlin. "Yes. She's a really nice girl, but I can't quite make her out, although she's been here for over a year now."

"And the lover?" asked the buyer, with a glance across the long square room where autumn costumes of every description were displayed upon stands, or hanging by the hundred in long rows, while ranged round the walls were many expensive evening-dresses exhibited in glass cases. It was afternoon, and the place was full of customers, the assistants in their neat black holding ready-made skirts to their sides to try the effect, or conducting the prospective purchaser to the fitting-rooms. And yet they were not what Mr Warner termed "busy."

"The man, too, is a mystery, like Miss Rolfe. Nobody knows his name. He comes in sometimes, goes up to her, and asks to be served with a skirt or something, and has it sent to Mr Evans at some chambers in Dover Street. The name is, of course, not the right one," said the head assistant. "But Miss Rolfe knows it, of course?"

"Probably she does."

"And she meets him after business hours?"

"I think so. But she keeps herself very much to herself, and is always at home early."

Mr Warner glanced across at the tall, fair-haired, handsome girl, whose figure showed to such advantage in her black satin gown. At that moment she was displaying a cheap tweed skirt to two middle-aged women. Her face, as he caught its profile, was very soft and refined, the contour of her cheeks perfect, and the stray wisp of hair across the brow gave a softness to her countenance that was charming. Many a stage girl whose photograph was displayed in the shop-windows was not half so beautiful as the demure, hard-working shop-assistant, Marion Rolfe.

The air of mystery surrounding her, Mr Warner found interesting, and the love-romance now in progress he intended to watch. Towards his assistants, he was always lenient. Unlike some "buyers," he was never hard, and never bullied them. He believed that by treating them with kindliness and with the courtesy every man should show towards a woman he obtained the best of their business abilities, as no doubt he did. "Warner of the Costumes" was known through the whole "house" as one of the most considerate of men, and one of the most trusted of old Mr Cunnington's advisers. Those in his department were envied by all the other seven hundred odd assistants in the employment of the great firm.

While Mr Warner and Miss Thomas were speaking, a smart-looking, fair-haired, fair-moustached young man of about twenty-five, in frock coat and silk hat, entered, and walking up to the little office, greeted the buyer saying—

"Mr Warner, I'm sorry to worry you, but may I speak to my sister for a moment on some important family business? I won't keep her but a few moments, for I see she's busy."

"Why, certainly, Mr Rolfe," was the good-humoured reply, as Miss Thomas went away to serve a customer. "It's against our rules, as you know, but for my own part I can never see why a young lady need be debarred from speaking to her own brother."

"You're always very good, Mr Warner," responded the young man, "and I'd like to thank you for many little kindnesses you've shown to Marion."

"Oh, nothing, nothing, my dear Mr Rolfe," Warner said. "Your sister is an excellent business woman—one of the best I have, I may tell you. But look! She's disengaged now. Go over to her." And he watched the young man crossing the department.

Marion, surprised when her brother stood before her, immediately asked whether he had received Mr Warner's permission.

"Of course I have," was his quick reply in rather an excited manner, she thought. "I just ran up to tell you that I have to go abroad suddenly to-night, and to say good-bye. Old Sam Statham is sending me out to Servia. He only told me at one o'clock that I must go, and I've been buying some things necessary."

"To Servia!" exclaimed the girl, amazed that her brother, to whom she was devoted, was to go so far from her.

"Yes. We have some mining interests and some other things out there, and old Sam suddenly decided to send me out to make certain inquiries. I shall be away a month or two, I daresay, as I have to go to see a new mine in the course of preparation down on the banks of the Danube somewhere."

"But do take care of yourself, Charlie," urged the girl, looking up into her brother's face. "I've heard that it's an unsafe country."

"Unsafe! Why that's quite a fallacy. Servia is as safe as the Strand nowadays. Bland, our chief clerk, was out there a year, and he's been telling me how delightful the people are. Servia is entirely misjudged by us."

"Then you'll go to-night?"

"Yes, by the mail from Charing Cross," he replied. "But don't come and see me off. I hate people to do that. And when you see dear old Max, tell him that I'm sorry I had no time to go round before leaving. I've just telephoned, and his man says he won't be back till seven. That will be too late for me."

"Very well," replied his sister. "But—"

"But what?"

"Well, Charlie, I'm sorry you're going. I feel—well, I feel that you are going to a place where an accident might happen to you. I know nothing about Servia, and besides—"

"Well?"

"The mystery about old Sam Statham always haunts me. I don't somehow like that man."

"You only met him once, and he was very courteous to you. Besides, he is my master. Were it not for him I should most probably be going about London penniless."

"I know, I know," she said. "Have you been to his house in Park Lane lately?"

"I was there this morning, but only for five minutes. He gave me some instructions about a call I had to make in the city."

"I wish you could leave him and get some other work as secretary. I don't like him. He isn't what he pretends to be, I'm sure he isn't."

"He pretends to be nothing," laughed her brother. "Old Sam is a millionaire, and millionaires need no pretence. He could buy up this show twice over, and then leave a million for the death duties. You've taken a prejudice against him."

"A woman's prejudice—which often is not very far wrong."

"I know that you women see much further than we men do, but in this, Marion, you are quite wrong. Old Sam is eccentric and mean, but at heart he's not at all a bad old fellow."

"Well, I tell you frankly, I don't half like your going to Servia under his auspices."

Charlie Rolfe laughed aloud.

"My dear Marion, of what are you apprehensive?" he asked. "I go in a very responsible position, as his confidential secretary, to inquire into certain matters in his interests. If I carry out my mission successfully, I shall get a rise of salary."

"Granted. But you know what you're told me about the queer stories afloat regarding Samuel Statham and his house in Park Lane."

"I've never believed them, although they are, of course, curious. Yet you must remember that every man of great wealth has mysterious stories put about by his enemies. Every man and every woman has enemies. Who has not?"

"But you've admitted yourself that you've never been in more than one room in the mansion," she said, looking him straight in the face.

"That's true. But it doesn't prove anything, does it?" he asked. And Marion saw that he was nervous and agitated, quite unlike his usual self. Perhaps, however, it was on account of her apprehensions, she thought.

She had only seen Samuel Statham, the well-known millionaire, on one occasion. She had called at the offices in Old Broad Street one afternoon to see her brother, who was his confidential secretary, when the old fellow had entered, a short, round-shouldered, grey-bearded old man, rather shabbily-dressed, who, looking at her, bluntly asked who she was and what she wanted there.

One of his eccentricities was that he hated women, and Marion knew that.

In a faltering tone she replied that she was sister of his secretary, whereupon his manner instantly changed. He became the acme of politeness, asked her into his private room, offered her a glass of port—which, of course, she refused—and chatted to her most affably till her brother's return.

Why she had taken such a violent dislike to the old man she herself could not tell. Possibly it was his sudden change of manner, and that his pleasant suavity was feigned. And this, combined with the extraordinary rumours regarding his past, and the mystery of his great mansion in Park Lane, had caused her to view him with bitter prejudice.

Several customers were waiting to be served, and Marion saw Mr Warner's eye upon her.

"Well, Charlie," she said, "perhaps I'll get down to Charing Cross to see you off. You go to Paris first, I suppose?"

"Yes. I take the Orient Express from there, by way of Vienna and Budapest to Belgrade. But," he added, "don't come and see me off, there's a good girl."

"Why? I've been before, when you've gone to the Continent."

"Yes, I know," he answered impatiently; "but—well, it makes me feel as if I shan't come back. Don't come, will you?"

Marion smiled. His anxiety that she should not come struck her as distinctly curious.

He was not himself. Of that she was convinced. To her, ever since her father's death, he had been a good friend, and for a year prior to her engagement at Cunnington's he had divided his salary with her. No girl ever had a better brother than he had been, yet of late she had noticed a complete change in his manner. He was no longer frank with her, as he used to be, and he seemed often to hide from her facts which, with her woman's keen intelligence, she afterwards discovered.

"Miss Rolfe!" exclaimed Mr Warner, emerging from his office. "Disengaged?" And he pointed to a pair of somewhat obese ladies who were examining a costume displayed on a stand.

"Well, good-bye, Charlie," she said, shaking his hand. "I must go. We're very busy this afternoon. Perhaps I shall see you at Charing Cross. If not—then take care of yourself, dear. Good-bye."

And she turned and left him to attend to the two ladies, while he, with a nod across to Mr Warner, strode out of the shop.

"I hope to goodness Marion doesn't come," he muttered to himself. "Women are so infernally inquisitive. And if she does go to Charing Cross she's sure to suspect something!"

Chapter Two
Concerns a Silent Secret

That same afternoon, while Charlie Rolfe was bidding farewell to his sister Marion, Max Barclay was sitting in the cosy study of one of the smaller houses in Cromwell Road, smoking cigarettes with a thin-faced, grey-haired, grey-bearded man whose cast of features at once betrayed him to be a foreigner.

The well-furnished room was the typical den of a studious man, as its owner really was, for about it was an air of solid comfort, while upon the floor near where the elder man was lying back in his leather easy-chair were scattered some newspapers with headings in unfamiliar type—the Greek alphabet.

The air was thick with cigarette smoke, giving forth an aroma unusual to English nostrils—that pleasant aroma peculiar to Servian tobacco.

The younger man, dressed in well-fitting, dark grey flannels, his long legs sprawled out as he lay back in his chair taking his ease and gossiping with his friend, was, without doubt, a handsome fellow. Tall beyond the average run of men, with lithe, clean-cut limbs, smart and well-groomed, with closely-cropped dark hair, a pair of merry dark eyes, and a small dark moustache which had an upward trend, his air was distinctly military. Indeed, until a few months before he had held a commission, in a cavalry regiment, but had resigned on account of the death of his father and his consequent succession to the wide and unencumbered Barclay estates in Lincolnshire and up in the Highlands.

Though now possessor of a fine old English home and a seventeenth-century castle in Scotland, Max Barclay preferred to divide his time between his chambers in Dover Street and wandering about the Continent. There was time enough to "settle down," he always declared. Besides, both the houses were too big and too gloomy to suit his rather simple bachelor tastes. His Aunt Emily, an old lady of seventy, still continued to live at Water Newton Hall, not far from that quaint, old world and many-spired town, Stamford; but Kilmaronock Castle was unoccupied save for six weeks or so when he went up with friends for the shooting season.

Agents were frequently making tempting offers to him to let the place to certain wealthy Americans, but he refused all inducements. The fine old place between Crieff and Perth had never been let during his father's lifetime, and he did not intend that any stranger, except his own friends, should enjoy the splendid shooting now.

"My dear Petrovitch," he was saying between whiffs of his cigarette, "It is indeed reassuring what you tell me regarding the settled state of the country. You have surely had sufficient internal troubles of late."

"Ah, yes!" sighed the elder man, a deep, thoughtful expression upon his pleasant, if somewhat sallow, countenance. "Servia has passed through her great crisis—the crisis through which every young nation must pass sooner or later; and now, heaven be thanked, a brighter day has dawned for us. Under our new *régime* prosperity is assured. But"—and pausing, he looked Max straight in the face, and in a changed voice, a voice of increased earnestness and confidence, he added with only a slight accent, for he spoke English very well—"I did not ask you here to discuss politics. We Servians are, I fear, sad gossips upon our own affairs. I wanted to speak to you upon a subject of greatest importance to myself personally, and of someone very dear to me. Now we have been friends, my dear Max, you and I, through some years, and I feel—nay, I know, that you will regard what I say in entire confidence."

"Most certainly," was the young Englishman's reply, though somewhat surprised at his friend's sudden change of manner.

It was true that he had known Dr Michael Petrovitch for quite a number of years.

Long ago, when he had first visited Belgrade, the Servian capital, the man before him, well-known throughout the Balkans as a patriot, was occupying the position of Minister of Finance under King Milan. Both his Excellency and his wife had been extremely kind to him, had introduced him to the smart social set, had obtained for him the *entrée* to the Palace festivities, and had presented him to Queen Nathalie. Thus a firm friendship had been established between the two men.

But affairs in Servia had considerably changed since then. Madame Petrovitch, a charming English lady, had died, and his Excellency, after becoming Minister of Commerce and subsequently Foreign Minister in several succeeding Cabinets, had gone abroad to represent his country at foreign Courts, first St. Petersburg, then Berlin, and then Constantinople, finally returning and coming to live in England.

Even now he was not more than fifty, and it had long ago been whispered that his Majesty was constantly urging him to return and accept the portfolio of Finance or of Commerce. But he steadily declined. As a statesman, his abilities had long ago been recognised by Europe, and none knew his value or appreciated him more than his own sovereign; yet for private reasons he preferred to live quietly in the Cromwell Road to returning to all the worries of State and those eternal bickerings in the Servian Skuptchina.

He was a man of even temper, of charming manner, and of scrupulous honesty. Had he been dishonest in his dealings he might have amassed a great fortune while occupying those posts in the various ministries. But he had preferred to remain as he was, upright, even though comparatively poor.

"Well?" asked Max, after a long silence. "I am waiting."

"It is a matter to which I refer not without some hesitation," declared his friend. "I want to speak to you about Maud."

"About Maud. Well?"

"I am worried about the child—a good deal."

"For what reason?" asked Max, considerably surprised.

Maud was Petrovitch's only daughter, a very beautiful girl, now nineteen years of age, who had been brought up in England and to whom he was entirely devoted.

"Well, she has fallen in love."

"All girls do sooner or later," replied Max, philosophically.

"But she's too young yet—far too young. Twenty-five is quite early enough for a girl to marry."

"And who's the man?"

"Your friend—Charlie Rolfe."

"Charlie!" he exclaimed, in great surprise. "And he's in love with Maud. Are you quite sure of this?"

"Quite. She meets him in secret, and though Rolfe is your friend, Max, I tell you I don't like it," he declared.

"I am not surprised. Secret affections never meet with a parent's approbation. If Charlie is in love with her, and the affection is mutual, why doesn't he come straight and tell you?"

"Exactly my argument," declared Petrovitch, lighting a fresh cigarette with the end of one half-consumed. "But tell me, Rolfe is an intimate friend of yours, is he not?"

"Very," was Max's reply, though he did not inform his friend of his love for Marion.

"What is his exact position?"

"As far as I know, he is private secretary to old Samuel Statham, the great financier. His position is quite a good one—as far as confidential secretaryships go."

"Statham! I've heard of him. There's some extraordinary story about his house in Park Lane, isn't there? Nobody has ever been inside, or something."

"There is, I believe, some cock and bull story," responded Max. "The old fellow is a bit eccentric, and doesn't care for people prying all over his house. He lives alone, and has no friends. Do you know, one can be very lonely in London. It is a perfect Sahara to those who are friendless."

"Yes," said Petrovitch, huskily. "I know it by experience myself. When I was a youth I lived here. I was a foreign clerk in an insurance office in the city, and I lived perfectly alone—among all these millions. I remember it all as though it were only yesterday. I was indeed glad to get back to Servia."

"But why are you worried about Maud, old fellow?" Max asked. "Don't you like Rolfe—or what?"

"I like him very much, indeed I took a great fancy to the young fellow when you introduced him to me last year at Aix-les-Bains. From the very first I noticed that he was attracted towards the child, and I did not object because I thought a little flirtation would amuse her. These secret meetings, however, I don't like. It is not right. She's met him in St. James's Park, and at other places of late, and they have gone for long walks together without my knowledge or sanction."

Max thought for a moment.

"Does she know that you are aware of the meetings?"

"No."

"Well, I must admit that I had no idea matters had gone so far as they evidently have," he said. "I, of course, knew that he has greatly admired Maud from the very first. He was, in fact, always speaking of her in admiration, yet I believed that he did not consider his position to be sufficiently established in warranting him to declare his love to her. Shall I throw out a gentle hint to him that the secret meetings would be best discontinued?"

"If he were to discontinue his visits here altogether it would, I think, be best," said Petrovitch in a hard voice, quite unusual to him.

Max was surprised at this. Had any unpleasantness occurred between the two men, which his friend was concealing, knowing that Rolfe was his most intimate chum?

"Does he come often?"

"He calls about once a week—upon me, ostensibly, but really in excuse to see the child."

"And now—let us speak frankly, old fellow," Max said, bending slightly towards the man seated opposite him. "Do you object to Rolfe paying his attentions to your daughter?"

"Yes—I do."

"Then I very much regret that I ever introduced him. We were together at Aix-les-Bains for three weeks last summer, and, as you know, we met. You were my old friend, and I could not help introducing him. I regret it now, and can only hope you will forgive me such an indiscretion."

"It was not indiscreet at all—only unfortunate," he answered, almost snappishly.

"But tell me straight out—what do you wish me to do?" Max urged. "Recollect that if I can serve you in any way you have only to command me."

"Even at the expense of your friend's happiness?" asked Petrovitch, his sharp eyes fixed upon the young man.

"If he really loves her, the circumstances of the cue are altered," was the diplomatic answer.

"And if he does not? If it is, as I suspect, a mere flirtation—what then?"

"Then I think you should leave the matter to me, to act with my discretion," young Barclay replied. He recollected that Charlie was Marion's brother, and he saw himself already in a somewhat difficult position. "My own idea is," he went on, "that it is something more than a mere flirtation, and that the reason of the secret meetings is because he fears to ask your consent to be allowed to pay court to your daughter."

"What makes you think so?"

"From some words that his sister Marion let drop the other day."

"Ah! Marion is a sweet and charming girl," the elder man declared. "What a pity she should be compelled to drudge in a shop!"

"Yes," replied Max, quickly. "It is a thousand pities. She's far too refined and good for that life."

"A matter of unfortunate necessity, I suppose."

Necessity! Max Barclay bit his lips when he recollected how very easily she might leave that shop-life if she would only accept money from him. But how could she? How could he offer it to her without insult?

No. Until she consented to be his wife she must still remain there, at the beck and call of every irritating tradesman's wife who cared to enter the department to purchase a ready-made costume or a skirt "with material for bodice."

"I'm sorry for Marion," Dr Petrovitch went on. "She frequently comes here of an evening, and often on Sundays to keep Maud company. They get on most excellently together."

"Yes; she is devoted to Maud. She has told me so."

"I believe she is," Petrovitch said. "And yet it is unfortunate, for friendliness with Marion must also mean continued friendliness with her brother."

"Ah! I see now that you do not like him," Max said, openly, for he could not now fail to see from his friend's expression that something had occurred. What it was he was utterly unable to make out.

"No, I don't," was the ex-Minister's plain, determined answer. "And to tell you the truth, I have other views regarding Maud's future. So just tell the young man whatever you think proper. Only request him neither to call here, nor to attempt to see the child again!"

Chapter Three
Tells of a Woman's Love

In the dull hazy London sunset Fopstone Road, which leads from Earl's Court Road into Nevern Square, was quite deserted.

There is a silence and monotony in the eminently respectable thoroughfares in that particular district that, to their residents, is often very depressing. Traffic there is none save a stray hansom or a tradesman's cart at long intervals, while street organs and even the muffin men avoid them because, unlike the poorer districts, they find no stray coppers and no customers.

On the same evening as the events recorded in the previous chapters, about six o'clock, just as the red dusky after-glow was deepening into twilight, Charlie Rolfe emerged from Earl's Court Station, walked along to the corner of Fopstone Road, and, halting, looked eagerly down it.

But there was not a soul. Indeed there was no sound beyond that of a distant cab whistle somewhere in Nevern Square.

For about five minutes he waited, glancing impatiently at his watch, and then, turning upon his heel, strolled along in the direction of the Square.

A few moments later, however, there hurried up behind him a sweet-faced, smartly-dressed girl who, as he turned to meet her, laughed merrily, saying:

"I do hope, Charlie, I haven't kept you waiting, but I've had such trouble to get out. Dad asked me to write some private letters in English for him; I really believe he suspects something. We meet too often."

"No, darling," answered Rolfe, raising his hat and taking her small gloved hand. "We don't meet frequently enough for me. And I think that your father is entirely unsuspicious. I was with him last night, and he did not strike me as possessing any knowledge of these secret meetings of ours."

"Yes, but you know how dangerous it is," replied the pretty girl, glancing round. "Somebody might pass, recognise me, and tell dad."

"And what then, dearest?" he laughed. "Why your fears are utterly groundless."

"I know, but—"

"But what?"

"Well, dad would be annoyed—that's all—annoyed with both of us."

"He must already have seen, darling, that I love you. He isn't blind," said Charlie Rolfe, moving slowly along at her side.

Hers was, indeed, a face that would attract attention anywhere, oval, delicately moulded, slightly flushed by the momentary excitement of meeting her lover. Her hair was well-dressed, her narrow-waisted figure still girlish; her dress, a pale biscuit-coloured cloth, which, in its refined simplicity, suited well the graceful contour of the slender form, and contrasted admirably with the soft white skin; the dark hair, a stray coquettish little wisp of which fell across her brow beneath her neat black hat, and the dark brown eyes, so large, luminous, and expressive.

Her gaze met his. Every sensitive feature, every quiet graceful movement told plainly of her culture and refinement, while on her face there rested an indescribable charm, a look of shy, sweet humility, of fond and all-consuming love for the man beside her.

As she lifted her eyes at the words of affection he was whispering into her ear as they went along the quiet, deserted street, she perceived how tall and athletic he was, and noticed, woman-like, the masculine perfection of his dress, alike removed from slovenliness and foppery.

"No," she said at last, her eyes gazing in abstraction in front of her. "I don't suppose dad is in any way blind. He generally is too wide-awake. I have to make all sorts of excuses to get out—dressmakers, painting-lessons, buying evening gloves, a broken watch—and all sorts of thing like that. The fact is," she declared, laughing sweetly and glancing again at him, "I have almost exhausted all the subterfuges."

"Ah, dearest, a woman can always find some excuse," he remarked, joining in her laughter.

"Yes, but that's all very well; you haven't a father," she protested, "so you don't know."

She had only left school at Brighton two years before, therefore her clandestine meetings with Charlie Rolfe were adventures which she dearly loved. And, moreover, they both of them were devoted to each other. Charlie absolutely adored her. Hitherto women had never attracted him, but from the day of their introduction on the gravelled walk in front of the Villa des Fleurs at Aix, his whole life had changed. He was hers—hers utterly and entirely.

For three months he had existed in constant uncertainty, until one warm evening at Scarborough—where she and her father were staying at the Grand—while they were alone together in the sloping garden of the Spa he summoned courage to tell her the secret of his heart, and to his overwhelming joy found that his passion was reciprocated. Thus had they become lovers.

As Max rightly guessed, he had feared for the present to tell Dr Petrovitch the truth lest he should object and a parting be the result. His position was not what he wished it to be. As secretary to the eccentric old financier, his salary was an adequate one, but not sufficient to provide Maud with a home such as her own. He therefore intended in a little while to tell old Statham the truth, and to ask for more. And until he had done so, he hesitated to demand of the Doctor his daughter's hand.

Together they strolled slowly on, chatting as lovers will. At the bottom of Fopstone Road they continued round the crescent of Philbeach Gardens, along Warwick Road, and crossing Old Brompton Road, entered that maze of quiet, eminently respectable streets in the neighbourhood of Redcliffe Square, strolling slowly on in the falling gloom.

"Do you know, darling," he exclaimed at last, "I wanted to see you very particularly this evening, because I am leaving London to-night for Servia."

"For Servia!" she cried, halting and fixing her great eyes upon his in quick surprise.

"Yes."

Her countenance fell.

"Then you—you are leaving me?"

"It is imperative, my darling," he said, in a low, tender voice, taking her hand in his. He wished to kiss her sweet lips, but there in the open street such action was impossible. Courtship in our grimy, matter-of-fact London has many drawbacks, even though every house contains its life-romance and every street holds its man or woman with a broken heart.

"But you never told me," she complained. "You've left it until the last minute. Do you start from Charing Cross to-night?"

"Yes. I would leave to-morrow at nine, and catch the Orient express from Calais for Belgrade, but I have business to do in Paris to-morrow."

"Ah! Belgrade!" sighed the girl. "I wonder if I shall ever see it again? Long ago I used to be so fond of it, and we had so very many good friends.

Dear old dad is so popular. Why, when we drove out the people in their brown homespun clothes used to run after the carriage and cheer 'Petrovitch the Patriot,' as they call dad."

"Of course you will return soon," Charlie said. "No doubt your father will be induced to enter the new Pashitch Cabinet."

The girl shook her head dubiously.

"I know the King has several times asked him to return to Servia, but for some mysterious reason he has always declined."

"But he is the most popular man in the country, and he cannot remain away much longer. It is his duty to return and assist in the Government."

"Yes. But my mother died in Belgrade, you know, and I think that may be the reason he does not care to return," replied the girl. "Why are you going there?" she asked.

"On a mission for Statham—regarding a mining concession," he answered. "You know we have a lot of interests out there. Perhaps I shall be away only a week or two—perhaps six months."

"Six months!" she cried in a blank voice. "It is such a long, long time to look forward to."

"I have no desire to leave you, my own darling," he declared, looking straight into her beautiful face. "But the mission is confidential, and for that reason I have received orders to go."

"Your train leaves at nine," she said, "and it is already nearly seven—only two hours! And those two remaining hours I cannot spend with you, for I must be in to dinner at seven. I must leave you in a moment," she added, and the faint flush in her face died away.

Her voice ceased. He looked down musing, without replying. He was impressed by her utter loneliness—impressed, too, without knowing it by the time and place. The twilight of the short evening was gathering fast. A cold damp feeling was mingled with the silence of the dull, drab London street. It struck him that it felt like a grave.

A slight nervous trembling came over his well-beloved, and a weary little sigh escaped her lips.

That sigh of hers recalled him to a sense of her distress at his departure, and the face that met her troubled eyes was, in an instant, as full as ever of resolute hopefulness.

"What matters, my own, if I am away?" he asked with a smile. "We love each other, and that is all-sufficient."

All the pity of his strong, tender nature went forth to the lovely girl whom he loved with such strong passionate devotion.

"What matter, indeed!" she cried, hoarsely, tears springing to her eyes. "Is it no matter that I see you, Charlie? Ah! you do not know how I count the hours when we shall meet again—how—how—" And unable to further restrain her emotion, she burst into tears.

He was silent. What, indeed, could he say?

Reflections, considerations, possibilities crowded in upon his mind, already disturbed and perplexed. The sweetness of the hours passed in her society had increased insensibly ever since that well-remembered afternoon in Aix; the tones of her voice, the notes of those melodious old Servian songs she so often sang, her slightest action held a charm for him such as his earnest nature had never experienced before.

And they must part.

Within himself he doubted whether they would ever meet again. He had secret fears—fears of something that was in progress—something that might entirely change his life—something he held secret from her.

But he put the thought away. It was a horrible reflection—a qualm of conscience. What would she think of him if she actually knew the truth?

He bit his lip, and in resolution again took her white-gloved hand.

"No, darling," he said, softly, in an earnest effort to cheer her. "I will return very soon. Be brave, and remember that my every thought is of you always—of you, my love."

"I know," she sobbed. "I know, Charlie, but—but I cannot really help it. Forgive me."

"Forgive you! Of course I do, sweetheart; only do not cry, or they will certainly suspect something when you sit down to dinner."

His argument decided her, and she slowly dried her tears, saying:

"I only wish I could go to Charing Cross to see you off. But an hour ago I telephoned to your sister Marion to come and dine with us, and go with me to a concert at Queen's hall."

"And she accepted?" he asked, quickly, almost breathlessly.

Rolfe gave a sigh of relief. At any rate neither his sister nor his well-beloved would be at Charing Cross at nine that evening.

"I must try and bring her to the station, if possible. Does she know you are going?" asked the girl.

"Oh, yes. But I particularly asked her not to see me off."

"In order that I might come alone. Oh! how very good of you, Charlie!"

"No. Forgive me for saying so, but like a good many men who travel a lot I never like being seen off—not even by you, yourself, my darling!"

"Very well," she sighed, looking up into his serious eyes. "I must, I suppose, act as you wish. May God protect you, my dearest, and bring you back again in safety to me." Then as he whispered into her ear words of courage and ardent affection, with linked arms they re-traced their steps back to Earl's Court Road, where, with lingering reluctance, he took affectionate leave of her.

Having watched her turn the corner, he went slowly back towards Earl's Court Station, and as he did so, beneath his breath he murmured "Ah! if she knew—if she knew! But she must never know—she shall never know—never as long as I have breath. I love her—love her better than my life—and she is mine. Yet—yet how can I, after—after—"

And he sighed deeply without concluding the sentence, while his face went ashen pale at the thought which again crossed his mind—a thought, secret and terrible.

Chapter Four
Which is Distinctly Mysterious

Max Barclay, on leaving Dr Petrovitch, had taken a cab straight to Charlie's chambers in Jermyn Street, arriving there shortly before six. Green, his man, had told him, however, that his master had returned soon after luncheon, ordered two big bags to be packed, and had left with them upon a hansom, merely saying that he should be absent a week, or perhaps two, and that no letters need be forwarded.

Max was not surprised at this sudden departure, for old Statham had a habit of sending his confidential secretary hither and thither at almost a moment's notice. The old fellow's financial interests were enormous, and widely dispersed. Some of them were in Servia and Bulgaria, where he held concessions of great value.

He had had a finger in most of the financial undertakings in the Near East during the past fifteen years or so. Out of the Oriental Railway extension from Salonica to the Servian frontier alone he had, it was said, made a huge fortune, for he was the original concessionaire. For some years he had lived in the Balkans, looking after his interests in person, but nowadays he entrusted it all to his agents with occasional visits by this confidential secretary.

Therefore Max suspected that Charlie had left for the East, more especially that at the hour he had left Jermyn Street he could have caught the afternoon Continental service from Charing Cross *viâ* Boulogne.

So he went on to his own rooms, changed, dined at the Automobile Club, his mind being full of what the Doctor had told him concerning Charlie and Maud. He had, of course, suspected it all along. Marion knew the truth, but, loyal to her brother, she had said no word. Yet when he had seen Rolfe with the ex-statesman's pretty daughter, he had long ago guessed that the pair were more than mere friends.

That the Doctor disapproved of the affair was somewhat disconcerting, more especially as he had openly declared that he had other ideas of Maud's future. What were they? Was her father hoping that she would marry some young Servian—a man of his own race?

He sat in the club over a cigar till nearly nine o'clock, wondering how he could assist the man who was not only his dearest friend but brother of the girl to whom he was so entirely devoted and whom he intended to make his wife.

He sighed with regret when he thought of her undergoing that shop drudgery to which she had never been accustomed. The early rising, the eternal drive of business, the calm, smiling exterior towards those pettish, snapping women customers, and those hasty scrambles for meals. He had seen her engaged in her business, and he had met her after shop hours, pale, worn, and fagged out.

And yet he—the man who was to be her husband—lived in that ease and idleness which an income of twelve thousand a year secured.

Had Petrovitch not told him that Marion was dining at Cromwell Road and going to a concert with Maud afterwards, he would have wired to her to meet him. But he knew how devoted the two girls were to each other, notwithstanding the difference of their stations, and how Maud welcomed Marion's company at concerts or theatres to which her father so seldom cared to go.

Suddenly it occurred to him that if he returned to the Doctor's he would meet Marion there later on, when she came back from Queen's Hall, and be able to drive her home to that dull street at the back of Oxford Street where the assistants of Cunnington's, Limited, "lived in."

This reflection aroused him, and, glancing at the smoking-room clock, he saw it wanted a quarter to ten.

Two other men, friends of his, were sitting near, discussing motoring matters, and their eternal chatter upon cylinders, tyres, radiators, and electric horns bored him. Therefore he rose, put on his coat, and, hailing a cab, told the man to drive to Victoria, where he took the underground railway to Gloucester Road Station.

From there to the house of the ex-Minister was only a very short walk. The night was mild, bright, and starlight, for the haze of sundown which had threatened rain had been succeeded by a brilliant evening. Cromwell Road is always deserted at that hour before the cabs and carriages begin to return from restaurants and theatres, and as he strolled along, knowing that he was always welcome at the Doctor's house to chat and smoke, his was the only footfall to be heard in the long open thoroughfare.

Ascending the steps beneath the wide portico, he pressed the visitors' bell, but though he waited several minutes, there was no response. Again and again he rang, but the bell was apparently out of order, so he gave a sounding rat-tat with the knocker.

Then he listened intently; but to his surprise no one stirred.

Over the door was a bright light, as usual, revealing the number in great white numerals, and through the chinks of the Venetian blinds of the dining-room he could see that the electric lamps were on.

Again and again he rang and knocked. It was surely curious, he thought, that all the servants should be out, even though the Doctor might be absent. The failure to arouse anybody caused him both surprise and apprehension. Though the electric bell might be out of order, yet his loud knock must be heard even up to the garrets. London servants are often neglectful in the absence of their masters, and more especially if there is no mistress, yet it seemed hardly creditable that they would go out and leave the place unattended.

Seven or eight times he repeated his summons, standing upon the door-steps with his ears strained to catch the slightest sound.

Once he thought he heard distinctly the noise of stealthy footsteps in the hall, and he held his breath. They were repeated. He was quite certain that his ears had not deceived him, for in the street all was silent as the grave. He heard someone moving within as though creeping slowly from the door.

What could it mean? Were thieves within?

He examined the door to see if the lock had been tampered with, but, so far as he could discern, it was untouched. He was undecided how to act, though now positively certain that something unusual was in progress.

He glanced up and down the long road, with its rows of gas lamps, but no one was visible. The only sound was the far-distant rat-tat of the postman on his last round.

For the Doctor to be out of an evening was very unusual; and that stealthy footstep had alarmed him. If there were actually thieves, then they had probably entered by the area door. Max was by no means a coward. There was a mystery there—a mystery he intended to at once investigate.

Doctor Petrovitch was one of his dearest friends and he meant to act as a friend should act.

What puzzled him most of all was the absence of the servants. All of them were apparently highly trustworthy, yet the foreigner in London, he remembered, often engaged servants without sufficient inquiry into their past.

For a few moment he stood motionless, his ears strained, at the door.

The movement was repeated. Someone seemed to be leaving the dining-room, for he distinctly heard the light footfall.

Therefore, with scarce a sound, he crept down the steps to the pavement and descended the winding flight to the area door. With great caution he turned the handle, but alas! the knob went right round in his hand, the door remaining still fastened.

A light showed in the kitchen, but whether anyone was there he of course could not tell. Again he tried the door, but without avail. It was securely fastened, while, as far as he could ascertain, there were no marks of any forcible entry.

Should he rap at the door? Or would that further alarm the intruders? He had knocked many times at the front door, it was true, but they would no doubt wait until they believed he had gone. Or else they might escape by the rear of the premises.

What should he do?

He hesitated again, with bated breath.

Next instant, however, he heard upon the stone steps above him, leading from the pavement to the front door, the light tread of feet quickly descending. Someone, having watched him descend there, was leaving the house! And yet so noiselessly that at first Max believed himself mistaken.

In a second he had dashed up the area steps and stood upon the pavement. But already he realised the truth. The front door stood ajar, and the intruder was flying as fast as his feet could carry him in the direction of the Brompton Road.

Swiftly, without looking back, the man sped lightly along the pavement to the next corner, which he turned and was a moment later lost to view.

Max Barclay did not follow. He stood there like a man in a dream.

"What—in Heaven's name—is the meaning of this?" as, held powerless, he stood staring in the direction the fugitive had taken.

His first impulse had been to follow, but next moment, as the escaping intruder had passed beneath a street lamp he recognised the figure unmistakably, both by the clothes and hat, as none other than his friend Charles Rolfe!

He fell back, staggered by the discovery.

For quite a brief space he stood unable to move. Then, seeing the door ajar, he ascended the steps and entered the house. The lights were switched on everywhere, but, on going in, something—what it was he could never describe—struck him as peculiar. Hardly had he crossed the threshold than he became instinctively aware that some mystery was there.

In a few seconds the amazing truth became apparent, for when he entered the dining-room, to the left of the hall, he started, and an involuntary exclamation of surprise escaped him. The place was empty, devoid of every stick of furniture!

From room to room he dashed, only to find that everything had been mysteriously removed. In the few brief hours or his absence Doctor Petrovitch had apparently fled, taking with him all his household effects.

He stood in the hall utterly dumbfounded.

Why had Rolfe been there? What had he been doing in the empty house?

The swift manner in which the removal had been effected increased the mystery, for he had not left the Doctor till five o'clock. Besides, he had no doubt dined with his daughter Maud and with Marion, and they would not leave until about eight o'clock.

Again, a removal of that magnitude, requiring at least two vans, after dark could not possibly be effected without attracting the notice of the constable on duty!

Perhaps the police really did know who carried out the sudden change of residence. Anyhow, the whole affair was a complete enigma which amazed and stupefied him.

Presently, when he had somewhat recovered from his surprise, he ascended the stairs, his footsteps now echoing strangely through the empty place, and there found that the drawing-room, and, in fact, all the other rooms, had been completely and quickly cleared. The carpets had in some cases been left, but in the hasty removal curtains had been torn down from the rings, leaving cornices and poles, and the grand piano remained, it being apparently too large and heavy for rapid transit.

He ascended, even to the servants' rooms on the top floor, but found scarcely a vestige of furniture left.

In one back room, a small half-garret with a slightly eloping roof, he noticed a cupboard which curiosity led him to open, as he had opened other cupboards. As he did so, he saw a bundle upon the floor, as though it had been hastily thrown there.

As he pulled it forth it unrolled, and he then saw that it was a woman's light grey tweed skirt and coat.

The latter felt damp to his touch, and as he held it up to examine it he saw that the breast and sleeve were both saturated with blood!

It dropped from his nerveless fingers. Some secret crime had been committed in that house, so suddenly and mysteriously divested of its furniture.

But what?

Max Barclay, pale as death, stood gazing around him, staggered, bewildered, horrified, scarce daring to breathe.

Why had Charles Rolfe fled so hurriedly and secretly from the place?

Chapter Five
What a Constable Saw

Slowly Max Barclay regained possession of his senses. The discovery had so staggered him that, for a few moments, he had stood there in that room, staring at the woman's tweed coat, transfixed in horror.

There was some great and terrible mystery there, and with it Charlie Rolfe, the man whom he had so implicitly trusted, his most intimate friend, and brother of the woman who was all the world to him, was closely associated.

He glanced around the bare garret in apprehension. All was so weird and unexpected that a queer, uncanny feeling had crept over him. What could have occurred to have caused this revolution in the Doctor's house?

Here in that house, only a few hours ago, he had smoked calmly with Petrovitch, the studious Servian patriot, the man whom the Servians worshipped, and who was the right hand of his sovereign the King. When they had chatted of Maud's flirtation there had been no suggestion of departure. Indeed, the Doctor had invited him to return after dinner, as he so often did. Max was an easy, gay, careless man of the world, yet he was fond of study, and fond of the society of clever men like Petrovitch. The latter was well-known in literary circles on the Continent by reason of having written a most exhaustive history of the Ottoman Empire. That night Marion, his well-beloved, had no doubt dined at that house, prior to going to the concert with Maud. At least she would be aware of something that might give a clue to this extraordinary and hurried flight, if not to the ugly stain upon the woman's dress lying upon the floor at his feet.

He was undecided how next to act. Should he go to the police-station and inquire of the inspector whether removing vans had been noticed by the constable on the beat, or should he take a cab to Queen's Hall to try and find Marion and Maud?

He glanced at his watch, and saw that by the time he got to the concert they would in all probability have left. Marion was compelled to be in by eleven o'clock, therefore Maud would no doubt come out with her. Indeed, in a quarter of an hour his friend's daughter would be due to return there.

This decided him, and, without more ado, he left the house. Was it worth while at present, he reflected, saying anything to the police regarding the blood-stained garment? Charlie might give the explanation. He would see him before the night was out.

Therefore, finding a constable at the corner of Earl's Court Road, he inquired of him if he had noticed any removing vans before the house in question. The man replied that he had only come on duty at ten, therefore, it would be best if he went to the police-station, to which he directed him.

"If the man on duty saw any removing vans in the evening, he would certainly report it," the constable added politely, and Barclay then went in the direction he indicated.

A quarter of an hour later he stood in the police-office, while the inspector turned over the leaves of the big book in which reports of every untoward or suspicious occurrence are entered for reference, in case of civil actions or other eventualities.

At first he could find nothing, but at last he exclaimed:

"There's something here. I suppose this is it. Listen: P.C. Baldwin, when he came off duty, reported to the station-sergeant that two large pantechnicon vans and a small covered van of Harmer's Stores, Knightsbridge, drove up at 8:10 to Number 127a, Cromwell Road, close to Queen's Gate Gardens, and with seven men and a foreman removed the whole of the furniture. The constable spoke to the foreman, and learned that it was a sudden order given by the householder, a Dr Petrovitch, a foreigner, for his goods to be removed before half-past ten that night, and stored at the firm's depository at Chiswick."

"But they must have done it with marvellous alacrity!" Max remarked, at the same time pleased to have so quickly discovered the destination of the Doctor's household goods.

"Bless you, sir," answered the inspector, "Harmer's can do anything. They'd have sent twenty vans and cleared out the place in a quarter of an hour if they'd contracted to do so. You know they can do anything, and supply anything from a tin-tack to a live monkey."

"Then they've been stored at Chiswick, eh?"

"No doubt, sir. The constable would make all inquiry. You know Harmer's place at Chiswick, not far from Turnham Green railway station? At the office in Knightsbridge they'd tell you all about it. This foreign doctor was a friend of yours, I suppose?"

"Yes, a great friend," replied Barclay. "The fact is, I'm much puzzled over the affair. Only late this afternoon I was in his study, smoking and talking, but he told me nothing about his sudden removal."

"Ah, foreigners are generally pretty shifty customers, sir," was the officer's remark. "If you'd seen as much as I have of 'em, when I was down at Leman Street, you'd think twice before you trusted one. Of course, no reflection intended on your friend, sir."

"But there are foreigners who are gentlemen," Max ventured to suggest.

"Yes, there may be. I haven't met many, and we have to deal with all classes, you know. But tell me the circumstances," added the inspector, scenting mystery in this sudden flight. "Petrovitch might be some City speculator who had suddenly been ruined, or a bankrupt who had absconded."

Max Barclay was, however, not very communicative. Perhaps it was because of Charlie's inexplicable presence in that deserted house, or perhaps on account of the inspector's British antipathy towards foreigners; nevertheless, he said nothing regarding that woman's coat with the tell-tale mark of blood.

Besides, the Doctor and Maud must be somewhere in the vicinity. No doubt he would come round to Dover Street in the morning and explain his unusual removal. The discovery of Rolfe's presence there was nevertheless inexplicable. The more he reflected upon it, the more suspicious it seemed. The inspector's curiosity had been aroused by Max's demeanour. The latter had briefly related how he had called, to find the house empty, and both occupier, his daughter, and the servants gone.

"Did you see any servant when you were there this evening?"

"Yes; the man-servant Costa."

"Ah, a foreigner! Old or young?"

"Middle-aged."

"A devoted retainer of his master, of course."

"I believe so."

"Then he may have been in his master's secret—most probably was. When a master suddenly flies he generally confides in his man. I've known that in many instances. What nationality was this Petrovitch?"

"Servian."

"Oh, we don't get many of those people in London. They come from the East somewhere, don't they—a half-civilised lot?"

"Doctor Petrovitch is perfectly civilised, and a highly-cultured man," Max responded. "He is a statesman and diplomat."

"What! Is he the Minister of Servia?"

"He was—in Berlin, Constantinople, and other places."

"Then there may be something political behind it," the officer suggested, beaming as though some great flash of wisdom had come to him. "If so, it don't concern us. England's a free country to all the scum of Europe. This doctor may be flying from some enemy. Russian refugees often do. I've heard some queer tales about them, more strange than what them writers put in sixpenny books."

"Yes," remarked Barclay, "I expect you've had a pretty big experience of foreigners down in Whitechapel."

"And at Vine Street, too, sir," was the man's reply, as he leaned against the edge of his high desk, over which the flaring gas jets hissed. "Nineteen years in the London police gives one an intimate acquaintance with the undesirable alien. Your story to-night is a queer one. Would you like me to send a man round to the house with you in order to give it a look over?"

Max reflected in an instant that if that were done the woman's dress would be discovered.

"Well—no," he replied. "At present I think it would be scarcely worth while. I think I know where I shall find the Doctor in the morning. Besides, a friend of mine is engaged to his daughter, so he'll be certain to know their whereabouts."

"Very well—as you wish. But," he said, "if you can't find where they're all disappeared to, give us a call again, and we'll try to assist you to the best of our ability."

Max thanked him. A ragged pickpocket, held by two constables, was at that moment brought in and placed in the railed dock, making loud protests of "I'm quite innocent, guv'nor. It warn't me at all. I was only a-lookin' on!"

So Barclay, seeing that the inspector would be occupied in taking the charge, thanked him and left.

Outside, he reflected whether he should go direct to Charlie's chambers in Jermyn Street. His first impulse was to do so, but somehow he viewed Rolfe with suspicion. If his friend had not seen him—and he believed he had not—then for the present it was best that he should hold his secret.

Perhaps the Doctor had sent a telegram to his own chambers. He would surely never leave London without sending him word. Therefore Max hailed a passing cab and drove to Dover Street.

His chambers, on the first floor, were cosy and well-furnished, betraying a taste in antique of the Louis XIV period. Odd articles of furniture he had picked up in out-of-the-way places, while several of the pictures were family portraits brought from Kilmaronock Castle.

The red-carpeted sitting-room, with its big inlaid writing-table, bought from an old château on the Loire, its old French chairs and modern book-case, was lit only by the green-shaded reading lamp, beneath which were some letters where his man had placed them.

On a small table at the side was a decanter of whisky, a syphon, glasses, and cigars, and beside them his letters. Eagerly he turned them over for a telegram, but there was none. Neither was there a letter from the Doctor. On the writing-table stood the telephone instrument. It might have been rung while his man Gustave had been absent. That evening he had sent him on a message down to Croydon, and he had not yet returned.

He pushed his opera-hat to the back of his head, and stood puzzled as to how he should act. Green had told him that is master had left for the Continent, and yet had he not with his own eyes seen him fly from that house in Cromwell Road?

Yes; there was a mystery—a deep, inexplicable mystery. There was not a doubt of it!

Chapter Six
Mentions a Curious Confession

When about ten o'clock next morning Mr Warner, buyer of the costumes at Cunnington's, noticed the tall, athletic figure of the young man in brown tweeds known as Mr Evans of Dover Street advance across the drab carpet with which the "department" was covered, he smiled within himself.

The "young ladies" of Cunnington's were not allowed any flirtations. It was "the sack" at a moment's notice for any girl being found flirting either with one of the male assistants or with an outsider, though he be a good customer. Cunnington's hundred and one rules, with fines ranging from threepence to half-a-crown, were stringent ones. Mr Cunnington himself, a short, black-bearded man, of keen business instinct, was a kindly master; but in such a huge establishment with its hundreds of employees, rules must of necessity, be adhered to. Nevertheless, the buyers or headmen of the various departments each controlled their own assistants, and some being more lenient than others towards the girls, rules were very often broken.

Cunnington's was, therefore, known to be one of the most comfortable "cribs" in the trade. Assistants who came up to London in search of a billet always went to see Mr Cunnington, and happy he or she who obtained a personal introduction to him. He had earned his success by dint of hard work. Originally an assistant himself in a Birmingham shop, he had gone into business for himself in Oxford Street, in one small establishment, and had, by fair dealing and giving good value, prospered, until great rows of windows testified to the fortune he had amassed.

Unlike most employers in the drapery trade, he was generous to a degree, and he appreciated devoted service. In his great shops he had many old hands. Some, indeed, had been with him ever since his first beginning. Those were his trusted lieutenants, of whom "Warner of the Costumes" was one.

What Warner said was never queried, and, being a kindly man, the girls in his department did pretty much as they liked.

Max Barclay, or Mr Evans as he had several times given his name, had run the gauntlet of the shopwalkers of the outer shops, and penetrated anxiously to the costumes. At that hour there were no customers. Before eleven there is but little shopping in Oxford Street. Buyers then see travellers, who come in their broughams, and assistants re-arrange and display their stocks.

On entering the department, Max at once caught sight of the tall fair-haired girl who, with her back to him, was arranging a linen costume upon a stand.

Two other girls glanced across at him, but, knowing the truth, did not ask what he required. He was Miss Rolfe's admirer, they guessed, for men did not usually come in alone and buy twenty-guinea ready-made costumes for imaginary relatives as he had done.

He was standing behind her before she turned suddenly, and blushed in surprise. Warner, sitting in his little glass desk, noticed the look upon the girl's face and fully realised the situation. He liked Marion's brother, while the girl herself was extremely modest and an excellent saleswoman. He knew that Charles Rolfe and this Mr Evans were friends, and that fact had prevented him from forbidding the flirtation to continue.

Evans was evidently a gentleman. Of that he had no doubt.

"Why!" she exclaimed to her lover. "This is really a great surprise. You are early?"

"Because I wanted to see you, Marion," he answered, quickly.

She noticed his anxiety, and in an instant grew alarmed.

"Why, what's the matter?" she asked, glancing round to see whether the other girls were watching her. "You ought not to come here, you know, Max. I fear Mr Warner will object to you seeing me in business hours."

"Oh! never mind him, darling," he replied, in a low voice. "I want to ask you a question or two. Where did you see Maud last night?"

"I met her at the door at Queen's Hall. I was to go to Cromwell Road to call for her, but she telegraphed to me at the last moment. She was with Charlie, she told me."

"And where is Charlie?"

"Gone to Servia. He left Charing Cross by the mail last night."

Max reflected that his friend had not left as his sister supposed.

"And where did you leave Maud?"

"I walked to the 'tube' station at Piccadilly Circus, and left her there. She went to Earl's Court Station, and I took a bus home. She told me that you'd been to see the Doctor earlier in the evening. But why do you ask all this?"

"Because—well, because, Marion, something unusual has occurred," he replied.

"Unusual!" she echoed. "What do you mean?"

"Did Maud tell you anything about her future movements last night—or mention her father's intentions?"

"Intentions of what?"

"Of leaving the house in Cromwell Road."

"No; she told me nothing. Only—"

"Only what?"

"Well, it struck me that she had something on her mind. You know how bright and merry she usually is. Well, last night she seemed very thoughtful, and I wondered whether she had had any little difference with Charlie."

"You mean that they may have quarrelled?"

"I hardly think that likely," she said, quickly. "Charlie is far too fond of her, as you know."

"And her father does not altogether approve of it," Max remarked. "He has told me so."

"Poor Charlie!" the girl said, for she was very fond of her brother. He was always a good friend to her, and gave her money to buy her dresses and purchase the few little luxuries which her modest stipend as a shop-assistant would not allow her to otherwise possess. "I'm sure he's devoted to Maud. And she's one of the best girls I know. They'd make a perfect pair. But the Doctor's a foreigner, and doesn't really understand Englishmen."

"Perhaps that's it," Max said, trying to assume a careless air, for he felt that a hundred eyes were upon him.

Their position was not a very comfortable one, to say the least. He knew that he ought not to have come there during business hours, but the mystery had so puzzled him that he felt he must continue his inquiries. He had fully expected the morning post to bring him a line from the Doctor. But there had been nothing.

Both he and Maud had disappeared suddenly, leaving no trace behind—no trace except that woman's coat with the stain of blood upon the breast.

Was it one of Maud's dresses, he wondered. In the band he had noticed the name of its maker—Maison Durand, of Conduit Street—one of the best dressmakers in London. True he had found it in the servants' quarters, but domestics did not have their clothes made by Durand.

"But tell me, Max," said the girl, her fine eyes fixed upon her lover, "what makes you suggest that the Doctor is about to leave Cromwell Road."

"He has left already," was Max's reply. "That's the curious part of it."

"Left! Moved away!"

"Yes. I came to ask you what you know about it. They've gone away without a word!"

"How? Why, you were there last evening!"

"I was. But soon after I left, and while Maud was with you at the concert, three vans came from Harmer's Stores and cleared out the whole of the furniture."

"There wasn't a bill of sale, or something of that sort, I suppose?" she suggested.

"Certainly not. The Doctor is a wealthy man. The copper mines of Kaopanik bring him in a splendid income in themselves," Max said. "No; there's a mystery—a very great mystery about the affair."

"A mystery! Tell me all about it!" she cried, anxiously, for Maud was her best friend, while the Doctor had also been *extremely* kind to her.

"I don't know anything," he responded. "Except that the whole place by half-past ten last night had been cleared out of furniture. Only the grand piano and a few big pieces have been left. Harmer's have taken the whole of it to their depository at Chiswick."

"Well, that's most extraordinary, certainly," she said, opening her eyes in blank surprise. "Maud must have known what was taking place. Possibly that is why she was so melancholy and pensive."

"Did she say nothing which would throw any light upon their sadden disappearance?"

Marion reflected for a few moments, her brows slightly knit in thought.

"Well, she said something about her father being much worried, but she did not tell me why. About a fortnight ago she told me that both she and her father had many enemies, one of whom would not hesitate to kill him if a chance occurred. I tried to get from her the reason, but she would not tell me."

"But you don't think that the Doctor has been the victim of an assassin, do you?" Max asked in apprehension.

"No; but Maud may have been," she answered. "Killed?"

"I hope not, yet—"

"Why do you hesitate, Marion, to tell me all you know?" he urged. "There is a mystery here which we must fathom."

"My brother knows nothing yet, I suppose."

Barclay hesitated.

"I suppose not," was his reply.

"Then, before I say anything, I must see him."

"But he's away in Servia, is he not? He won't be back for six months."

"Then I must wait till he returns," she answered, decisively.

"Maud has told you something. Come, admit it," he urged.

The girl was silent for a full minute.

"Yes," she sighed. "She did tell me something."

"When?"

"Last night, as we were walking together to the station—something that I refused to believe. But I believe it now."

"Then you know the truth," he cried. "If there had not been some unfair play, the Doctor would never have disappeared without first telling me. He has many times entrusted me with his secrets."

"I quite believe that he would have telegraphed or written," she said. "He looked upon you as his best friend in London."

"And, Marion, this very fact causes me to suspect foul play," he said, the recollection of that fugitive in the night flashing across his brain. "What do you, in the light of this secret knowledge, suspect?"

Her lips were closed tightly, and there was a strange look in her eyes.

"I believe, Max," she replied, in a low, hard voice, "that something terrible must have happened to Maud!"

"Did she apprehend something?"

"I cannot tell. She confessed to me something under a bond of secrecy. Before I tell you I must consult Charlie—the man she loved so dearly."

"But are we not lovers, Marion?" he asked, in a low intense voice. "Cannot you tell me what she said, in order that I may institute inquiries at once. Delay may mean the escape of the assassin if there really has been foul play."

"I cannot betray Maud's confidence, Max," was her calm answer.

This response of hers struck him as implying that Maud had confessed something not very creditable to herself, something which she, as a woman, hesitated to tell him. If this were actually true, however, why should she reveal the truth to Maud's lover? Would she not rather hide it from him?

"But you will not see Charlie for months," he exclaimed, in dismay. "What are we to do in the meantime?"

"We can only wait," she answered. "I cannot break my oath to my friend."

"Then you took an oath not to repeat what she told you?"

"She told me something amazing concerning—"

And she hesitated.

"Concerning herself," he added. "Well?"

"It was a confession, Max—a—a terrible confession. I had not a wink of sleep last night for her words rang in my ears, and her face, wild and haggard, haunted me in the darkness. Ah! it is beyond credence—horrible!—but—but, Max—leave me. These people are noticing us. I will see you to-night, where you like. Only go—go! I can't bear to talk of it! Poor Maud! What that confession must have cost her! And why? Ah, I see it all now! Because—because she knew that her end was near!"

Chapter Seven
Contains Several Revelations

Max Barclay re-traced his steps along Oxford Street much puzzled. What Marion had told him was both startling and curious in face of the sudden disappearance of the Doctor and his daughter. If the latter had made a confession, as she apparently had, then Marion was, after all, perfectly within her right in not betraying her friend.

Yet what could that confession be? Marion had said it was "a terrible confession," and as he went along he tried in vain to imagine its nature.

The morning was bright and sunlit, and Oxford Street was already busy. About the Circus the ebb and flow of traffic had already begun, and the windows of the big drapery shops were already attracting the feminine crowds with their announcements of "summer sales" and baits of "great bargains."

For a moment he paused at the kerb, then, entering a hansom, he drove to Mariner's Stores, the great emporium in Knightsbridge, which had been entrusted with the removal of the Doctor's furniture.

Without much difficulty he found the manager, a short, dapper, little frock-coated freckled-faced business man, and explained the nature of his inquiry.

The man seemed somewhat puzzled, and, going to a desk, opened a big ledger and slowly turned the pages.

"I think there must be some mistake, sir," was his reply. "We have had no removal of that name yesterday."

"But they were at Cromwell Road late last night," Max declared. "The police saw them there."

"The police could not have seen any of our vans removing furniture from Cromwell Road last night," protested the manager. "See here for yourself. Yesterday there were four removals only—Croydon to Southsea, Fitzjohn's Avenue to Lower Norwood, South Audley Street to Ashley Gardens, and Elgin Avenue to Finchley. Here they are," and he pointed to the page whereon the particulars were inscribed.

"The goods in question were removed by you from Cromwell Road, and stored in your depository at Chiswick."

"I think, sir, you really must be mistaken," replied the manager, shaking his head. "Did you see our vans there yourself?"

"No. The police did, and made inquiry."

"With the usual result, I suppose, that they bungled, and told you the wrong name."

"They've got it written down in their books."

"Well, all I can say is, that we didn't remove any furniture from the road you mention."

"But it was at night."

"We do not undertake a job at night unless we receive a guarantee from the landlord that the rent is duly paid, and ascertain that no money is owing."

Max was now puzzled more than ever.

"The police say that the effects were sent to your depository," he remarked, dissatisfied with the manager's assurance.

"In that case inquiry is very easy," he said, and walking to the telephone he rang up the depository at Chiswick.

"Is that you, Merrick?" he asked over the 'phone. "I say! Have you been warehousing any goods either yesterday or to-day, or do you know of a job in Cromwell Road, at the house of a Doctor Petrovitch?"

For a full minute he waited the reply. At last it came, and he heard it to the end.

"No," he said, putting down the receiver and turning to Barclay. "As I expected. They know nothing of the matter at the depository."

"But how do you account for your vans—two pantechnicons and a covered van—being there?" he asked.

The manager shook his head.

"We have here the times when each job in London was finished, and when the vans returned to the yard. They were all in by 7:30. Therefore, they could not have been ours."

"Well, that's most extraordinary."

"Is it somebody who has disappeared?"

"Yes."

"Ah! the vans were, no doubt, painted with our names specially, in order to mislead the police," he said. "There's some shady transaction somewhere, sir, depend upon it. Perhaps the gentleman wanted to get his things away, eh?"

"No. He had no necessity for so doing. He was quite well off—no debts, or anything of that kind."

"Well, it's evident that if our name is registered in the police occurrences the vans were painted with our name for some illegal purpose. The gentleman's disappeared, you say."

"Yes. And—well, to tell you the truth, I suspect foul play."

"Have you told the police that?" asked the man, suddenly interested.

"No; not yet. I've come to you first."

"Then if I were you I'd tell the police the result of your inquiries," the manager said. "No doubt there's a crooked incident somewhere."

"That's just what I fear. Quite a number of men most have been engaged in clearing the place out."

"Have you been over it? Is it entirely cleared?"

"Nearly. The grand piano and a big book-case have been; left."

"I wonder if it's been done by professional removers, or by amateurs?" suggested the manager.

"Ah! I don't know. If you saw the state of the place you'd know, wouldn't you?"

"Most probably."

"Then if you'll come with me I'll be delighted to show you, and you can give me your opinion."

So the pair entered a cab, and a quarter of an hour later were passing along the hall of the empty house. The manager of Harmer's removals inspected room after room, noticed how the curtains had been torn down, and noted in the fire grate of the drawing-room a quantity of tinder where a number of papers seemed to have been burned.

"No," he said presently. "This removal was carried out by amateurs, who were in a very violent hurry. Those vans were faked—bought, perhaps, and repainted with our name. It's evident that they deceived the constable very cleverly."

"But the whole affair is so extraordinary?" gasped Max, staring at his companion.

"Yes. It would appear so. Your friend, the Doctor, evidently wished to get his goods away with the least possible delay and in the greatest secrecy."

"But the employment of so many men did not admit of much secrecy, surely!"

"They were only employed to load. They did not unload. Only the three drivers probably know the destination of the furniture. It was valuable old stuff, I should say, if one is to judge by what is remaining."

"Yes, the place was well and comfortably furnished."

"Then I really think, sir, that if you suspect foul play it's your duty to tell the police. In cases like this an hour's delay is often fatal to success in elucidating the mystery." Max was undecided how to act. It was his duty to tell the police his suspicions and show them that blood-stained coat. And yet he felt so certain that the Doctor must in the course of the day take him into his confidence that he hesitated to make a suggestion of foul play and thus bring the affair into public prominence.

The fact that Harmer's name had been upon vans not belonging to that firm was in itself sufficient proof that there had been a conspiracy somewhere.

But of what nature was it? What could possibly have been its object? What was Maud's "terrible confession!"

The expert in removals was examining some litter in the dining-room.

"They evidently did not stop to pack anything," he remarked, "but simply bundled it out with all possible speed. One fact strikes me as very peculiar."

"What is that?"

"Well, if they wanted to empty the place they might have done so, leaving the curtains up, and the palms and things in the windows in order to lead people to believe that the house was still occupied. Apparently, however, they disregarded that precaution altogether."

"Yes. That's true. The object of the sudden flight is a complete mystery," Max remarked. He had not taken the man to the top room, where, in the cupboard, the woman's dress was hidden.

"You say that the Doctor was rich. Therefore, it wasn't to escape from an execution threatened by the landlord."

"Certainly not."

"Well, you may rest assured, sir, that the removal was not effected by professional men. The way in which carpets have been torn up and damaged, curtains torn from their rings, and crockery smashed in moving, shows them to have been amateurs."

They had ascended to the front bedroom, wherein remained a large, heavy old-fashioned mahogany chest of drawers, and he had walked across to them.

"Indeed," he added. "It almost looks as though it were the work of thieves?"

"Thieves! Why?"

"Well—look at this. They had no keys, so they broke open the drawers, and removed the contents," he answered. "And look across there!"

He pointed to a small iron fireproof safe let into the wall—a safe evidently intended originally as a place for the lady of the house to keep her jewels.

The door stood ajar, and Max, as he opened it, saw that it was empty.

The curious part of the affair was that Max was convinced within himself that when he had searched the house on the previous night that safe was not there. If it was, then the door must have been closed and concealed.

He remembered most distinctly entering that room and looking around. The chest of drawers had been moved since he was last there. When he had seen them they had been standing in their place concealing the iron door of the safe, which, when shut, closed flush with the wall. Someone had been there since! And whoever it was, had moved the heavy piece of furniture and found the safe.

He examined the door, and from its blackened condition, the twisted iron, and the broken lock, no second glance was needed to ascertain that it had been blown open by explosives.

Whatever valuables Dr Petrovitch had kept there had disappeared.

The theory of theft was certainly substantiated by these discoveries. Max stood by the empty safe silent and wondering.

"I noticed downstairs in the study that a board had been prised up, as though somebody has been searching for something," the man from Harmer's remarked. "Probably the Doctor had something in his possession of which the thieves desired to get possession."

"Well," said Max, "I must say that this safe being open looks as though the affair has actually been the work of thieves. If so, then where is the Doctor, where is his daughter Maud, and where are the servants?"

"Yes. I agree. The whole affair is a complete mystery, sir," the other replied. "There have been thieves here without a doubt. Perhaps the Doctor knows all about it, but for some reason dare not utter a word of complaint. Indeed, that's my theory. He may be in fear of them, you know. It's a gang that have done it, without a doubt."

"And a pretty ingenious gang, too," declared Max, with knit brows.

"They evidently made short work of all the furniture. I wonder why they took it, and where it is at present."

"If it has gone to a sale room the police could trace it," Max suggested.

"Certainly. But suppose it was transferred from the vans it was taken away in to the vans of some depository, and removed, say, to Portsmouth or Plymouth, and there stored? It could be done quite easily, and would never be traced."

"Yes. But it's a big job to have made a whole houseful of furniture disappear in a couple of hours."

"It is not so big as it first seems, sir. I'd guarantee to clear a house of this size in one hour, if necessary. And the way they turned out the things didn't take them very long. They were in a desperate hurry, evidently."

"Do you think that thieves did the work?"

"I'm very strongly of that opinion. Everything points to it. If I were you I'd go back to the police and tell them about the safe, about that chest of drawers, and the flooring in the study. Somebody's been prying about here, depend upon it."

Max stood, still undecided. Did it not seem very much as though the thieves had visited there after Charles Rolfe had fled so hurriedly?

Chapter Eight
The Pauper of Park Lane

About half-way up Park Lane—the one-sided row of millionaires' residences that face Hyde Park—not far from the corner of that narrow little turning, Deanery Street, stood a great white house, one of a short row. The windows were protected from the sun by outside blinds of red and buff-striped holland, and the first floor sills were gay with, geraniums.

The house was one of imposing importance, and dwarfed its neighbours, being both higher, larger, and more artistic. On the right side dwelt one of Manchester's cotton kings, and on the other a duke whose rent-roll was one of the biggest in the United Kingdoms. The centre house, however, was far more prosperous-looking than the others, and was often remarked upon by country cousins as they passed up and down upon omnibuses. It was certainly one of the finest in the whole of that select thoroughfare where rents alone were ruinous, and where the possession of a house meant that one's annual income must run into six figures. The mere nobility of England cannot afford to live in Park Lane nowadays. It is reserved for the kings of Britain's commerce, the Stock Exchange speculator, or the get-rich-quick financier.

Those who read these lines know well the exterior of many of the houses of notable people who live there. Some are in excellent taste, while others betray the blatant arrogance of the man who, risen from penury, has suddenly found himself a controller of England's destinies, a Birthday Knight, and the husband of a woman whom the papers have suddenly commenced to dub "the beautiful Lady So-and-So." Other houses are quiet and sober in their exterior, small, modest, and unobstructive, the town residences of men of great wealth, who, posing as gentlemen, are hoping for a peerage.

The hopes in Park Lane are many. Almost every household possesses a secret ambition, some to shine in Society, other in politics, and some even in literature. The really wealthy man sneers at a baronetcy, an honour which his tea-merchant received last year, and as for a knighthood, well, he can plank down his money this afternoon and buy one just as he bought a cigar half an hour ago in Bond Street. He must have a title, for his wife wants to be known by the name of his country place, and he has secret ambitions for a seat in the Lords. And so in every house in that long, one-sided row are hopes eternal which rise regularly every year towards the end of June.

Diamond, copper, soap, pork, and railway "kings" who dwell there are a curious assortment, yet the combined wealth of that street alone would be sufficient to pay off our National Debt and also run a respectable-sized kingdom for a year or two.

Almost every man could realise a million sterling, and certainly one of the very wealthiest among them was old Samuel Statham, the man who owned and lived in that house with the red-striped sun-blinds.

While Max Barclay was engaged in his investigations at the deserted house in Cromwell Road, old Sam was standing at the window of his study, a large front room on the ground floor overlooking the Park. It was a quiet, soberly-furnished apartment, the carpet of which was so soft that one's feet fell noiselessly, while over the mantelshelf was a large life-sized Venus by a modern French artist, the most notable picture in the Salon five years ago.

The leather-covered chairs were all heavy and old-fashioned, the books in uniform bindings of calf and gold, and the big writing-table of the early Victorian period. Upon the table stood a great silver candelabra fitted with electric lamps, while littered about the floor were quantities of folded papers and business documents of various kinds.

There was but little comfort about the room. Artistic taste and luxury are commonly associated with Park Lane, therefore the stranger would have been greatly surprised if he had been allowed a peep within. But there was a curious bet about the house.

No stranger had ever been known to pass beyond the big swing-glass doors half-way down the hall. No outsider had ever set foot within.

Levi, the hook-nosed old butler, in his well-cut clothes and spotless linen, was a zealous janitor. No one, upon any pretext whatsoever, was allowed to pass beyond the glass doors. His master was a little eccentric, it was said, and greatly disliked intruders. He hated the inquisitiveness of the modern Press, and always feared lest his house should be described and photographed as those of his neighbours constantly were. Therefore all strangers were rigorously excluded.

Some gossip had got about concerning this. A year ago the wealthy old financier had been taken suddenly ill, and his doctor was sent for from Cavendish Square. But even he was not allowed to pass the rigidly-guarded frontier. His patient saw him in the hall, and there he diagnosed the ailment and prescribed. The doctor in question, a well-known physician, remarked upon old Sam's eccentricity over a dinner-table in Mayfair, and very soon half smart London were talking and wondering why nobody was ever invited to the table of Samuel Statham.

In the City, as head of Statham Brothers, foreign bankers, whose offices in Old Broad Street are known to every City man, he was always affable, yet very shrewd. He and his brother could drive hard bargains, but they were always charitable, and the name of the firm constantly figured for a substantial amount in the lists in response to any charitable appeal.

From small beginnings—the early days of both brothers being shrouded in mystery—they had risen to become what they now were, a house second only to the Rothschilds in financial power, a house whose assistance was sought by kings and emperors, and whose interests were world-wide.

That morning old Sam Statham appeared unusually agitated. Rising at five o'clock, as was his habit summer and winter, he had been hard at work for hours when Levi brought him his tiny cup of black Turkish coffee. Then, glancing at the clock upon his desk, he had risen, gone to the window, and gazed out eagerly, as though in search of someone.

It was eight o'clock, and there were plenty of people about. But, though he looked up and down the thoroughfare, he was disappointed. So he snapped his thin fingers impatiently and returned to his writing.

His personal appearance was truly insignificant. When, in the street, he was pointed out to people as the great Samuel Statham, they invariably expressed astonishment. There was nothing of the blatant millionaire about him. On the contrary, he was a thin, grey, sad-looking man, rather short of stature, with a face very broad in the brow and very narrow at the chin, ending with a small, scraggy white beard clipped to a point. His cheeks were hollow, his dark eyes sunken, the skin upon his brow tightly stretched, his lips pale and thin, and about his clean-shaven upper lip a hardness that was in entire opposition with his generous instincts towards his less fortunate fellow men.

One of his peculiarities of dress was that he always wore a piece of greasy black satin ribbon, tied loosely in a bow as a cravat. The same piece did duty both by day and at evening.

His clothes, for the most part, hung upon his lean, shrunken limbs as though they had been made for a much more robust man, and his hats were indescribably greasy and out of date. When he went to the City Levi compelled him to put on his best silk hat and a decent frock coat, but often of an afternoon he might be seen sitting alone in the Park and mistaken for some poor, broken-down old man the sadness of whose face compelled sympathy.

This carelessness of dress appears to be one of the inevitable results of great fortune. A man should never be judged by his coat nowadays. The struggling clerk who lives in busy Brixton or cackling Croydon usually gives himself greater airs, and dresses far better than the head of the firm, while the dainty typewriter wears prettier blouses and neater footgear than his own out-door daughters, with their slang, their "pals," and their distorted ideas of maiden modesty.

But old Sam Statham had neither kith nor kin. He was a lonely man—how utterly lonely only he himself knew. He had only his perpetual calculations of finance, his profit and loss accounts, and occasional chats with the ever-faithful Levi to occupy his days. He seldom if ever left London. Even the stifling August days, when his clerks went to the mountains or the sea, he still remained in London, because, as he openly declared, he hated to mix with strangers.

Curiously enough, almost the only man he trusted was his private secretary, Charlie Rolfe, the smart young man who came there from ten o'clock till two each day, wrote his private letters, and was paid a very handsome salary.

Usually old Sam was a very quiet-mannered man whom nothing disturbed. But that morning he was distinctly upset. He had scarcely slept a single wink, and his deep-sunken eyes and almost haggard face told of a great anxiety wearing out his heart.

He tried to add up a long column of figures upon a sheet of paper before him, but gave it up with a deep sigh. Again he rose, glanced out of the window, audibly denounced in unmeasured terms a motor-'bus which, tearing past, caused his room to shake, and then returned to his table.

But he was far too impatient to sit there long, for again he rose and paced the room, his grey brows knit in evident displeasure, his thin, bony hands clenched tightly, and from his lips escaping muttered imprecations upon some person whom he did not name.

Once he laughed—a hard little laugh. His lip curled in exultant triumph as he stuck his hands into the pockets of his shabby jacket and again went to look over the *brisé-brisé* curtains of pale pink silk into the roadway.

For a moment he looked, then, with a start, he stood glaring out. Next instant he sprang back from the window with a look of terror upon his blanched cheeks. He had caught sight of somebody whose presence there was both unwelcome and unexpected, and the encounter had filled him with anxiety and dismay.

As he had gazed inquiringly forth, with his face close to the window-pane, his eyes had met those of a man of about his own age, shabby, with grey, ragged hair, threadbare clothes, broken boots, and a soft grey felt hat, darkly stained around the band—a tramp evidently. The stranger was leaning idly against the park railings, evidently regarding the house with some wonder, when the sad face of its master had appeared.

The pair glared at each other for one single second. Then Sam Statham, recognising in the other's crafty eyes a look of cruel, relentless revenge, started back into the room, breathless and deathly pale. He staggered to his chair, supporting himself by clutching at its back.

"Then they did not lie!" he gasped aloud. "He—he's alive—therefore so it's all over! I—I saw his intentions plainly written in his face. I've played the game and lost! He has returned, therefore I must face the inevitable. Yes," he added, with that same bitter laugh, only this time it was the hoarse, discordant laugh of a man who found himself cornered, without any possible means of escape. "Yes—this is the end—I must die!—to-day!" And he whispered, glancing round the room as though in terror of his own voice, "Yes—before the sun sets."

Chapter Nine
In which Levi Gives Advice

For fully five minutes Samuel Statham stood steadying himself by the back of his chair. His face was white and rigid, his jaw set, his breathing quick and excited, his hands trembling, his face full of a sudden horror.

He had entirely changed. The sight of that shabby stranger had filled him with fear.

Once or twice he glanced furtively at the window. Then, straightening himself in a vain endeavour to remain calm, he bent and crept back to the window in order to ascertain whether the man still remained. Bent and out of sight he approached the lace-edged curtain and peered through unseen.

Yes; the fellow was still there. He had lit his pipe with calm unconcern, and was leaning back against the railings in full view of the house. The man's attitude was that of complete triumph. Ah! what a fool he had been to have shown himself so openly as he had done! To think that this man of all men was still alive!

He crept back again, trembling. His face was haggard and bloodless, the countenance of a man whose future was but a blank—the dismal blank of the grave.

His whole body trembled as he sank into his writing-chair, and, leaning his elbows upon the desk, he buried his face in his hands and sobbed. Yes; he, the hard-headed financier, whose influence was felt in every corner of the world, the man who controlled millions and who loaned great sums to certain of the rulers of Europe, sobbed aloud.

"Ah!" he cried to himself, "I was a fool when I disbelieved them. I thought that blackmail was their object in telling me the story of how that man was alive and had been seen. Therefore I only laughed at them and took no precaution. Ah! I was a fool, and my foolishness must end fatally. There is no way out of it for me—only death. I've been a fool—a confounded fool. I ought to have made certain; I ought not to have taken any risk. I'm wiser now than I was then. Age has brought me wisdom as well as destroying my belief in the honesty of men and the loyalty of friends"; and as he sighed heavily, his brow still bent upon his hand, he touched the bell, and old Levi appeared.

"Levi," he said, in a low unusual voice, "go quietly to that window and, without attracting attention, look outside at a man opposite."

The faithful old servant, somewhat surprised at these rather unusual instructions, walked stealthily to the window and peered through the lace insertion of the brisé-brisé.

Scarcely had he done so than, with a cry, he withdrew, and facing his master, stood staring at him.

"Did you see anyone, Levi?" asked his master, raising his head suddenly.

"Yes," was the hoarse whisper of the man who stood there, white-faced in fear. "It's him! I—I thought you said he was dead."

"No; he isn't! He's there in the flesh."

"And what are we to do?"

"What can we do? He recognised me a moment ago, and he's watching the house."

"Which means that you had better leave England for a considerable time."

"What!" cried Statham, in quick reproof. "What—run away? Never!"

"But—well, in the circumstances, don't you scent danger—a very grave danger?" asked the old servant whose devotion to his master had always been so marked.

"When I am threatened I always face my accuser. I shall do so now," was the great man's calm reply, even though it were in absolute contradiction to his attitude only a few moments before. Perhaps it was that he did not wish old Levi to know his fear.

"But—but that can only result in disaster," remarked the old servant, who never addressed his master as "sir"—the pair were on too intimate terms for that. "If I might presume to advise, I think—"

"No, Levi," snapped the other; "you haven't any right to give advice in this affair. I know my own business best, surely?"

"And that man knows as much as you do—and more."

"They told me he was alive, and I—fool that I was—disbelieved them!" the old millionaire cried. "And there he is now, watching outside like a terrier outside a rat-hole. And I'm the rat, Levi—caught in my own trap!"

"Is there no way out of this?" asked the other. "Surely you can escape if you so desire—get away to America, or to the Continent."

"And what's the use. He'd follow. And even if he didn't, think of what he can tell if he goes to the police."

"Yes; he could tell sufficient to cause Statham Brothers to close their doors—eh?" remarked the old servant very seriously.

"That's just it. I've been a confounded idiot. Rolfe warned me only the other day that the fellow was in London, but I said I wouldn't believe him until I saw the man with my own eyes. To-day I have actually seen him, and there can be no mistake. He's the man that—that I—"

His sentence remained unfinished, for he sank into his chair and groaned, covered his face again with his hands in an attitude of deep remorse, while Levi stood by watching in silence.

"Rolfe could help you in this matter," the man exclaimed at last. "Where is he?"

"I don't know. I sent him yesterday to Belgrade, but last night he telephoned that he had lost the train."

"Then he may have left at nine o'clock this morning?"

"Most probably."

"Then you must recall him by wire."

"No telegram can reach him till he gets to Servia, for I don't know whether he's gone from Ostend or Paris."

"They'd know in the City. Why not ask them?"

"No; they wouldn't know."

"Why?"

"Because Rolfe had with him a big sum in German notes and a quantity of securities belonging to the National Bank of Servia. In that case he would not let anyone know his route, for fear of thieves. It is one of my strictest orders to him. Why he lost the train last night I can't tell."

"Well, it's a thousand pities we can't get at him, for he's the only man to help you out—of this difficulty."

"Yes; I quite agree. That shabby, down-at-heel man waiting outside is my master, Levi—the master of Statham Ltd. My future is in his hands!"

He had raised his head, and sat staring at the beautiful picture upon the wall before him, the picture with its wonderful tints which had been copied in a hundred different places.

His countenance was haggard and drawn, and in his eyes was a look of unspeakable terror, as though he were looking into his own grave, as indeed at that moment he was.

The sombre melancholy-looking Levi stood watching for a moment, and then, creeping to the window, looked out into the sunshine of Park Lane.

The ragged tramp was still there, idling against the railings, and smoking a short, dirty pipe quite unconcernedly. He was watching for the re-appearance of that white, startled face at the window—the face of the great Samuel Statham. "He's still outside, I suppose?" queried the man at the other end of the room.

Levi replied in the affirmative, whereat old Samuel clenched his teeth and muttered something which sounded like an oration. He was condemning himself for his disbelief in his secretary's warnings.

"Had I listened to him I could easily have saved myself—I could have prevented him from coming here," he said in a meaning voice.

"Yes; it would not have been difficult to have prevented this. After what has occurred that blackguard has no right to live."

"Aha! then you believe me, Levi?" cried the wretched man. "You do not blame me?" he asked, anxiously.

"He was to blame—not you."

"Then I was right in acting as I did, you think—right to protect my interests."

"You were right in your self-defence," the man answered, somewhat grey, sphinx-like, for Levi was a man whose thoughts one could never read from his thin, grey, expressionless face. "But you were injudicious when you disregarded Rolfe's warning."

"I thought he had his own interests to serve," was Statham's reply.

"Frankly, you believed it to be an attempt at blackmail. I quite follow you. But do you think Rolfe would be guilty of such a thing?"

"My dear Levi, when a poor man is in love, as Rolfe is, it is a sore temptation to obtain by any means, fair or foul, sufficient to marry and support a wife. You and I were both young once—eh? And we thought that our love would last always. Where is yours to-day, and"—he sighed—"where is mine?"

"You are right," replied the old servant slowly, with a slight sigh. "You refer to little Marie. Ah! I can see her now, as plainly as she was then, forty years ago. How beautiful she was, how dainty, how perfect, and—ah!—how well you loved her. And what a tragedy—the tragedy of your life—the tragedy that has ever been hidden from the world—the—"

"No! Enough, Levi!" cried his master hoarsely, staring straight before him. "Do not recall that to me, especially at this moment. It was the great tragedy of my life, until—until this present one which—which threatens to end it."

"But you are going to face the music. You have said!"

"I may—and I may not."

Levi was silent again. Only the low ticking of the dock broke the quiet, and was followed by the rumble of a motor-'bus and the consequent tremor in the room.

"At any rate, Samuel Statham will never act the coward," the millionaire remarked at last, in a soft but distinct voice.

"Rolfe can help you. Where is he—away just at the moment that he's wanted," Levi said.

"My fault! My fault, Levi!" his master declared. "I disbelieved him, and sent him out to Servia to show him that I did not credit what he told me."

"You were a fool!" said Levi, bluntly. He never minced words when his master spoke confidentially.

"I know I was. I have already admitted it," exclaimed the financier. "But what puzzles me is that that man outside is really alive and in the flesh. I never dreamed that he would return to face me. He was dead—I could have sworn it."

"So you saw him dead—eh?"

Old Statham drew a quick breath, and his face went ashen, for he saw how he had betrayed himself. Next instant he had recovered from his embarrassment and, bracing himself with an effort, said:

"No—no, of course not. I—I only know what—well, what I've been told. I was misled wilfully by my enemies."

Levi looked straight into his face with a queer expression of disbelief. Statham noticed it, and it unnerved him.

He had inadvertently made confession, and Levi did not credit his denial.

The peril of the situation was complete!

Chapter Ten
Shows a Woman's Peril

Several hours had gone by, hours which Samuel Statham spent, seated in a deep easy-chair near the empty fire grate, reviewing his long and eventful life.

With his head buried in his hands, he reflected upon all the past—its tragedy and its prosperity. True, he had grown rich, wealthier than he had ever dreamed, but, ah! at what a cost! The world knew nothing. The world of finance, known in the City, looked upon him as a power to be reckoned with. By a stroke of that stubby, ink-stained pen which lay upon the writing-table he could influence the markets in Paris or Berlin. His aid and advice were sought by men who were foremost in the country's commerce and politics, and he granted loans to princes and to kingdoms. And yet the tragedy of his own heart was a bitter one, and his secret one that none dreamed.

He, like many another world-famous man, had a skeleton in his cupboard. And that day it had seen the light, and the sight of it had caused him to begin the slow and painful process of putting his house in order, prior to quitting it for ever—prior to seeking death by his own hand.

For nearly an hour he had been huddled up in the big leather armchair almost immovable. He had scrawled two or three letters, and written the superscription upon their envelopes, and from his writing-table he had taken a bundle of letters tied with a faded blue ribbon. One by one he had read them through, and then, placing them in the grate, he had applied a match and burnt them all. Some other business documents followed, as well as an old parchment deed, which he first tried to tear, but at last burned until it was merely twisted tinder.

It was now afternoon, and the silence of that house of mystery, wherein no one save Charles Rolfe ever penetrated, was unbroken. Across the soft green carpet lay a bar of warm sunlight that seemed strangely out of place in that sombre apartment, with its despairing owner, while outside the shabby stranger was no longer to be seen.

He might be lurking in the vicinity, but Levi had an hour ago entered and informed his master that the patient vigil had been relaxed.

Old Sam had dismissed him with a grunt of dissatisfaction. Those last hours of his life he wished to spend alone.

He had been trying to see some way out of the *cul-de-sac* in which he found himself, but there was none. That shabby wayfarer—his worst enemy, had found him. Years ago he had sworn a terrible vengeance, but for secret reasons, known only to Statham himself, he had laughed his threats to scorn. Then came his death, and Statham was free, free to prosper, become rich and powerful, and use his great wealth for good or for evil as he felt so inclined.

He had, however, used it for good. His contributions to charities were many and handsome. Among other things, he had built and endowed a wing of the London Hospital, for which his Majesty signified his intention of conferring a baronetcy upon him. But that honour he declined. To his brother in the City he had said, "I don't wish for any honour, and I'll remain plain Sam to the end of my days." There was a reason—a secret reason—why he was unable to receive the distinction. None knew it—none even dreamed.

The papers expressed wonder at the refusal, and people called him a fool. In Old Broad Street men were envious, and laughed in their sleeves. Yet if they had known the real reason they would surely have stood aghast.

One day, however, his private secretary, young Rolfe, had come to him with a strange and improbable tale. His enemy was alive and well, and was, moreover, actually in England! He questioned the young man, and found certain discrepancies in the statement. Therefore, shrewd and far-seeing, he refused to believe it, and suspected blackmail to be the ultimate intention. He did not, however, suspect Rolfe of any inclination that way. He was both faithful and devoted.

Five years before, Rolfe's father, a man of considerable means who had been interested in his financial undertakings, burnt his fingers badly over a concession given by the Persian Government and became bankrupt. A year later he died, a ruined man, leaving a son Charles and a daughter Marion. The latter had been compelled, he understood, to earn her living in a London shop, and the former, who had only recently come down from Oxford, he had engaged as his confidential secretary.

He had indeed done this because he had felt that Charlie's father had made the ruinous speculation upon his advice, and it therefore behoved him to do some little for the dead man's children. Few men in the City of London in these modern days are possessors of consciences, and those who have are usually too busy with their own affairs to think of the children of ruined friends.

Old Sam Statham was a hard man, it must be admitted. He would drive a bargain to the last fraction of percentage, and in repayment of loans he was relentless sometimes. Yet the acts of private charity that he did were many, and he never sought to advertise them.

In Charles Rolfe he had not been disappointed. Never once had he disobeyed the orders he had given, and, what was more, never once had he sought to penetrate beyond the door at the head of the staircase which shut off the ground floor from the one above.

The first day that Rolfe came to attend to his correspondence he had told him that he must never ascend those stairs, and that if he did he would be discharged at a moment's notice.

This prohibition struck the young man as curious and lent additional colour to the whispers of mystery concerning the fine fashionable house. A thousand weird suggestions arose within his mind of what was concealed upstairs, yet he was powerless to investigate, and, after a few weeks, grew to regard his master's words as those of an eccentric man whose enormous wealth had rendered a trifle extraordinary at times.

Old Levi was janitor of that green baize door. Situated round the corner, no one standing in the hall could see it. Therefore its existence was unsuspected. But it was an iron door covered with green baize, and always kept locked. Levi kept the key, and to all Rolfe's inquisitiveness he was dumb.

"The master allows nobody upstairs," was always his reply. "I sleep downstairs because I am not permitted to ascend."

What other servants might be there he knew not. Levi was the only other person he ever saw. The curtains at the upper windows always looked fresh and smart, and often as he went up Park Lane at night and glanced up at them, he saw lights in them, showing that they must be inhabited.

At first all this puzzled him sorely. He had told Marion about it, and also Maud Petrovitch, both girls being intensely interested in the mystery of the house and the character of the unseen occupants of its upper floors.

But as Charlie declared that old Statham was eccentric in everything, the mystery had gradually worn off and been forgotten.

The old man's face had sadly changed since early morning. His countenance now was that of a man in sheer despair. He had looked up the Continental Bradshaw and had scrawled half a dozen telegrams, addressed to his secretary, now on his way to Servia, and these had been taken to the post-office by Levi.

But it was all in vain. The message to Belgrade could not possibly reach Rolfe for another three days, and then, alas! it would be too late.

Before then he would be finished with all earthly things, and the world would denounce him as a coward. Yet even that would be preferable to standing and hearing his enemy's denunciation than facing exposure, ridicule, and ruin.

"Levi was right when he suggested flight," he was murmuring to himself. "Yet where can I go? I'm too well-known. My portrait is constantly in the papers, and, save Greece, there is no country in which I could obtain sanctuary. Again, suppose I got safely to Greece, what about the firm's credit? It would be gone. But if I die to-day, before this man returns, they cannot accuse the dead, and the firm, being in a sound financial position, cannot be attacked. No, only by my own death can I save the situation. I must sacrifice myself. There is no help for it! None! I must die!"

He gazed wildly around the big old-fashioned room as though his eyes were searching for some means of escape.

But there was none. His past had that day risen against him, and he was self-condemned.

His chin sank again upon his chest, and his deep-set eyes were fixed upon the soft, dark-green carpet. The marble clock chimed the hour of four, and recalled him to a sense of his surroundings.

He stretched himself, sighing deeply. He was wondering, when that shabby watcher, who held his life in his dirty talons, would return.

Thoughts of the past, tragic and bitter, arose within him, and a muttered imprecation escaped his thin, white lips. He was faced with a problem that even the expenditure of his millions could not solve. He could purchase anything on earth, but he could not buy a few more years of his own life.

He envied the man who was poor and struggling, the man with a cheerful wife and loving children, the man who worked and earned and had no far-reaching interests. The wage-earner was to him the ideal life of a man, for he obtained an income without the enormous responsibility consequent upon being a "principal." His vast wealth was but a millstone about his neck.

That little leather book, with its brass lock, wherein was recorded his financial position in a nutshell, was lying upon the table. When he had consulted it he had been appalled. He was worth far more than he had ever imagined. And yet, by an irony of fate, the accumulation of that wealth was now to cost him his life!

The long bar of sunlight had been moving slowly across the carpet, all the afternoon. Old Sam Statham has risen and crossed again to his writing-table, searching among some papers in a drawer, and finding a silver cigarette case, much tarnished by long neglect. This he opened, and within was displayed one tiny object. It was not a cigarette, but a tiny glass tube with a glass stopper, containing a number of very small white pilules.

He was gazing thoughtfully upon these, without removing the tube from its hiding-place, when, of a sudden, the door opened, and Levi, his pale face flushed with excitement and half breathless, entered, exclaiming in a low whisper:

"Rolfe is here! Shall I show him in?"

"Rolfe!" gasped the millionaire in a voice of amazement. "Are you serious, Levi?"

"Serious? Of course. He has just called and asked if you can see him."

"Show him in instantly," was Statham's answer, as hope became at that instant renewed. "We may find a way out of this difficulty yet—with his aid."

"We may," echoed Levi, closing the door for a moment behind him, so that the young man might not overhear his words. "We may; but recollect that he is a man in love."

"Well?"

"And he loves that girl Maud Petrovitch. Don't you understand—eh?" asked Levi, with an evil flash in his eyes.

"Ah! I see," replied his master, biting his under lip. "I follow you, Levi. It is good that you warned me. Leave the girl to me. Show him in."

"You know what I told you a few days ago—of his friendship with Petrovitch," the old servant went on. "Recollect that what I said was the truth, and act upon the confidential information I gave you. In this matter you've a difficult task before you, but don't be chicken-hearted and generous, as you are so very often. You're in a tight corner, and you must get out of it somehow, by hook or by crook."

"Trust me to look after myself," responded the millionaire, with a sudden smile upon his pale, haggard face, for he saw that with his secretary in London he might after all escape, and he had already closed the tarnished cigarette case that contained those pilules by which he had been contemplating ending his stormy existence. "Tell him to come in."

"But I beg of you to be firm. You're not a fool," urged Levi, bending earnestly towards him. "What is a woman's honour as compared with your future? You must sacrifice her—or yourself. There are many women in the world, recollect—but there is only one Samuel Statham!"

Chapter Eleven
Samuel Statham Makes Confession

When Rolfe entered old Sam's presence he saw that something was amiss.

Was it possible that his employer knew his secret—the secret of his visit to Cromwell Road on the previous night? Perhaps he did. The suggestion crossed his mind, and he stood breathless for a few seconds.

"I thought you had left for Servia, Rolfe," exclaimed the old man in his thin, weak voice. He had seated himself at the writing-table prior to his secretary's appearance, and had tried to assume a businesslike air. But his face was unusually drawn and haggard.

"I missed the train last night," was the young man's reply. "It is useless to leave till to-night, as I can then catch the Orient Express from Paris to-morrow morning. Therefore I thought I'd call to see if you have any further instructions."

The old man grunted. His keen eyes were fixed upon the other's face. The explanation was an unsatisfactory one.

Samuel Statham, as became a great financier, had a wonderful knack of knowing all that passed. He had his spies and secret agents in every capital, and was always well informed of every financial move in progress. To him, early information often meant profits of many thousands, and that information was indeed paid for generously.

In London, too, his spies were ever at work. Queer, mysterious persons of both sexes often called there in Park Lane, and were admitted to private audience of the king of the financial world. Rolfe knew them to be his secret agents, and, further, that his employer's knowledge of his own movements was often wider than he had ever dreamed.

No man in the whole City of London was more shrewd or more cunning than old Sam Statham. It was to the interest of Statham Brothers to be so. Indeed, he had once remarked to his secretary that no secret, however carefully kept, was safe from his agents, and that he could discover without difficulty anything he wanted to know.

Had he discovered the truth regarding the strange disappearance of the Doctor and his daughter?

"Why did you lose the train last night, Rolfe?" asked the great financier. "You did not go to Charing Cross," he added.

Rolfe held his breath again. Yes, as he had feared, his departure had been watched for.

"I—well, it was too late, and so I didn't attempt to catch the train."

"Why too late?" asked Statham, reprovingly. "In a matter of business— and especially of the magnitude of yours at this moment—one should never be behindhand. Your arrival in Belgrade twenty-four hours late may mean a loss of about twenty thousand to the firm."

"I hope not, sir," Rolfe exclaimed, quickly. "I trust that the business will go through all right. I—I did my best to catch the train!"

"Your best! Why, you had half a day in which to pack and get to Charing Cross!"

"I quite admit that, but I was prevented."

"By what?" asked Statham, fixing his eyes upon the young man before him.

"By a matter of private business."

"Yes—a woman! You may as well admit it, Rolfe, for I know all about it. You can't deceive me, you know."

The other's face went ghastly white, much to Statham's surprise. The latter saw that he had unconsciously touched a point which had filled his secretary with either shame or fear, and made a mental note of it.

"I don't deny it, sir," he faltered, much confused. He had no idea that his employer had any knowledge of Maud.

"Well—you're an idiot," he said, very plainly. "You'll never get on in the world if you're tied to a woman's shoe strings, depend upon it. Girls are the ruin of young men like you. When a man is free, he's his own master, but as soon as he becomes the slave of a pretty face then he's a lost soul both to himself and to those who employ him. Take the advice of an old man, Rolfe," he added, not unkindly. "Cast off the trammels, and be free to go hither and thither. When I was your age, I believed in what men call love. Bah! Live as long as I have, and watch human nature as I have watched it, and you'll come to the same conclusion as I have arrived at."

"And what is that?" asked Rolfe, for such conversation was altogether unusual.

"That woman is man's ruin always—that the more beautiful the woman the more complete the ruin," he answered, in the hard, unsympathetic way which he sometimes did when he wished to emphasise a point.

Charlie Rolfe was silent. He was familiar with old Sam's eccentricities, one of which was that he must never be contradicted. His amazing prosperity had induced an overbearing egotism. It was better to make no reply.

At heart the old man was beside himself with delight that his secretary had not left London, but it was his policy never to betray pleasure at anything. He seldom bestowed a single word of praise upon anyone. He was silent when satisfied, and bitterly sarcastic when not pleased.

"I do not think, sir, that whatever you may have heard concerning the lady in question is to her detriment," he could not refrain from remarking.

"All that I have heard is very favourable, I admit. Understand that I say nothing against the lady. What I object to is the principle of a young man being in love. Why court unhappiness? You'll meet with sufficient of it in the world, I can assure you. Look at me! Should I be what I am if I had saddled myself with a woman and her worries of society, frocks, children, petty jealousies, flirtations, and the thousand and one cares and annoyances which make a man's life a burden to him.

"No. Take my advice, and let those fools who run after trouble go their own way. Sentimentalists may write screeds and poets sonnets, but you'll find, my boy, that the only true friend you'll have in life is your own pocket."

Charlie was not in the humour to be lectured, and more especially upon his passionate devotion to Maud. He was annoyed that Statham should have found it out, and yet, knowing the wide-reaching sources of information possessed by the old millionaire, it was scarcely to be wondered at.

¬ "Of course," he admitted, somewhat impatiently, "there is a good deal of truth in your argument, even though it be a rather blunt one. Yet are not some men happy with the love of a good wife?"

"A few—alas! a very few," Statham replied. "Think of our greatest men. Nearly all of them have had skeletons in their cupboards because of their early infatuations. Of some, their domestic unhappiness is well-known. Others have, however, hidden it from the world, preferring to suffer than to humiliate themselves or admit their foolishness," he said, with a calm cynicism. "To-day you think me heartless, without sentiment, because you are inexperienced. Twenty years hence recollect my words, and you will be fully in accord with me, and probably regret deeply not having followed my advice."

With his thin hand he turned over some papers idly, and then, after a moment's pause, his manner changed, and he said, with a good-humoured laugh:

"You won't listen to me, I know, Rolfe. So what is the use of expounding my theory?"

"It is very valuable," the young man declared, deferentially. "I know that you are antagonistic towards women. All London is aware of that."

"And they think me eccentric—eh?" he laughed. "Well, I do not want them. Society I have no use for. It is all too shallow, too ephemeral, and too much make-believe. If I wished to go into Society to-morrow, it would welcome me. The door of every house in this neighbourhood would be opened to me. Why? Because my money is the key by which I can enter.

"The most exclusive set would be delighted to come here, eat my dinners, listen to my music, and borrow my money. But who among the whole of that narrow, fast-living little world would care to know me as a poor man? I have known what it is to be poor, Rolfe," he went on; "poorer than yourself. The world knows nothing of my past—of the romance of my life. One day, when I am dead, it may perhaps know. But until then I preserve my secret."

He was leaning back in his padded chair, staring straight before him, just as he had been an hour ago.

"Yes," he continued; "I recollect one cold January night, when I passed along the pavement yonder," and jerked his finger in the direction of the street. "I was penniless, hungry, and chilled to the bone. A man in evening-dress was coming from this very house, and I begged from him a few coppers, for I had tasted nothing that day, and further, my poor mother was dying at home—dying of starvation. The man refused, and cursed me for daring to beg charity. I turned upon him and cursed him in return; I vowed that if ever I had money I would one day live in his house. He jeered at me and called me a maniac.

"But, strangely enough, my words were prophetic. My fortune turned. I prospered. I am to-day living in the house of the man who cursed me, and that man himself is compelled to beg charity of me! Ah, yes!" he exclaimed suddenly, rising from his chair with a sigh. "The world little dreams of what my past has been. Only one man knows—the man whom you told me, Rolfe, a little time ago, is in England and alive."

"What—the man Adams?" exclaimed Rolfe, in surprise.

"Yes," replied his employer, in a hoarse, changed voice. "He knows everything."

"Things that would be detrimental to you?" asked his private secretary slowly.

"He is unscrupulous, and would prove certain things that—well, I—I admit to you in strictest confidence, Rolfe, that it would be impossible for me to face."

Charlie stared at him in utter amazement.

"Then you have satisfied yourself that what I told you is correct?"

"I disbelieved you when you told me. But I no longer doubt."

"Why?"

"Because I have seen him to-day—seen him with my own eyes. He was standing outside, there against the railings, watching the house."

"And did he see you?"

"He saw and recognised me."

Charlie gave vent to a low whistle. He recognised the seriousness of the situation. As private secretary he was in old Statham's confidence to a certain extent, but never before had he made such an admission of fear as that he had just done.

"Where is he now?"

"I don't know. Gone to prepare his coup for my ruin, most probably," was the old man's response, in a strained unnatural voice. "But listen, Rolfe. I have told you to-day what I would tell no other man. In you I have reposed many confidences, because I know you well enough to be confident that you will never betray them."

"You honour me, sir, by those words," the young man said. "I endeavour to serve you faithfully as it is my duty. I am not forgetful of all that you have done for my sister and myself."

"I know that you are grateful, Rolfe," he said, placing his bony hand upon the young man's shoulder. "Therefore I seek your aid in this very delicate affair. The man Adams has returned from the grave—how, I do not know. So utterly bewildering is it all that I was at first under the belief that my eyes were deceiving me—that some man had been made up to resemble him and to impose upon me. Yet there is no imposture. The man whom I know to be dead is here in London, and alive!"

"But did you actually see him dead?" asked Rolfe, innocently.

Old Statham started quickly at the question.

"Er—well—no. I mean, I didn't exactly see him dead myself," he faltered.

"Then how are you so very positive that he died?"

"Well, there was a funeral, a certificate, and insurance money was, I believe, paid."

"That does not prove that he died," remarked Rolfe. "I thought I understood you to say distinctly when we spoke of it the other day that you had actually stood beside the dead body of John Adams, and that you had satisfied yourself that life was extinct."

"No! no!" cried the old man, uneasily, his face blanched. "If I led you to suppose that, I was wrong. I meant to imply that, from information furnished by others, I was under the belief that he had died."

Charlie Rolfe was silent. Why had his employer altered his declaration so as to suit the exigencies of the moment?

He raised his eyes to old Sam's countenance, and saw that it was the face of a man upon whom the shadow of a crime had fallen.

Chapter Twelve
In which a Woman's Honour is at Stake

"John Adams has seen you!" exclaimed Rolfe, slowly. "Therefore the situation is, I understand, one of extreme peril. Is that so?"

"Exactly," responded the millionaire, in a thin, weak voice. "But by your aid I may yet extricate myself."

The younger man saw that the other was full of fear. Never had he seen his employer so nervous and utterly unstrung. The mystery of it all fascinated him. Statham had unwittingly acknowledged having been present at the presumed death of John Adams, and that in itself was a very suspicious circumstance.

"Whatever assistance I can give I am quite ready to render it," he said, little dreaming what dire result would attend that offer.

"Ah, yes!" cried the old man, thankfully, grasping his secretary's hand. "I knew you would not refuse, Rolfe. If you succeed I shall owe my life to you; you understand—my life!" And he looked straight into the young man's face, adding, "And Samuel Statham never forgets to repay a service rendered."

"I look for no repayment," he said. "You have been so very good to my sister and myself that I owe you a deep debt of gratitude."

"Ah! your sister. Where is she now?"

"At Cunnington's, in Oxford Street."

"Oh, yes! I forgot. I wrote to Cunnington myself regarding her, didn't I? I hope she's comfortable. If not, tell me. I'm the largest shareholder in that business."

"You are very kind," replied the young man. "But she always says she is most comfortable, and all the principals are very kind to her. Of course, it was hard for her at first when she commenced to earn her own living. The hours, the confinement, and the rigorous rules were irksome to a girl of her character, always been used as she had to freedom and a country life."

"Yes," replied the old man rather thoughtfully. "I suppose so. But if she's getting on well, I am quite satisfied. Should she have any complaint to make, don't fail to let me know."

Rolfe thanked him. The old fellow, notwithstanding his eccentricities, was always a generous master.

There was a pause, during which the millionaire walked to the window, peered out to see if the shabby watcher had returned, and then came back again to his table.

"Rolfe," he commenced, as he seated himself, with surprising calmness, "I have spoken more openly to you this afternoon than I have spoken to anyone for many years. First, you must remain in London. Just ring them up in the City, and tell them to send Sheldon here, and say that he must leave for Belgrade to-night. I will see him at seven o'clock."

The secretary took up the transmitter of the private telephone line to the offices of Statham Brothers in Old Broad Street, and in a few moments was delivering the principal's message to the manager.

"Sheldon will be here at seven for instructions," he said, as he replaced the transmitter.

"Then sit down, Rolfe—and listen," the old man commanded, indicating a chair at the side of the table. The younger man obeyed, and the great financier commenced.

"You have promised your help, and also complete secrecy, have you not?"

"I shall say nothing," answered the other, at the same time eager to hear some closed page in the old man's history. "Rely upon my discretion."

He was wondering whether the grey-faced old fellow was aware of the startling events of the previous evening in Cromwell Road. His spies had told him of Maud. They perhaps had discovered that amazing truth of what had occurred in that house, now deserted and empty.

Was it possible that old Statham, being in possession of his secret, did not now fear to repose confidence in him, for he knew that if he were betrayed he could on his part make an exposure that must prove both ruinous and fatal. The crafty old financier was not the person to place himself unreservedly in the hands of any man who could possibly turn his enemy. He had an ulterior motive, without a doubt. But what it was Charles Rolfe was unable to discover.

"The mouth of that man Adams must be closed," said the old man, in a slow, deliberate voice, "and you alone are able to accomplish it. Do this for me, and I can afford to pay well," and he regarded the young man with a meaning look.

Was it possible that he suggested foul play. Rolfe wondered. Was he suggesting that he should lurk in some dark corner and take the life of the shabby wayfarer, who had recently returned to England after a long absence?

"It is not a question of payment," Rolfe replied. "It is whether any effort of mine can be successful."

"Yes; I know. I admit, Rolfe, that I was a fool. I ought to have listened to you when you first told me of his re-appearance, and I ought to have approached him and purchased his silence. I thought myself shrewd, and my cautiousness has been my undoing."

"From the little I know, I fear that the purchase of the fellow's silence is now out of the question. A week ago it could have been effected, but now he has cast all thought of himself to the winds, and his only object is revenge."

"Revenge upon myself," sighed the old man, his face growing a trifle paler as he foresaw what a terrible vengeance was within the power of that shabby stranger. "Ah! I know. He will be relentless. He has every reason to be if what has been told him had been true. A man lied—the man who is dead. Therefore the truth—the truth that would save my honour and my life—can never be told," he added, with a desperate look upon his countenance.

"Then you have been the victim of a liar?" Rolfe said. "Yes—of a man who, jealous of my prosperity, endeavoured to ruin me by making a false statement. But his reward came quickly. I retaliated with my financial strength, and in a year he was ruined. To recoup himself he committed forgery, was arrested, and six months later died in prison—but without confessing that what he had said concerning me was a foul invention. John Adams believed it—and because of that, among other things, is my bitterest enemy."

"But is there no way of proving the truth?" asked Rolfe, surprised at this story.

"None. The fellow put forward in support of his story proofs which he had forged. Adams naturally believed they were genuine."

"And where are those proofs now?"

"Probably in Adams' possession. He has no doubt hoarded them for use at the moment of his triumph."

Rolfe did not speak for several moments.

"A week ago those proofs might, I believe, have been purchased for a round sum."

"Could they not be purchased now? From the man's appearance he is penniless."

"Not so poor as you think. If what I've heard is true, he is in possession of funds. His shabbiness is only assumed. Have you any knowledge of a certain man named Lyle—a short man slightly deformed."

"Lyle!" gasped his employer. "Do you mean Leonard Lyle? What do you know of him?"

"I saw him in the company of Adams. It is he who supplies the latter with money."

"Lyle!" cried Statham, his eyes glaring in amazement. "Lyle here—in London?"

"He was here a week ago. You know him?"

"Know him—yes!" answered the old millionaire, hoarsely. "Are you certain that he has become Adams' friend?"

"I saw them together with my own eyes. They were sitting in the Café Royal, in Regent Street. Adams was in evening-dress, and wore an opera-hat. They'd been to the Empire together."

"Why didn't you tell me all this before?" asked Statham, in a tone of blank despair. "I—I see now all the difficulties that have arisen. The pair have united to wreak their vengeance upon me, and I am powerless and unprotected."

"But who is this man Leonard Lyle?" inquired the secretary.

"A man without a conscience. He was a mining engineer, and is now, I suppose—a short, white-moustached man, with a slightly humped back and a squeaky voice."

"The same."

"Why didn't you tell me this before? If Lyle knows Adams, the position is doubly dangerous," he exclaimed, in abject dismay. "No," he added, bitterly; "there can be no way out."

"I said nothing because you had refused to believe."

"You saw them together after you had told me of Adams' return, or before?"

"After," he replied. "Even though you refused to believe me, I continued to remain watchful in your interests and those of the firm. I spent several evenings in watching their movements."

"Ah! you are loyal to me, I know, Rolfe. You shall not regret this. Hitherto I have not treated you well, but I will now try and atone for the manner in which I misjudged you. I ask your pardon."

"For what?" inquired Rolfe, in surprise.

"For believing ill of you," was all the old man vouchsafed.

"I tried to do my duty as your secretary," was all he said.

"Your duty. You have done more. You have watched my enemies even though I sneered at your well-meant warning," he said. "But if you have watched, you perhaps know where the pair are in hiding."

"Lyle lives at the First Avenue Hotel, in Holborn. Adams lives in a small furnished flat in Addison Mansions, close to Addison Road railway station."

"Lives there in preference to an hotel because he can go in and out shabby and down-at-heel without attracting comment—eh?"

"I suppose so. I had great difficulty in following him to his hiding-place without arousing his suspicions."

"Does he really mean mischief?" asked the principal of Statham Brothers, bending slightly towards his secretary.

"Yes; undoubtedly he does. The pair are here with the intention of bringing ruin upon you and upon the house of Statham," was Rolfe's quiet reply.

"Then only you can save me, Rolfe," cried the old man, starting up wildly.

"How? Tell me, and I am ready to act upon your instructions," Rolfe said.

The millionaire placed his hand upon the young man's shoulder and said:

"Repeat those words."

Rolfe did so.

"And you will not seek to inquire the reason of a request I may make to you, even though it may sound an extraordinary and perhaps mysterious one?"

"I will act as you wish, without desiring to know your motives."

The great financier stood looking straight into his secretary's eyes. He was deeply in earnest, for his very life now depended upon the other's assent. How could he put the proposal to the man before him?

"Then I take that as a promise, Rolfe," he said at last. "You will not withdraw. You will swear to assist me at all hazards—to save me from these men."

"I swear."

"Good! Then to-day—nay, at this very hour—you must make what no doubt will be to you a great sacrifice."

"What do you mean?" asked Rolfe, quickly.

"I mean," the old man said, in a very slow distinct voice—"I mean that you must first sacrifice the honour of the woman you love—Maud Petrovitch."

"Maud Petrovitch!" he gasped, utterly mystified.

"Yes," he answered. "You have promised to save me—you have sworn to assist me, and the sacrifice is imperative! It is her honour—or my death!"

Chapter Thirteen
Describes the Man from Nowhere

Late that same night, in the small and rather well-furnished dining-room of a flat close to Addison Road station, the beetle-browed man known to some as John Adams and to others as Jean Adam was seated in a comfortable armchair smoking a cigarette.

He was no longer the shabby, half-famished looking stranger who had been watching outside Statham's house in Park Lane, but rather dandified in his neat dinner jacket, glossy shirt-front, and black tie. Adventurer was written all over his face. He was a man whose whole life history had been a romance and who had knocked about in various odd and out-of-the-way corners of the world. A cosmopolitan to the backbone, he, like his friend Leonard Lyle, whom he was at that moment expecting, hated the trammels of civilised society, and their lives had mostly been spent in places where human life was cheap and where justice was unknown.

Alone in that small room where the dinner-cloth had been removed and a decanter and glasses had been placed by his one elderly serving-woman, who had now gone for the night, he was muttering to himself as he smoked—murmuring incoherent words that sounded much like threats.

It was difficult to recognise in this well-groomed, gentlemanly-looking man, with the diamond in his shirt-front and the sparkling ring upon his finger, the low-looking tramp whose eyes had encountered those of the man whose ruin he now sought to encompass.

In half a dozen capitals of the world he was known as Jean Adam, for he spoke French perfectly, and passed as a French subject, a native of Algiers; but in London, New York, and Montreal he was known as the wandering and adventurous Englishman John Adams.

Whether he was really English was doubtful. True, he spoke English without the slightest trace of accent, yet sometimes in his gesture, when unduly excited, there was unconsciously betrayed his foreign birth.

His French was as perfect as his English. He spoke with an accent of the South, and none ever dreamed that he could at the same time speak the pure, unadulterated Cockney slang.

He had just glanced at his watch, and knit his brows when the electric bell rang, and he rose to admit a short, triangular-faced, queer-looking little old man, whose back was bent and whose body seemed too large for his legs. He, too, was in evening-dress, and carried his overcoat across his arm.

"I began to fear, old chap, that you couldn't come," Adams exclaimed, as he hung his friend's coat in the narrow hall. "You didn't acknowledge my wire."

"I couldn't until too late. I was out," the other explained, in a tone of apology. "Well," he asked, with a sigh, as he stretched himself before he seated himself in the proffered chair, "what has happened?"

"A lot, my dear fellow. We shall come out on top yet."

"Be more explicit. What do you mean?"

"What I say," was Adams' response. "I've seen old Statham to-day."

"And he's seen you—eh?"

"Of course he has. And he's scared out of his senses—thinks he's seen a ghost, most likely," he laughed, in triumph. "But he'll find I'm much more than a ghost before he's much older, the canting old blackguard."

Lyle thought for a second.

"The sight of you has forearmed him! It was rather injudicious just at this moment, wasn't it?"

"Not at all. I meant to give him a surprise. If I'd have gone up to the house, rung the bell, and asked to see him, I should have been refused. He sees absolutely nobody, for there's a mystery connected with the house. Nobody has ever been inside."

"What!" exclaimed the old hunchbacked mining engineer. "That's interesting! Tell me more about it. Is it like the haunted house in Berkeley Square about which people used to talk so much years ago?"

"I don't think it's ever been alleged to be haunted," responded Adams. "Yet there are several weird and amazing stories told of it, and of the grim shadows which overhang it both night and day."

"What stories have you heard?" asked his companion, taking a cigarette from the box, for he had suddenly become much interested.

"Well, it is said that the place is the most gorgeously furnished of any house in that select quarter, and that it is full of art treasures, old silver, miniatures, and antique furniture, for old Statham is a well-known collector and is known to have purchased many very fine specimens of antiques during the past few years. They say that, having furnished the place from kitchen to garret in the most costly manner possible, he sought out the old love of his earlier days—a woman who assisted him in the foundation of his fortune, and invited her to inspect the house. They went round it together, and after luncheon he proposed marriage to her. To his chagrin, she declined the honour of becoming the wife of a millionaire."

"She was a bit of a fool, I should suppose," remarked the hunchback.

"They were fond enough of each other. She was nearly twenty years his junior, and though they had been separated for a good many years, he was still devoted to her. When she refused to marry him, there was a scene. And at last she was compelled to admit the truth—she was the wife of another! A quarter of an hour later she left the house in tears, and from that moment the beautiful mansion, with the exception of two or three rooms, has been closed. He will allow nobody to pass upstairs, and the place remains the same as on that day when all his hopes of happiness were shattered."

"But you said there were stories concerning the house," Lyle remarked, between the whiffs of his cigarette.

"So there are. Both yesterday and to-day I've been making inquiries and been told many curious things. A statement, for instance, made to me is to the effect that one night about a month ago the chauffeur of the great Lancashire cotton-spinner living a few doors away was seated on the car at two o'clock in the morning, ready to take two of his master's guests down to their home near Epsom, when he noticed Statham's windows all brilliantly lit.

"From the drawing-room above came the sounds of waltz music—a piano excellently played. This struck the man as curious, well knowing the local belief that the upper portion of the house was kept rigorously closed. Yet, from all appearances, the old millionaire was that night entertaining guests, which was further proved when a quarter of an hour later the door opened and old Levi, the man-servant, came forth. As he did so, a four-wheeled cab, which had been waiting opposite, a little further up the road, drew across, and a few moments later both Levi and Statham appeared, struggling with a long, narrow black box, which, with the cabman's aid, was put on top of the vehicle. The box much resembled a coffin, and seemed unusually heavy.

"So hurried and excited were the men that they took no notice of the motor car, and the cab next moment drove away, the man no doubt having previously received his orders. The music had ceased, and as soon as the cab had departed the lights in the windows were extinguished, and the weird home remained in darkness."

"Very curious. Looks about as though there had been some foul play, doesn't it?" Lyle suggested.

"That's what the chauffeur suspects. I've spoken with him myself, and he tells me that the box was so like a coffin that the whole incident held him fascinated," Adams said. "And, of course, this story getting about, has set other people on the watch. Indeed, only last night a very curious affair occurred. It was witnessed by a man who earns his living washing carriages in the mews close by, and who has for years taken an interest in the mysterious home of Samuel Statham.

"He had been washing carriages till very late, and at about half-past two in the morning was going up Park Lane towards Edgware Road, where he lives, when his attention was drawn to the fact that as he passed Statham's house the front door was slightly ajar. Somebody was waiting there for the expected arrival of a stranger, and, hearing the carriage washer's footstep, had opened the door in readiness. There was no light in the hall, and the man's first suspicion was that of burglars about to leave the place.

"Next instant, however, the reputation for mystery which the place had earned, occurred to him, and he resolved to pass on and watch. This he did, retiring into a doorway a little farther down, and standing in the shadow unobserved he waited.

"Half an hour passed, but nothing unusual occurred, until just after the clock had struck three, a rather tall, thin man passed quietly along. He was in evening-dress, and wore pumps, for his tread was noiseless. The man describes him as an aristocratic-looking person, and evidently a foreigner. At Statham's door he suddenly halted, looked up and down furtively to satisfy himself that he was not being watched, and then slipped inside."

"And what then?" inquired Lyle, much interested.

"A very queer circumstance followed," went on the cosmopolitan. "There was, an hour and a half later, an exact repetition of the scene witnessed by the chauffeur."

"What! the black trunk?"

"Yes. A cab drove up near to the house, and, at signal from Levi, came up to the kerb. Then the long, heavy box was brought out by the servant and his master, heaved up on to the cab, which drove away in the direction of the Marble Arch."

"Infernally suspicious," remarked the hunchback, tossing his cigarette end into the grate. "Didn't the washer take note of the number of the cab?"

"No. That's the unfortunate part of it. Apparently he didn't notice the crawling four-wheeler until he saw Levi come forth and give the signal."

"And the aristocratic-looking foreigner? Could he recognise him again?"

"He says he could."

"That was last night—eh?"

"Yes."

"There may be some police inquiries regarding a missing foreigner," remarked Lyle, thoughtfully. "If so, his information may be valuable. How did you obtain it?"

"From his own lips."

"Then we had better wait, and watch to see if anybody is reported missing. Certainly that house is one of mystery."

"Sam Statham is unscrupulous. I know him to my cost," Adams remarked.

"And so do I," Lyle declared. "If what I suspect is true, then we shall make an exposure that will startle and horrify the world."

"You mean regarding the foreigner of last night?"

"Yes. I have a suspicion that I can establish the identity of the foreigner in question—a man who has to-day been missing?"

Chapter Fourteen
Reveals a Clever Conspiracy

"And who was he?" asked Adams, quickly.

"For the present that is my own affair," the hunchback replied. "Suffice it for you to know that we hold Samuel Statham in the hollow of our hand."

"I don't know so much about that," remarked Adams, dubiously. "I thought so until this morning."

"And why, pray, has your opinion changed?"

"Because when he came a second time to the window and looked out at me, there was a glance of defiance in his eye that I scarcely lie. He's wealthy and influential—we are not, remember."

"Knowledge is power. We shall be the victors."

"You are too sanguine, my dear fellow," declared the other. "We are angling for big game, and to my idea the bait is not sufficiently attractive."

"Statham is unscrupulous—so are we. We can prove our story—prove it up to the hilt. Dare he face us? That's the question."

"I think he dare," Adams replied. "You don't know him as well as I do. His whole future now depends upon his bluff, and he knows it. We can ruin both the house of Statham Brothers and its principal. In the circumstances, it is only natural that he should assume an air of defiance."

"Which we must combat by firmness. We are associated in this affair, and my advice is not to show any sign of weakness."

"Exactly. That's the reason I asked you here to-night, Lyle—to discuss our next step."

The hunchback was silent and thoughtful for a few moments. Then he said:

"There is but one mode of procedure now, and that is to go to him and tell him our intentions. He'll be frightened, and the rest will be easy."

"Sam Statham is not very easily frightened. You wouldn't be, if you were worth a couple of million pounds." Adams remarked, with a dubious shake of the head.

"I should be if upon me rested the burden of guilt."

"Then your suggestion is that I should go and tell him openly my intentions?"

"Decidedly. The more open you are, the greater will be the old man's terror, and the easier our ultimate task."

"He'll refuse to see me."

"He goes down to the City sometimes. Better call there and present a false card. He won't care to be faced in the vicinity of his managers and clerks. It will show him from the first that the great home of Statham is tottering."

"And it shall fall!" declared Adams, with a triumphant chuckle. "We hold the trump cards, it is true. The only matter to be decided is how we shall play them."

"They must be played very carefully, if we are to win."

"Win?" echoed the other. "Why, man, we can't possibly lose."

"Suppose he died?"

"He won't die, I'll take care of that," said Adams, with a fierce expression upon his somewhat evil countenance. "No; the old blackguard shall live, and his life shall be rendered a hell of terror and remorse. He made my life so bitter that a thousand times I've longed for death. He taunted me with my misfortunes, ruined me and laughed in my face, jeered at my unhappiness and flaunted his wealth before me when I was penniless. But through all these years I have kept silence, laughing within myself because of his ignorance that I alone held his secret, and that when I chose I could rise and crush him.

"He had no suspicion of my knowledge until one blazing day in a foreign city I betrayed myself. I was a fool, I know. But very soon afterwards I repaid the error by death. I died and was buried, so that he then believed himself safe, and has remained in self-satisfied security until this morning, when his gaze met mine through the window. I have risen from the dead," he added, with a short, dry laugh; "risen to avenge myself by his ruin."

"And his death," added the hunchback.

"Don't I tell you he shall not die?" cried Adams. "What satisfaction should I have were he to commit suicide? No; I mean to watch his agony, to terrify him and drive him to an existence constantly fearing exposure and arrest. He shall not enjoy a moment's peace of mind, but shall be tortured by conscience and driven mad by terror. I will repay his evil actions towards me and mine a hundredfold."

"How can you prevent him escaping you by suicide?"

"He'll never do that, for he knows his suicide would mean the ruin of Statham Brothers, and perhaps the ruin of hundreds of families. The canting old hypocrite would rather do anything nowadays than ruin the poor investor."

"Yet look at his operations in earlier days! Did he not lay the foundation of the house by the exercise of cunning and unscrupulous double-dealing? Was it not mainly by his influence that a great war was forced on, and did he not clear, it is declared, more than half a million by sacrificing the lives of thousands? And he actually has the audacity to dole out sums to charities, and contributions to hospitals and convalescent homes!"

"The world always looks at a man's present, my dear old chap, never at his past," responded the hunchback.

"Unfortunately that is so, otherwise the truth would be remembered and the name of Statham held up to scorn and universal disgust. Yet," Adams went on, "I grant you that he is not much worse than others in the same category. The smug frock coat and light waistcoat of the successful City man so very often conceals a black and ungenerous heart."

"But if you really make this exposure as you threaten, it will arouse the greatest sensation ever produced in England in modern years," Lyle remarked, slowly lighting a fresh cigarette.

"I will make it—and more!" he declared, bringing his fist down heavily upon the table. "I have waited all these years for my revenge, and, depend upon it, it will be humiliating and complete."

For a few moments neither man spoke. At last Lyle said: "I have more than once wondered whether you are not making a mistake in your association with that young man Barclay."

"Max Barclay is a fool. He doesn't dream the real game we are playing with him."

"No. If he did, he wouldn't have anything to do with us."

"I suppose he wouldn't. But the whole thing appears to him such a gilt-edged one that we've fascinated him—and he'll be devilish useful to us in the near future."

"You've inquired about that girl, I suppose?"

"Yes. She's in a drapery shop—at Cunnington's, in Oxford Street, and, funnily enough, is sister of old Sam's secretary."

"His sister! By Jove! we ought to know her—one of us. She might be able to find out something."

"No: we must keep away from her at present," Adams urged. Then, in a curious voice, he added: "We may find it necessary to become her enemy, you know. And if so, she ought not to be personally acquainted with either of us. Do you follow me?"

"You mean that we may find it necessary to secure Max Barclay's aid at sacrifice of the girl—eh?"

His companion smiled meaningly.

"We must be careful how we use Barclay," Lyle said. "The young man has his eyes open."

"I know. I'm well aware of that," Adams said, quickly. "He will be of the greatest assistance to us."

"If he has no suspicions."

"What suspicion can he have?" laughed the other. "All that we've told him he believes to be gospel truth. Only the night before last we dined together at Romano's, and after an hour at the Empire he took me to his club to chat and smoke."

"He, of course, believes the story of the railway concession to be genuine," Lyle suggested. "Let me see, the concession is somewhere in the Balkans, isn't it?"

"Yes; the railroad from Nisch, in Servia, across Northern Albania, to San Giovanni di Medua, on the Adriatic. A grand scheme that's been talked of for years, and which the Sultan has always prevented by refusing to allow the line to pass through Turkish territory.

"Our story is," added Adams, "that his Majesty has at last signed an iradé granting permission, and that within a month or so the whole concession will be given over to an English group of whom I am the representative. I saw that the scheme appealed to him from the very first. He recognised that there was money in it, for such a line would tap the whole trade of the Balkans, and by a junction near the Iron Gates of the Danube, take the trade of Roumania, Hungary, and South-Western Russia to the Adriatic instead of as at present into the Black Sea.

"For the past week I've met Barclay nearly every day. He suggested that, as the railway would be a matter of millions, he should approach old Sam Statham and ask him to lend us his support."

"Does he know Statham?"

"Slightly. But I at once declined to allow him to speak about the scheme."

"Why?"

"Because old Sam, with the aid of his spies and informants in diplomatic circles, could in three days satisfy himself whether our story was true or false. It would have given the whole story away at once. So I made an excuse for continued secrecy."

"Quite right. We must not court failure by allowing any inquiry to be prematurely made," said Lyle. "Make the project a secret one, and speak of it with bated breath. Hint at diplomatic difficulties between Turkey and England, if the truth were known."

"That's just what I have done, and he's completely misled. I explained that Germany would try and bring pressure upon the Sultan to withdraw the iradé as soon as it were known that the railway had fallen into British hands. And he believed me implicitly!"

"He had no suspicion of whom you really are?"

"Certainly not. He believes that I've never met Statham but that I have the greatest admiration for his financial stability and his excellent personal qualities," Adams replied: "He knows me as Jean Adam, of Paris, as they do here in these flats—a man who has extensive business relations in the Near East, and therefore well in with the pashas of the Sublime Porte and the officials of the Yildiz. I tell you, Lyle, the young fellow believes in me."

"Because you're such a confoundedly clever actor, Adams. You'd deceive the cutest business man in London, with your wonderful documents, your rosy prospectuses, and your tales of fortunes ready to be picked up if only a few thousands are invested. You've thoroughly fascinated young Max Barclay, who, believing that you've obtained a very valuable concession, is seized with a laudable desire to share the profits and to obtain a lucrative occupation as a director of the company in question."

"Once he has fallen entirely in our power, the rest will be easy," answered the adventurer. "I mean to have my revenge, and you receive thirty thousand as your share."

"But what form is this revenge of yours to take?" the hunchback inquired. "You have never told me that."

"It is my own affair," answered Adams, leaning back against the mantelshelf.

"Well, I think between friends there should not be any distrust," Lyle remarked. "You don't think I'd give you away, do you? It's to my interest to assist you and obtain the thirty thousand."

"And you will, if you stick to me," Adams answered.

"But I'd like to know your main object."

"You know that already."

"But only yesterday you told me that you don't want a farthing of old Statham's money."

"Nor do I. His money has a curse upon it—the money filched from the pockets of widows and orphans, money that has been obtained by fraud and misrepresentation," cried Adams. "To-day he is respected and lauded on account of his pious air and his philanthropy; yet yesterday he floated rotten concerns and coolly placed hundreds of thousands in his pocket by reason of the glowing promises that he never fulfilled. No!" cried the man, clenching his strong, hard fist; "I don't want a single penny of his money. You, Lyle, may have what you want of it—thirty thousand to be the minimum."

"You talk as though you contemplated handling his fortune," the other remarked, in some surprise.

"When I reveal to him my intentions, his banking account will be at my disposal, depend upon it," Adams said. "But I don't want any of his bribes. I shall refuse them. I will have my revenge. It shall be an eye for an eye, and a tooth for a tooth. He showed me no mercy—and I will show him none—none. But it is Max Barclay who will assist me towards that end, and the girl at Cunnington's, Marion Rolfe, who must be made the catspaw." ˍ

Lyle remained thoughtful, his eyes upon the carpet.

"Yes," he said, slowly, at last. "I quite follow you and divine your intentions. But, remember she's a woman. Is it just—is it human?"

"Human!" echoed the cosmopolitan, removing his cigarette as he shrugged his shoulders with a nonchalant air. "To me it matters nothing, so long as I attain my object. Surely you are not chicken-hearted enough to be moved by a woman's tears."

"I don't understand you," his friend declared.

"No; I suppose you don't," he answered. "And, to be frank with you, Lyle, I don't intend at this moment that you shall. My intention is my own affair. I merely foreshadow to you the importation into the affair of a woman who will, through no fault of her own, be compelled to suffer in order to allow me to achieve the object I have in view."

The hunchback turned slightly towards the curtained window. He moved quickly in order to conceal an expression upon his face, which, had it been detected by his companion, the startling and amazing events recorded in the following chapters would surely never have occurred.

But John Adams, standing there in ignorance, was chuckling over the secret of the terrible triumph that was so very soon to be his—a triumph to be secured by the sacrifice of an honest woman!

Chapter Fifteen
More about Marion

The following Sunday afternoon was warm and bright, perfect for up-river excursions, and, as was their usual habit, Max and Marion were spending the day together.

Released from the eternal bustle of Oxford Street, the girl looked forward with eager anticipation to each Saturday afternoon and Sunday—the weekly period of rest and recreation. To the assistant in shops where the "living-in" system pertains, Sunday is the one bright interval in an otherwise dull, dreary, and monotonous life, the day when he or she gets away from the weariness of being businesslike, the smell of the "goods," and the keen eye of the buyer or shop-walker, and when one is one's own master for a few happy hours.

To those not apprenticed in their youth to shop-life who, being born in a higher status, have been compelled to enter business as a means of livelihood, the long hours are terribly irksome, especially in winter, when artificial light is used nearly the whole day. The work is soul-killing in its monotony and the pay very meagre, therefore customers need hardly be surprised when a tired assistant does not take the trouble to exert herself unduly to satisfy her requirements.

In summer, Marion loved the river. The air was fresh and healthful, after the vitiated atmosphere of the costume department at Cunnington's. Usually Max brought his little motor-boat from Biffen's, at Hammersmith Bridge, where he kept it, up to Kew, and there they would embark in the morning and run up to Hampton Court, Staines, or even Windsor, getting their luncheon or tea at one or other of the old riverside inns, and spending a lazy afternoon up some quiet, leafy backwater, where, though so near the metropolis, the king-fishers skimmed the surface of the stream and the water-lilies lay upon their broad, green leaves.

Those lazy hours spent together were always delightful, therefore, to the devoted pair, a wet Sunday was indeed a calamity. On the afternoon in question they had met at Kew Bridge at four o'clock, and as she sat upon the crimson cushions in the stern, they were ascending the broad Thames, the motor running as evenly as a clock, and leaving a small wash in their wake. Marion could not meet her lover before, because she had spent the morning with a poor girl who had been a fellow assistant at Cunnington's, and was now in Guy's Hospital. The girl was friendless and in a dangerous condition, therefore Marion had given up her morning and taken her some grapes.

There were not many people on the river, for pleasure-seekers usually prefer the reaches above Richmond. The craft they passed was mostly sailing boats, belonging to the club Chiswick, and the inevitable launch of the Thames Conservancy.

In a well-cut gown of plain white cotton, with lace and muslin at the throat, a straw hat of mushroom shape, with a band of pale blue velvet, and a white sunshade over her shoulder, she looked delightfully fresh and cool. He was in navy serge suit and a peaked cap, and in his mouth a pipe.

Seated sideways in the boat, with the throbbing motor at his feet, he thought he never had seen her looking so chic and indescribably charming. Those stiff black dresses, which custom forced her to wear in business, did not suit her soft beauty. But in her river dress she looked delightfully dainty, and he tried to conjure up a vision of what figure she would present in a well-cut evening gown. The latter, however, she did not possess. The shop-assistant has but little need of décolleté, and, indeed, its very possession arouses comment among the plainer, more prudish, and more elderly section of the girls in the "house."

More than once Max had wanted to take her to the stalls of a theatre in an evening gown, but she had always declared that she preferred wearing a light blouse. As a man generally is, he was a blunderer, and she could not well explain how, by the purchase of evening clothes, she would at once debase herself in the eyes of her fellow-assistants. As was well-known, her salary at Cunnington's certainly did not allow of such luxuries as theatre gowns, and from the very first she had always declined to accept Max's well-meant presents.

The only present of his that she had kept was the pretty ring now upon her slim, white hand, a ring set with sapphires and diamonds and inscribed within "From Max to Marion," with the date.

As she leaned back enjoying the fresh air, after the dust and stifling heat of London, she was relating how pleased the poor invalid had been at her visit, and he was listening to her description of her friend's desperate condition. A difficult operation had turned out badly, and the surgeons held out very little hope. Not a soul had been to see the poor girl all the week, the nurse had said, for she had no relatives, and all her friends were in business and unable to get out, except on Sunday.

"I very much fear she won't live to see next Sunday," Marion was saying, with a sigh, a cloud passing over her bright face. "It is so very sad. She's only twenty, and such a nice girl. Her father was a naval officer, but she was left penniless, and had to earn her own living."

"Like you yourself, dearest," he answered. "Ah! how I wish I could take you from that life of drudgery. I can't bear to think of you being compelled to slave as you do, and to wait upon those crotchety old cats, as many of your customers are. It's a shame that you should ever have gone into Cunnington's."

"Mr Statham, Charlie's employer, holds the controlling interest in our business. It was through him that I got in there. Without his influence they would never have taken me, for I had no experience. As a matter of fact," she added, "I'm considered very lucky in obtaining a situation at Cunnington's, and Mr Warner, our buyer, is extremely kind to me."

"I know all that; but it's the long hours that most wear you out," he said, "especially in this close, muggy weather."

"Oh! I'm pretty strong," she declared lightly, her beautiful eyes fixed upon him. "At first I used to feel terribly tired about tea-time, but nowadays I can stand it very much better."

"But you really must leave the place," Max declared. "Charlie should so arrange things that you could leave. His salary from old Statham is surely sufficient to enable him to do that!"

"Yes; but if he keeps me, how can he keep a wife as well?" asked Marion. "Dear old Charlie is awfully good to me. I never want for anything; but he'll marry Maud before long, I expect, and then I shall—"

"Marry me, darling," he exclaimed, concluding her sentence.

She blushed slightly and smiled.

"Ah!" she said, in mock reproof. "That may occur perhaps in the dim future. We'll first see how Charlie's marriage turns out—eh?"

"No, Marion," he cried. "Come, that isn't fair! You know how I love you—and you surely recollect your promise to me, don't you?" he asked seriously.

"Of course I do," she replied. "You dear old boy, you know I'm only joking."

He seemed instantly relieved at her words, and steered across to the Middlesex banks as they approached Brentford Dock in order to get the full advantage of the rising tide.

"Has Charlie seen Maud of late?" he asked, a few moments later.

"I don't know at all. I suppose he's in the East. I haven't seen him since he came to the shop to say good-bye to me."

"I wonder if the Doctor and his daughter have returned to their own country?" he suggested.

"What! Have you heard nothing of them?"

"Nothing," he replied. "I have endeavoured to discover where their furniture was taken, or where they themselves went, but all has been in vain. Both they and their belongings have entirely disappeared."

The girl did not utter a word. She was leaning back, with her fine eyes fixed straight before her, reflecting deeply.

"It is all very extraordinary," she remarked at last.

"Yes. I only wish, darling, you were at liberty to tell me the whole truth regarding Maud, and what she has told you," he said, his gaze fixed upon her pale, beautiful face.

"I cannot do that, Max," was her prompt answer, "so please do not ask me. I have already told you that in this matter my lips are sealed by a solemn promise—a promise which I cannot break."

"I know! Yet I somehow cannot help thinking that you could reveal to me some fact which might expose the motive of this strange and unaccountable disappearance," he said. "Do you know, I cannot get rid of the suspicion that the Doctor, and possibly Maud herself, have been victims of foul play. Remember that as a politician he had many enemies in his own country. A political career in the Balkans is not the peaceful profession it is here at St. Stephen's. Take Bulgaria, for instance, and recall the political assassinations of Stambuloff, Petkoff, and a dozen others. The same in Servia and in Roumania. The whole of the Balkans is permeated by an air of political conspiracy, for there life is indeed cheap, more especially the life of the public man."

"What! Then you really suspect that both Maud and her father have actually been the victims of some political plot?" she asked, regarding him with a strange expression.

"Well—how can I conjecture otherwise? The Doctor would never have left suddenly without sending word to me. Have you written to Charlie telling him of the sudden disappearance?"

"Yes. I wrote the same day that you told me, and addressed the letter to the Grand Hotel, at Belgrade."

"Then he has it by now?"

"Certainly. I'm expecting a wire from him asking for further particulars. He should have got my letter the day before yesterday, but up to the present I've received no acknowledgment."

Max did not tell her that her brother had not left London on the night when he was believed to have done so, and that it was more than probable he had never started from Charing Cross. He kept his own counsel, at the same time wondering what was the real reason why Marion so steadfastly refused to tell him the nature of Maud's confession. That it had been of a startling nature she had already admitted, therefore he could only suppose that it had some direct connection with the astounding disappearance of both father and daughter.

On the other hand, however, he was suspicious of some ingenious plot, because he felt convinced that the Doctor would never have effaced himself without giving him confidential news of his whereabouts.

"Have you written to Maud?" he asked, after a fen; moments.

"No. I don't know her address."

"And you have not seen her?"

"No."

"But you don't seem in the least alarmed about her disappearance?"

"Why should I be? I rather expected it," she answered; and it suddenly occurred to him whether, after all, she had been with Maud to the concert at Queen's Hall on the night of the sudden removal.

A distinct suspicion seized him that she was concealing from him some fact which she feared to reveal—some fact that concerned herself more than Maud. He could see, in her refusal to satisfy him as to the girl's confession, an attempt to mislead and mystify him, and he was just a trifle annoyed thereby. He liked open and honest dealing, and began to wonder whether this pretended promise of loyalty to her friend was not being put forward to hide some secret that was her own!

The two girls had, during the past few months, been inseparable. Had Maud really made a startling confession, or was the girl seated before him, with that strangely uneasy expression upon her beautiful countenance, endeavouring to deceive him?

He tried to put such thoughts behind him as unworthy of his devotion to her. But, alas! he could not.

Mystery was there—mystery that he was determined to elucidate.

Chapter Sixteen
On Dangerous Ground

In the glorious sundown glinting across the river, and rendering it a rippling flood of gold, Max and Marion were seated in the long upstairs room of that old-fashioned riparian inn, the "London Apprentice," at Isleworth, taking their tea at the open window.

Before them was the green ait, with the broad, tree-fringed river beyond, a quiet, peaceful old-world scene that, amid the rapidly changing metropolitan suburbs, remains the same to-day as it has been for the past couple of centuries or so.

They always preferred that quiet, old-fashioned upstairs room—the club-room, it was called—of the "London Apprentice," at Isleworth, to the lawns and string bands of Richmond, the tea-gardens of Kew, or the pleasures of Eel Pie Island.

That long, silent, old, panelled room with its big bow-window commanding a wide reach of the river towards St. Margaret's was well suited to their idyllic love. They knew that there they would at least be alone, away from the Sunday crowd, and that after tea they could sit at the window and enjoy the calm sundown.

The riverside at Isleworth does not change. Even the electric trams have passed close by it on their way to Hampton Court from Hammersmith but they have not modernised it. The old square-towered church, the row of ancient balconied houses, covered with tea-roses and jasmine, and the ancient waterman's hostelry, the "London Apprentice," are just the same to-day as they have ever been in the memory of the oldest inhabitant; and the little square in the centre of the riverside village is as silent and untrodden as in the years when Charles II loved to go there on his barge and dine in that very room at the inn, and when, later, David Garrick and Pope sang its praises.

Max and his well-beloved had finished their tea, and, with her hat and gloves off, she was lying back in a lounge chair in the deep bay window, watching the steamer *Queen Elizabeth*, with its brass band and crowd of excursionists, slowly returning to London. Near her he was seated, lazily smoking a cigarette, his eyes upon her in admiration, but still wondering, as he always wondered.

The truth concerning Maud Petrovitch had not been told.

He was very fond of the Doctor. Quiet, well-educated, polished, and pleasant always, he was, though a foreigner, and a Servian to boot, the very essence of a gentleman. His dead wife had, no doubt, influenced him towards English ways and English thought, while Maud herself—the very replica of his lost wife, he always declared—now held her father beneath her influence as a bright and essentially English girl.

The disappearance of the pair was an enigma which, try how he would, he could not solve. His efforts to find Rolfe had been unavailing, and Marion herself had neither seen nor heard from him. At Charlie's chambers his man remained in complete ignorance. His master had left for Servia—that was all.

Max had been trying in vain to lead the conversation again up to the matter over which his mind had become so much exercised; but, with her woman's keen ingenuity, she each time combated his efforts, which, truth to tell, only served to increase his suspicion that her intention was to shield herself behind her friend.

Why this horrible misgiving had crept upon him he could not tell. He loved her with his whole heart and soul, and daily he deplored that, while he lived in bachelor luxury in artistic chambers, and with every whim satisfied, she was compelled to toil and drudge in a London drapery store. He wished with his whole heart that he could take her out of that soul-killing business life, with all its petty jealousies and its eternal make-believe towards customers, and put her in the companionship of some elderly gentlewoman in rural peace.

But he knew her too well. The mere offer she would regard as an insult. A hundred times she had told him that, being compelled to work for her living, she was proud of being able to do so.

Charlie, her brother, he could not understand. He had just made a remark to that effect, and she had asked—"Why? He's awfully good to me, you know. Lots of times he sends me unexpectedly five-pound notes, and they come in very useful to a girl like me, you know. I dare say," she laughed, "you spend as much in a single evening when you go out with friends to the theatre and supper at the Savoy as I earn in a month."

"That's just it," he said. "I can't understand why Charlie, in his position, secretary to one of the wealthiest men in England, allows you to slave away in a shop."

"He does so because I refuse to leave," was her prompt answer. "I don't care to live on the charity of anybody while I have the capacity to work. My parents were both proud in this respect, and I take after them, I suppose."

"That is all to your credit, dearest," he said; "but I am looking forward to the future. I love you, as you well know, and I can't bear to think that you are bound to serve at Cunnington's from nine in the morning till seven at night—waiting on a set of old hags who try to choose dresses to make them appear young girls."

She laughed, her beautiful face turned towards him. "Aren't you rather hard on my sex, Max?" she asked. "We all of us try to present ourselves to advantage in order to attract and please."

"All except yourself, darling," he said courteously. "You look just as beautiful in your plain black business gown as you do now."

"That's really very sweet of you," she said, smiling. Then a moment later a serious look overspread her countenance, and she added: "Why worry yourself over me, Max, dear. I am very happy. I have your love. What more can I want?"

"Ah! my darling!" he cried, rising and bending till his lips touched hers, "those words of yours fill me with contentment. You are happy because I love you! And I am happy because I have secured your affection! You can never know how deeply I love you—or how completely I am yours. My only thought is of you, my well-beloved; of your present life, and of your future. I have friends—men of the world, who spend their time at clubs, at sport, or at theatres—who scoff at love. I scoff with them sometimes, because there is but one love in all the world for me—yours!"

"Yes," she said, slowly fixing her eyes upon his, and tenderly stroking his hair. "But sometimes—sometimes I am afraid, Max—I—"

"Afraid!" he echoed. "Afraid of what?"

"That you cannot trust me."

He started. Was it not the unconscious truth that she spoke? He had been doubting her all that afternoon.

"Cannot trust you!" he cried. "What do you mean? How very foolish!"

But she shook her head, and a slight sigh escaped her. She seemed to possess some vague intuition that he did not entirely accept her statement regarding Maud. Yet was it, after all, very surprising, having in view the fact that she had admitted that Maud had made confession. It was the truth regarding that admission on the part of the Doctor's daughter that he was hoping to elicit.

"Marion," he said presently, in a low, intense voice, "Marion, I love you. If I did not trust you, do you think my affection would be so strong for you as it is?"

She paused for a moment before replying.

"That all depends," she said. "You might suspect me of double-dealing, and yet love me at the same time."

"But I do not doubt you, darling," he assured her, at the same time placing his arm around her slim waist and kissing her upon the lips. "I love you; surely you believe that?"

"Yes, Max, I do," she murmured. "I do—but I—"

"But what?" he asked, looking straight into her fine eyes and waiting for her to continue.

She averted his gaze, and slowly but firmly disengaged herself from his embrace, while he, on his part, wondered.

She was silent, her face pale, and in her eyes a look of sudden fear.

"Tell me, darling," he whispered. "You have something to say to me—is not that so?"

He loved her, he told himself, as truly as any man had ever loved a woman. It was only that one little suspicion that had arisen—the suspicion that she had not been to Queen's Hall with his friend's daughter.

He took her hand lightly in his and raised it courteously to his lips, but she drew it away, crying, "No! No, Max! No."

"No?" he gasped, staring at her. "What do you mean, Marion. Tell me what you mean."

"I—I mean that—that though we may love each other, perfect trust does not exist between us."

"As far as I'm concerned it does," he declared, even though he knew that his words were not exactly the truth. "Why have you so suddenly changed towards me, Marion? You are my love. I care for no one save yourself. You surely know that—have I not told you so a hundred times? Do you still doubt me?"

"No, Max. I do not doubt you. It is you who doubt me!"

"I do not doubt," he repeated. "I have merely made inquiry regarding Maud, and the confession which you yourself told me she made to you. Surely, in the circumstances, of her extraordinary disappearance, together with her father, is it not strange that I should be unduly interested in her?"

"No, not at all strange," she admitted. "I am quite as surprised and interested over Maud's disappearance as you are."

"Not quite so surprised."

"Because I view the whole affair in the light of what she told me."

"Did what she tell you in any way concern the Doctor?" he asked eagerly.

"Indirectly it did—not directly."

"Had you any suspicion that father and daughter intended to suddenly disappear?"

"No; but, as I have before told you, I am not surprised."

"Then they are fugitives, I take it?" he remarked, in a changed tone.

"Certainly. They were no doubt driven to act as they have done. Unless there—there has been a tragedy!"

"But the men who removed the furniture must be in some way connected with the Doctor's secret," he remarked. "There were several of them."

"I know. You have already described to me all that you have discovered. It is very remarkable and very ingenious."

"A moment ago you were about to tell me something, Marion," he said, fixing his gaze upon hers; "what is it?"

"Oh!" she answered uneasily. "Nothing—nothing, I assure you!"

"Now, don't prevaricate!" he exclaimed, raising his forefinger in mock reproof. "You wanted to explain something to me. What was it?"

She tried to laugh, but it was only a very futile attempt, and it caused increased suspicion to arise within his already overburdened mind. Here he was, endeavouring to elucidate the mystery of the disappearance of a friend, yet she could not assist him in the least. His position was sufficiently tantalising, for he was convinced that by her secret knowledge she held the key to the whole situation.

Usually, women are not so loyal to friends of their own sex as are men. A woman will often "give away" another woman without the least compunction, where a man will be staunch, even though the other may be his enemy. This is a fact well-known to all, yet the reason we may leave aside as immaterial to this curious and complex narrative which I am endeavouring to set down in intelligible form.

Marion, the woman he loved better than his own life, was assuring him that she had nothing to tell, while he, at the same moment, was convinced by her attitude that she was holding back from him some important fact which it was her duty to explain. She knew how intimate was her lover's friendship with the missing man, and the love borne his daughter by her own brother. If foul play were suspected, was it not her bounden duty to relate all she knew?

The alleged confession of Maud Petrovitch struck him now more than ever as extraordinary. Why did Marion not openly tell him of her fears or misgivings? Why did not she give him at least some idea of the nature of her companion's admissions? On the one hand, he admired her for her loyalty to Maud; while, on the other, he was beside himself with chagrin that she persistently held her secret.

In that half-hour during which they had sat together in the crimson sundown, her manner seemed to have changed. She had acknowledged her love for him, yet in the same breath she had indicated a gulf between them. He saw in her demeanour a timidity that was quite unusual, and he put it down to guiltiness of her secret.

"Marion," he said at last, taking her hand firmly in his again, and speaking in earnest, "you said just now that you believed I loved you, but—something. But what? Tell me. What is it you wish to say? Come, do not deny the truth. Remember what we are both to each other. I have no secrets from you—and you have none from me!"

She cast her eyes wildly about her, and then they rested upon his. A slight shudder ran through her as he still held her soft, little hand.

"I know—I know it is very wrong of me," she faltered, casting her eyes to the floor, as though in shame. "I have no right to hold anything back from you, Max, because—because I love you—but—ah!—but you don't understand—it is because I love you so much that I am silent—for fear that you—"

And she buried her head upon his shoulder and burst into tears.

Chapter Seventeen
In which a Scot Becomes Anxious

That same Sunday evening, at midnight, in a cane chair in the lounge of the Central Station Hotel, in Glasgow, Charlie Rolfe sat idly smoking a cigar.

Sunday in Glasgow is always a dismal day. The weather had been grey and depressing, but he had remained in the hotel, busy with correspondence. He had arrived there on Saturday upon some urgent business connected with that huge engineering concern, the Clyde and Motherwell Locomotive Works, in which old Sam Statham held a controlling interest, but as the manager was away till Monday, he had been compelled to wait until his return.

The matter which he was about to decide involved the gain or loss of some 25,000 pounds, and a good deal of latitude old Statham had allowed him in his decision. Indeed, it was Rolfe who practically ran the big business. He reported periodically to Statham, and the latter was always satisfied. During the last couple of years, by his clever finance, Rolfe had made much larger profits with smaller expenditure, even though his drastic reforms had very nearly caused a strike among the four thousand hands employed.

He had spent a most miserable day—a grey day, full of bitter reflection and of mourning over the might-have-beens. The morning he had idled away walking through Buchanan Street and the other main thoroughfares, where all the shops were closed and where the general aspect was inexpressibly dismal. In the afternoon he had taken a cab and gone for a long drive alone to while away the hours, and now, after dinner, he was concluding one of the most melancholy days of all his life.

There were one or two other men in the lounge, keen-faced men of commercial aspect, who were discussing, over their cigars, prices, freights, and other such matters. In the corner was a small party of American men and women, stranded for the day while on their round tour of Scotland—the West Highlands, the Trossachs, Loch Lomond, Stirling Castle, the Highlands, and the rest—anxious for Monday to come, so as to be on the move again.

Rolfe stretched his legs, and from his corner surveyed the scene through the smoke from his cigar. He tried to be interested in the people about him, but it was impossible. Ever and anon the words of old Sam Statham rang in his ears. If the house of Statham—which, after all, seemed to be but a house of cards—was to be saved, it must be saved at the sacrifice of Maud Petrovitch!

Why? That question he had asked himself a thousand times that day. The only reply was that the charming half-foreign girl held old Statham's secret. But how could she? As far as he knew, they had only met once, years ago, when she was but a child.

And Statham, the elderly melancholy man who controlled so many interests, whose every action was noted by the City, and whose firm was believed to be as safe as the Bank of England, actually asked him to sacrifice her honour. What did he mean? Did he suggest that he was to wilfully compromise her in the eyes of the world?

"Ah, if he knew—if he only knew!" murmured Rolfe to himself, his face growing pale and hard-set. "Sam Statham believes himself clever, and so he is! Yet in this game I think I am his equal." And he smoked on in silence, his frowning countenance being an index to his troubled mind.

He was reviewing the whole of the curious situation. In a few years he had risen from a harum-scarum youth to be the private secretary, confidant, and frequent adviser to one of the wealthiest men in England. Times without number, old Sam, sitting in his padded writing-chair in Park Lane, had commended him for his business acumen and foresight. Once, by a simple suggestion, daring though it was, Statham had, in a few hours, made ten thousand pounds, and, with many words of praise the dry, old fellow took out his chequebook and drew a cheque as a little present to his clever young secretary. Charlie Rolfe was however, unscrupulous, as a good many clever men of business are. In the world of commerce the dividing-line between unscrupulousness and what the City knows as smartness is invisible. So Marion's brother was dubbed a smart man at Statham Brothers' and in those big, old-fashioned, and rather gloomy offices he was envied as being "the governor's favourite."

Charlie intended to get on. He saw other men make money in the City by the exercise of shrewdness and commonsense, and he meant to do the same. The business secrets of old Sam Statham were all known to him, and he had more than once been half tempted to take into partnership some financier who, armed with the information he could give, could make many a brilliant coup, forestalling even old Statham himself. Up to the present, however, he had never found anybody he could implicitly trust. Of sharks he knew dozens, clever, energetic men, he admitted, but there was not one of these who would not give away their own mother when it came to making a thousand profit. So he was waiting—waiting until he found the man who could "go in" with him and make a fortune.

Again, he was reflecting upon old Sam's appeal to him to save him.

"Suppose he knew," he murmured again. "Suppose—" and his eyes were fixed upon the painted ceiling of the lounge.

A moment later he sighed impatiently, saying, "Phew! how stifling it is here!" and, rising, took up his hat and went down the stairs and out into the broad street to cool his fevered brain. He was haunted by a recollection—the tragic recollection of that night when the Doctor and his daughter had so mysteriously disappeared.

"I wonder," he said aloud, at last, "I wonder if Max ever dreams the extraordinary truth? Yet how can he?—what impressions can he have? He must be puzzled—terribly puzzled, but he can have no clue to what has actually happened!" and then he was again silent, still walking mechanically along the dark half-deserted business street. "But suppose the truth was really known!—suppose it were discovered? What then? Ah!" he gasped, staring straight before him, "what then?"

For a full hour he wandered the half-deserted streets of central Glasgow, till he found himself down by the Clyde bank, and then re-traced his steps to the hotel, hardly knowing whither he went, so full was he of the terror which daily, nay, hourly, obsessed him. Whether Max Barclay had actually discovered him or not meant to him his whole future—nay his very life.

"I wonder if I could possibly get at the truth through Marion?" he thought to himself. "If he really suspects me he might possibly question her with a view of discovering my actual movements on that night. Would it be safe to approach her? Or would it be safer to boldly face Max, and if he makes any remark, to deny it?"

Usually he was no coward. He believed in facing the music when there was any to face. One of the greatest misfortunes of honest folks is that they are cowards.

As he walked on he still muttered to himself—

"Hasn't Boileau said that all men are fools, and, spite of all their pains, they differ from each other only more or less, I'm a fool—a silly, cowardly ass, scenting danger where there is none. What could Max prove after all? No! When I return to London I'll go and face him. The reason I didn't go to Servia is proved by Statham himself. Of excuses I'm never at a loss.

It's an awkward position, I admit, but I must wriggle out of it, as I've wriggled before. Statham's peril seems to me even greater than my own, and, moreover, he asks me to do something that is impossible. He doesn't know—he never dreams the truth; and, what's more, he must never know. Otherwise, I—I must—"

And instinctively his hand passed over his hip-pocket, where reposed the handy plated revolver which he always carried.

Presently he found himself again in front of the Central Station Hotel, and, entering, spent an hour full of anxious reflection prior to turning in. If any had seen him in the silence of that hotel room they would have at once declared him to be a man with a secret, as indeed he was.

Next morning he rose pale and haggard, surprised at himself when he looked at the mirror; but when, at eleven o'clock, he took his seat in the directors' office at the neat Clyde and Motherwell Locomotive Works his face had undergone an entire change. He was the calm, keen business man who, as secretary and agent of the great Samuel Statham, had power to deal with the huge financial interests involved.

The firm had a large contract for building express locomotives for the Italian railways, lately taken over by the State, and the first business was to interview the manager and sub-manager, together with the two engineers sent from Italy, regarding some details of extra cost of construction.

The work of the Clyde and Motherwell Company was always excellent. They turned out locomotives which could well bear comparison with any of the North-Western, Great Northern, or Nord of France, both as to finish, power, speed, and smoothness of running. Indeed, to railways in every part of the world, from Narvik, within the Arctic circle, to New Zealand, Clyde and Motherwell engines were running with satisfaction, thanks to the splendid designs of the chief engineer, Duncan Macgregor, the white-bearded old Scot, who at that moment was seated with Statham's representative.

The conference between the engineers of the Italian *ferrovia* and the managers was over, and old Macgregor, who had been engineer for years to Cowan and Drummond, who owned the works before Statham had extended them and turned them into the huge Clyde and Motherwell works, still remained.

He was a broad-speaking Highlander, a native of Killin, on Loch Tay, whose services had long ago been coveted by the London and North-Western Railway Company, on account of his constant improvements in express engines, but who always refused, even though offered a larger salary to go across the border and forsake the firm to whom, forty years ago, he had been apprenticed by his father, a small farmer.

As a Scotsman, he believed in Glasgow. It was, in his opinion, the only place where could be built locomotives that would stand the wear and tear of a foreign or colonial line. An engine that was cleaned and looked after like a watch, as they were on the English or Scotch main lines, was easily turned out, he was fond of saying; but when it became a question of hauling power, combined with speed and strength to withstand hard wear and neglect, it was a very different matter.

Managers and sub-managers, secretaries and accountants there might be, gentlemen who wore black coats and went out to dine in evening clothes, but the actual man at the head of affairs at those great works was Duncan Macgregor—the short, thick-set man, in a shabby suit of grey tweed, who sat there closeted with Rolfe.

"You wrote to London asking to see me, Macgregor," exclaimed the young man. "We're always pleased to hear any suggestions you've got to make, I assure you," said Charlie, pleasantly. "Have a cigarette?" and he pushed the big box over to the man who sat on the other side of the table.

"Thank ye, no, Mr Rolfe, sir. I'm better wanting it," replied Macgregor, in his broad tongue. And then, with a preliminary cough, he said "I—I want very badly to speak with Mr Statham."

"Whatever you say to me, Macgregor, I will tell him."

"I want to speak to him ma'sel'."

"I'm afraid that's impossible. He sees nobody—except once a week in the city, and then only for two hours."

"'E would'na see me—eh?" asked the man, whose designs had brought the firm to the forefront in the trade.

"I fear it would be impossible. You would go to London for nothing. I'm his private secretary, you know; and anything that you tell me I shall be pleased to convey to him."

"But, mon, I want to see 'im ma'sel'!"

"That can't be managed," declared Rolfe. "This business is left to Mr Smale and myself. Mr Statham controls the financial position, but details are left to me, in conjunction with Smale and Hamilton. Is it concerning the development of the business that you wish to see Mr Statham?"

"No, it ain't. It concerns Mr Statham himself, privately."

Rolfe pricked up his ears.

"Then it's a matter which you do not wish to discuss with me?" he said. "Remember that Mr Statham has no business secrets from me. All his private correspondence passes through my hands."

"I know all that, Mr Rolfe," Macgregor answered, with impatience; "but I must, an' I will, see Mr Statham! I'm coming to London to-morrow to see him."

"My dear sir," laughed Rolfe, "it's utterly useless! Why, Mr Statham has peers of the realm calling to see him, and he sends out word that he's not at home."

"Eh! 'E's a big mon, I ken; but when 'e knows ma' bizniss e'll verra soon see me," replied the bearded old fellow, in confidence.

"But is your business of such a very private character?" asked Rolfe.

"Aye, it is."

"About the projected strike—eh? Well, I can tell you at once what his attitude is towards the men, without you going up to London. He told me a few days ago to say that if there was any trouble, he'd close down the works entirely for six months, or a year, if need be. He won't stand any nonsense."

"An' starve the poor bairns—eh?" mentioned the old engineer, who had grown white in the service of the firm. "Ay, when it was Cowan and Drummond they wouldna' ha' done that! I remember the strike in '82, an' how they conciliated the men. But it was na' aboot the strike at all I was wanting to see Mr Statham. It was aboot himself."

"Himself! What does he concern you? You've never met him. He's never been in Glasgow in his life."

"Whether I've met 'im or no is my own affair, Mr Rolfe," replied the old fellow, sticking his hairy fist into his jacket pocket. "I want to see 'im now, an' at once. I shall go to the London office an' wait till 'e comes."

"And when he comes he'll be far too busy to see you," the secretary declared. "So, my dear man, don't spend money unnecessarily in going up to London, I beg of you."

By the old man's attitude Rolfe scented that something was amiss, and set himself to discover what it was and report to his master.

"Is there any real dissatisfaction in the works?" he asked Macgregor, after a brief pause.

"There was a wee bittie, but it's a' passed away."

"Then it is not concerning the works that you want to see Mr Statham?"

"Nay, mon, not at all."

"Nor about any new patent?"

"Nay."

Rolfe was filled with wonder. The attitude of the old fellow was sphinx-like and yet he seemed confident that the millionaire would see him when he applied for an interview. For a full half-hour they chatted, but canny Macgregor told his questioner nothing—nothing more than that he was about to go to London to have a talk with the great financier upon some important matter which closely concerned him.

Therefore by the West Coast evening express, Rolfe left Glasgow for the south, full of wonder as to what the white-bearded old fellow meant by his covert insinuations and his proud confidence in the millionaire's good offices. There was something there which merited investigation—of that he was convinced.

Chapter Eighteen
The Outsider

On the left-hand side of Old Broad Street, City, passing from the Royal Exchange to Liverpool Street Station, stands a dark and dingy building, with a row of four windows looking upon the street. On a dull day, when the green-shaded lamps are lit within, the passer-by catches glimpses of rows of clerks, seated at desks poring over ledgers. At the counter is a continual coming and going of clerks and messengers, and notes and gold are received in and paid out constantly until the clock strikes four. Then the big, old doors are closed, and upon them is seen a brass plate, with the lettering almost worn off by continual polishing, bearing the words "Statham Brothers."

Beyond the counter, through a small wicket, is the manager's room—large, but gloomy, screened from the public view, and lit summer and winter by artificial light. In a corner is a safe for books, and at either end big writing-tables.

In that sombre room "deals" representing thousands upon thousands were often made, and through its door, alas! many a man who, finding himself pressed, had gone to the firm for financial aid and been refused, had walked out a bankrupt and ruined.

Beyond the manager's room was a narrow, dark passage, at the end of which was a door marked "Private," and within that private room, punctually at eleven o'clock, three mornings after Rolfe's conversation with Macgregor, old Sam Statham took his seat in the shabby writing-chair, from which the stuffing protruded.

About the great financier's private room there was nothing palatial. It was so dark that artificial light had to be used always. The desk was an old-fashioned mahogany one of the style of half a century ago, a threadbare carpet, two or three old horsehair chairs, and upon the green-painted wall a big date-calendar such as bankers usually use, while beneath it was a card, printed with old Sam's motto:—

"TIME FLIES; DEATH URGES."

That same motto was over every clerk's desk, and, because of it, some wag had dubbed the great financier, "Death-head Statham."

As he sat beneath the lamp at his desk, old Sam's appearance was almost as presentable as that of his clerks. Levi always smartened his master up on the day he went into the City, compelling him to wear a frock coat, a light waistcoat, a decent pair of trousers, and a proper cravat, instead of the bit of greasy black ribbon which he habitually wore.

"And how much have we gained over the Pekin business, Ben?" Mr Samuel was asking of the man who, though slightly younger, was an almost exact replica of himself, slightly thinner and taller. Benjamin Statham, Sam's brother, was the working manager of the concern, and one of the smartest financiers in the whole City of London. He was standing with his back to the fireplace, with his hands thrust deep in his trousers-pockets.

"Ah!" he laughed. "When I first suggested it you wouldn't touch it. Didn't owe for Chinese business, and all that! You'd actually see the French people go and take the plums right from beneath our noses—and—"

"Enough, Ben. I own I was a little short-sighted in that matter. Perhaps the details you sent me were not quite clear. At any rate," he said, "I was mistaken, for you say we've made a profit. How much?"

"Twelve thousand; and not a cent of hazardous risk."

"How did we first hear of the business?"

"Through the secret channel in Paris."

"The woman?"

"Yes."

"Better send her something."

"How much? She's rather hard-up, I hear."

"Women like her are always hard-up," growled old Sam. "Leave it to me. I'll get Rolfe to send her something to-morrow."

"I promised her a couple of hundred. You mustn't send her less, or we shall queer business for the future."

"I shall send her five hundred," responded the head of the firm. "She's a very useful woman—and pretty, too, Ben—by Jove! she is! She called on me in her automobile at the Elysée Palace about eighteen months ago, and I was much struck by her. She knows almost everybody in Paris, and can get any information she wants from her numerous male admirers."

"She's well paid—gets a thousand a year from us," Ben remarked.

"And we sometimes make twenty out of the secret information she obtains for us," laughed old Sam. "Remember the Morocco business, and how she gave us the complete French programme which she got from young Delorme, at the Quai d'Orsay. We were as much in the dark as the newspapers till then, and if we hadn't have got at the French intentions, we should have made a terribly heavy loss. As it was, we left it to others—who went under."

"She got an extra five hundred as a present for that," Ben pointed out.

"And it was worth it."

"Delorme doesn't know who gave the game away to us. If he did, it would be the worse for Her Daintiness."

"No doubt it would. But she's a fly bird, and as only you and I and Rolfe know the truth, she's pretty confident that she'll never be given away."

"She's in town—at Claridge's—just now, so you need not write her to Paris. She asked me to call the night before last, and I went," said Ben. "She wanted to get further instructions regarding a matter about which I wrote her. I dined with her."

Sam grunted as he turned slightly in his chair.

"Rather undesirable company—eh—Ben?" he exclaimed, with some surprise. "Suppose you were seen by anyone who knows her? And recollect that all Paris knows her. It is scarcely compatible with our standing in the City for you to be seen in her company."

"My dear Sam, I took very good care not to be seen in her company. I'm not quite a fool. I accepted her invitation with a distinct purpose. I wanted to question her about one of her friends—a man who may in future prove of considerable use to us. He's, as usual, in love with her, and she can twist him inside out."

"Ah! any man's a fool who allows himself to fall under the fascination of a woman's smiles," remarked the dry-as-dust old millionaire. "We've been wise, Ben, to remain bachelors. It's the unmarried who taste the good things of this world."

Benjamin sighed, but said nothing. He, like Sam himself, had had his love-romance years ago, and it still lingered within him, lingered as it does within the heart of every man who has loved a woman that has turned out false and broken her pledge of affection. Ben Statham's was a sorry story. Before his eyes, even now that thirty years had gone, there often arose the vision of a sweet, pale-faced, slim figure in white muslin, girdled with blue; of green meadows, where the cattle stood knee-deep in the rich grass, and of a cool Scotch glen where the trees overhung the rippling burn and where the trout darted in the pools.

But it had all ended, as many another love-romance has, alas! ended, in the woman forsaking the man who loved her, and in marrying another for his money.

Three years later her husband—the man whom she had wedded because of his position—was in the bankruptcy court, and six months afterwards he had followed her to her grave. But the sweet recollection of her still remained with Ben, and beneath that hard and wizened countenance beat a heart foil of tender memories of a day long since dead.

His brother Samuel's romance was even more tragic. Nobody knew the story save himself, and it had never passed his lips. The society gossips who so often wrote their tittle-tattle about him never dreamed the strange story of the life of the great financier, nor the extraordinary romance that underlay his marvellous success. What a sensation would be produced if they ever learnt the truth! In those days long ago both of them had been poor, and had suffered in consequence. Now that they were both wealthy, the bitterness of the past still remained with them.

They were discussing another matter, concerning a project for an electric tramway in a Spanish city, the concession for which had been brought to them. They both agreed that the thing would not pay, therefore it was dismissed.

During their discussion Rolfe entered, and, taking his seat at the small table near his master, busied himself with some letters.

Suddenly Benjamin Statham exclaimed—

"Oh! by the way, there's a queer-looking Scot from the Clyde and Motherwell works who's been hanging about for a couple of days to see you, Sam. Says he must see you at all coats."

"I don't want to see anybody from Glasgow," snapped Statham. "Tell him I'm not here, whoever he is."

"He's the old engineer, Macgregor," Rolfe said. "He mentioned to me when I was in Glasgow the other day that he particularly wished to see you, and that he was coming up on purpose. I told him it was a wild-goose chase."

"Engineer? What does he do? Mind the engine—one of the men who threaten to go on strike, I suppose," remarked old Sam.

"No," laughed Rolfe. "He's a little more than engineer. It is he who has designed nearly every locomotive we've turned out."

"Oh! valuable man—eh? Then raise his salary, Rolfe, and send him back to Glasgow to make a few more engines."

"He's waiting outside at the counter now, and won't go away," exclaimed the secretary.

"Then go to him and say he shall have fifty pounds more a year. I can't be bothered to see the fellow."

Rolfe rose and went to the outer office, where Macgregor stood patiently. He had waited there for best part of two days and, with a Scot's tenacity, refused to be put off by any of the clerks. He wanted to see Mr Samuel Statham, "an' I mean to see 'im, mon," he told everybody, his grey beard bristling fiercely as he spoke.

He was evidently a man with a grievance. Such men came to Old Broad Street sometimes, and on rare occasions Mr Benjamin saw them. There were hard cases of men ignorant of the ways of business as the City to-day knows it, having been deliberately swindled out of their rights by sharks, concessions filched from their rightful owners, and patents artfully stolen and registered. But old Duncan Macgregor, with his white beard, was of a different type—the type of honest, hard-working plodder, out of whose brains the great Clyde and Motherwell works were practically coining money daily.

As Rolfe advanced to him he said:—

"I'm sorry, Macgregor, that Mr Statham is quite unable to see you to-day. He's engaged three deep. I've told him you wished to see him, and he says that he much appreciates the great services you've rendered to the firm, and that you are to receive a rise of salary of fifty pounds a year, beginning the first of last January."

"What!" cried the old man. "What—'e offers me another fifty pounds! 'E's guid an' generous; but I have na' come here for that. I've come to London to see him—ye hear!—to see him—d'ye hear, Mr Rolfe, an' I must."

"But, my dear sir, you can't!"

"Tell him I don't want his fifty pound," cried the old man so derisively that the clerks looked up from their ledgers. "I must speak to him, an' him alone."

"Impossible," exclaimed Rolfe, impatiently.

"Why impossible?" asked the old fellow. "When Mr Statham knows the business I've come upon he won't thank ye for keepin' us apart. D'ye ken that, mon?" and his beard wagged as he spoke.

"I know nothing, Macgregor, because you've told me nothing," was the other's reply.

"Well, I tell ye I mean to see him, an' that's sufficient for Duncan Macgregor."

"Mr Duncan Macgregor will, if he continues to create a scene here, find himself discharged from the employ of the Clyde and Motherwell works," remarked Rolfe, drily.

"An' Duncan Macgregor can go to the North-Western to-morrow at a bigger rise than the fifty pounds a year. D'ye ken that?" replied the man from Glasgow.

"Then you refuse to accept Mr Statham's offer to you?"

"Of course, mon. Ye don't think that I come to London a cringin' for more pay, do ye? If I wanted it I could ha' got it from another company years ago," replied the independent old fellow. "No, I must see Mr Statham. Go back an' tell him so. I'm here to see him on a very important matter," and, dropping his voice, he added, "a matter which closely concerns himself."

"Then tell me its nature."

"It's private, sir. Until Mr Statham gives me leave to tell you, I can't."

"But he wants to know the nature of the business," answered the secretary, again struck by the old fellow's pertinacity. It was not every man who would decline a rise of a pound a week in his salary. Rolfe was puzzled, but he knew old Sam well enough to be aware that even if a duke called he would refuse to see him. He only came to the City once a week to discuss matters with his brother Ben, and saw no outsider.

"I can't tell ye why I want to see Mr Statham; that's only his business and mine," replied the bearded Scot. The clerks were now smiling at Rolfe's vain attempts to get rid of him.

"Will you write it? Here—write on this slip of paper," the secretary suggested.

The old fellow hesitated.

"Yes—if you'll let me seal it up in an envelope."

Rolfe at once assented, and, with considerable care, the old fellow wrote some pencilled lines, folded the paper, sealed it in the envelope, and wrote the superscription.

A few moments later, when Rolfe handed it to the old millionaire, who was still at his table chatting with his brother, he asked, in the snappish way habitual to him:—"Who's this from—eh? Why am I bothered?"

"From the man Macgregor, from Glasgow. He won't go away."

"Then discharge the brute," he replied, and with the note in his hand he finished a remark he had addressed to his brother.

At last, mechanically, he opened it, and his eyes fell upon the scribbled words.

His jaw dropped. The colour left his cheeks, and, sitting back, he glared straight at Rolfe as though he had seen an apparition.

For a few moments he seemed too confused to speak. Then, when he recovered himself, he said, half apologetically:—"Ben, I must see this man alone—a—a private matter. I—I had no idea—I—"

"Of course, Sam," exclaimed his brother, leaving the room. "Let me know when he's gone."

"Rolfe, show him in," the millionaire ordered. The instant his secretary had gone he sprang to his feet, examined his face in the small mirror over the mantelshelf for a moment, and then stood bracing himself up for the interview.

Chapter Nineteen
The Man who Loved

A few nights later Max Barclay was seated in the stalls of the Empire Theatre with Marion.

They never went to the legitimate theatre because she had no evening-dress. Even to be seen in one would have caused comment among her fellow employés at Cunnington's. The girls were never very charitable to each other, for in the pernicious system of "living-in" there is no privacy or home life, no sense of responsibility or of freedom.

The average London shop girl has but little leisure and little rest. Chronically over-tired, she cares little to go out of an evening after the long shop hours, and looks forward to Sunday as the day when she can read in bed till noon if she chooses, snooze again in the afternoon, and perhaps go to a café in the evening. It was so with Marion. The sales were on, and there were "spiffs," or premiums, placed by Mr Warner upon some out-of-date goods which it was every girl's object to sell and thus earn the commission. So she was working very hard, and already held quite a respectable number of tickets representing "spiffs."

In a dark blue skirt, white silk blouse and black hat, she looked extremely pretty and modest as she sat beside her lover in the second row of the stalls, watching the ballet with its tuneful music, clever groupings, and phantasmagoria of colour. She glanced at the watch upon her wrist, and saw that it was nearly ten o'clock. In half an hour she would have to be "in."

The bondage of his well-beloved galled Max, yet he could say nothing. Her life was the same as that of a hundred thousand other girls in London. Indeed, was she not far better off that those poor girls who came up from their country homes to serve a year or two's drudgery without payment in order to learn the art and mystery of "serving a customer" — girls who were orphans and without funds, and who very soon found the actual necessity of having a little pocket-money for dress and for something with which to relish the stale bread and butter doled out to them.

The public have never yet adequately realised the hardships and tyranny of shop-life, where man is but a mere machine, liable to get the "sack" at a moment's notice, and where woman is but an ill-fed, overworked drudge, liable at any moment to be thrown out penniless upon the great world of London.

Some day ere long the revelation will come. There are certain big houses in London with pious shareholders and go-to-meeting directors which will earn the opprobrium of the whole British public when the naked truth regarding their female assistants is exposed. In "the trade" it is known, and one day there will arise a man bolder and more fearless than the rest, who will speak the truth, and, moreover, prove it.

If in the meantime you want to know the truth concerning shop-life, ask the director of any of the numerous rescue societies in London. What you will be told will, I assure you, open your eyes.

The couple of hours Max had spent with Marion proved delightful ones, as they always were. Promenading in the lounge above were many men-about-town whom he knew, and who, seeing him with the modest-looking girl, smiled knowingly. They never guessed the truth—that he loved her and intended to make her his wife.

"Charlie is back from Glasgow," she was saying. "He came to the shop this afternoon to ask if I had seen you, and to explain how the other night he, by a most fortunate circumstance, missed the Continental train, for next morning Mr Statham wanted him to do some very important business, and was delighted to find that he had not left. Another man has gone out to the East."

"If he wanted to know my movements he might have called at Dover Street," Max remarked thoughtfully, the recollection of that night in Cromwell Road arising within him.

"He seemed very busy, and said he had not a moment to spare. He was probably going north again. They have, he told me, some big order from Italy at the locomotive works."

"I thought Statham couldn't do without him," remarked Max. "Nowadays, however, he seems always travelling."

"He's awfully kind to me—gave me a five-pound note this afternoon."

"What did he say about me?" inquired Max.

"Oh! nothing very much. He asked me, among other things, whether I knew where you were on the night of the disappearance of the Doctor and his daughter."

Max started.

"And what did you reply?"

"That I hadn't the slightest idea. I never saw you that evening," was the girl's frank response.

Her lover nodded thoughtfully. It was now plain that Charlie suspected that he had detected him leaving the house and was endeavouring to either confirm his suspicion or dismiss it.

"Did he tell you to-day where he was going?"

"Back to Glasgow, I believe—but only for two days."

Max was seated at the end of the second row of the stalls, and beyond Marion were three or four vacant seats. At this juncture their conversation was interrupted by a man in well-cut evening-dress, his crush hat beneath his arms, advancing down the gangway and putting his hand out heartily to Max, exclaiming—

"My dear Barclay! Excuse me, but I want very much a few words with you to-night, on a matter of great importance." Then, glancing at Marion, he added: "I trust that Mademoiselle will forgive this intrusion?"

The girl glanced at the new-comer, while her lover, taking the man's hand, said—

"My dear Adam, I, too, wanted to see you, and intended to call to-morrow. You are not intruding in the least. Here's a seat. Allow me to introduce Miss Rolfe—Mr Jean Adam."

The man of double personality bowed again, and passing Marion and her lover, seated himself at her side, commencing to chat merrily, and explaining that he had recognised Max from the circle above. He had, it appeared, been to Dover Street an hour before, and Max's man had told him where his master was spending the evening.

Marion rather liked him. Max had already told her of this Frenchman who spoke English so well, and with whom he was doing business. In his speech he had the air and polish of the true cosmopolitan, and he also possessed a keen sense of humour.

Presently Marion, glancing again at her watch, declared that she must leave. Max scarcely ever took her home. He always put her into a cab, and she descended at the corner of the street off Oxford Street, where Cunnington's assistants had their big barrack-like dwelling, and walked home alone. It was her wish to do so, and he respected it.

Therefore all three rose, and Max went outside with her and put her into a cab, promising to meet her on the following evening. In the bustle of Leicester Square at that hour, he could not kiss her; but as their hands grasped, their eyes met in a glance which both knew was one of trust and mutual affection.

And so they parted, Max returning to the lounge where the Frenchman, Jean Adam, *alias* the Englishman John Adams, awaited him.

They had a drink at the American bar, and then promenaded up and down in the gay crowd that nightly assembles in that popular resort. Max nodded to one or two men he knew—clubmen and *habitués* like himself, and then, after the show was over, they took a cab down to the Savoy to supper.

The gay restaurant, with its crimson carpet and white decorations was crowded. To Gustave, who allotted the tables, Max was well-known, therefore a table for two in the left-hand corner of the big room—the table he usually occupied—was instantly secured, and the couple who had engaged were moved elsewhere. In the season Max had supper there on an average three nights a week, for at the Savoy one meets all one's friends, and there is always music, life, and brightness after the theatre, until the licensing regulations cut off the merriment so abruptly.

That night was no exception. The place was filled to overflowing with the smart world, together with many American visitors, the latest musical-comedy actresses and their male appendages, country cousins, men whose names were household words, and women whose pasts had appeared in black and white in the newspapers. A strange crowd, surely. Half the people were known to each other by sight, if not personally, and the other half were mere onlookers, filled with curiosity when Lord This or Dolly That were pointed out to them.

Max and Jean Adam were seated with a bottle of Krug between them when the former exclaimed—

"Well, how does our business go?"

"That's the reason I wanted to see you to-night," was his companion's reply with just a slight French accent. "I had some news from Constantinople to-day—confidential news from the Palace," he added in an undertone, bending across the table. "I want you to read it and give your opinion." And producing an envelope and letter on thin paper closely written in French, he handed it across to Barclay, as he added: "Now what is written there is the bed-rock fact, I know from independent inquiries I have made in an entirely different quarter."

Between mouthfuls of the perfectly-cooked *filet de sole* placed before him Max read the letter carefully. It was signed "your devoted friend Osman," and was evidently from a Turkish official at the Yildiz Kiosk. Briefly, it was to the effect that the *iradé* of the Sultan for the construction of the railway from Nisch in Servia to San Giovanni di Medua, on the Adriatic, was in the hands of Muhil Pasha, one of his Majesty's most intimate officials, and had been granted to him for services rendered in the Asiatic provinces.

Muhil had offered to part with it for twelve thousand pounds sterling, and that the agent of a French Company had arrived in Constantinople in order to treat with him. Muhil, however, had no love for the French, since he was Ottoman Ambassador in Paris a few years ago, and got into disgrace there, hence he would be much more ready to sell to an English syndicate.

The letter of Osman concluded by urging Adam to send instructions at once to a certain box at the British post-office in Constantinople, and to if possible secure the valuable document which would enable a line of railway to be built which would pay its shareholders enormously.

"Well," exclaimed Max, as he replaced the letter in its envelope, noting the surcharge in black—"1 piastre"—upon the blue English stamp. "What shall you do?"

"Do? Why we must get the twelve thousand, of course. It's a mere bagatelle compared with the magnitude of the business. I've got some reports in my overcoat pocket which I'll show you after supper. We must get the thing through, my dear Barclay. There's a big fortune in it for both of us—a huge fortune. Why, for the past ten years every diplomat at the Sublime Porte has been at work to get it through, but has been unsuccessful. The Sultan has always refused to let the line run through Turkish territory, fearing lest it should be used for military transport in the event of another war. His Majesty is not particularly partial to Austria, Servia, or Bulgaria, you know," he laughed.

"And hardly surprising, in view of past events, eh?" exclaimed Max, entirely ignorant of the real character of this man, who seemed a smart man of business combined with a genial companion. Adam was a past-master in the art of fraud. He did not press the point, but merely went on with his supper, swallowed a glass of champagne, and turned the conversation by admiring the graceful carriage of the head of a girl sitting near with a wreath of forget-me-nots across her fluffy fair hair.

"Yes," replied Max. "The poise of her head is full of grace, but—well, her face is like the carved handle of an umbrella!" Whereat his companion laughed heartily. Barclay was full of quaint expressions, and of a quiet but biting sarcasm. Some of his *bons mots* had been repeated from month to mouth in the clubs until they became almost popular sayings. He was now in love entirely and devotedly with Marion, and no other woman of the thousand who passed before his eyes and smiled into his face had the least attraction for him.

A moment later a pretty girl in pink, the Honourable Eva Townley, who was at supper with her mother and same friends, bowed to him and laughed, while another woman, the rather go-ahead wife of a leader at the Chancery Bar, waved a menu at him.

Society knew Max, and many a woman had set her cap at him, hoping to capture the tall, well-set-up and easy-going young fellow, together with the ease and comfort which his substantial estates would afford.

Max, however, had done a few years of town life. He had become *blasé* and nauseated. Since he had met Marion Rolfe the quiet, modest, unassuming and hard-working shop-assistant, the *haute monde* bored him more than ever. He went only where he was compelled, yet he nowadays preferred the cheap Italian restaurant and Marion's society to the tables of the rich with their ugly women striving to fascinate, and their small-talk of scandal, gossip and cruel innuendo.

There is surely no world in the world like that of London—nothing so complex, so tragic, and yet so grimly humorous, so soul-killing, and yet so reckless as our little, lax world of vanity and display that calls itself Society, the world which the *nouveau riche* are ever seeking to enter by the back-door, and which the suburbs rush to see portrayed upon the stage of the theatre.

Everywhere the manner and morals of Mayfair are aped nowadays. Mrs Browne-Smythe, the City clerk's wife of tattling Tooting, has her "day," and gives her bridge-parties just as does the Duchess of Dorsetshire in Grosvenor Square; and Mrs Claude Greene, the wife of the wholesale butcher, who was once a barmaid near the Meat Market, and now lives in matrimonial felicity in cliquey Clapham, "requests the company of" upon the self-same cards and with the self-same formula as the wife of Jimmy James the South African magnate in Park Lane.

Max, glad that supper was over, rose and walked with his friend out into the big lounge where the Roumanian band were playing weird gipsy melodies, and sat at one of the little tables to smoke and sip Grand Marnier cordon rouge, being joined a few moments later by a couple of men whom he knew at the club, and who appeared to be at a loose end.

At last the lights were turned down as signal that in five minutes it would be closing time, and then rifling, Max, ignorant of the ingenious plot, invited his friend Adam round to Dover Street for a final smoke.

Chapter Twenty
Explains Jean Adam's Suggestion

Over whiskey and soda in Barclay's chambers, Jean Adam pushed his sinister plans a trifle further.

He was aware that Max had taken the opinion of a man he knew on the Stock Exchange as to the probable value of the concession for the Danube-Adriatic Railway, and that his reply had been highly favourable. Therefore he was confident that such an opportunity of making money by an honest deal Max would not let slip.

They had known each other several months, and Adam, with his engaging manner and courteous bearing, had wormed himself into the younger man's confidence. A dozen times Max had been his host, but on each occasion the other took good care to quickly return the hospitality. To Max he represented himself as resident in Constantinople. A few years ago he had been fortunate enough to obtain a concession from the Ottoman Government which, being floated in Paris, had placed him in a very comfortable position; and he was now about to aim for bigger and more lucrative things.

"You see," he was saying as he produced an official report to the Foreign Office—a pamphlet-like document in a blue paper cover—"here is what our consul in Belgrade reported on the scheme two years ago. Such a line, he says, would tap nearly half the trade that now goes to Odessa, besides giving Servia a seaport. It will be the biggest thing in railways for years, depend upon it."

Max went to the writing-table, where the lamp was burning, and glanced through the paragraphs of the consular report and several other printed documents which his friend handed to him in succession. Then Adam produced a map, and upon it traced the route of the proposed line.

"Well," Barclay said at last, rising and lighting a cigar.

"It all seems pretty plain sailing. I'll go to-morrow and see old Statham about it. His secretary, Rolfe, is a friend of mine."

"No, Mr Barclay," said the wily Adam. "If I were you I would not."

"Why?"

"Well, if you do, you'll queer all our plans—both yours and mine," he mused vaguely.

"How?"

"Sam Statham has agents in Constantinople—agents who could offer Muhil double the price immediately, and the ground would be cut from under our feet. Statham knows a good thing when he sees it, you bet, and if he knew anything about this he wouldn't stick at a thousand or two."

"Then he doesn't know?"

"At present he can't know. It is a secret between Muhil, Osman, and myself?"

"And what about the French people?"

"Of course they know; but they're not such fools as to let out the secret," replied Adam.

"Well, what do you suggest?" Max asked, taking a pull at the long tumbler.

"That we keep the affair strictly to ourselves. Once we have the concession in our hands there'll be a hundred men in the City ready to take it up. Why, old Statham would give us a big profit on it, especially if, as you say, you know his secretary."

"That was his secretary's sister whom you met with me to-night," Max remarked.

"What an extremely pretty girl," exclaimed Adam enthusiastically.

"Think so?" asked Barclay with a smile of satisfaction. "Why, of course. A face like here isn't seen every day. I was much struck with it when I first noticed you from the circle, and wondered whom she might be. Rolfe's her name, is it?" he added with a feigned air of uncertainty.

"Yes. Charlie Rolfe is old Sam's confidential secretary."

"Well, afterwards, through him, we might interest Sam," remarked Adam. "What we have first to do is to get hold of the concession."

"But how?"

"By buying it."

The two men smoked in silence. Adam's quick eye saw that the affair was full of attraction for the man he had marked down as victim.

"You mean that I should put twelve thousand into it?" he said.

"Not at all," responded the wily Adam at once. "In any case I do not propose that you should put up the whole sum. My idea is that we should put up six thousand each."

"And go shares?"

"And go shares," repeated Adam, knocking the ash from his cigar. "But prior to doing so I think it would be only right for you to go out to Constantinople, see Muhil, and ascertain the truth of the whole affair. You have only my word for it all—and the letter. I quite admit that they are not sufficient guarantee for you to put down six thousand. You are too good a business man for that."

Max was flattered by that last sentence.

"Well," he said smiling, "I really think it would be more satisfactory if I had—well, some confirmation of all these comments."

"You can obtain that at once by going out to Constantinople," declared Adam. "You'll be out and home in ten days, and I'll go with you," he added persuasively.

"Well, I shall have to consider it," the younger man replied after a brief pause.

"There is very little time to consider," Adam said. "The French people are at work, and if they raise the purchase price to Muhil we shall be compelled to do the same."

"But we can get an option, I suppose?"

"I have it. But it expires in ten days from to-morrow. After that Muhil will make the best terms he can with the French. The latter will have to pay through the nose, no doubt, but they'll get it, without doubt. Their Embassy is helping them."

"And how long can I have to decide?"

"To reach Constantinople in time we have six days more. We might then take the Orient Express from Paris and just do it. But," he added, "of course if your inclination is against the journey and inquiry I hope you'll allow me to assess it before somebody else. Personally," he laughed, "I can't afford to miss this chance of making a fortune. This, remember, is no wild mining speculation: it's solid, bed-rock enterprise. The Servians surveyed the line four years ago and got out plans and estimates. There's a printed copy of them at the Servian Consulate here in London. So it's all cut-and-dried."

"Well I hope, Adam, you'll allow me a little time to reflect. Six thousand is a decent sum, you know."

"I don't want it until you've been out there and seen Muhil, Mr Barclay," Adam declared. "Indeed, I refuse to touch it until you have personally satisfied yourself of the *bonâ fides* of the scheme. Muhil himself must first assure you of the existence of the *iradé*, and that it is actually in is possession. Then I will put up six thousand if you will put up the balance."

"And if it is more than twelve?"

"Why, we share the increase equally, of course."

"Very well. So far as it goes it is agreed," said Max. "It only remains whether I go out to Turkey, or not."

"That's all. The sooner you can decide, the better for our plans," Adam remarked. "Only take good care that old Statham does not learn what's in the wind. You know him, I believe?"

"Yes, slightly. He's a queer old fellow—very eccentric."

"So I've heard," said the other, betraying ignorance. What would Max Barclay have thought if he had witnessed that scene so recently when the millionaire had glanced out of his cosy library and seen the shabby stranger lounging against the railings of the Park? What, indeed, would he have thought if he had witnessed old Sam's consequent agitation, or overheard his confession to Rolfe?

But he knew nothing of it all. Adam had shown him the best side of his nature—the easy-going and keen money-making cosmopolitan whose manner was so gentlemanly and so very charming. He had not seen the other—the side which Samuel Statham knew too well.

Adam, seated there in the big saddle-bag chair, in the full enjoyment of the excellent cigar, knew that with the exercise of a little further ingenuity he would make the first step towards the goal he had in view. He was a man who took counsel of nobody, and even the old hunchback Lyle, his closest friend, knew nothing of his object in drawing Max Barclay, until recently a perfect stranger, into the fatal net spread for him.

He smiled within himself as he calmly contemplated his victim through the haze of tobacco smoke. The dock upon the mantelshelf had struck two.

He took a final drink, slipped on his coat, and with a merry *bon soir* and an injunction to make up his mind and wire him at the earliest moment, he shook his friend's hand and went out.

Max sat alone for a long time, still smoking. In his ignorance he was reflecting that the business seemed a sound one. Adam had not asked him to put down money before full inquiry, and had, at the same time, offered to put up half. This latter fact, in itself, showed that his friend had confidence in the scheme.

And so, before he turned in that night, he had practically made up his mind to pay a flying visit to the Sultan's capital. There could be no harm done, he argued. He had never been in Constantinople, and to go there with a resident like Adam was in itself an opportunity not to be missed.

Meanwhile the astute concession-hunter, as he drove to Addison Road in a cab, was calmly plotting a further step in the direction he was slowly but surely following. His daring and ingenuity knew no bounds. He was a man full of energy and resource, unabashed, undaunted, unscrupulous, and yet to all, even to his most intimate friend, a perfect sphinx.

The second step in his progress he took on the evening of the day after.

In the afternoon, about four, a shabbily-dressed man called upon him at his flat, and they remained together for ten minutes or so. At half-past eight, as Marion was about to enter a 'bus at Oxford Circus to take her up to Hampstead for a blow—a trip she frequently took in the evening when alone—she heard her name uttered, and turning, found Max's polite French friend behind her, about to mount on the same conveyance.

To avoid him was impossible, therefore they ascended to the top together, he declaring that he was on his way to Hampstead.

"I'm going there too," she told him, although he already knew it quite well. "Have you seen Mr Barclay to-day?"

"Not to-day. I have been busy in the City," Adam explained. He glanced at her, and could not refrain from noting her neat appearance, dressed as she was in a black skirt, white cotton blouse, and a black hat which suited her beauty admirably. He knew that she was at Cunnington's, but, of course, appeared in ignorance of the fact. He was most kind and courteous to her, and so well had he arranged the meeting that she believed it to be entirely an accident.

Presently, after they had chatted for some time, he sighed, saying—

"In a few days I suppose I must leave London again."

"Oh! are you going abroad?"

"Yes, to Constantinople. I live there," he said.

"In Constantinople! How very strange it must be to live among the Turks!"

"It is a very charming life, I assure you, Miss Rolfe," he answered. "The Turk is always a gentleman, and his country is full of beauty and attraction, even though his capital may be muddy under foot."

"Oh, well," she said laughing, "I don't think I should care to live there. I should be afraid of them!"

"Your fears would be quite ungrounded," he declared. "A lady can walk unmolested in the streets of Constantinople at any hour of the day or night, which cannot be said, of your London here."

Then, after a pause, he added—

"I think your friend Mr Barclay is coming with me."

"With you?—to Constantinople?" she exclaimed in dismay. "When?"

"In two or three days," he replied. "But you mustn't tell him I said so," he went on. "We are going out on business—business that will bring us both a sum of money that will be a fortune to me, if not to Mr Barclay. We are in partnership over it."

"What nature is the business?"

"The building of a railroad to the Adriatic. We are obtaining permission from the Sultan for its construction."

"And Max—I mean Mr Barclay—will make a large sum?" she asked with deep interest.

"Yes, if he decides to go," replied Adam; "but I fear very much one thing," and he fixed his dark eyes upon hers.

"What do you fear?"

"Well—how shall I put it, Miss Rolfe?" he asked. "I—I fear that he will refuse to go because he does not wish to leave London just now."

"Why not?"

"He has an attraction here," the man laughed—"yourself."

She coloured slightly. Max had probably told this friend that they were lovers.

"Oh! that's quite foolish. He must go, if it is really in his interests."

"Exactly," declared Adam. "I have all my life been looking for such a chance to make money, and it has at last arrived. He must go."

"Most certainly. I will urge him strongly."

"A word from you, Miss Rolfe, would decide him—but—well, don't you think it would be best if you did not tell him that we had met. He might not like it if he knew we had discussed his business affairs—eh?"

"Very well," she said. "I will say nothing. When he speaks to me about the suggested journey I will strongly advise him to go in his own interests."

"Yes; do. It will be the means of putting many thousands of pounds into both our pockets. The matter is, in fact, entirely in your hands. May I with safety leave it there?"

"With perfect safety, Mr Adam," was her reply. "It is, perhaps, fortunate that we should have met like this to-night."

"Fortunate!" he echoed. "Most fortunate for all of us. If you are really Mr Barclay's friend you will see that he goes with me."

"I am his friend, and he shall go if it is to his interest to do go."

"Ask him, and he will tell you," was the reply of the man who had lounged in Park Lane as a shabby stranger, and of whom old Sam Statham went in such deadly fear.

He went with Marion to the end of her journey, and then left her in pretence of walking to his destination.

But after he had raised his hat to her so politely, and bent over her hand, he turned on his heel muttering to himself—

"You think you are his friend, my poor, silly little girl! No. You will compel him to go with me to the East, and thus become my catspaw—the tool of Jean Adam."

And giving vent to a short, dry laugh of triumph, he went on his way.

Chapter Twenty One
Shows Mr Statham at Home

Many a man and many a woman, as they passed up Park Lane on motor-'buses, in cabs, or on foot, glanced at the white house of Samuel Statham, and wondered.

The mystery concerning it and its owner always attracted them. Many were the weird stories afloat concerning it, stories greatly akin to those already told in a previous chapter. Men had watched, it was said, and had seen queer goings and comings. But as the matter concerned nobody in particular it merely excited public curiosity.

That Sam Statham was eccentric all the world knew. Society gossips in the papers were fond of referring to the millionaire as "the recluse of Park Lane" when recording some handsome donation to a charitable institution, or expressing a surprise that he was never seen at public functions such as the opening of hospitals or children's homes which he had himself endowed.

But the word "eccentric" explained it all. As regards the mansion in Park Lane they were always silent, for the elastic law of libel is ever before the eyes of the journalist who deals in tittle-tattle.

Though the stories concerning the millionaire's residence were curious and sometimes sensational—many of them of course invented—yet colour was certainly lent to them by the fact that the old man saw nobody except Levi and his secretary, and nobody had ever been known to pass that closed door at the head of the staircase.

Anyone, however, catching a glimpse of the interior of the hall when passing, saw old Levi in black, with his strip of spotless shirt-front, and behind, a wide hall with thick Turkey carpet, huge blue antique vases, carved furniture, and several fine pictures, the whole possessing an air of solidity and wealth. Beyond, however, was the Unknown and the Mysterious.

In the clubs and over dinner-tables the mystery of that Park Lane house was often spoken of. Men usually shook their heads and said little, but women expressed their opinion freely, and formed all sorts of wild theories.

Among the men who had always been attracted by the stories afloat were Charlie Rolfe, because of his close association with the old man, and Max Barclay, because of his intimate friendship with Rolfe. The latter had always been full of suspicion. Sam and Levi, master and man, were the only two who knew the truth of what lay behind that locked door. And the servant guarded his master's secret well. He was janitor there, and no one passed the threshold into old Sam's library without a very good cause, and without the permission of the master himself.

A thousand times, as Rolfe had gone in and out of the place, he had glanced up the broad, well-carpeted stairs, at the foot of which stood the fine marble Aphrodite, holding the great electrolier, and at the head, to the corner out of sight, was the locked door upon which half London had commented.

Had Samuel Statham thrown open his house only once, and given a reception, all gossip would be allayed. Indeed, as Rolfe sat with his master in the library the morning following Adam's meeting with Marion, he, without telling Sam the reason, suggested an entertainment in November. He said that Society were wondering he did not seek to make their acquaintance. There were hundreds of people dying to know him.

"Yes," snapped the old man, glancing around the darkened room, for the morning sun was full upon the house. "I know them. They'd come here, crush and guzzle, eat my dinners, drink my wine, and go away without even remembering my name. Oh! I know what the so-called aristocracy we like, never fear. Most of them live upon people like myself who are vain-glorious enough to be pleased to number the Earl of So-and-So and the Countess of Slush among their personal friends.

"Men with wives can't help being drawn into it. The womenfolk like to speak of 'dear Lady Longneck,' slobber over some old titled hag at parting, or find their names in the 'Court and Society' column of the *Daily Snivel*. It's their nature to be ambitious; but when a man's single, like myself, Rolfe, he can please himself. That's why I shut my door in their faces."

"Of course, you can afford to," the secretary replied, leaning both his elbows on the table and looking straight into his master's face. "Few men could do as you do. It would be against their interests."

"It may be even against my interests," the old man said thoughtfully, leaning back in his chair, "for I might get a good deal of fun out of watching them trying to squeeze a little money out of me, or worm from me what men call 'tips' regarding investments. Why, my dear Rolfe, once my door is opened to them, my life would no longer be worth living. Instead of one secretary I'd want a dozen, and Levi would be at the door all day long answering callers. Other men who live in this street on either side of me have done it to their cost."

"I've heard it said in the clubs that you, with your vast means and huge interests, owe a duty to Society," Rolfe remarked.

"I owe no duty to Society," the old fellow declared angrily. "Society owes nothing to me, and I owe nothing to it. You know, Rolfe, how—well—how I hate women—and I won't have a pack of chatterboxes about my place. If I was a man with five hundred a year they wouldn't want to know me."

"That's very true," Rolfe remarked with a slight sigh. "Nowadays, when a man has money he is at once called a gentleman. A lady is the wife of a man with money, whatever may have been her past—or her present."

The old man laughed.

"And there is the 'perfect lady,'" he said. "A genus usually associated with the police-court. But you are quite right, Rolfe, nowadays, according to our modern code, a poor man cannot be a gentleman. No, as long as I live, the needy aristocracy which calls itself Society shall never my threshold. I will remain independent of them, for I have no womankind, and no fish to fry. I don't want a baronetcy, or a peerage. I don't want shooting, or deer-stalking, or yachting, or hunting, or any of those pastimes. I merely want to be left alone here in peace—if it is possible." And he drew a long breath as the ugly recollection of the shabby stranger crossed his mind.

Rolfe knew well that the old man's objections were because he dare not throw open the mansion. Some secret was hidden there which he could not reveal. What was it? Why were those brilliant lights sometimes at night in the upper windows? He had seen them himself sometimes as he passed along near midnight on his way to his chambers in Jermyn Street, and had been sorely puzzled. More than once he had been convinced that somebody lived in the upper floors—somebody who was never seen. Yet if that were so, why should there be such secrecy regarding it. The occupant, whoever it was, could easily vacate the place while a reception was held.

As he sat there listening to the old man's tirade against the West-End and its ways he felt that there must be some far greater mystery than an unseen tenant.

That old Sam knew quite well the rumour concerning the house, was evident. Keeping secret agents in every capital as he was forced to do—agents, male and female, who knew everything and reported exactly what he wished to know—it was certain that public opinion concerning him was well-known to him. Yet, as in a scandal, the man most concerned is always the last to get wind of it. Perhaps after all he might be in ignorance of what people were saying, although it was hardly credible that Ben, his brother, would not tell him.

For craft and cunning few men in London could compare with Sam Statham, yet at the same time he was just in his judgment and honest in his transactions. The weak and needy he befriended, but woe betide any who endeavoured to mislead him or impose upon his generosity.

More than one man had, by receiving a word of good advice from Sam Statham and the temporary loan of a few thousand as capital, awakened in a week's time to find himself wealthy. One man in particular, now a well-known baronet, had risen in ten years from being a small draper in Launceston to his present position with an estate in Suffolk and a town house in Green Street, merely by taking Sam Statham's advice as to certain investments.

It was owing to this fact, and others, that old Sam, as he rose from the table and crossed the room to the window, where he pulled aside the blind to look out upon the sunny roadway, said—

"I myself, Rolfe, have made one or two so-called gentlemen. But," he added, drawing a deep breath, "let's put all that aside and get on with the letters. I'm expecting that Scotch friend of yours, the locomotive designer of Glasgow."

"Oh, Macgregor!" remarked the secretary. "He was most pertinacious the other day."

"All Scots are," replied the old man simply. "Let's get on." And returning to the table he took up letter after letter and dictated replies in his sharp, snappy way which, to those who did not know him, would have appeared priggish and uncouth.

_ The reason of Macgregor's visit to Old Broad Street had caused Rolfe a good deal of curiosity. He recollected how, on the instant his master had read the old engineer's scribbled lines, his face fell. The visitor was at all events not a welcome one. Yet, on the other hand, he had seen him without delay, and they had been closeted together for quite a long time.

When the bearded Scot left, and he had re-entered the millionaire's room, two facts struck him as peculiar. One was that a strong smell of burnt paper and a quantity of black tinder in the empty grate showed that some papers had been burned there, while the other was that old Sam was in the act of lighting a cigar, in itself showing a buoyancy of mind.

He never smoked when down at the bank, and very seldom when at home. His cigars, too, were of a cheap quality which even his clerks would be ashamed to offer their friends. Indeed, while all connected with the house in Old Broad Street possessed an air of solid prosperity, the head of the firm was usually of a penurious and hard-up aspect, as though he had a difficulty in making both ends meet. His smart electric brougham he used only once a week to take him to the City and back again. At other times he strolled about the streets so shabby as to pass unnoticed by those desirous of making his acquaintance and worming themselves into his good graces; or else he would idle in the park where he passed for a lounger who, crowded out by reason of his age, was down on his luck.

Samuel Statham loved the Park. Often and often he would get into conversation with the flotsam and jetsam of London life—the unemployed, and the men who, in these days of hustle, alas! find themselves too old at forty. The ne'er-do-wells he knew quite well, and they believed him to be one of themselves. But he was ever on the look-out for a deserving case—the starving, despondent man with wife and children hungry at home. He would draw the man's story from him, hear his complaint against unfair treatment, listen attentively to his wrongs, and pretending all the time to have suffered in a similar way himself.

Usually the man would, in the end, invite him to the home or the lodging-house where his wife and children were, and then, on ascertaining that the case was genuine, he would suddenly reveal himself as the good Samaritan.

To such men he gave himself out as Mr Jones, agent of a benevolent society which was nameless, and which did its work without advertisement, and extracted a pledge of secrecy. By such means many a dozen honest, hard-working men, who through no fault of their own had been thrown out of employment, had been "put upon their legs" again and gained work, and yet not one of them ever suspected that the shabby, down-at-heel man Jones was actually the millionaire Samuel Statham, who lived in the white house in fall view of the seat whereon they had first met.

Even from Rolfe he sought to conceal this secret philanthropy, yet the young man had guessed something of it. He had more than once caught him talking to strange men whose pinched faces and trim appearance told the truth.

The man whose vast wealth had brought him nothing but isolation and loneliness, delighted in performing these good works, and in rescuing the unfortunate wives and families of the deserving ones who were luckless. He loved to see the brightness overspread those dark, despairing faces, and to hear the heartfelt thanks which he was told to convey to the mythical "society."

Never but once did he allow a man to suspect that the money he gave came from his own pocket. That single occasion was when, after giving a man whom he believed to be deserving a sovereign, he next evening found him in the park the worse for liquor.

He said nothing that night, but a few days later, when he met him, he gave him a piece of his mind which the plausible good-for-nothing would not quickly forget.

"Such frauds as you," he had said, "prevent people from assisting the deserving poor. I've made inquiry into your story, and found it false from beginning to end. You have no wife, and the four children starving and ill that you described to me do not exist. You live for the most part in the bar of the 'Star,' off the Edgware Road, and on the night after I gave you the money you were so drunk that they wouldn't serve you. Such men like you," he went on with withering sarcasm, his grey beard bristling as he spoke, and his fist clenched fiercely, "are a disgrace to the human race, for you are a liar, a drunkard, and a blackguard—a man who deserves the death that will, I hope, overtake you—death in the gutter."

And he turned upon his heel, leaving the accused man standing staring at him open-mouthed, utterly unable to offer a single word in self-defence.

This secret charity was Sam Statham's only recreation. By it he made many friends whom he had taken out of the slums—friends who were perhaps more devoted and true to him than those to whom he had given financial "tips," and who had made many thousands thereby. In many a modest home was Mr Jones a welcome guest whenever he called to see how "his friends" were progressing, and many a time had he drunk a humble glass of bitter "sent out" for by his thankful and devoted host who was all unconscious of who his guest really was. The world would have laughed at the idea of a working man standing Samuel Statham a glass of ale.

One case was old Sam's particular pride. About eighteen months before, in the park one day, he came across a despairing but well-educated, middle-aged man, who at first was not at all communicative, but whose bearing and manner was that of refinement and culture. Three times they met, and it was very evident that the sad-faced man was starving.

At last Sam offered to "stand him" a meal, and over it the man told a pathetic story, how that he was a fully-qualified medical man in practice in York, but owing to his unfortunate habit of drinking he had lost everything, sold his practice, and had been compelled to leave the city. The proceeds of his practice had soon gone in drink, and now, with all the bitter remorse upon him, he and his wife and two small children were faced with starvation.

Friends and relations would not assist him because of his intemperance. There was only one way out of it all, he declared—suicide.

Sam had taken him in hand. He had seen the wife and children, and then explained, as usual, that he was Mr Jones. Small sums he first gave them, and finding that his charity was never abused, and that the doctor withstood the temptation to drink, he had gone to an agency, the address of which he had found in the *Lancet*, and bought a comfortable little practice with a furnished house in West Norwood, where the doctor and his family were now installed and doing well.

In West Norwood to-day that doctor is the most popular and the most sought after. His practice is ever increasing, and already he has nearly repaid the whole of the sum which Mr Jones lent him, and has been compelled to take an assistant.

The doctor is still in ignorance, however, for he has never identified Mr Jones with Statham the millionaire. But was it surprising that at his house no guest was more welcome than the man who had rescued him from ruin and from death?

Truly money, if properly applied, can do much to alleviate the sufferings of the world, and as it is the "root of all evil," so it is also the root of all good.

Chapter Twenty Two
Tells of the Three

"Well?"

"Weel?" asked Duncan Macgregor, who was seated in an easy attitude in Sam Statham's library. At the table sat the millionaire himself, while near by, in the enjoyment of a cigar, sat old Levi. The latter was still in his garb of service, but his attitude was certainly more like that of his master's intimate friend than that of butler.

It was from his thin lips that the query had escaped in response to a fact which the Scot had emphasised with his hairy fist.

"Well," exclaimed Statham after a pause, "and what do you suppose should be done, Mr—"

"Macgregor—still Duncan Macgregor," exclaimed the bearded man, concluding the millionaire's sentence. "That's the verra thing that puzzles me, mon. P'raps we'd best wait a wee bittie an' see."

Levi dissented. He knew that whatever his position in that strange household, his master always listened to him and took his advice— sometimes when it involved the risk of many thousands. He was a kind of oracle, for generally when Ben came there to consult his brother upon some important point, the old servant remained in the room to hear the discussion and to give his dry but candid opinion.

"My own opinion is that we should act at once—without fear. The slightest hesitation now will be our undoing, depend upon it," he said.

"Ah! Mr Levi," exclaimed the Scot, "I'm a'ways for caution. Hasna' our ain Bobbie said that facts are chiels that winna ding, and downa be disputed?"

"Yes; but we've not yet quite established the facts yet, you see," Statham said.

"Why, mon, isn't it as plain as plain can be? What mair d'ye want?"

"A good deal," Levi chimed in in his squeaky voice. "We can't act on that. It's too shadowy altogether."

"I tell ye it isn't!" cried Duncan, shaking his clenched fist again. "Mr Statham is in sair peril, I tell ye he is, an' I've proved it."

"Mr Statham must be allowed to be the best judge of that," Levi said, placing his hands together, and holding his cigar between his teeth.

"Mr Statham knows me weel. He knows I'd nae tell him what I didn't ken ma'sel'."

The great financier rose thoughtfully and stood with his back to the mantelshelf.

"Look here, Macgregor," he said, fixing his eyes upon the man seated before him. "When you called at the office and was fool enough not to give your proper name you had a difficulty in getting an interview with me. I hadn't any idea till I received your note that—well, that you were in the land of the living. When we met before it was under different circumstances—very different, weren't they?" and the millionaire smiled. "Shall I recall to your memory one scene—long ago—a scene that lives in my memory this moment as though the events happened but yesterday. We were both younger, and more active then—you and I—and—"

"Nae, Mr Statham. We're better not bearin' it," he protested, holding up his hands. "I jalouse what you're again' to say."

"To you, my friend, I owe much," the old man went on. "The place was in a sun-baked South American city, the time was sunset, fierce and blood-red like the deeds of that never-to-be-forgotten day. There was war—a revolution was in progress, and the Government forces had been that day driven back into the capital followed by us. I remember you, with that great bullet furrow down your cheek and the blood streaming from it as you fought at my side. I see you bear the scar even now." Then, with a quick movement he pulled up his sleeve and showed on his right forearm a great cicatrice, asking: "Do you remember how I received this?"

"Nae, nae, Mr Statham, enough!" cried the Scot. "Our days of war are long since past. They'll come again nae mair."

"You remember how we followed the troops of Hernandez into the capital, shooting and killing as we drove them before us, and how you and I and a few more of the younger bloods made a dash for the Palace to secure the President himself. I recollect the wild excitement of those moments. I was tearing along the street shouting and urging on my men, when of a sudden I found myself surrounded by a dozen soldiers of Hernandez. I fought for life, though well knowing I was lost. As a prisoner I should be tortured, for they had long sworn to serve me as they had served our friends José and Manuel. This recollection flashed across me, and with my back to the wall I fired my pistol full in a man's face and blew it out of all recognition. A man had raised his rifle and covered me, but next moment I gave him an upward cut with my sword.

"At the same instant I felt a sharp twinge upon my right arm, and my sword dropped from my grasp. I was maimed, and stood there at their mercy. A dark-faced, beetle-browed fellow raised his sabre with a fierce Spanish oath to cut me down, but in the blood-red sunlight another blade flashed high, and the man sank dying in the dust.

"It was you, Macgregor—you alone had come to my aid, and four of my attackers fell beneath your blows in that hand-to-hand struggle as you, with your own body placed before mine, fought on, keeping them back and yet without assistance. Shall I ever forget those moments, or how near both of us were to death? I was already half-fainting, but you shouted to me to keep courage, and in the end we were discovered by our men and saved. If ever a deed deserved the Victoria Cross, yours did. You, Macgregor—as you now call yourself—saved my life."

"An' I'm here, Mr Statham, to save it again, if ye'll only let me," was the Scot's dry reply.

"Years have gone since that day," the millionaire went on, with a distinct catch in his voice. "I lost sight of you soon afterwards, and heard once that you were in Caracas. Then there was no further news of you. We drifted apart—our lives lay in opposite directions. Yet to you—and to you alone—I owe my present life, for were it not for your aid at that moment I should have been put to the torture in that terrible castle where Hernandez did his prisoners to death, and my body given to the rats like others of our friends."

"Eh, mon, ye really make me blush," laughed Macgregor. "So please don't talk of it. That's all over the noo. Let the past take care of itsel'. We've got the present to face."

"I have never ceased reflecting upon the past," Sam declared in a rather low and husky voice. "I never dreamed that the man Macgregor, in the employ of the Clyde and Motherwell Works, was the same man to whom I am indebted for my life."

"Ah! man's a problem that puzzles the devil hissel'," laughed Macgregor. "I'd nae ha kenned ye were the Statham I knew out there in the old days till I saw the picture of ye in the *Glasgie News* one nicht when I bought it at the corner of Polmadie Street on me way hame. An' there was a biography of ye—which didn't mention very much. But it was the real Sam Statham—and Sam Statham was my friend of long ago."

"Most extraordinary!" remarked Levi, who had been smoking quietly and listening to the conversation. "I had so idea of all this!"

"There are many incidents in my career, Levi, of which you are unaware," remarked his master drily.

"I have no doubt," retorted the servant in a tone quite as dry as that of his master's. This was Duncan Macgregor's first visit to Park Lane, and Levi did not approve of him. He always looked askance at any friend of Mr Samuel's of the old days. Everybody who had ever known him in the unknown and struggling period, now claimed his acquaintance as his intimate friend, and various and varied were the ruses adopted in order to endeavour to obtain an interview.

He suspected this hairy Scot—whose bravery in his youth had saved Sam's life—of working for his own ends.

"This is a strange story of yours, Duncan," remarked the millionaire a few moments later, his eyes fixed upon the seated man—"so strange that I should not believe it, but for one thing."

"An' what's that?"

"Other information in my possession goes to prove that your surmise is actually correct, and that your apprehension has foundation. I know that Adam is in London. I've seen him!"

"An' he's seen you—eh?" cried Macgregor, starting up in alarm.

"Yes, he's seen me."

"Did he speak to ye?"

"No. He watched me through the window from yonder pavement outside."

A silence fell in that warm room where the blinds were still down to exclude the sun, a silence unbroken save by the buzzing of the flies and the low, solemn ticking of the clock.

At last the Scot spoke.

"He means mischief. Depend on it."

"I quite believe he does," Statham admitted.

"That is why we should act at once," Levi chimed in.

"And perhaps by a premature move spoil the whole of our chance of victory!" remarked the millionaire, very thoughtfully.

"Remember that Adam holds very strong cards in the game," the butler urged, knocking the ash slowly from his cigar. Surely it was a queer, unusual scene, this conference of three!

"I have suspected something for some time past, Levi," was his master's response. "And I took steps to combat my enemies; but, unfortunately, I was not sufficiently wary, and I failed."

"What, mon!" gasped the man from Glasgow; "ye don't say ye're at the mercy of those devils?"

"I tell you, Macgregor, that my position is more insecure than even you believe it to be," was the response, in a low voice, almost of despair.

Levi and Duncan exchanged glances. The millionaire's words were somewhat enigmatical, but the truth was apparent. Samuel Statham was in fear of some revelation which could be made by that shabby stranger whom he had seen idling at the Park railings.

"Tell me, Macgregor. Does Adam know you?"

"No."

"You've seen him, and you know him?"

"Perfectly weel. I kept ma eye on him when he didn't dream that anybody was nigh him."

"And what you told me in the City you are prepared to stand by?"

The Scot put out his big hands, saying:

"Mr Statham, what I've told ye I stick to."

"Duncan," said the great man, clasping the hand offered him. "You were my friend once—my best friend—and you will be so again."

"If ye'll let me be," answered the other warmly. Statham could read a man's innermost character at a glance. He was seldom, if ever, mistaken. He looked into Macgregor's eyes, and saw truth and friendship there.

As Levi watched the two men his lip curled slightly. He was a cynic, and did not approve of this outburst of sentimentality on the part of his master. Samuel Statham, the man of millions and the controller of colossal interests, should, he declared within himself, be above such an exhibition of his own heart.

"Is it not strange," remarked Statham, as though speaking to himself, "that you should actually have been engaged in my works without knowing that it was the head of the firm who was indebted to you for his life?"

"Ay, the world's only a sma' space, after all," Duncan replied. "I was apprenticed to the firm, but soon got sick of a humdrum life. So I went out to South America to try ma fortune, an' we met. After the war I went to Caracas, and then back to Glasgie to the old firm, where I've been ever since. I thought that when the new company took the place over I'd be discharged as too old. Indeed, more than once Mr Rolfe has hinted at it."

"I don't think you'd need fear that, Duncan. Both you and I recollect scenes set in strong remembrance—scenes that are never to return. I had no idea it was you to whom the creditable work turned out at Glasgow was due until Rolfe told me all about you," and as he uttered those words a twinge of conscience shot through his mind as he recollected how he had ordered the man to be summarily discharged for daring to seek an interview. And then how, when he had entered his presence, he had handed him something that was far better destroyed. They had indeed destroyed it together.

He saw that Macgregor had no great love for Rolfe, but put it down to the fact that his secretary, being practically in charge of the works, had become out of favour with the men over the question of labour. The Scot had said nothing derogatory regarding Charlie, but merely expressed surprise that he had not been accorded an interview at once. Then he had urged that he had something of importance and of interest to impart.

"Well, you see, Macgregor," replied the millionaire, half apologetically; "the fact is I have to make it a rule to see nobody. Of course, to old friends, like yourself, I am always accessible, and delighted to have a chat, but if it were known that I received people, I should be besieged here all day long. I make it a rule not to allow anybody here in my house."

"Why?" asked the Scot, quite unconscious of the gravity of his inquiry. He was in entire ignorance of the strange stories concerning the house wherein he was at that moment. The papers never mentioned them for fear of an action for libel. As far as he had seen there was nothing peculiar or extraordinary about the place. The hall and the library were very handsomely furnished, as befitted the home of one of England's wealthiest men. The fact that Levi had been called into conference even was not remarkable, for the reason had already been explained to him briefly, in half-a-dozen words.

"But you have your ain circle of good friends here, I suppose?" suggested the Scot, as the great man had not replied to his question.

"No," replied Statham. "Nobody comes here—nobody enters my door."

"But why?"

Master and servant exchanged glances. It was a direct question to which it was impossible to give a truthful reply without the revelation of a secret.

And so Samuel Statham lied to his best, humble yet most devoted friend.

Chapter Twenty Three
London Lovers

Nearly three weeks had now passed since the extraordinary disappearance of Dr Petrovitch and his daughter from the house in Cromwell Road.

The cleverness with which the removal of their household goods had been effected, and the cunning and ingenuity displayed regarding them, showed Max Barclay plainly that the disappearance had been carefully planned, and that those assisting had been well paid for keeping their secret.

And yet, after all, it was quite possible that the men who had removed the furniture from the house were merely hired for the job, and had gone away thinking they had acted quite legitimately. Harmer's Stores often engage extra hands, and what would have been easier than for the foreman to have paid them, and driven the van with the false name upon it to another part of London. That was, no doubt, what had really been done.

Max had devoted the greater part of his time to endeavouring to elucidate the mystery, but had failed ignominiously. The statement made by Marion concerning what seemed to be some confession of Maud's greatly puzzled him. His well-beloved was loyal to her friend, and would not betray her. Times without number he had reverted to the question, but she always evaded his questions.

Only a few evenings before, while they were seated at one of the little tables on the lawn of the Welcome Club at the Earl's Court Exhibition, of which he was a member, he had again referred to Maud, and asked her, in the interests of his inquiry, to give him some idea of what she had stated on that night when they last met.

"I really cannot tell you, Max," was her reply, as she lifted her eyes to his in the dim light shed by the coloured lamps with which the place was illuminated. "Have I not already told you of the promise I gave her? You surely do not wish me to break it! Would it be fair, or just? I'm sure you, who are always loyal to a woman, would never wish me to mention what she told me."

"Of course. If it is anything against her reputation—her honour—then it is certainly best left unsaid," he replied quickly. "Only—well, I—I thought, perhaps, it might give us a clue to the motive of their unaccountable flight."

"Perhaps it might," she admitted; "and yet I cannot tell you."

"Does Charlie know? Would he tell me, do you think?"

"I don't think Charlie knows. At any rate, she would not tell him. If he does know, it must be through some other source."

"And you anticipate that what Maud told you had some connection with their sudden disappearance?" he asked, looking steadfastly into the face of the woman he dearly loved.

"I've already told you so."

"But when you parted from her that night, did you believe that you would not meet her again?"

She was silent, looking straight before her at the crowd of idlers circulating around the illuminated bandstand and enjoying the music and the cool air after the stifling London day.

At last she spoke, saying in a low, rather strained voice:

"I can hardly answer that question. Had I suspected anything unusual I think I should have mentioned my apprehension to you."

"Yes, I feel sure you would have done, dearest," he declared. "I quite see the difficulty of your present position. And you understand, I'm quite sure, how anxious I feel regarding the safety of the doctor, who was such a dear friend of mine."

"But why are you so anxious, Max?" she asked.

"Because if—well, if there had not been foul play, I should have heard from the doctor before this!" he said seriously.

"Foul play?" she gasped, starting forward. "Do you suspect some—some tragedy, then?"

"Yes, Marion," was his low, earnest reply. "I do."

"But why?" she queried. "Remember that the doctor was a diplomat and statesman. In Servia politics are very complex, as they are, I'm told, in every young nation. Our own English history was a strange and exciting one when we were the present age of Servia. The people killed King Alexander, it is true; but did we not kill King Charles?"

"Then you think that some political undercurrent is responsible for this disappearance?" he suggested.

"That has more than once crossed my mind."

"Yet would he not have sent word to me in secret?"

"No. He might fear spies. You yourself have told me how secret agents swarm in the Balkan countries, and that espionage is as bad there as in Russia."

"But we are in London—not in Servia."

"There are surely secret agents of the Servian Opposition party here in London!" she said. "You were telling me something about them once— some facts which the doctor had revealed to you."

"Yes, I remember," he remarked thoughtfully, feeling that in her argument there was much truth. "Yet I have a kind of intuition of the occurrence of some tragedy, Marion," he added, recollecting how her brother had stolen in secret from that denuded house.

"Well, I think, dear, that your fears are quite groundless," she declared. "I know how the affair is worrying you, and how much you respected the dear old doctor. But, if I were you, I would wait in patience. He will surely send you word some day from some remote corner of the earth. Suppose he had sailed for India, South America, or South Africa, for instance? There would have been no time for him to write to you from his hiding-place."

"Then he is in hiding—eh?" asked Max, eager to seize on any word of hers that might afford a clue to the strange statement of Maud.

"He may be."

"Is that your opinion?"

"I suspect as much."

"Then you do not believe there has been a tragedy?"

"I believe only in what I know," replied the girl with wisdom.

"And you know there has not been a tragedy?"

"Ah! no. There you are quite mistaken. I have no knowledge whatsoever."

"Only surmise?"

"Only surmise."

"Based upon what Maud told you—eh?" he asked at last, bringing the conversation to the point.

"What Maud told me has nothing whatever to do with my surmise," was her quick reply. "It is a surmise, pure and simple."

"And you have no foundation of fact for it?"

"None, dear."

Max was disappointed. He sat smoking, staring straight before him. At the tables around, beneath the trees, well-dressed people were chatting and laughing in the dim light, while the military band opposite played the newest waltz. But he heard it not. He was only thinking of how he could clear up the mystery of the strange disappearance of his dearest friend. He glanced at the soft face of the sweet girl at his side, that was so full of affection and yet so sphinx-like.

She would tell him nothing. Again and again she had refused to betray the confidence of her friend.

For the thousandth time he reflected upon that curious and startling incident which he had seen with his own eyes in Cromwell Road, and of the inexplicable discovery he had made. He had not met Rolfe. That he should keep away from him was, in itself, suspicious. Without a doubt he knew the truth.

Max wondered whether Charlie had told his sister anything—whether he had told her the truth, and the reason of her determination not to speak was not to incriminate him. He knew in what strong affection she held her brother—how she always tried to shield his faults and magnify his virtues. Yet was it not only what might be very naturally supposed that she would do? Charlie was always very good to her. To him, she owed practically everything.

And so he pondered, smoking in silence while the band played and the after-dinner idlers gossiped and flirted on that dimly-lit lawn. He pondered when later on he took her to Oxford Street by the "tube," and saw her to the corner of the street in which Cunnington's barracks were situated, and he pondered as he drove along Piccadilly to the Traveller's to have a final drink before going home.

Next morning, about eleven, he was in his pleasant bachelor sitting-room in Dover Street going over some accounts from his factor up in Scotland, when the door opened and Charlie Rolfe entered, exclaiming in his usual hearty way:

"Hulloa, Max, old chap, how are you?"

Barclay looked up in utter surprise. The visit was entirely unexpected, and so intimate a friend was Rolfe that he always entered unannounced.

In a moment, however, he recovered himself.

"Why, Charlie," he exclaimed, motioning him to a low easy-chair on the other side of the fireplace, "you're quite a stranger. Where have you been all this long time?"

"Oh! I thought you knew through Marion. I've been up in Glasgow. Had a lot of worries at the works—labour trouble and all that sort of thing," he replied. "Those Scotch workmen are utterly incorrigible, but I must say that it's due to agitators from our side of the border."

"Yes; I saw something in the papers the other day about an impending strike. Have a cigar?" and he pushed the box towards his friend.

"There would have been a strike if the old man hadn't put his foot down. The men held a meeting and reconsidered their position. It's well for them they did, otherwise I had orders to close down the whole works for six months—or for a year, if need be."

"But you'd have lost very heavily, wouldn't you?"

"Lost? I should rather think so. We should have had to pay damages for breach of contract with the Italian railways to the tune of a nice round sum. But what does it matter to the guv'nor. When he takes a stand against what he calls the tyranny of labour he doesn't count the cost."

"Well," sighed Max, looking across at Marion's brother, "it's rather nice to be in such a position, and yet—"

"And yet it isn't all honey to be in his shoes—eh? No, Max, it isn't," he said. "I know more about old Sam than most men, and I tell you I'd rather be as I am than stifled by wealth as he is. He's a millionaire in gold, but a pauper in happiness."

"I can't help thinking that his unhappiness must, in a great measure, be due to himself," Max remarked, wondering why Charlie had visited him after this length of time. "I think if I had his money I should try and get some little enjoyment out of it. Other wealthy men have yachts, or motor cars, or other hobbies. Why doesn't he?"

"Because he doesn't care for sport. He told me once that in his younger days abroad he was as keen a sportsman as anybody. But now-a-days he's too old for it, and prefers his armchair."

"And yet he isn't a very old man, is he?"

"Sometimes wealth rejuvenates a man, but more often the worry of it ages him prematurely," Rolfe remarked. "I only got back from Glasgow again last night, and I thought I'd look in and see you. Seen Marion lately?"

"I was with her at Earl's Court last night. She's all right."

Then a silence fell between the pair. Rolfe lit the cigar he had been slowly twisting between his fingers. Max looked furtively into his friend's face, trying to read what secret thought lay behind. Charlie, however, preserved his usual easy, nonchalant air as he leaned back in his chair, his weed between his teeth and his hands clasped behind his head.

"Look here, Charlie," Max exclaimed at last, in a tone of confidence. "I want to ask you something."

The other started visibly, and his cheeks went just a trifle paler.

"Well, go on, old chap." He laughed uneasily. "What is it?" And then he held his breath.

"It's about old Statham."

"About old Statham!" the other echoed, breathing freely again.

"Yes. Do you know that there are going about London a lot of queer stories regarding that house of his in Park Lane—I mean a lot more stories."

"More stories!" laughed the private secretary. "Well, what are people saying now?"

"Oh, all sorts of weird and ridiculous thing."

"What is one of them? I'm interested, for they never tell me anything."

"Because they know you to be connected with the place," Max remarked. "Well, just now there are about a dozen different tales going the rounds, and all sorts of hints against the old man."

"Set about by those with whom he has refused to associate—eh?"

"Probably concocted by spiteful gossips, I should think. Some of them bear upon the face of them their own refutation. For instance, I've heard that the reason lights are seen upstairs is because there's a mysterious Mrs Statham and her family living there in secret. Nobody has seen them, and they never go out."

"Oh! And what reason is given for that?"

"Because they say she's a Turkish woman, and that he still keeps her secluded as she has been ever since a child. The story goes that she's a very beautiful woman, daughter of one of the most powerful Pashas in Constantinople, who escaped from her mother's harem and got away over the frontier into Bulgaria, where Statham joined her, and they were married in Paris."

Rolfe laughed aloud. The idea of old Sam being an actor in such a love-romance was distinctly amusing.

"They call him Statham Pasha, I suppose! Well, really, it is the very latest, just as though there may not be lights upstairs when the old man goes to bed."

"Of course," said Max. "But the fact that the old man refuses to allow anybody in the house has given rise to all these stories. You really ought to tell him."

"What shall I tell him? Is there any other gossip?"

"Yes," replied Max, looking the secretary straight in the face in suspicion that he knew more about the mysteries of that house than he really did. "There's another strange story, which I heard two or three days ago, to the effect that one night recently a person was seen to go there secretly, being admitted at once. Then, after the lapse of an hour or so, old Levi came forth, signalled to a four-wheeled cab which was apparently loitering about on the chance of a fare. Then from out of the house was carried a long, heavy box, which was placed on the cab and driven away to an unknown destination."

"A box!" gasped Rolfe in surprise, bending quickly across to the speaker. "What do you mean—what do you suggest?"

"Well the natural suggestion is that the body of the midnight visitor was within that box?"

Charlie Rolfe did not reply. He sat staring open-mouthed, as though Max's story had supplied the missing link in a chain of suspicions which had for a long time existed in his mind—as though he now knew the terrible and astounding truth.

Chapter Twenty Four
Truth or Untruth

The two men exchanged glances, each suspicious of the other.

Max tried to imagine the motive of his friend's visit, while Rolfe, on his part, was undecided as to the extent of the other's knowledge. To come there and boldly face Max had cost him a good many qualms. At one moment he felt certain that Max suspected, but at the next he laughed at his own fears, and declared himself to be a chicken-hearted fool. And so days had gone on until, unable to stand it further, he had at last resolved to call at Dover Street.

"You're quite a stranger, Charlie," Max remarked at last. "I haven't seen you since the doctor disappeared so mysteriously."

He watched Rolfe's face as he spoke, yet save a very slight flush upon the cheeks he was in no way perturbed.

"Well, I've been away nearly the whole time," was the other's reply. "The whole affair is most curious."

"And haven't you seen Maud since?"

He hesitated slightly, and in that hesitation Max detected falsehood.

"No," was his reply.

"What? And haven't you endeavoured to find out her whereabouts?" cried Max, staring at him. "If Marion had disappeared, I think I should have left no stone unturned in order to discover the truth."

"I have tried to solve the mystery, and failed," was his rather lame response.

"But where are they—where can they be? It's most extraordinary that the doctor should not send me word in confidence of their secret hiding-place. I was his most intimate friend."

"Well," he said. "The fact is that until this moment I believed you were well aware of their whereabouts, but could not, in face of your friendship, betray them."

Max looked him straight in the face. Was he lying?

Such a statement was, indeed, ingenious, to say the least. Yet how, recollecting that he had left the empty house in secret, could he believe that Max knew the truth and was concealing it? Was it really possible that he was in ignorance? Barclay thought. Had he gone to Cromwell Road expecting to find the doctor at home, just as he had done? If he had, then why had he crept out of the place and made his escape so hurriedly?

Again, he recollected the result of the search in company with the man from Harmer's, and the finding of the open safe. Somebody had been there after his visit; somebody who had robbed the safe! That person must have been aware of the departure of the doctor. Who was it if not the man seated there before him?

"Well, Rolfe," Max remarked at last. "You're quite mistaken. I haven't the slightest notion of where they are. I've done my best to try and discover some clue to the direction of their flight, but all in vain. The more I have probed the affair, the more extraordinary and more mystifying has it become."

"What have you discovered?" asked Charlie quickly.

"Several strange things. First, I have found that the furniture was removed in vans painted with the name of Harmer's Stores, but they were not Harmer's vans. The household goods were spirited away that night, nobody knows whither."

"And with them the Doctor and Maud."

"Exactly. But—well, tell me the truth, Charlie. Have you had no message of whatever sort from Maud?"

"None," he replied, his face full of pale anxiety.

"But, my dear fellow she loved you, did she not? It was impossible for her to conceal it."

"Yes, I know. That's why I can't make it out at all. I sometimes think that—"

"That what?"

"Well, that there's been foul play, Max," he said hoarsely. "You know what the people of those Balkan countries are—so many political conspirators in every walk of life. And the doctor was such a prominent politician in Servia."

Was he telling an untruth? If so, he was a marvellous actor.

"Then you declare that you have received no word from either Maud or the Doctor."

"I have heard nothing from them."

"But, Charlie," he said slowly, "has it not struck you that Marion knows something—that if she liked she could furnish us with a clue to the solution of the mysterious affair?"

"Yes," he said, his face brightening at once. "How curious! That thought struck me also. She knows something, evidently, but refuses to say a word."

"Because she is Maud's most intimate friend."

"Yet she ought, merely to set my mind at rest. She knows how fondly I love Maud."

"What has she told you?"

"She's merely urged me to be patient. That's all very well, because I feel sure that if Maud were allowed to do so she would write to me."

"Her father may prevent her. He does not write to me, remember," said Max.

"I can't understand Marion; she is so very mysterious over it all. Each time I've seen her I've tried to get the truth from her, but all in vain," Rolfe declared. "My own idea is that on the night in question, when they went together to Queen's Hall, Maud told Marion something—something that is a secret."

Max pondered. His friend's explanation tallied exactly with his own theories; but the point still remained whether or not there had been foul play.

"But why doesn't the Doctor send me word of his own safety?" asked Barclay. "I was with him only a few hours before, smoking and chatting. He surely knew then of his impending flight. It had all been most ingeniously and cleverly arranged."

"No doubt. When I knew of it I was absolutely staggered," Rolfe said.

It was curious, thought his friend, that he did not admit visiting the house after the furniture had been removed.

"I thought you left at nine that night to go to Belgrade. Marion told me you had gone," Max remarked.

"Yes. I had intended to go, but I unfortunately missed my train. The next day the old gentleman sent somebody else, as he wanted me at home to look after affairs up in Glasgow."

"And how did you first know of Maud's disappearance?" asked Max, thinking to upset his calm demeanour.

"I called at the house," he replied, vouchsafing no further fact.

"And after that?" Max inquired, recollecting that tell-tale stain upon the woman's bodice.

"I made inquiries in a number of likely quarters, without result."

"And what's your theory?" Max asked, looking him straight in the face, now undecided whether he was lying or not.

"Theory? Well, my dear fellow, I haven't any. I'd like to hear yours. The doctor and his daughter have suddenly disappeared, as though the earth has swallowed them, and they've not left the least trace behind. What do you believe the real truth to be?"

"At present I'm unable to form any actual theory," his friend replied. "There has either been foul play, or else they are in hiding because of some act of political vengeance which they fear. That not a word has come from either tends to support the theory of foul play. Yet if there has been a secret tragedy, why should the furniture have been made to disappear as well as themselves?" Then, after a pause, he fixed his eyes suspiciously upon Charlie, and added, "I wonder if the Doctor kept any valuables or securities that thieves might covet in his house?"

Rolfe shrugged his shoulders. Mention of that point in no way disturbed him.

"I have never heard Maud speak of her father having any valuable possessions there," he said simply.

"But he may have done so, and a theft may have been committed!"

"Of course. But the whole affair from beginning to end is most puzzling. I wonder the papers didn't get hold of it. They could have concocted lots of theories if it had become known."

"And now, at this lapse of time, the Press could not mention it for fear of libel. They'll think that the Doctor had done a moonlight flit, instead of paying his rent."

"It certainly looks like that," remarked Max with a laugh. "But I only wish we could induce Marion to tell us all she knows."

Charlie sighed.

"Yes," he said. "I only wish she would say something. But she refuses absolutely, and so we're left entirely in the dark."

"Well, all I can say is, that the Doctor would never wilfully leave me in ignorance of his whereabouts, especially at this moment. We have certain business matters together involving a probable gain of a good round sum. Therefore, it was surely to his interest to keep me in touch with him!" Max declared.

The man before him was silent.

Was it possible that he had misjudged him? Was he lying; or had he really gone to Cromwell Road in search of the Doctor and found the house untenanted and empty?

"It is a complete mystery," was all that Rolfe could say.

"Do you know, Charlie, a curious thought struck me the other day, and I mention it to you in all confidence. It may be absurd—but—well, somehow I can't get it out of my head."

"And what is it?" asked his friend with an eagerness just a little unusual.

Max paused. Should he speak? Or should he preserve silence? The mystery now held him bewildered. What had become of the dear old Doctor and the pretty girl with the tiny wisp of hair straying across her white brow? Yes. He would speak the vague impression that had, of late, been uppermost in his mind.

"Well," he said, "old Statham has financial interests in Servia, has he not?"

"Certainly. Quite a number. He floated their loan a few years ago."

"And has it not struck you then that he and the Doctor might be acquainted?"

"They were strangers," he exclaimed quickly, darting a strange look across at Barclay.

Max was somewhat surprised at the vehement and decisive nature of Charlie's declaration.

"And Maud never met the old fellow?"

"Never—to my knowledge."

"Statham has a number of friends and acquaintances whom you do not know. The Doctor may have been one of them."

"Oh, Sam has very few secrets from me. I am his confidential secretary," was the other's rather cold response.

"I know—I know. But would it not be to Statham's interest to be on friendly terms with such a powerful factor in the Servian political world as Dr Petrovitch?"

"Well, it might. But you know how independent he is. He never goes into society, and has no personal friends. He's utterly alone in the world—the loneliest man in London."

"Then let us go a trifle further," said Max at last. "Answer me one question. Is it or is it not, a fact that you were at the house in Cromwell Road on the night of—of their disappearance?"

Rolfe's countenance changed in an instant. His lips went white.

"Why?" he faltered—"what do you mean to imply?—why—?"

"Because, Rolfe," the other said in a hard, determined voice, "because I saw you there—saw you with my own eyes!"

Chapter Twenty Five
Two Men and a Woman

The face of Charlie Rolfe went pale as death.

He was in doubt, and uncertain as to how much, or how little, was known by this man who loved his sister.

"I saw you there, Rolfe, with my own eyes," repeated Max, looking straight into his face.

He tried to speak. What could he say? For an instant his tongue clave to the roof of his mouth.

"I—I don't quite understand you," he faltered. "What do you mean?"

"Simply that I saw you at the Doctor's house on the night of their disappearance."

"My dear fellow," he laughed, in a moment, perfectly cool, "you must have been mistaken. You actually say you saw me?"

"Most certainly I did," declared Max, his eyes still upon his friend.

"Then all I can say is that you saw somebody who resembled me. Tell me exactly what you did see."

Max was for a moment silent. He never expected that Rolfe would flatly deny his presence there. This very fact had increased his suspicions a hundredfold.

"Well, the only person I saw, Charlie, was you yourself—leaving the house. That's all."

"Somebody who closely resembled me, I expect."

"Then you deny having been at the house that evening?" asked Max in great surprise.

"Why, of course I do. You're absolutely mistaken, old chap," was Charlie's response. "Of course, I can quite see how this must have puzzled you. But what now arises in my mind is whether someone has not endeavoured to personate me. It seems very much as though they have. You say that I left the house. When?"

"After the removal. You were in the empty house, which you left secretly."

"And you were there also, then?" he asked.

"Of course. I called, ignorant that they had left." Charlie Rolfe did not speak for several moments.

"Well," he exclaimed at last, "it seems that somebody has been impersonating me. I certainly was not there."

"Why should they impersonate you?"

"Who knows? Is there not mystery in the whole affair?"

"But if somebody went there dressed to resemble you, there must have been a motive in their visit," Max said.

"Well, old fellow, as you know, I have kept away from the house of late—at Maud's request. She feared that her father did not approve of my too frequent visits."

"And so you met her at dusk in the quiet streets about Nevern Square and the adjacent thoroughfares?"

"Certainly. I told you so. I made no secret of it to you. Why should I?"

"Then why make a secret about your visit to the house on that particular evening?"

"I don't make any secret of it," he protested. "As I've already told you, I was not there."

"But you didn't leave Charing Cross, as you made people believe you had done. You didn't even go to the station," returned Max.

"Certainly I did not."

"You had no intention, when you saw Marion at Cunnington's, of leaving at all. Come, admit that."

"You are quite right. I did not intend to leave London."

"But Statham had given you orders to go."

"I do not always obey his orders when it is to his own interest that I should disregard them," he replied enigmatically.

"Then you had a reason for not going to Servia?"

"I had—a very strong one."

"Connected with Maud Petrovitch?"

"In no way whatever. It was a purely personal motive."

"And you thought fit to disregard Statham's injunctions in order to attend to your own private business!"

"It was his business, as well as mine," declared Charlie, who, after a pause, asked: "Now tell me, Max, why are you cross-examining me like a criminal lawyer? What do you suspect me of?"

"Well—shall I be frank?"

"Certainly. We are old enough friends for that."

"Then I'm sorry to say, Charlie, that I suspect you of telling a lie."

"Lies are permissible in certain cases—for instance, where a woman's honour is at stake," he replied, fixing his eyes steadily upon those of his friend.

"Then you admit that what you have just told me is not the truth?"

"I admit nothing. I only repeat that I was not in Cromwell Road on the evening in question."

"But my eyes don't deceive me, man! I saw your face, remember."

"If it was actually my face, it was not in Cromwell Road. That's quite certain?" laughed old Statham's secretary. "But it was your face."

"It was, I repeat, somebody who resembled me," he declared. "But you haven't told me what the person was doing in the empty house."

"That's just what I don't know," Barclay replied. "I only know this: When I entered that night I saw nothing of a safe let into the wall. But on going there the next day the safe stood revealed, the door was open, and it was empty."

"And so you charge me with being a thief!" cried Rolfe, his cheek flushing.

"Not at all. You asked me for the truth, and I've told you."

"Well, it's evident that you suspect me of sneaking into the house, breaking open the Doctor's safe, and taking the contents," he said plainly, annoyed.

"The Doctor may have returned himself in secret," Max replied. "But such could hardly be the case, for the door had been blown open by explosives."

"That would have created a noise," Charlie remarked quickly. "Shows that whoever did it was a blunderer."

"Exactly. That's just my opinion. What I want to establish is the motive for the secret visit, and who made it."

"Well, I can assure you that I'm in entire ignorance of the existence of any safe in the Doctor's house."

"And so was I. It was concealed by the furniture until my second visit, on the following morning."

"Curious," Rolfe said. "Very curious indeed. The whole thing is most remarkable—especially how both father and daughter got away without leaving the least trace of their flight."

"Then you don't anticipate foul play?" Max asked quickly.

"Why should one?"

"The Doctor had a good many political enemies."

"We all have enemies. Who has not? But they don't come and murder one and take away one's household goods."

"Then I am to take it that it was not you I saw at Cromwell Road, Charlie?" asked his friend in deep earnestness, at the same time filled with suspicion. He felt that his eyes could not deceive him.

"In all seriousness," was the other's reply. "I was not there. This personation of myself shows that there was some very clever and deeply-laid scheme."

"But you've just declared that a falsehood was permissible where a woman's honour was concerned?"

"Well, and will not every man with a sense of honour towards a woman hold the same opinion? You yourself, Max, for instance, are not the man to give a woman away?"

"I know! I know—only—"

"Only what? Surely you do not disagree with me!"

"In a sense I don't, but I'm anxious to clear up this matter as far as you yourself are concerned."

Rolfe saw that he had shaken his friend's fixed belief that he had seen him in Cromwell Road. Max was now debating in his mind whether he had not suspected Charlie unjustly. It is so easy to suspect, and so difficult to satisfy one's self of the actual truth. The mind is, alas! too apt to receive ill-formed impressions contrary to fact.

"It is already cleared up," Rolfe answered without hesitation. "I was not there. You were entirely mistaken. Besides, my dear chap, why should I go there when I had been particularly asked by Maud not to visit the house?"

"When did she ask you?"

"Only the night before. That very fact is, in itself, curious. She urged me that whatever might occur, I was not to go to the house."

"Then she anticipated something—eh?"

"It seems as though she did."

"And she told Marion something on the night when she and her father disappeared."

"I know."

"You know what she told her?"

"No. Marion refuses to tell me, I wish I could induce her to speak. Marion knows the truth—that's my firm belief."

"And mine also."

"The two girls have some secret in common," Rolfe said. "Can't you get Marion to tell you?"

"She refuses. I've asked her half a dozen times already."

"I wonder why! There must be some reason."

"Of course there is. She is loyal to her friend. But tell me honestly, Charlie. Do you know the Doctor's whereabouts?"

"I tell you honestly that I haven't the slightest idea. The affair is just as great a mystery to me as to you."

"But why have you kept away from me till to-day?" Barclay asked. "It isn't like you."

"Well," answered Rolfe, with a slight hesitation, "to tell you the truth, because I thought your manner had rather changed towards me of late."

"Why, my dear fellow, I'm sure it never has."

"But you suspected me of being in that house on the night of the disappearance!"

"Of course, because I saw you."

"Because you thought you saw me," Charlie said, correcting him. "You surely would not misjudge me for that."

"No. But your theory regarding falsehoods has, I must admit, caused some suspicion in my mind."

"Of what?"

"Well, of prevaricating in order to shield a woman—Maud it may be."

"I am not shielding her!" he declared. "There is nothing to shield. I love her very dearly indeed, and she loves me devotedly in return. Cannot you imagine, Max, my perturbed state of mind now that she has disappeared without a word?"

"Has she sent you no secret message of her safety?" Max asked, seriously.

"Not a word."

"And you do not know, then, if she has not met with foul play?"

"I don't. That's just it! Sometimes—" And he rose from his chair and paced the room in agony of mind. "Sometimes—I—I feel as if I shall go mad. I love her—just as you love Marion! Sometimes I feel assured of her safety— that she and her father have been compelled to disappear for political or other reasons—and then at others a horrible idea haunts me that my love may be dead—the victim of some vile, treacherous plot to take from me all that has made my life worth living!"

"Stop!" cried Max, starting to his feet and facing him. "You love her— eh?"

"Better—ah! better than my own life!" he cried in deep earnestness, his troubled face being an index of his mind.

"Then—then upon her honour—the honour of the woman you love— swear to me that you have spoken the truth!"

He looked into his friend's eyes for a moment. Then he answered:

"I swear, Max! I swear by my love for Maud that I have spoken the truth!"

And Barclay stood silent—so puzzled as to be unable to utter a word.

Chapter Twenty Six
Which Puts a Serious Question

At last Max spoke, slowly and with great deliberation.

"And you declare yourself as ignorant as I am myself of their whereabouts?"

"I do," was Rolfe's response. Then after a second's hesitation he added in a changed voice: "I really think, Max, that you are scarcely treating me fairly in this matter. Sorely it is in my interests to discover the whereabouts of Maud! I have done my best."

"Well?"

"And I've failed to discover any clue whatever—except one—that—"

And he broke off, without finishing his sentence.

"What have you discovered? Tell me. Be frank with me."

"I've not yet established whether it is a real clue, or whether a mere false surmise. When I have, I will tell you."

"But cannot we join forces in endeavouring to solve the problem?" Max suggested, his suspicion of his friend now removed.

"That is exactly what I would wish. But how shall we begin? Where shall we commence?" asked Rolfe.

"The truth that it was not you whom I saw leaving the house in Cromwell Road adds fresh mystery to the already astounding circumstance," Max declared. "The man who so closely resembled you was purposely made up to be mistaken for you. There was some strong motive for this. What do you suggest it could be?"

"To implicate me! But in what?"

The thought of that blood-stained bodice ever haunted Max. It was on the tip of his tongue to reveal his discovery to his friend, yet on second thoughts he resolved to at present retain his secret. He had withheld it from the police, therefore he was perfectly justified in withholding it from Charlie.

The flat denial of the latter regarding his visit to Cromwell Road caused him deep reflection. He watched his friend's attitude, and was compelled to admit within himself that now, at any rate, he was speaking the truth.

"The only reason for the visit of the man whom I must have mistaken for yourself, Charlie," he said, "must have been to open that safe."

"Probably so."

Then Max explained, in detail, the position of the safe, and how he had discovered it being open, and its contents abstracted.

"On your first visit, then, the safe was hidden?"

"Yes. But when I went in the morning it stood revealed, the door blown open by some explosive."

"By an enemy of the Doctor's," remarked Charlie.

Max did not reply. The Doctor's words regarding his friend on the last occasion they had sat together recurred to him at that moment with a queer significance. The Doctor certainly did not like Rolfe. For what reason? he wondered. Why had he taken such a sudden dislike to him?

Hitherto, they had been quite friendly, ever since the well-remembered meeting at the Villa des Fleurs, in Aix-les-Bains, and the Doctor had never, to his knowledge, objected to Maud's association with the smart young fellow whose keen business instincts had commended him to such a man as old Sam Statham. The Doctor held no doubt, either secret knowledge of something detrimental to Rolfe, or else entertained one of those sudden and unaccountable prejudices which some men form, and which they are unable to put behind them.

"The one main point we have first to decide, Charlie," he said at last, standing at the window and gazing thoughtfully down into the narrow London street, "is whether or not then has been foul play."

Rolfe made no reply, a circumstance which caused him to turn and look straight into his friend's face. He saw a change there.

His countenance was blanched; but whether by fear of the loss of the woman he loved, or by a guilty knowledge, Max knew not.

"Marion can tell us," he answered at last. "But she refuses."

"You, her brother, can surely obtain the truth from her?"

"Not when you, her lover, fail," Charlie responded, his brows knit deeply.

"But a moment ago you said you had a clue?"

"I think I have one. It is only a surmise."

"And in what direction does it trend?"

"Towards foul play," he said hoarsely.

"Political?"

"It may be."

"And were both victims of the plot?"

"I cannot tell. At present I'm making all the secret inquiries possible—far afield in a Continental city. It takes time, care, and patience. As soon as I obtain anything tangible, I will tell you. But first of all, Max," he added, "I wish to have your assurance that you no longer suspect me. I am not your enemy—why should you be mine?"

"I am not, my dear fellow," declared Barclay. "How can I be the enemy of Marion's brother? I was only suspicious. You would have been the same in similar circumstances, I'm sure."

"Probably," laughed Charlie. "Yet what you've told me about the endeavour to implicate myself in the affair is certainly extraordinary. I don't see any motive."

"Except that you were known by the conspirators, whoever they are, to be Maud's lover."

"If so, then they intend, most probably, to bring some false charge against me. And—and—"

"And what?" asked Max in some surprise.

"Why, don't you see?" he said hoarsely, staring straight into his friend's face with a horrified expression as a terrible truth arose within him. "Don't you see that you yourself, Max, would become the principal witness against me!"

Max stood wondering at the other's sudden anticipation of disaster. What could he dread if this denial of his was the actual truth?

Again he grew suspicious.

"How can I be witness against you if you are innocent of any connection with the affair?" he queried.

"Because the Doctor's enemies have done this, in order to shield themselves."

"But if the Doctor is really still alive, what have you to fear?"

"Is he alive? That is the point."

"Marion gives me to understand that both he and Maud are safe," Max responded quickly.

The other shook his head dubiously, saying: "If she has told you that, then it is exactly contrary to what she has given me to understand."

"What? She has expressed a suspicion of foul play?"

"Yes—more than a suspicion."

"Well—this is certainly strange," Max declared. "Marion has all along been trying to allay my fears."

"Because she feared to upset you, perhaps. With me it is different. She does not mind my feelings."

"I'm sure she does, Charlie. She's devoted to you. And she ought to be. Few brothers would do what you have done."

"That's quite outside the question," he said, quickly pacing anxiously up and down the room. "She told me distinctly the other day that her fears were of the worst."

"Ah! if you could only induce her to tell us what Maud confessed to her. It was a confession—a serious and tragic one, I believe."

"Yes. It was, no doubt; and if she would only speak we could, I believe, quickly get at the truth," Rolfe said. "To me it seems incredible that the Doctor, your most intimate friend, should not have found some secret manner by which to communicate with you, and assure you of his safety."

There was a pause. Suddenly Max turned to the speaker and exclaimed—

"Tell me, Charlie. Be perfectly frank with me. Have you, do you think, at any time recently given some cause for offence to the Doctor?"

"Why do you ask that?" inquired the other in quick surprise.

"I have reasons for asking. I'll tell you after you've answered my question."

"I don't know," he laughed uneasily. "Some men, and especially foreigners, are very easily offended."

"But have you offended the Doctor?"

"Perhaps. A man never knows when he gives unintentional offence."

"Are you aware of having done anything to offend him?"

"No, except that Maud asked me not to visit there so often, as her father did not approve of it."

"Did she ever tell you that the Doctor had suddenly entertained a dislike of you?"

"Certainly not. I always believed that he was very friendly disposed towards me. But—well—why do you ask all this?"

"I merely ask for information."

"Of course, but you promised to tell me the reason."

"Well, the fact is this. On the afternoon prior to their disappearance, the Doctor expressed feelings towards you that were not exactly friendly. It seemed to me that he had formed some extraordinary prejudice. Fathers do this often towards the men who love their daughters, you know. They are sometimes apt to be over-cautious, with the result that the girl loses a very good chance of marriage," he added. "I've known several similar cases."

"Well," said Charlie thoughtfully, "that's quite new to me. I had flattered myself that the Doctor was very well disposed towards me. This is quite a revelation?"

"Didn't Maud ever tell you?"

"Not a word."

"She feared, of course, to hurt your feelings. It was quite natural. She loves you."

"If what we fear be true, you should put your words into the past tense, Max," was his reply in a hard voice. Barclay knew that his friend loved the sweet-faced girl with the stray, unruly wisp of hair which fell always across her white brow and gave her such a piquante appearance. And if he loved her so well, was it possible that he could have been author of, or implicated, in a foul and secret crime?

Recollection of that dress-bodice with the ugly stain still wet upon it flashed upon him. Was it not in itself circumstantial evidence that some terrible crime had been committed?

The man before him denied all knowledge of the disappearance of his well-beloved, and yet Max, with his own eyes, had seen him slinking from the house!

Had he spoken the truth, or was he an ingenious liar?

Such was the problem which Max Barclay put to himself—a question which was the whole crux of the extraordinary situation. If what Rolfe had declared was the truth, then the mystery became an enigma beyond solution.

But if, on the other hand, he was now endeavouring to shield himself from the shadow of guilt upon him, then at least one fact was rendered more hideous than the rest.

The question was one—and only one.

Had this man, brother of his own dear Marion, sworn falsely upon what he had held to be most sacred—his love for Maud?

What was the real and actual truth?

Chapter Twenty Seven
In the Web

It was four o'clock on the following afternoon, dark and threatening outside, precursory of a thunderstorm.

In that chair in Max's room, where Charlie Rolfe had sat on the previous morning, was the polished cosmopolitan, Jean Adam, lazily lolling back, smoking a cigarette.

Max had lunched over at White's, and just come in to find Adam awaiting him. The Frenchman had risen and greeted him merrily, took the proffered Russian cigarette, and they; had settled themselves to chat.

"I've been expecting every day to hear from you," Adam exclaimed at last. "When do you propose starting for Constantinople?"

"Well, I've been thinking over the matter, and I've come to the conclusion that just at present it is impossible for me to leave London. I have other interests here."

Adam stirred uneasily in his chair. This reply filled him with chagrin, yet so clever was he, and such a perfect type of ingenious adventurer, that he never showed the least trace of surprise.

"Really," he laughed, "that's very unfortunate—for you!"

"Why, for me?"

"Well, the missing of such a chance would be unfortunate, even to a Rothschild," he said. "There's hundreds of thousands in the deal, if you'll only go out with me. You're not a man of straw. You can afford to risk a thousand or two, just as well as I can—even better."

"I would willingly go if it were not for the fact that I find I must remain in London."

Adam laughed, with just a touch of sarcasm.

"Ah! the lady! I quite understand, my dear fellow. The charming young lady whom I met with you the other night does not wish you to leave her side—eh? We have all of us been through that stage of amorous ecstasy. I have myself, I know that; and if I may tell you with the frankness of a friend, I've regretted it," he added, holding up his white palms.

"All men do not regret I hope to be the exception," remarked Max Barclay, pensively watching the smoke from his lips rise to the ceiling.

"Of course. But is it wise to turn one's back upon Fortune in this way?" asked Adam, in that insidious manner by which he had entrapped many a man. "Review the position calmly. Here is a project which, by good luck, has fallen into my hands. I want somebody to go shares with me in it. You are my friend, I like you. I know you are an upright man, and I ask you to become my partner in the venture. Yet you refuse to do so because—well, merely because a woman's pretty face has attracted you, and you think that you please her by remaining here in London!

"Is it not rather foolish in your own interests? Constantinople is not the Pole. A fortnight will suffice for you to get there and back and clinch the bargain. Muhil is awaiting us. I had a wire only yesterday. Do reconsider the whole question—there's a good fellow."

Max had said nothing about the meeting with Marion. Therefore he believed that she had not told her lover. Adam was reflecting whether she might not, after all, be a woman to be trusted. This refusal of Max's to go out to Turkey interfered seriously with the plans he had formed. Yet what those plans actually were he had not even told the hunchback. He was a man who took counsel of nobody. His ingenious schemes he evolved in his own brain, and carried them into effect by his own unaided efforts.

The past history of Jean Adam, alias John Adams, had been one of amazing ups-and-downs and clever chicanery. He knew that Samuel Statham held him in awe, and was now playing upon his fears, and gloating over the success which must inevitably be his whenever he thought fit to deal the blow. It would be irresistible and crushing. He held the millionaire in his power. But before he moved forward to strike, he intended that Max should be induced to go abroad. And if he went—well, when he thought of his victim's departure his small, near-set eyes gleamed, and about the corners of his mouth there played an expression of evil.

"My decision does not require any reconsideration," said the young fellow, after a pause. "I shall remain in London."

"And lose the chance of a lifetime—eh?" exclaimed Adam, as though perfectly unconcerned.

"I have some very important private matters to attend to."

"I, too, used to have when I was your age."

"They do not concern the lady," Max said quickly. "It is purely a personal matter."

"Of business? Why, you'd make as much in an hour over this Railway business as you'd make in twenty years here in London," Adam declared. "Besides, you want a change. Come out to the Bosphorus. It's charming beside the Sweet Waters."

"All sounds very delightful; but even though I may let the chance of a fortune slip through my fingers, I cannot leave London at present."

"But why?"

"A purely private matter," was his reply, for he did not wish to tell this man anything concerning the strange disappearance of the Doctor and his grave suspicions of Charlie Rolfe. "I can tell you nothing more than that."

"Well, I'm sure the lady, if she knew that it was in your interests to go to Turkey, would urge you to go," declared Adam. "She would never keep you here if she knew that you could pull off such a deal as I have put before you."

"She does know."

"Oh! And what does she say?"

"She suggested that I should go with you."

"Then why not come?"

"Because, as I've already told you, it is impossible. I am kept in London by something which concerns the welfare of a very dear friend," Max answered. "You must put it before somebody else. I suppose the affair cannot wait?"

"I don't want to put it before anybody else. If we do business, I want you and I to share the profits."

"Very good of you, I'm sure; but at present I am quite unable to leave London."

Max was wondering for the first time why this man was so pressing. If the thing was a really good one—as it undoubtedly was, according to the friend he had consulted in the City—then there could not be any lack of persons ready to go into the venture. Was it sheer luck that had led this man Adam to offer to take him into it, or had the man some ulterior motive? Max Barclay was no fool. He had sown his wild oats in London, and knew the ways of men. He had met many a city shark, and had been the poorer in pocket through the meeting. But about this man Adam was something which had always fascinated him. The pair had been drawn together by some indescribable but mutual attraction, and the concession by the Sultan which must result in great profits was now within his reach. Nevertheless, he felt that in the present circumstances it was impossible to leave London. Before doing so he was desirous of solving the problem of the disappearance of Doctor Petrovitch, and clearing up the question of whether or not there had been foul play.

Rolfe's denial of the previous day had complicated matters even further. He was convinced, now that he had reflected calmly, that his friend was concealing something from him—some fact which had an important bearing upon the astounding affair.

Was Charlie playing a straight game? After long consideration he had come again to the conclusion that he was not!

In his ear was the voice of the tempter Jean Adam. Fortune awaited him in that sunlit city of white domes and minarets beside the Bosphorus—the city of veiled women and of mystery he had always hoped to visit. Would he not spare fourteen days, travel there, and obtain it?

It was a great temptation. The concession for that railway would indeed have been a temptation to any man. Did not the late Baron Hirsch lay the foundation of his huge fortune by a similar iradé of his Majesty the Sultan?

The man seated in the deep armchair with the cigarette between his lips looked at his victim through his half-closed eyes, as a snake watches the bird he fascinates.

Jean Adam was an excellent judge of human nature. He had placed there a bait which could not fail to attract, if not to-day, then to-morrow—or the next day. He had gauged Max Barclay with a precision only given to those who live upon their wits.

To every rule there are, of course, exceptions. Every man who lives upon his wits is not altogether bad. Curious though it may be, there are many adventurers to be met with in every capital in Europe, who, though utterly unscrupulous, have in their nature one point of the most scrupulous honour—one point which redeems them from being classed as utter blackguards.

Many a man, who will stick at nothing where money can be made, is loyal, honest, and upright towards a woman; while another will with one hand swindle the wealthy, and with the other give charity to the poor. Few men, indeed, are altogether bad. Yet when they are, they are, alas! outsiders indeed.

Adam was a man who had no compunction where men were concerned, and very little when a woman stood in his way. His own adventures would have made one of the most interesting volumes ever written. Full of ingenuity and tact, fearless when it came to facing exposure, and light-hearted whenever the world smiled upon him, he was a marvellous admixture of good fellow and scoundrel.

He knew that his clever story had fascinated the man before him, and that it was only a question of time before he would fall into the net so cleverly spread.

"When do you anticipate you could go East—that is, providing I can get the matter postponed?" asked Adam at last, as he placed his cigarette end in the ash-tray.

"I can't give you a date," replied Max. "It is quite uncertain. Why not go to somebody else?"

"I tell you I have no desire to do so, my dear friend," was the Frenchman's reply. "I like you. That is why I placed the business before you. I know, of course, there are a thousand men in the City who would only jump at this chance of such a big thing."

"Then why not go to them?" repeated Max, a little surprised and yet a little flattered.

"As I have told you, I would rather take you into partnership. We have already decided to do the thing on a sound business basis. Indeed, I went to my lawyers only yesterday and gave orders for the agreement to be drawn up between us. You'll receive it to-night or to-morrow."

"Well," replied Max with some hesitation, "if it is to be done, it must be done later. At present I cannot get away. My place is in London."

"Beside the lady to whom you are so devoted, eh?" the Frenchman laughed.

Max was irritated by the man's veiled sarcasm.

"No. Because I have a duty to perform towards a friend, and even the temptation of a fortune shall not cause me to neglect it."

"A friend. Whom?"

"The matter is my own affair. It has nothing to do with our business," was Max's rather sharp response.

"Very well," said the other, quite unruffled. "I can only regret. I will wire to-night to Muhil Pasha, and endeavour to obtain a postponement of the agreement."

"As you wish," Max said, still angered at this importation of the woman he loved into the discussion. "I may as well say that it is quite immaterial."

"To you it may be so. But I am not rich like yourself," the other said. "I have to obtain my income where I can by honest means, and this is a chance which I do not intend to lose. I look to you—I hold you to your promise, Barclay—to assist me."

"I do not intend to break my promise. I merely say that I cannot go out to Turkey at once."

"But you will come—you will promise that in a few days—in a week— or when you have finished this mysterious duty to your friend, that you will come with me?" he urged. "Come, give me your hand. I don't want to approach anybody else."

"Well, if you really wish it," Max replied, and he gave the tempter his hand in pledge.

When, a few seconds later, Jean Adam turned to light a fresh cigarette there was upon his thin lips a smile—a sinister smile of triumph.

Max Barclay had played dice with the Devil, and lost. He had, in his ignorance of the net spread about him, in that moment pledged his own honour.

Chapter Twenty Eight
Old Sam has a Visitor

It was past midnight.

At eleven o'clock old Sam Statham had descended from the mysterious upper regions, emerged from the green baize door upon the stairs, which concealed another white-enamelled door—a door of iron, and, passing down to the study, had switched on the electric light, thrown himself wearily into an armchair, and lit a cigar.

Upon his grey, drawn countenance was a serious apprehensive look, as of a man who anticipated serious trouble, and who was trying in vain to brave himself up to face it. For nearly half an hour he had smoked on alone, now and then muttering to himself, his bony fingers clenched as though anticipating revenge. The big room was so silent at that hour that a pin if dropped might have been heard. Only the clock ticked on solemnly, and striking the half-hour upon its silvery bell.

The old millionaire who, on passing through that baize-covered door, had locked the inner door so carefully after him, seemed strangely agitated. So apprehensive was he that Levi, entering some time afterwards, said in his sharp, brusque manner:

"I thought you had retired long ago. What's the matter?"

"I have an appointment," snapped his master; "an important one."

"Rather late, isn't it?" suggested the old servant. "Remember that there are spies about. That little affair the other night aroused some curiosity—I'm certain of it."

"Among a few common passers-by. Bah! my dear Levi, they don't know anything."

"But they may talk! This house has already got a bad name, you know."

"Well, that's surely not my fault," cried the old man with a fiery flash in his eyes. "It's more your fault for acting so infernally suspiciously and mysteriously. I know quite well what people say of me."

"A good deal that's true," declared old Levi in open defiance of the man in whose service he had been so long.

Sam Statham grinned. It was a subject which he did not wish to discuss.

"You can go to bed, Levi. I'll open the door," he said to the man who was his janitor.

"Who's coming?" inquired Levi abruptly.

"A friend. I want to talk to him seriously and alone."

"What's his name?"

"Don't be so infernally inquisitive, Levi. Go to bed, I tell you," he croaked with a commanding wave of the hand.

The servant never thwarted his master's wishes. He knew Sam Statham too well. A strange smile played about the corners of his mouth, and he looked around to see that the whisky, syphons and glasses were on the side table. Then with a rather ill-grace said:

"Very well—good-night," and, bowing, he retired.

When the door had closed the old millionaire ground his teeth, muttering:

"You must always poke your infernal long nose into my affairs. But this matter I'll keep to myself just for once. I'm tired of your constant interference and advice. Ah!" he sighed. "How strange life is! Samuel Statham, millionaire, they call me. I saw it in the *Pall Mall* to-night. Rather Sam Statham, pauper—the Pauper of Park Lane! Ah! If the public only knew! If they only knew!" he gasped, halting suddenly and staring wildly about him. "What would be my future—what will it be when my enemies, like a pack of wolves, fall upon me and tear me limb from limb? Yes, yes, they'll do that if I am unable to save myself.

"But why need I anticipate failure? What does the sacrifice of one woman matter when it will mean the assurance of my future—my salvation from ruin?" he went on, speaking to himself in a low, hoarse voice. "It's a thing I cannot tell Levi. He must find it out. He will—one day—when the police inquiries give him the clue," and he snapped his own white fingers nervously and glanced at the clock in apprehension.

He threw down his cigar, for it had gone out a long time ago. Sam Statham's life had been made up of many crises, and one of these he was passing through on that hot, breathless night after the motor-'buses had ceased their roar in Park Lane and tinkling cab-bells were few and far between.

One o'clock, the sound of the gong arousing him. He switched off the light, and, walking to the window, raised one of the slats of the Venetian blinds and peered out upon the pavement where so recently he had first recognised that man from the grave—the man Jean Adam.

He stood behind the blue brocade curtains, watching eagerly. The passers-by were few—very few. Lower-class London was mostly at Margate and Ramsgate, while "the West-End" was totally absent, in Scotland or at the sea.

He was wondering if Levi had really gone to bed. Or was he lurking there to ascertain who might be the visitor expected? Old Sam crept noiselessly to the door, and, opening it, peered out. The wide hall was now in darkness. Levi had, apparently, obeyed his orders and gone below to bed. And yet, so faithful was he to his trust that nobody could ever enter that house without him being aware of the identity of the visitor.

Sometimes old Sam would regret the brusque manner in which he treated the man who was so entirely devoted to him and who shared so many of his secrets.

But the secret of that night he did not intend Levi to share. It was his— and should be his alone. And for that person he was waiting to himself open the door to his midnight caller.

He was about to close the study door again when he fancied he heard a slight movement in the darkness of the hall. "Levi!" he exclaimed angrily. "What are you doing here when I ordered you to retire?"

"I'm doing my duty," responded the old servant, advancing out of the shadow. "I do not wish you to go to the door alone, and at night. You do not take sufficient care of your personal safety."

"Rubbish! I have no fear," he answered as both stood there in the darkness.

"Yes, but, you are injudicious," declared the old servant. "If not, you would have heeded young Rolfe's warning, and your present dangerous position might have been avoided. Adams means mischief. You surely can't close your eyes to that!"

"I know he does," answered the millionaire in a voice that seemed harsh and hollow. "I know I was a fool."

"You took a false step, and can't retrace it. If you had consulted me I would have given you my views upon the situation."

"Yes, Levi. You're far too fond of expounding your view on subjects of which you have no knowledge. Your incessant chatter often annoys me," was his master's response. "If I have committed an error, it is my affair — not yours. So go to bed, and leave me alone."

"I shall not," was Levi's open reply.

"I'm master here. I order you to go!" cried Sam Statham in an angry, commanding tone.

"And I refuse. I will not allow you to run any further risk."

"What do you anticipate?" his master asked with sarcasm. "Are you expecting that my enemies intend to kill me in secret. If so, I can quickly disabuse your mind. It would not be to their interests if I were dead, for they could not then bleed me, as is, no doubt, their intention. I know Adams and his friends."

"So do I," declared Levi. "Whatever plot they have formed against you is no doubt clever and ingenious. They are not men to act until every preparation is complete."

"Then why fear for my personal safety?" asked the millionaire. "I always have this — and I can use it," and he drew from his pocket something which glistened in the darkness — a neat plated revolver.

"I fear, because of late you've acted so injudiciously."

"Through ignorance. I believed myself to be more shrewd than I really am. You see I admit my failing to you, Levi. But only to you — to nobody else. The City believes Sam Statham to possess the keenest mind and sharpest wits of any man between Temple Bar and Aldgate. Strange, isn't it, that each one of us earns a reputation for something in which really does not excel?"

"You excel in disbelieving everybody," remarked Levi outspokenly. "If you believed that there was some little honesty in human nature you might have been spared the present danger."

"You mean I'm too suspicious — eh? My experience of life has made me so," he growled. "Of the thousand employees I possess, is there a man among them honest? And as for my friends, is there one I can trust — except Ben and yourself, of course?"

"What about Rolfe?"

Sam Statham hesitated. It was a question put too abruptly — a question not easily decided on the spur of the moment. Of course, ever since his failure to go to Belgrade, he had entertained some misgivings regarding his secretary. There was more than one point of fact which did not coincide with Rolfe's statements. The old man was quickly suspicious, and when he scented mystery, it was always a long time before his doubts were allayed.

Like every man of great wealth, he had been surrounded by sycophants, who had endeavoured to get rich at his expense. The very men he had helped to fortune had turned round afterwards and abused and libelled him. It was that which had long ago soured him against his fellow men, and aroused in his heart a disbelief in all protestation of honesty and uprightness.

Levi recognised his master's lack of confidence in Rolfe, and it caused him to wonder. Hitherto he had been full of praise of the clever and energetic young secretary by whose smart business methods several great concerns in which he had controlling interest had been put into a flourishing condition. But now, quite of a sudden, there was a hesitancy which told too plainly of lack of confidence. Was the star of Rolfe's prosperity on the wane?

If so, Levi felt sorry, for he was attached to the young man, whom he felt confident had the interests of his master thoroughly at heart. Old Levi was a queer fish. He had seldom taken to anybody as he had done to Mr Rolfe, who happily cracked a joke with him and asked after his rheumatics.

"Levi," exclaimed Statham after a few moments of silence, "is it not absurd for us to chatter here, in the darkness? It's past one. I wish you to go downstairs and leave me alone."

"Why?" demanded the old retainer.

"Because I have a strong reason for opening the door myself. I—well I promised that my visitor should be seen by no one except myself. Now, do you understand?"

Levi did not answer for a few moments.

"Then in that case," he said with reluctance, "I suppose I must do as you wish, only I'm very much against you opening the door yourself. You know that!"

And grunting, his dark figure moved along the hall, and he disappeared down the stairs, wishing his master "good-night."

Statham, having listened to his retreating footsteps, re-entered the library, which was still unlit, and, going again to the window, peered forth into Park Lane.

Rain was falling, and the street-lamps cast long lines of light upon the shining pavements. In the faint ray of light that fell across the room from without he bent and looked at his watch. It was half-past one—the hour of the appointment.

The old fellow raised both hands to his head and smoothed back his grey hair. Then he drew a long sigh, and waited in patience, peering forth in eager expectancy.

For another ten minutes he remained almost motionless until at last his ear caught the sound of a footstep coming from the direction of Oxford Street, and a dark figure, passing the window, stopped beneath the porch.

Next second he flew along the hall to the door, opening it noiselessly to admit a woman in a black tailor-made gown and motor-cap, her features but half concealed by a thin veil of grey gauze.

She crossed the threshold without speaking, for he raised his finger as though to command her silence. Then, when he had closed the door behind her and slipped the bolt into its socket, he conducted her along to the dark study, without uttering a word.

Her attitude and gait was that of fear and hesitancy; as though she already regretted having come there, and would fain make her escape—if escape were possible.

Chapter Twenty Nine
In which Marion is Indiscreet

On entering, old Statham switched on the electric light quietly, the soft glow revealing the pale countenance of his guest.

The blanched face, with its apprehensive, half-frightened expression, was that of Marion Rolfe.

"Well," he said in his thin, rather squeaky voice, after he had closed the door behind her and drawn forward a chair, "you have at last summoned courage to come—eh?" He smiled at her triumphantly. "Why have you refused my invitation so many times? My house, I know, bears a reputation for mystery, but I am no ogre, I assure you, Miss Rolfe."

"Whispers have come back to me that I am believed by some to be a modern Blue Beard, or by others a kind of seducer; but I trust you will disbelieve the wild rumours put out by my enemies, and regard me as your friend."

She had sunk into the soft depths of the green silk upholstered chair, and, with her motor-veil thrown back, was gazing at the old man, half in fear, half in wonder. To his words she made no response.

"I hope the car I sent came for you as arranged?" he said, at once changing the subject.

"Yes. The man arrived punctually," she answered at last. "But—"

"But what?"

"I ought never to have come here," she declared uneasily. "I will have to go before Mr Cunnington to-morrow for being absent all night, and shall certainly be discharged. He will never hear excuse in any case. Instant dismissal is the hard and fast rule."

"Not in your case, Miss Rolfe," replied the old millionaire. "Remember that it is not Mr Cunnington who controls Cunnington's, Limited. I have asked you here in order to speak to you in strictest confidence. Indeed, I want to take you into my confidence, if you'll allow me. Perhaps you will be absent from Oxford Street a week—perhaps a month. But when you return you will not find the vacancy filled." His cold eyes were fixed upon hers. She found a strange fascination in the old man's glance, for he seemed to fix her and hold her immovable. Now, for the first time she experienced what Charlie had so often told her, namely, that Samuel Statham could, when he so desired, exercise an extraordinary power over his fellow men.

"Absent a month?" she echoed, staring at him. "What do you mean?"

"What I say. The car is awaiting you at the Marble Arch, isn't it?"

"I suppose so. The chauffeur put me down there—at your orders, I believe."

"I told you to put on a thick coat and motor-veil. I see you have done as I wished. I want you to go on a long journey." She looked at the grey, immovable face before her in sheer astonishment. To this man both her brother Charlie and she herself owed their present happiness. And yet he was a man of millions and of mystery. Charlie had always been reticent regarding the strange tales concerning the house in which she now found herself, a visitor there under compulsion. Max, on the other hand, had often expressed wonder whether or not there was really any substratum of truth.

As she sat there she recollected how, only a fortnight before, Max had told her the latest queer story regarding the mysterious mansion and its eccentric owner. What would he say if he knew that she had dared to go alone there—that she was seated in the old man's private room?

Dared! If the truth were told, Sam Statham had written to her fully half-a-dozen times, asking her to call upon him in secret in the evening when her brother would have left, as he wished to speak with her. Each time she had replied making excuses, for within herself she could not imagine upon what business he wished to see her. She had only met him once, on the day her brother took her to the City and asked his master to secure her a berth at Cunnington's. The interview only lasted five minutes, and the impression he left upon her was that of a peevish, snappy old man who held all women in abhorrence.

"Very well, very well, Rolfe," he had replied impatiently, "I'll write to Cunnington's about your sister. Remind me to-morrow." Then, turning to her, he had wished her a hasty good-bye, and resumed his writing. He had hardly taken the trouble to look at her.

Now, for the first time, he was gazing straight into her face, and she thought she detected in his eyes an expression of sadness, combined with kindliness. An expert in the reading of character, however, would have noticed beneath that assumed kindliness was an expression of triumph. He had brought her there against her will. She was there at his bidding, merely because she dare not offend the man to whom both Charlie and herself owed their daily bread.

For a long time she had held out against all his strongly-expressed desires to see her. His letters had been placed in her hand by a special messenger, and Mr Warner, "the buyer," had on two occasions witnessed their delivery, and wondered who might be his assistant's correspondent. He never dreamed that it was Samuel Statham, the man who held the controlling interest in the huge concern.

The writer of those letters particularly requested her not to mention the matter to her brother, therefore she more than once thought of consulting Max. But Statham's instructions was that she should regard the matter as confidential so she had refrained, and at the same time had met all his invitations with steady excuses.

At last on the previous day came a tersely worded note, which made it plain that the millionaire would brook no refusal. She was to purchase a motor-cap and veil, and, wearing them, was, at an hour he appointed, to meet a dark red motor car that would be awaiting her at Addison Road station. In it she was to drive back to the Marble Arch, where he was to alight and walk along Park Lane direct to the house, where he himself would admit her in secret. The writer added that she was to ask no questions, and that no reply was needed. He would be expecting her.

And so she had come there in utter ignorance of his motive for inviting her, and as she sat before him she became filled with apprehension. Hers was, she knew, an adventure of which neither Charlie nor Max would approve.

The clever old man read the girl's mind like an open book, and at once sought to allay her misgivings.

"I see," he said, smiling, "that you are not altogether at your ease. You're afraid of what people might say—eh? Your fellow-assistants wouldn't approve of you coming to see me at this hour, I suppose. Yes," he laughed. "What is considered discreditable among the middle classes is deemed quite admissible in society. But who need know unless you yourself tell them?"

"It will be known to-morrow morning that I was absent," she said.

"Leave that to me. Only one person will know—Cunnington himself. So make your mind quite easy upon that point, my dear young lady. I can quite understand your hesitation in coming here. It is, of course, only natural. But you must remember in what high esteem I held your father, and how for the sake of his memory I have taken your brother into my service."

"Before we go further, Mr Statham," exclaimed the girl, "I would like to take this opportunity of thanking you for all you've done for both of us. Had it not been for your generosity I'm sure Charlie would never have been in such a position."

"Ah! you're very fond of your brother, eh?" he asked in his quick, brusque way, leaning back in his armchair and placing his hands together.

"Yes. He is so very good to me."

"And you probably know something of his affairs?"

"Very little. He doesn't tell me much."

"He talks of me sometimes, I suppose?" remarked the old man with a good-humoured smile.

"With the greatest admiration always, Mr Statham. He is devoted to you," she declared.

The old man moved uneasily, and gave a sniff of suspicion combined with a low grunt of satisfaction.

"He's engaged to some foreign woman, I hear," he said. "You know her, of course."

"You mean Maud Petrovitch. Yes, she is my friend."

"Petrovitch—Petrovitch," he repeated, as though in ignorance of the fact. "I've heard that name before. Sounds like a Russian name."

"Servian. She is the daughter of Doctor Petrovitch, the well-known Servian statesman."

"Of course. I recollect now. He's been in the Ministry once or twice. I recollect having some dealings with him over the Servian Loan. He was Finance Minister then. And so he is in love with her!" he said, reflectively. "If I remember aright, she's the only daughter. His Excellency invited me to dine at his house in Belgrade one night a few years ago, and I saw her—a very pretty, dark-haired girl; she looked more French than Servian."

"Her mother was English."

"Ah!"

And a dead silence fell, broken only by the low tinkle of a cab-bell outside.

"So your brother is in love with the pretty daughter of the ex-Minister! What a happy circumstance is youth!" sighed the old man. "And you yourself?" he went on, staring straight at her. "You have a lover also! How can I ask? Of course, a beautiful girl like you must have a lover."

Marion blushed deeply—dropping her eyes from his. She was annoyed that he should make such an outspoken comment, and yet she forgave him, knowing full well what an eccentric person he was.

The truth was that the old man now, for the first time, realised how extremely good-looking was the sister of his secretary. He had been told so by Mr Cunnington on one occasion, but he had heard without paying attention. Yet as he now sat with his gaze fastened upon her he saw how uneasy she was, and how anxious to escape from his presence.

This rather piqued him. He had a suspicion that her brother might have said something to prejudice him in her estimation; therefore he exerted all his efforts to place her at her ease—efforts which, alas! had but little avail. The silence of that sombre but gorgeous room, the weird mystery of the house itself, and the thin-faced man of millions himself all combined to fill her with some instinctive dread. Alone there at that hour, she felt herself completely in that man's power.

Only three days before she had read a paragraph in "M.A.P." regarding his enormous wealth and his far-reaching power and influence. The writer said that Samuel Statham was a man who seldom smiled, and whose own secretary scarcely knew him, so aloof did he hold himself from the world. And it was added that he, possessor of millions, preferred hot baked potatoes on a winter's night to the finest dishes which a French chef could contrive.

He was a man of simplest tastes, yet strangely erratic in his movements; a man whose foresight in business matters was little short of miraculous, and whose very touch seemed to turn dross to gold. He had declined half-a-dozen invitations to meet royalty at royalty's express wish, and when offered a peerage by the Prime Minister before the late Government went out of office he had respectfully declined the preferred honour. Sam Statham sneered at society, and turned a cold shoulder to it—a fact which caused society to be all the more eager to know him.

Marion recollected every word of this as she sat in wonder at the actual motive of her visit. Her eyes wandered around the fine room with its beautiful pictures, its priceless pieces of statuary, and its great Chinese vases that were loot from the Summer Palace at Pekin. The air of wealth and luxury impressed her, while even the arrangement of the electric lights, placed out of sight behind the book-cases and reflected into the centre of the apartment, was so cunningly devised that the illumination was bright without being glaring.

"And so you have a lover in secret—eh?" he laughed, leaning back and regarding her with half-closed eyes. "Like every other girl, you dream of marriage and happiness—a shadowy dream, I can assure you. Happiness is as tangible as the moonbeams, and love as fleeting as the sunset. But you are young, and will disbelieve me. I don't ask you to heed me, indeed, for I am old and world-weary and soured of life. I only urge upon you to pause, and think deeply, very deeply and earnestly, before you plight your troth to any man. Most men are unworthy, and all men are liars."

Had he brought her there at that unusual hour to deliver a discourse upon the perils of affection?

She sat listening to him without uttering a word. But she thought of Max—her Max, who loved her so dearly and so well—and she laughed within herself at the old man's well-meant warnings.

His words were those of a man whose happiness had been wrecked by some woman, vain and worthless.

Why had he insisted that she should visit him in secret? To her, his motive was a complete enigma, rendered the more complicated by his vigorous denunciation of affection, and all that appertained to it.

Chapter Thirty
The Spider's Parlour

"What you have told me, Miss Rolfe, concerning your brother's engagement, interests me greatly," the old fellow said at last. "He is entirely in my confidence, and a most valuable assistant, therefore I, naturally, am very anxious that he should not make an unhappy marriage."

"I—I hope that you will not say that I have told you," exclaimed the girl quickly. "I know I ought not to—"

"Whatever is said between us in this room, Miss Rolfe, is said in strictest confidence," the millionaire declared. "I have a good many secrets in my keeping, you know. Therefore rest assured that whatever you tell me goes no further."

"You are against his marriage," she suggested, looking him boldly in the face.

"I have not said so. I am only seeking information abort the lady—Maud Petrovitch, I think you said was her name?"

"Whatever I can tell you is only in her favour. She was a dear—a very dear friend of mine."

"Ah! then you have quarrelled—eh?" he said, looking at her sharply.

"You said she was your friend—you used the past tense."

"I know."

"Why?"

"Because,"—and she grew confused—"well, because something has happened."

"To interrupt pure friendship?"

She did not reply. He had craftily led up the conversation to Maud, and was, as he had openly told her, seeking information. He watched the flush upon her cheeks, and the nervous manner in which she picked at her skirt.

"And yet, though you are friends no longer, you are in favour of your brother's marriage with the lady? That appears strange. I suppose he loves her. Every man loves at his age, and lives to regret it at forty," he added with that touch of biting sarcasm that was never absolutely absent from his remarks.

"Yes; Charlie does love her. I'm convinced of that. And her devotion to him has always been very marked, from the first time they were introduced at Aix-les-Bains. She has told me how deep is her affection for him."

"At Aix-les-Bains," Statham exclaimed in surprise: "I thought Doctor Petrovitch lived in London?"

"And so he did—until recently."

"Where is he now? I would much like to meet him again."

"I do not know. He left London suddenly with his daughter."

"Your brother would know, of course."

"No. He also is unaware of their present whereabouts," she answered quickly, adding: "Recollect your promise not to mention the matter to him."

"When I make a promise, Miss Rolfe, I keep it," was his grave response. "Only forgive me for saying so, but you appear to be a little evasive regarding the Doctor's daughter."

"Evasive?" she echoed. "I don't understand you, Mr Statham."

"Well, you are trying to mislead me," he answered, knitting his brows and looking her straight in the face. "And let me say that when you try to mislead Sam Statham you have a difficult task."

She started at his sudden change of manner, and again became confused.

"Now," he said, bending forward to her from his chair, "let us understand each other at the outset. You were the most intimate friend of this girl Maud who, with her father, suddenly disappeared from London. The facts of their disappearance are already known to me, I may as well tell you that much. They vanished, and took their household goods with them. Perhaps they were afraid of anarchists or political enemies, or perhaps the Doctor is wanted by the police. Who knows? It was a mystery, and as such remains, is not that so?"

She nodded. This knowledge of his astounded her. She had believed that the disappearance was only known to the two or three persons who had been the Petrovitchs' personal friends. She little dreamed of the many spies in the pay of the great financier, men and women who reported to him any political move at home or abroad which might influence the markets. The world had often believed that Sam Statham was omnipresent. They knew nothing of his agents, or of their secret visits.

"Now, Miss Rolfe, let us advance one step further," the old man said, still keeping his keen gaze upon hers. "If you will kindly carry your mind back to the day of their disappearance, you will remember that you accompanied the Doctor's daughter to a concert at Queen's Hall."

"How do you know that?" she cried, starting up from her chair.

"How I know it is immaterial," he said firmly. "Kindly re-seat yourself."

"I will not," she declared boldly. "You are cross-examining me as though I were a criminal. This is outrageous!"

"I politely request you to sit down, Miss Rolfe," he said, never moving a muscle.

Her beautiful face was flushed with resentment and anger, as, standing erect before him, she faced him in open defiance.

"I see no further point in this interview," was her cool reply. "I will go."

"I think it would be wiser for you to remain," he responded in a low, determined voice; "wiser for you to answer my questions."

"I have already answered them."

"I wish to know something further," he said, stirring again in his chair, and waving his hand with a repeated request that she would be re-seated.

"I have nothing to conceal," was her reply, attempting to smile. "Why should I?"

"Why, indeed," he said, "I may as well tell you that I have reasons— very strong business reasons—for elucidating this mystery concerning Doctor Petrovitch. To me it involves a question of many thousands of pounds. I have considerable interests out in Servia, as your brother may have explained to you. I must find the Doctor, and the reason I have asked you here to-night is to invoke your aid in assisting me to do so. Can I be more explicit?"

He looked in her face, but a shrewd observer would have known by the wavering smile at the corners of his mouth that he was not speaking the exact truth. There was some trick or motive underlying it all.

Though she did not detect this, she was still undecided. Anger was aroused within her by his commanding manner. His attitude had changed so suddenly that she had been taken thoroughly aback.

"I am afraid, Mr Statham, that I cannot render you any assistance in discovering the whereabouts of the Petrovitchs."

"But, my dear young lady!" he cried. "They had servants. Surely there is one who could give us some very valuable information."

"Perhaps so, if he or she could be found," she remarked. "They, no doubt, took every precaution against being followed. As a matter of fact, so great a care has the Doctor taken that his most intimate friend in London is in ignorance."

"And who is he, pray?" asked the millionaire quickly.

"A gentleman named Barclay—Mr Max Barclay."

"Max Barclay! I've heard of him. A friend of your brother's, eh? And so he was the Doctor's friend?"

"They were inseparable, but the Doctor left without a word of farewell."

"And also the daughter—except to you, Miss Rolfe," he said, looking at her meaningly.

"To me?"

"Yes," he went on, his keen gaze again upon her. "It is useless to assume ignorance. You know quite well that the doctor's daughter, on the night of their disappearance, made a statement to you—an important statement."

"My brother told you that!" she cried. "He has told you everything!"

"He has told me nothing," replied the old man coldly. "I only ask whether you deny that she made a statement."

The girl hesitated.

"She certainly spoke to me," she admitted at last. "I was her most intimate friend, and it was only natural perhaps that she told me what was most uppermost in her mind."

"And what was that?"

"I regret," she replied, "that I cannot repeat it; Mr Statham."

"What! You refuse to say anything?"

"Under compulsion—yes," was her firm answer. "I did not know," she added, "that you had invited me here to ply me with questions in this manner."

"Or you would not have come, eh?" he laughed. "Well, my dear young lady, you apparently don't quite realise how very important it is to me to discover Doctor Petrovitch. I have asked you here in order to beg a favour of you. I may be rough and matter-of-fact, but I trust you will pardon my apparent rudeness."

"There is nothing to forgive, Mr Statham," was her quiet, dignified response. "My reply, quite brief and at the same time unalterable, is that I have nothing to say."

"You mean you refuse to tell me?"

She nodded.

He thrust his hands deep into the pockets of his old grey trousers, and stared down at the carpet. Marion Rolfe was more difficult to question than he had anticipated. She possessed the same firm, resolute nature of her father and her brother. That Maud Petrovitch had made a statement to her which possessed a most important bearing upon the serious interests involved, he was absolutely certain. Ever since the day following the strange disappearance, certain secret agents of his had been at work, but they had discovered next to nothing. Marion Rolfe alone was in possession of the actual facts. He knew that full well, and was therefore determined that she should be compelled to speak and explain.

"I wish, Miss Rolfe, that I could impress upon you the extreme importance of this matter to myself personally," he said, assuming an air quite conciliatory in the hope that he might induce her to reveal the truth. "I have begged of you to assist me in a very difficult task—one which, if I fail in accomplishing, will mean an enormous financial revenue. Your brother is in my service, while you yourself are also indirectly in my service," he added; "and if, as result of your information, I am able to discover the Doctor, I need not tell you that I shall mark your services in an appreciable manner."

"You have already been very generous to us both, Mr Statham, but I think you cannot know much of me if you believe that for sake of reward I will betray the Doctor," was her dignified answer.

"It is not a question of betrayal," he hastened to reassure her. "It is to his own interest as well as to mine that we should meet. If we do not, it will mean ruin to him."

"And if he is dead?" suggested Marion.

"My own belief is that he is not dead," was the millionaire's reply. "I know more of him and of his past than you imagine. There is every reason why he should live."

"And Maud—what of her?"

He shrugged his shoulders, and replied:

"As regards her—you know best. She told you the truth."

"Yes—and which I will not repeat."

"Oh! but, my dear young lady, you must! Why waste time like this? Every day, nay every hour, causes the affair to assume increased gravity. I would have gone to the police long ago, only such a course would have brought the Doctor into a criminal dock. I have his interests, as well as my own at heart."

"I have given my promise of secrecy, Mr Statham, and I will not betray it," she repeated, again rising from her chair, anxious to leave the house.

"You still refuse!" he cried starting to his feet also, and standing before her. "You still refuse—even to save yourself!"

"To save myself!" she exclaimed. "I do not follow you, Mr Statham."

A sinister grin spread over his grey face.

"You are perfectly free to leave this place, Miss Rolfe," he said in a hard, meaning voice, "but first reflect what they will say at Cunnington's regarding your visit here to-night!"

"You—you will tell them!" she gasped, drawing back from him, pale as death as she realised, for the first time, how she had imperilled her good name, and how completely she was in his power. "I—I believed, Mr Statham, that you were an honourable man!"

"Where a man's life is concerned it is not a question of honour," was his reply. "You refuse to assist me—and I refuse to assist you. That is all!"

Chapter Thirty One
"His Name!"

"Not a question of honour, Mr Statham!" she cried. "Is it not a question of my own honour!" and she stood before him, erect and defiant.

"My dear young lady," he laughed, "pray calm yourself. Let us discuss the matter quietly."

"There is nothing to discuss," she exclaimed resentfully, looking straight into the old man's grey face. "You have threatened to divulge the secret of my visit to you to-night if—if I refuse to betray my friend! Is such an action honourable? Does such a threat against a defenceless woman do you credit?" she asked.

"You misunderstand me," he hastened to assure her, realising the mistake he had made.

"I understand that you ask me a question," she said. "You wish me to repeat what was told to me in confidence—the secret imparted to me by the girl who was my beat friend!"

"Yes; I wish to know what Maud Petrovitch told you," he answered, standing with his thin hands behind his back.

"Then I regret that I am unable to satisfy your curiosity," was her firm response. "I now realise your motive in inviting me here at this hour to see you in secret. You meant me to compromise myself—to remain away from Cunnington's and be punished for my absence—the punishment of dismissal," she went on, her fine eyes flashing in anger at his dastardly tactics. "You know quite well, Mr Statham, that the world is only too ready to think ill of a woman! You anticipate that I will betray my friend, in order to save myself from calumny and dismissal from the service of the firm. But in that you are mistaken. No word shall pass my lips, and I wish you good-night," she added with serve hauteur, moving towards the door.

"No, Miss Rolfe!" he cried, quickly intercepting her. "Surely it is unnecessary to create this scene. I hate scenes. Life is really not worth them. You have denounced what you are pleased to call my ungentlemanly tactics. Well, I can only say in my defence that Samuel Statham, although he is not all that he might be, has never acted the blackguard towards a woman, and more especially, towards the daughter of his dear friend."

"You have told me that you will refuse to assist me further!" she said. "In other words, you decline to preserve the secret of my visit here, although you made a promise that my absence to-night from Cunnington's should not be noted!"

"I have given you a promise, Miss Rolfe, and I shall keep it," was his quiet and serious response.

She looked at him with distrust.

"You have asked me a question, Mr Statham—one to which I am not permitted to reply," she said.

"Why not?"

"Because—well, because I have made a vow to regard what was told me as strictly in confidence."

Sam Statham pursed his lips. Few were the secrets he could not learn when he set his mind upon learning them. In every capital in Europe he had his agents, who, at orders from him, set about to discover what he wished to know, whether it be a carefully-guarded diplomatic secret, or whether it concerned the love affair of some royal prince to whom he was making a loan. He knew as much of the internal affairs of various countries as their finance ministers did themselves, and with the private affairs of some of his clients he was as well acquainted as were their own valets.

To the possession of sound but secret information much of the old man's success was due. The mysterious men and women who so often came and went to that house all poured into his ear facts they had gathered—facts which he afterwards duly noted in the locked green-covered book which he kept in the security of his safe.

Surely the contents of that book would, if published, have created a huge sensation; for there were noted there many ugly incidents in the lives of the men who were most prominent in Europe, together, be it said, with facts concerning them that were highly creditable, and sometimes counterbalanced the black pages in their history.

And this man of many secrets stood there thwarted by a mere chit of a girl!

He regarded her coldly with expressionless eyes. His gaze caused her to shudder. She withdrew from him with instinctive dislike. About this man of millions, whose touch turned everything to gold, there seemed to her something superhuman, something indescribably fearsome. His very gaze seemed to fascinate her, and yet at the same time she regarded him with distrust and horror. She was a fool, she told herself, ever to have listened to his appeal. She ought to have had sense enough to know that by bringing her there at that hour he had some sinister motive.

His motive was to wring from her the words of Maud Petrovitch.

Suddenly he altered his tactics, and, drawing her chair forward again, said:

"Let us sit down and talk of something else. You look pale. May I offer you something?"

"No, thank you," she replied. It was true that his threatening words a few moments ago had upset her, therefore she was glad to be seated again. He evidently did not intend that she should leave yet.

Having re-seated himself near his writing-table, he said: "As I explained, I want you, if you will, to go on a journey for me. The car is awaiting you round in Deanery Street."

"A journey? Is it far?"

"That all depends—if you are prepared to render me this service," he replied.

"I am prepared to render you any service, Mr Statham, that is within my power, and my conscience permits me," she said in a firm voice.

"Ah, now, that's better. We're beginning to be friends. When you know me, you will not accuse me of ungentlemanly conduct—especially towards a woman. But," he added with a laugh, "I'm a woman hater. I daresay you've heard that about me—eh?"

She smiled also.

"Well—yes. I've heard that you are not exactly a ladies' man. But surely you are not alone in the world in that!"

"If all men were like me, Miss Rolfe," he said, "there wouldn't be much work for the parsons in the matter of marrying."

"You've been unfortunate, perhaps, in your female acquaintances," she ventured to suggest. His manner towards her had altered, therefore she was again perfectly at her ease.

"Yes," he sighed. "You have guessed correctly—unfortunate."

And then a dead silence fell, and Marion, watching his face, saw that he was reflecting deeply.

Of a sudden, he looked straight into her face again, and said:

"You have a lover, Miss Rolfe—and you are happy. Is not that so?"

The girl blushed deeply at this unexpected statement. How could the old man possibly know, unless some of the people at Cunnington's had carried tales to him. Perhaps Mr Warner had told Mr Cunnington, and he had spoken to the millionaire!

"I see," he laughed, "that I've spoken the truth. Max Barclay loves you, doesn't he? He's a friend of your brother's. I know him, and allow me to congratulate you. He's a thoroughly good fellow, and would be better if he'd keep off hazardous speculation."

She did not reply. The old man's final sentence impressed her. Max's speculations were hazardous. This was news to her.

"You don't deny that you love young Barclay, do you?" the old man demanded.

She hesitated, her cheeks crimsoning.

"Well, why should I?" she asked. "He is very good to me—very good, indeed."

"That's right," he said approvingly. "If I did not think him an honest, upright fellow I should warn you against him. Girls in your dependent position, you know, are too frequently victims of men whom the world call gentlemen. You know that, don't you?"

"Yes," she answered in a low voice. She was impressed by his solicitude on her behalf. In his eyes was a kindly glance, and she began to declare within herself that she had misjudged him.

"Well," he went on, "when it came to my knowledge that Max Barclay was paying court to you, and that you were seen together of an evening and on Sundays, it gave me great satisfaction. I owe a debt of gratitude to your poor father, Miss Rolfe, and I am endeavouring to repay it to his children. Therefore I admit to you now that more than once I wondered what kind of lover would be yours. I anticipated annoyance, but, on the contrary, I have only the most complete satisfaction."

"I am sure, Mr Statham, it is very kind of you to say this. And surely it is very generous of you to take in interest in Charlie and myself."

"It is not a matter of kindness, but a matter of duty," he said. "We were talking of Barclay. How did you meet him?"

"Charlie introduced him to me one Sunday afternoon in the Park."

"And he has promised you marriage? Tell me frankly." She nodded, again blushing deeply.

"Then you have my very heartiest wishes for your future happiness," he declared with a pleasant smile. "Mind I am told the date, so that I can send you the usual teapot!"

Whereat they both laughed in chorus. The old man could be charming when he wished.

"Oh! we shan't be married for a long time yet, I suppose!" Marion exclaimed. "Max talks of going with a shooting party up the Zambesi next spring. They'll be away a full year, I expect."

"And you'll be left all alone?" he said in a tone of surprise. "No, I don't think he'll do that. He ought not to leave you alone at Cunnington's."

"Oh, but he's going out to Turkey now—in a few days I think. He has some financial business out there. Something which will bring him in a very big sum of money."

"Oh, what's its nature?" asked the old financier, instantly pricking up his ears.

"I believe it's a concession from the Sultan for the construction of a railway from some place on the Servian frontier, across Northern Albania, down to San Giovanni di Medua—if I pronounce the name aright—on the Adriatic."

"What!" cried Statham, starting up. "Are you quite certain of this?"

"Yes; why?" she asked, surprised at the sudden effect her words had produced upon him.

"Well—well, because this is a surprise to me, Miss Rolfe," he said. "Tell me the details, as far as you know them. Has he spoken to you about it?"

"Yes. He is hesitating to go, not wishing to leave me."

"Of course. Did I not tell you so a moment ago?" he remarked with a smile. "But are you aware that this concession, if the Sultan really gives it, is of the greatest importance to the commercial development of the Near East? There are big interests involved, and correspondingly big profits. Curious that I have not heard anything of the scheme lately! It's a dream that every Balkan statesman has had for the past fifteen years—the creating of an outlet for trade to the Adriatic; but the Sultan could never be induced to allow the line to run through his dominion. He is not too friendly with either Bulgaria or Servia. I thought I was being kept well informed of all the openings in Constantinople where British capital can be employed. Yet I haven't heard anything of this long discussed scheme for quite a year."

"Your informants believe, perhaps, that it would not interest you?"

"Interest me!" he echoed. "Why, they could not successfully carry it through in London without my aid—or, at least, without my consent. Whoever is getting the concession—if it is being obtained at all, which I very much doubt—knows full well that in the long run he must come to Sam Statham. Do you happen to know who, besides Barclay, is interested in the scheme?"

"There is a French gentleman—a friend of Max's—who wants him to go to Constantinople with him."

"What is his name? I may probably know him?"

"Adam—Jean Adam."

"Jean Adam!" gasped the old man. "Jean Adam—a friend of Max Barclay?"

"Yes," she answered, staring at him. "Why?"

"Why, girl!" he cried roughly. "Don't ask me why? But tell me all about it—tell me at once!"

Chapter Thirty Two
Man's Broken Promises

"I know very little of the details," replied the girl. "Max could, of course, tell you everything. He introduced me one night to Mr Adam, who seemed a very polite man."

"All bows and smiles, like the average Frenchman—eh? Oh, yes. I happen to know him. Well?"

"He seems a most intimate friend of Max's."

"Is he really?" remarked the millionaire. "Then Max doesn't know as much about him as I do."

"What?" asked Marion in quick alarm. "Isn't he all that he pretends to be?"

"No, he isn't. I must see Barclay to-morrow—the first thing to-morrow. I wonder if he's put any money into the venture?"

"Of that I don't know. He only told me that it would mean a big fortune."

"So it would—if it were genuine."

"Then isn't it genuine?" she asked anxiously.

"Genuine! Why, of course not! Nothing that Jean Adam has anything to do with, my dear young lady, is ever genuine. Depend upon it that his Majesty the Sultan will never grant any such concession. He fears Bulgaria far too much. If it could have been had, I may tell you at once I should already have had it. There is, as you say, a big thing to be made out of it—a very big thing. But while the Sultan lives the line will never be constructed. Pachitch, the Prime Minister of Servia, told me so the last time I was in Belgrade, and I'm entirely of his opinion."

"But what you tell me regarding Mr Adam surprises me."

"Ah! you are still young, Miss Rolfe! You have many surprises yet in store for you," he replied with a light laugh. "Do you know Adam personally?"

"Yes."

"Then beware of him, my girl—beware of him!" he snapped, his grey face darkening in remembrance of certain ugly facts, and in recollection of the sinister face of the shabby lounger against the park railings.

"Is he such a bad man, then?"

Sam Statham pressed his thin lips together.

"He is one of those men without conscience, and without compunction; a man whose plausible tongue would deceive even Satan himself."

"Then he has deceived Max—I mean Mr Barclay," she exclaimed, quickly correcting her slip of the tongue, her cheeks slightly crimsoning at the same time.

"Without doubt," was the millionaire's reply. "I must see Barclay to-morrow, and ascertain what are Adam's plans."

"He is persuading Mr Barclay to go to Constantinople. I know that because he asked me to use my influence upon him in that direction."

"Oh, so he has approached you, also, has he? Then there is some strong motive for this journey, without a doubt! Barclay will be ill-advised if he accepts the invitation. The bait held out is a very tempting one; but when I've seen your gentleman friend he will not be so credulous."

"I'm very surprised at what you told me. I thought Mr Adam quite a nice person—for a foreigner."

"No doubt he was nice to you, for he wished to enlist your services to induce your lover to go out to Turkey. For what reason?"

"How can I tell?" asked the girl. "Mr Barclay mentioned that the railway concession would mean the commercial development of the Balkan States, and that it would be one of the most paying enterprises in Europe."

"That is admitted on all hands. But as the concession is not granted, and never will be granted, I cannot see what object Adam has in inducing your friend to visit Constantinople. Was he asked to put money into the scheme, do you know?"

"Mr Adam did not wish him to put up any money until he had thoroughly satisfied himself regarding the truth of his statements."

Statham was silent.

"That's distinctly curious," he remarked at last, apparently much puzzled by her statement. "Underlying it all is some sinister motive, depend upon it."

"You alarm me, Mr Statham," the girl said, apprehensive of some unexpected evil befalling the man she loved.

"It is as well to be forearmed in dealing with Jean Adam," was the old man's response. "More than one good man owes the ruin of his life's happiness, nay his death, to the craft and cunning of that man, who, under a dozen different aliases, is known in a dozen different capitals of the world."

"Then he's an adventurer?"

"Most certainly. Tell Barclay to come and see me. Or better, I will write to him myself. It is well that you've told me this, otherwise—" and he broke off short, without concluding his sentence.

The pretty clock chimed the half-hour musically, reminding Marion of the unusual hour, and she stirred as if anxious to leave. Her handkerchief dropped upon the floor. The old man noticed it, but did not direct her attention to it.

"Then if you wish it, Mr Statham, I will say nothing to Mr Barclay," she remarked.

"No. You need say nothing. I will send him a message in the morning. But," he added, looking straight into the girl's beautiful face, "will you not reconsider your decision, Miss Rolfe?"

"My decision! Of what?" she asked.

"Regarding the statement made to you by Maud Petrovitch. She told you something. What was it? Come, tell me. Some very great financial interests are involved in the ex-Minister's disappearance. Your information may save me from very heavy losses. Will you not assist me?"

"I regret that it is impossible."

"Have I not even to-night been your friend?" he pointed out. "Have I not warned you against the man who is Max Barclay's secret enemy—and yours—the man Jean Adam?"

"I am very grateful indeed to you," she answered; "and if it were in my power, I would tell you what she told me."

"In your power!" he laughed. "Why, of course, it is in your power to speak, if you wish?"

"Maud made a confession to me," she declared, "and I hold it sacred."

"A confession!" he exclaimed, regarding her in surprise. "Regarding her father, I suppose?"

"No; regarding herself."

"Ah! A confession of a woman's weakness—eh?"

"Its nature is immaterial," she responded in a firm tone. "I was her most intimate friend, and she confided in me."

"And because it concerns her personally, you refuse to divulge it?"

"I am a woman, Mr Statham, and I will not betray anything that reflects upon another woman's honour."

"Women are not usually so loyal to each other!" he remarked, not without a touch of sarcasm. "You appear to be unlike all the others I have known."

"I am no better than anybody else, I suppose," she replied. "Every woman must surely possess a sense of what is right and just."

"Very few of them do," the old man snarled, for woman was a subject upon which he always became bitterly sarcastic. In his younger days he had been essentially a ladies' man, but the closed page in his history had surely been sufficient to sour him against the other sex.

The world, had it but known the truth, would not have pondered at Sam Statham's hatred of society, and more especially the feminine element of it. But, like many another man, he was misjudged because he was compelled to conceal the truth, and was condemned unjustly because it was not permitted to him to make self-defence.

How many men—and women, too—live their lives in social ostracism, and perhaps disgrace, because for family or other reasons they are unable to exhibit to the world the truth. Many a man, and many a woman, who read these lines, are as grossly misjudged by their fellows as was Samuel Statham, the millionaire who was a pauper, the man who lived that sad and lonely life in his Park Lane mansion, daily gathering gold until he became crushed beneath the weight of its awful responsibility, his sole aim and relaxation being the mixing with the submerged workers of the city, and relieving them by secret philanthropy.

The sinner assumes the cloak of piety, while too often the denounced and maligned suffer in silence. It was so in Samuel Statham's case; it is so in more than one case which has come under my own personal observation during the inquiries I made before writing this present narrative of east and west.

The old millionaire was surprised at the girl's admission that what the Doctor's daughter had told her was a confession. He realised how, in face of the fact that her brother loved Maud Petrovitch, it was not likely that she would betray her. Still, his curiosity was excited. The girl before him knew the truth of the ex-Minister's strange disappearance—knew, most probably, his whereabouts.

"Was the confession made to you by the Doctor's daughter of such a private nature that you really cannot divulge it to me?" he asked her, appealingly. "Remember, I am not seeking to probe the secrets of a young girl's life, Miss Rolfe. On the contrary, I am anxious—most anxious—to clear up what is at present a most mysterious and unaccountable occurrence. Doctor Petrovitch disappeared from London just at a moment when his presence here was, in his own interests, as well as in mine, most required. I need not go into the details," he went on, fixing her with his sunken eyes. "It is sufficient to explain to you that he and I had certain secret negotiations. He came here on many occasions, always in secret—at about this hour. He preferred to visit me in that manner, because of the spies who always haunted him and who reported all his doings to Belgrade."

"I was not aware that you were on friendly terms," Marion remarked. "Maud never told me that her father visited you."

"Because she was in ignorance," Statham replied. "The Doctor was a diplomatist, remember, and could keep a secret, even from his own daughter. From what I've told you, you can surely gather how extremely anxious I am to know the truth."

Marion was silent. She realised to the full that financial interests of the millionaire were at stake—that her statement might save huge losses if she betrayed Maud, and told this man the truth. He was her friend and benefactor. To him both she and Charlie owed everything. Without him they would be compelled to face the world, she friendless and practically penniless. The penalty of her silence he had already indicated. By refraining from assisting her, he could to-morrow cast her out of her employment, discredited and disgraced!

What would Max think? What would he believe?

If she remained silent she would preserve Maud's honour and Charlie's peace of mind. He was devoted to the sweet-faced, half-foreign girl with the stray little wisp of hair across her brow. Yet if he knew what she had told him he would hate her—he must hate her. Ah! the mere thought of it drove her to a frenzy of despair.

She set her teeth, and, with her face pale as death, she rose slowly to go. Her brows were knit, her countenance determined.

Come what might, she would be loyal to her friend. Charlie should never know the truth. Rather than that she would sacrifice herself—sacrifice her love for Max Barclay, which was to her the sweetest and most treasured sentiment in all the world.

"I have asked you to assist me, Miss Rolfe," the old man said, in a low, impressive voice, leaning his arm upon the edge of his writing-table and bending towards her. "Surely when you know all that it means to me, you will not refuse?"

"I refuse to betray my friend," was her firm response, her face white to the lips. "You may act as you think proper, Mr Statham. You may allow my friends to think ill of me; you may stand aside and see me cast to-morrow at a moment's notice out of Cunnington's employ because of my absence to-night, but my lips are closed regarding the confession made to me in confidence. In anything else I am ready to serve you. You have asked me to go upon a journey in your interests—in a motor car that is awaiting me. This I am willing and anxious to do. You are my benefactor, and it is my duty to do what you wish."

"It is your duty, Miss Rolfe, to tell me what I desire to know."

"No!" she cried, facing him boldly, her bright eyes flashing defiantly upon him. "It is not my duty to betray my friend—even to you!"

"Very well," he answered, with a smile upon his thin lips. "It is getting late. They may be wondering at Cunnington's. I will see you to the door."

And the expression upon his face showed her, alas! too plainly that for her there was no future.

The present was already dead, the future—?

Chapter Thirty Three
Against the Rules

"Miss Rolfe, Mr Cunnington wants you in the counting-house," exclaimed a youth approaching Marion just after ten o'clock the following morning. She had been in the department early, and was busy re-arranging an autumn costume upon a stand, with a ticket bearing the words, "Paris model, 49 shillings, 11 pence."

The dread words that broke upon her ear caused her young heart to sink within her. As she feared, she was "carpeted."

To be absent at night without leave was the "sack" at a moment's notice to any of Cunnington's girls. There was no leniency in that respect as in certain other large stores in London which I could name, where the girls are so very badly paid that it is a scandal and disgrace to the smug, church-going shareholders who grow fat upon their dividends. But who among those who bold shares in the big drapery concerns of London, or who among the millions of customers on the look-out for bargains at sales, care a jot for the poor girl-assistant, the drudgery she has to undergo, or the evils she suffers by the iniquitous system of "living-in?"

It is a dull, drab life indeed, the life of the London shop, with its fortnight's holiday each year and its constant strain of the telling of untruths in order to sell goods. But the supply of shop labour is always greater than the demand. Girls and youths are always coming up from the country in constant streams, "cribbing," as it is called—or on the lookout for a berth—and as soon as a girl loses her freshness, or a man's hair begins to show silver threads, he is thrown out in favour of a youth—from Scotland or Wales by preference.

London, alas! little dreams of the callous heartlessness of employers in the drapery trade.

Marion knew this. Since she had been at Cunnington's her eyes had been opened to the scant consideration she need expect. Girls who had worked in her department had been discharged merely because, suffering from a cold or from the stress of overwork, they had been absent a couple of days. And all the information vouchsafed them was that the firm could not afford to support invalids. Once, indeed, she had sat beside a dying girl in the Brompton Hospital—a girl to whom the close, vitiated atmosphere of the shop had brought consumption, and she had been sent forth, at a moment's notice, homeless, and to die.

And so, when the youth made the announcement, she knit her brows, brushed the hair from her brow, placed down the pincushion in her hand, and followed him through the several shops into another building where Mr Cunnington's private room was situated.

In the outer office of the counting-house several persons, buyers, callers, and others, were waiting audience with the chief.

One girl, a saucy, dark-haired assistant in the ribbons, exclaimed:

"Hullo, Rolfe! What are you up for?"

Marion flushed slightly, and answered:

"I—I hardly know."

"Well, I'm going in for a rise, and if the guv'nor don't give it to me I'm going to Westoby's to-morrow. I've got a good crib there. My young man is shop-walker, so I'll get on like a house on fire."

"Westoby's is a lot better than here," remarked a pale-faced male assistant. "I was there for a sale once. I only wish they'd have kept me."

"I've heard that the food is wretched," remarked Marion, for the sake of something to say.

"It isn't good," declared the young man, "but the girls get lots more freedom. They do as they like almost. Old Westoby don't care, as long as the business pays. It's a public company, like this, but they do a bit lower-class trade, which means more 'spiffs.'"

"I haven't made a quid this last three months out of 'spiffs'," declared the ribbon-girl. "That's why I want a rise."

Marion smiled within herself, for beyond the glass partition were quite a dozen girls, all of them young, several quite good-looking, waiting to see if any berths were vacant, and ready that very hour to take the ribbon-girl's place—and hers.

Every girl who came up to London went first to Cunnington's, for the assistants there were declared to be of better class than those of the other drapery houses that jostle each other on the north side of Oxford Street.

Marion waited, full of deep anxiety. Every detail of that midnight interview with the man who held controlling interest in the huge concern came back to her—his clever attempt to ingratiate himself with her in order to learn Maud's secret, and her curt dismissal when she had met his request with point-blank refusal.

One by one the applicants for a hearing were received by Mr Cunnington, again emerging from his room, some dark and angry, and others smiling and happy. At last her turn came, and she walked into the small office with the severe-looking writing-table and the dark blue carpet.

The dark-bearded man, by whose enterprise that big business had been built up, turned in his chair and faced her.

"Miss Rolfe!" he exclaimed. "Ah! yes," and he referred to a memorandum upon his desk. "You were absent without leave last night, the housekeeper reports. You are aware of rule seventy-three—eh?"

"Most certainly, sir," was the trembling girl's reply, for this meant to her all her future, and more. It meant Max's love. "But I think I ought to explain that—"

"I have no time, miss, for explanations. You know the rule. When you were engaged here you signed it, and therefore I suppose you've read it. It states as follows: 'Any assistant absent after eleven o'clock without previously obtaining signed leave from Mr Hemmingway or myself will be discharged on the following day.' The firm have, therefore, dispensed with your services. As regards character, Miss Rolfe, please understand that the firm is silent."

"But, Mr Cunnington," cried the girl, "I was absent at the express request of Mr Statham. He wished to see me." The head of the firm frowned slightly, answering:

"I have no desire to enter into the reasons of your absence. You could easily have asked for leave. If Mr Statham had wished to see you, he would have sent me a note, no doubt. It was at his request I engaged you, I recollect. Therefore, I think that the least said regarding last night the better."

"But Mr Statham promised me he would send you a message this morning," the girl declared in her distress.

"Parker, has Mr Statham been on the 'phone this morning?" asked Mr Cunnington of the young man seated near him.

"No, sir," was the prompt reply.

"But will you not ask him?" cried the girl. "He promised me he would communicate with you."

Mr Cunnington hesitated for a moment. He reflected that the girl was a *protégée* of the millionaire. Therefore he gave Parker orders to ring up the man whose millions controlled the concern.

Marion waited in breathless anxiousness. The secretary asked for Mr Statham, and spoke to him, inquiring if he knew anything of Miss Rolfe's absence from the firm's dormitory on the previous night. "Mr Statham says, sir," said Parker at last, "that he is too busy to be troubled with the affaire of any of Cunnington's shop-assistants."

The reply filled Mr Cunnington with suspicion. It showed him plainly that Statham had at least no further interest in the girl, and that her discharge would be gratifying.

"You hear the reply," he said to her. "That is enough." And he scribbled something upon a piece of paper. "Take it to the cashier, and he will pay your wages up to date."

"Then I am discharged!" asked the girl, crimsoning—"sent out from your establishment without a character?"

"By reason of your own action," was the rough reply. "You know the rules. Please leave. I am far too busy to argue."

"But Mr Statham wrote asking me to call and see him. I have his letter here."

"I have no desire or inclination to enter into Mr Statham's affairs," Cunnington replied. "You are discharged for being absent at night without leave. Will you go, Miss Rolfe?" he asked angrily.

"Mr Cunnington," she said, quite quietly, "you misjudge me entirely. Mr Statham asked me to call upon him in secret, because he desired me to give him some private information. He promised at the same time to send you word, so that my absence should not be mentioned. You are a man of honour, with daughters of your own," she went on appealingly. "Because I refused to betray a friend of mine, a woman, he has refused to stretch forth a hand to save me from the disgrace of this discharge," and tears welled in her fine eyes as she spoke.

"It is a matter that does not concern me in the least, Miss Rolfe, Mr Statham put you here, and if he wishes for your discharge I have nothing to say in the matter. Good morning."

And he turned from her and busied himself with the heap of papers on his desk.

She did not move. She stood as one turned to stone. Therefore he touched the electric button beneath the arm of his chair, and a clerk appeared.

"Send in Mortimer," he said coldly, disregarding the girl's presence. Then Marion, seeing that all appeal was in vain, turned upon her heel and went out—broken and bitter—a changed woman.

Mr Cunnington turned and watched her disappearing. Suddenly, as though half uncertain whether his action might not be criticised by Statham, he exclaimed:

"Call that young lady back!"

Marion returned, her face full of anger and dignity.

"Do I really understand you that Mr Statham invited you to his house?" he asked her. "I mean that you received letters from him?"

"Yes."

The dark-bearded man, alert and businesslike, eyed her critically, and asked:

"You have those letters, I presume."

"Certainly. I have them here," was her reply, as she fumbled in the pocket of her black skirt. "I refused to call upon him, but he pressed me so much that I felt it imperative. He has been so very good to me that I feared to displease him."

And she placed several letters upon Mr Cunnington's desk.

"I see they are marked 'private,'" he said, with a good deal of curiosity. "Have I your permission to glance at them?"

"Certainly," was the cool reply. "You refuse to hear me, therefore I am compelled to give you proof."

The man opened them one after the other, scanned them, and placed them aside. Statham's refusal to answer the query upon the telephone was for him all-sufficient.

"You had better leave these letters with me, Miss Rolfe," he said decisively, for he saw that at all hazards he must obtain that correspondence and hand it back to the writer.

"But—"

"There are no buts," he exclaimed, quickly interrupting her. "Had Mr Statham desired you to remain in our service he would have replied to that effect. Come, you are wasting my time. Good morning."

And a moment later, almost before she was aware of it, Marion found herself outside the room, with the door closed behind her.

She was no longer in the service of Cunnington's. She had been discharged in disgrace.

What would Charlie say? What explanation could she offer to Max?

Chapter Thirty Four
The Mysterious Mademoiselle

The future, nay, the very life, of Samuel Statham depended, according to his own admission to his secretary, upon the honour of Maud Petrovitch.

The position was, to say the least, strangely incongruous. Here was a man whose power and wealth were world-famous, a man whom kings and princes sought to conciliate and load with honours, which he steadfastly refused to accept, dependent for his life upon a woman, little more than a child.

Charlie Rolfe had thought over his master's strange, enigmatical words many times. Maud—his Maud whom he loved so dearly, and who had so suddenly and mysteriously gone out of his life—was to be sacrificed. Why? What did old Sam mean when he uttered those words, each of which had burnt indelibly into his soul.

"You have promised to save me; you have sworn to assist me, and the sacrifice is imperative?" Statham had said. "It is her honour—or my death!"

Each time he entered the grim portals of the silent house in Park Lane those fateful words recurred to him. The house of mystery seemed dark and chilly, even on those sunny days of early September, and old Levi seemed more sphinx-like and solemn. A dozen times had he been on the point of referring again to the matter, but each time he had refrained, for the millionaire's manner had now changed. He was less anxious, and far more bright and hopeful. The discovery of Duncan Macgregor seemed to have wrought a great change in him, for the old Scot frequently spent the evening there, being telegraphed for from Glasgow, ostensibly to discuss business matters.

On the day following Marion's visit to Park Lane Charlie was in Paris, having been sent there overnight upon a pressing message to the branch house in the Avenue de l'Opéra, for Statham Brothers were as well-known for their stability in France as in England.

Just before twelve o'clock, as he was issuing from the fine offices of the firm into the street, he stumbled against a rather short but well-dressed girl of about twenty-four. He raised his hat, and in English asked her pardon, whereupon, with a light laugh, she replied in the same tongue.

"Oh, really no apology is needed, Mr Rolfe."

He glanced at her inquiringly.

"I—I really haven't the pleasure of your name," he said, still upon the doorstep of the office. At all events, she was rather good-looking and well-bred, even if her stature was a trifle diminutive. Her gown was in excellent taste, too.

"My name really doesn't matter," she laughed. "I know you quite well. You are Mr Charles Rolfe, old Mr Statham's secretary."

Then, in an instant, the troth flashed across his mind. This girl must be one of old Sam's friends—one of his secret agents controlled and paid from the office in Old Broad Street.

"You wish to speak to me—eh?" he asked, in a quick, businesslike way.

"Yes; I do. Let us stroll somewhere where we can talk." Then after a moment's reflection she added: "The Tuileries Gardens would be a good place. We might avoid eavesdroppers there."

"Certainly," he said, and, rather interested in the adventure, he strolled along at her side. She put up her pale blue sunshade, for it was a hot day, and at that hour the Avenue was deserted, for the work-girls were not yet out from the numerous ateliers in the neighbourhood, and half Paris was away at the spas or at the sea.

Rolfe knew many of old Sam's spies, but had never seen this English girl before. That she was a lady seemed evident by her manner and speech, and that she had something of importance to tell him was plain. She had, no doubt, learned of his flying visit to Paris—for he meant to leave for London at four o'clock—and had come to the office in order that he could not escape her.

As he walked beside her, a well-set-up figure in dark grey flannel, he cast a furtive glance at the pretty, dark-complexioned face beneath the turquoise sunshade. She looked younger than she was, for her skirts only reached to her ankles, displaying a neat brown shoe tied with large bows. Across her brow was just a tiny wisp of stray hair, reminding him forcibly of the sweet countenance of his lost love. He recollected how he used to tease her about that unruly little lock, and how often he used to tenderly brush it back from her eyes.

"You live in Paris?" he asked as they walked together.

"Sometimes," was her rather vague reply. "I'm always fond of it, for it is so bright and pleasant after—" and she was on the point of giving him a clue to her place of abode, but stopped her words in time.

"After what?" he asked.

"After other places," she answered evasively.

He glanced at her again, wondering whom she might be. A girl of her age could scarcely act as secret agent in financial matters. Her white gown perhaps gave her a more girlish appearance than she otherwise possessed, but there could be no two opinions that she was really good-looking.

She had approached him with timidity and modesty, yet in those few minutes of their acquaintance she had already become quite friendly, and they were already laughing together as they crossed the Rue de Rivoli.

"I knew you were in Paris, and came here specially to meet you, Mr Rolfe," she said at last. "I'm afraid you must think me very dreadful to purposely compel you to apologise and speak to me."

"Not at all. Only—well, I think you know you have a rather unfair advantage of me. You ought to give me your name," he urged.

"I have my own reasons for not doing so," she laughed. "It is sufficient for you to know that I am your friend."

"And a very charming little friend, too," he laughed. "I only wish all my friends were so dainty as yourself."

"Ah! so you are a flatterer—eh?" she said, reproving him with a smile.

"Not flattery—but the truth," he declared, filled with curiosity as to whom she might be. Why, he wondered, had she sought him? Perhaps if he described her at the office they had just left, she might be known there.

Though out of the season, there was still life and movement in the Rue de Rivoli, as there always is between the Magasins du Louvre and the Rue Castiglione. The tweeds and blouses of the Cook's tourists were in evidence as usual, and the little midinette tripped gaily through the throng.

At last they entered the gate of the public gardens, which in the afternoons are given over to nurses in white caps and children with air-balls, and, walking some distance, still chatting, presently found a seat in full view of the Quai with its traffic and the sluggish Seine beyond.

Then as he seated himself beside her she, with her sunshade held behind her head, threw herself back slightly and laughed saucily in his face, displaying her red lips and even, pearly teeth.

"Isn't this a rather amusing meeting?" she asked, with tantalising air. "I know you are dying to know who I am. Just think. Have you never seen me before?"

Charlie was puzzled—sorely puzzled. He tried to think, but to his knowledge he had never previously set eyes upon the dark-haired little witch before in all his life.

"I—well I really don't recollect. You've asked me a riddle, and I've given it up."

"But think. Have you never seen me before?"

"In London?"

"No; somewhere else—a long way from here."

He shook his head. She was a complete enigma this girl not yet out of her teens.

"I must apologise to you, but I do not recollect," he said. "If you refuse to tell me who you are, you can surely give me your Christian name."

"Why?"

"Well, because—"

"Because of your natural curiosity!" she declared. "Men are always curious. They always want to get at hard facts. Half the romance of life is taken away by their desire to go straight to the truth of things. Women are fond of a little imagination."

Was she merely carrying on a mild flirtation with him because of a sheer love of romance? He had heard of girls of her age, overfed upon romantic novels and filled with daydreams, starting out upon adventures similarly perilous. He looked into her eyes, and saw that they danced with tantalising merriment. She was making fun of him!

"My curiosity is certainly natural," he said, a little severely, piqued by her superiority. "You have told me that you wish to speak with me in confidence. How can I repose equal confidence in you if you refuse me your name?"

"I do not ask you to repose confidence in me, Mr Rolfe," was her quick response, opening her eyes widely. "I have brought you here to tell you something—something which I know will greatly interest you, more so, indeed, than the question of whom and what I am."

"Then tell me your Christian name, so that I may address you by that."

For a moment she did not reply. Her gaze was fixed straight before her. The wind stirred the dusty leaves above them, causing them to sigh slightly, while before them along the Quai a big cream-coloured automobile sped swiftly, trumpeting loudly.

At last she turned to him, and with a smile upon her fresh dimpled cheeks, she said:

"My name is a rather unusual one—Lorena."

"Lorena!" he echoed. "What a very pretty name! Almost as charming as its owner!"

She moved with a gesture of mock impatience, declaring: "You are really too bad, Mr Rolfe! Why do you say these things?"

"I only speak the truth. I feel flattered that you should deign to take notice of such an unimportant person as myself."

"Unimportant!" she cried, again opening her eyes and making a quick gesture which showed foreign residence. "Is Mr Statham's secretary an unimportant man?"

"Certainly."

"But he is of importance to one person at least."

"To whom?"

For a moment she did not answer. Then, she turned her dark eyes full upon his, and replied:

"To the woman who loves him!"

Charlie started perceptibly. What could the girl mean? Did she mean that she herself entertained affection for him, or was she merely hinting at what she believed might possibly be the case—that he was beloved.

He was more than ever dumbfounded by her attitude. There was something very mysterious about her—a mystery increased by her own sweet, piquante and unconventional manner. In his whole career he had never met with a similar adventure. At one moment he doubted her genuineness, but at the next he reflected how, at the first moment of their meeting, she had been extremely anxious to speak with him alone. Her attitude was of one who had some confidential information to impart— something no doubt in the interests of the world-renowned firm of Statham Brothers.

Other secret agents of Sam Statham whom he had seen on their visits to Park Lane had been mostly men and women advanced in age, for the most part wearing an outward aspect of severe respectability. Some were, however, the reverse. One was a well-known dancer at the music-halls of Paris and Vienna, whose pretty face looked out from postcards in almost every shop on the Continent.

But the question was, who could be this dainty girl who called herself Lorena?

"What do you mean by the woman who loves me?" he asked her presently, after a pause. "I don't quite follow you. Who does me the great honour of entertaining any affection for me?"

"Who? Can you really ask that?" she said. "Ask yourself?"

"I have asked myself," he laughed, rather uneasily, meeting her glance and wavering beneath it.

"Ah! you will not admit the truth, I see," she remarked, raising her finger in shy reproof.

"Of what?"

"That you are beloved—that you are the lover of Maud Petrovitch!"

"Maud Petrovitch!" he gasped. "You know her? Tell me," he cried quickly.

"I have told you," she answered. "I have stirred your memory of a fact which you have apparently forgotten, Mr Rolfe."

"Forgotten—forgotten Maud!" he exclaimed. "I have never for a moment forgotten her. She is lost to me—and you know it. Tell me the truth. Where is she? *Where can I see her?*"

But the girl only shook her head slowly in sadness. Over her bright, merry face had fallen a sudden gloom, a look of deep regret and dark despair.

"Where is she?" he demanded, springing up from the seat and facing his companion.

But she made no response. She only stared blankly before her at the dark sluggish waters of the Seine.

Chapter Thirty Five
In which there is another Mystery

The girl puzzled him.

Her attitude was as though she delighted in tantalising him, as if she held knowledge superior to his own. And so she did. She was evidently aware of the whereabouts of Maud—his own lost love.

He repeated his question, his eyes fixed upon her pale, serious countenance. But she made no response.

"Why have you brought me here, Miss Lorena?" he asked. "You told me you had something to tell me."

"So I have," she answered, looking up at him again. "I don't know, Mr Rolfe, what opinion you must have of me, but I hope you will consider my self-introduction permissible under the circumstances."

"Why, of course," he declared, for truth to tell he was much interested in her. She seemed so charmingly unconventional, not much more than a schoolgirl, and yet with all the delightful sweetness of budding womanhood. "But you have mentioned the name of a woman—a woman who is lost to me."

"Ah! Maud Petrovitch," she sighed. "Yes. I know. I know all the tragic story."

"The tragic story?" he echoed, staring at her. "What do you mean?"

"I mean the tragic story of your love," was her slow, distinct reply. "Pray forgive me, Mr Rolfe, for mentioning a subject which must be most painful, but I have only done so to show you that I am aware of the secret of your affection."

"Then you are a friend of Maud?"

She nodded, without uttering a word.

"Where is she? I must see her," he said quickly, with a fierce, anxious look upon his countenance. "This suspense is killing me."

She was silent. Slowly she turned her fine eyes upon his, looking straight into his face.

"You ought surely to know," she said, unflinchingly.

"I—I know! Why? Why do you say that?"

"Because you know the truth—you know why they so suddenly disappeared."

"I know the truth!" he repeated. "Indeed I do not. You are speaking in enigmas, just as you yourself are an enigma, Miss Lorena."

Her lips relaxed into a smile of incredulity.

"Why, Mr Rolfe, do you make a pretence of ignorance, when you are fully aware of the whole of the combination of circumstances which led Doctor Petrovitch and his daughter to escape from London?"

"But, my dear girl!" he cried; "you entirely misjudge me. I am in complete ignorance."

"And yet you were present at Cromwell Road on the night in question!" she said slowly, fixing her eyes calmly upon him.

"Who are you, Miss Lorena, that you should make these direct allegations against me?" he cried, staring at her.

"I am your friend, Mr Rolfe, if you will allow me to act as such."

"My friend!" he cried. "But you are alleging that I have secret knowledge of the Doctor's disappearance—that I make a pretence of ignorance. If I were in possession of the facts, is it feasible that I should be so anxious of the welfare of Maud?"

"No anxiety is necessary."

"Then she is alive?"

"I believe so."

"And well?"

"Yes, she is quite well. But—"

"But what?" he demanded. "Speak, Lorena. Speak, I beg of you."

She had hesitated, and he saw by her contracted brow that anxiety had arisen within her mind.

"Well—she is safe, I believe, up to the present. Yet if what I fear be true, she is daily nay, hourly, in peril—in deadliest peril."

"Peril!" he gasped. "Of what?"

"Of her life. You know that the political organisations of the East are fraught with murder plots. Dr Petrovitch has opponents—fierce, dastardly opponents, who would hesitate at nothing to encompass his end. They have intrigued to induce the King to place him in disgrace, but at Belgrade the Petrovitch party are still predominant. It is only in the country—at Nisch and Pirot—where the Opposition is really strong."

"You seem to know Servia and the complication of Servian politics, mademoiselle?" he remarked.

"Yes, I happen to know something of them. I have made them a study, and I assure you it would be very fascinating if there were not quite so many imprisonments in the awful fortress of Belgrade, and secret assassination. But Servia is a young country," the girl added, with a philosophic air, "and all young countries must go through the same periods of unrest and internal trouble. At any rate, all parties in Servia acknowledge that King Peter is a constitutional monarch, and is doing his utmost for the benefit of his people."

"You are a partisan of the Karageorgevitch?"

"I am. I make no secret of it. Alexander and Draga were mere puppets in the hands of Servia's enemies. Under King Peter the country is once more prosperous, and, after all, political life there is no more fraught with danger than it is in go-ahead Bulgaria. Did they not kill poor Petkoff the other day in the Boris Garden in Sofia? That was a more cruel and dastardly murder than any in Servia, for Petkoff had only one arm, and was unable to defend himself. The other was shot away at the Shipka where he fought for his country against the Turk."

"How is it you know so much of Servia?" Charlie inquired, for he found himself listening to the girl's sound arguments with much interest. Her views upon the complicated situation in the Near East were almost identical with his. "Did you ever see Petkoff, for instance?"

"I knew him well. Twice I've dined at his house is Sofia. Strangely enough, he was with his bosom friend Stambuloff when the latter was assassinated, and for years was a marked man. As Prince Ferdinand's Prime Minister, which he was at the time he was shot, he introduced many reforms into Bulgaria, and was a patriot to the core."

He was surprised. Who could this girl be who dined with Prime Ministers, and who was, apparently, behind the scenes of Balkan politics?

"And you fear lest the same fate should befall Maud. Why?" he asked.

"Because the Opposition has a motive—a strong motive."

"For the secret assassination of the daughter of the man who has made Servia what she is!" he exclaimed.

"Yes. Maud is in peril."

"And for that reason, I suppose, is living incognito?"

"Possibly," she answered, not without hesitation. "There is, I believe, a second reason."

"What is that?"

"I scarcely like to tell you, Mr Rolfe. We are strangers, you and I."

"But do tell me. I am very anxious to know. If she is your friend, she has, no doubt, told you of our love."

"Well, she wishes to avoid you."

"Avoid me—why?"

"Because acquaintance with you increases her peril."

"How absurd!" he cried. "How can her love for me affect her father's political opponents in Servia?"

"I am ignorant of the reasons. I only know the broad facts."

"But the Doctor had retired from active political life long ago! He told me one day how tired he was of the eternal bickerings of the Skuptchina."

"Of course he had ostensibly retired, but he secretly directed the policy of the present Government. In all serious matters King Peter still consults him."

"And that is why you have brought me into the privacy of these gardens, Miss Lorena—to tell me this!" he laughed, bending to her and drawing a semi-circle in the gravel with the point of his stick.

"No," she replied sharply, with just a little frown of displeasure. "You do not understand me, Mr Rolfe. Have I not said, a few moments ago, that I wanted to be your friend?"

"You are a most delightful little friend," was his courteous reply.

"Ah! I see. You treat me as a child," was her rather impatient reply. "You are not serious."

"I am most serious," he declared, with a solemn face. "Indeed, I was never more serious in my life than I am at this moment."

She burst out laughing—a peal of light, merry, irresponsible, girlish laughter.

"And before I met you," she said, "I thought you a most terribly austere person."

"So I am—at times. I have to be, Miss Lorena. I'm secretary to a very serious old gentleman, remember."

"Yes. And that was the very reason why I threw the convenances to the winds—if there are any in the Anglo-French circle in Paris—and spoke to you—a perfect stranger."

"You spoke because I was Mr Statham's secretary?" he asked, somewhat puzzled.

"Yes. I wanted to speak to you privately."

"Well, nobody can overhear us here," he said glancing around, and noticing only a fat *bonne* wheeling a puny child in a gaudily-trapped perambulator.

"I wanted to speak to you regarding Mr Statham," she said, after a long pause. "I ascertained you were coming to Paris, and waited in order to see you."

"Why?" he asked, much surprised. The refusal of her name, her determination to conceal her identity, her friendship for Maud, and her intimate acquaintance with thing Servian, all combined to puzzle him to the verge of distraction. Who was she? What was she?

The mystery of the Doctor and his daughter was an increasing one. His pretended ignorance of certain facts had been unmasked by her in a manner which showed that she was aware of the actual truth. Was she really a secret messenger from the girl he loved so devotedly—the girl with whom he had last walked and talked with in the quietness of the London sundown in Nevern Square?

He glanced again at her pretty but mysterious face. She was a lady—refined, well-educated, with tiny white hands and well-shod feet. There was nothing of the artificial *chic* of the Parisienne about her, but a quiet dignity which seemed almost incongruous in one so young. Indeed, he wondered that she was allowed about in the streets of Paris alone, without a chaperone.

Her piquante manner, and her utter disregard of all conventionality, amused him. True, she was older than Maud but most possibly her bosom friend. If so, Maud was probably in hiding in Paris, and this pretty girl had been sent to him as Cupid's messenger.

"I wanted to see you on a matter which closely concerns Mr Statham."

"Anything that concerns Mr Statham concerns myself, Miss Lorena," he said. "I am his confidential secretary."

"I have ascertained that, otherwise I would not have dared to speak to you. I want to warn you."

"Of what?"

"Of a deeply-laid conspiracy to wreck Mr Statham's life," she said. "There have arisen recently two men who are now determined to lay bare the secret of the millionaire's past, in revenge for some old grievance, real or fancied."

"For the purposes of blackmail—eh?" he asked. "Every rich man is constantly being subjected to attempted blackmail in some form or other."

"No. They have no desire to obtain money. Their sole intention is to expose Mr Statham."

"Most men who are unsuccessful are eager to denounce the methods of their more fortunate friends," he said, smiling. "Mr Statham has no fear of exposure, I assure you." The girl looked him straight in the face with a long, steady gaze.

"Ah! I see?" she exclaimed, after a pause. "You treat me as an enemy, Mr Rolfe; not as a friend."

Chapter Thirty Six
The Locked Door in Park Lane

"Excuse me, Miss Lorena, I do not," he declared quickly. "Only we have heard so many threats of exposure that to cease to regard them seriously. Mr Statham's high reputation is sufficient guarantee to the public."

"I quite admit that," answered the girl. "It is not the present that is in question, but the past."

"In these days of hustle, a man's past matters but little. It is what he is, not what he was, which the public recognise."

"Personally," she said, "I hold Mr Statham in highest esteem. I have never met him, it's true, but I have knowledge of certain kind and generous actions on his part, actions which have brought happiness and prosperity to those who have fallen upon misfortune. For that reason I resolved to speak to you and warn you of the plot in progress. Do you happen to know a certain Mr John Adams?"

Rolfe started, and stared at her. What could she know of the Damoclean sword suspended over the house of Statham?

"Well," he answered guardedly, "I once met a man of that name, I think."

"Recently?"

"About a month ago."

"You knew nothing of him prior to that?"

Rolfe hesitated. "Well, no," he replied.

"He made pretence of being friendly with you."

"Yes. But to tell you the truth I was somewhat suspicions of him. What do you know of him? Tell me."

"I happen to be well acquainted with him," the girl responded. "It is he who has arisen like one from the grave, and intends to avenge the wrong which he declares that Mr Statham had done him."

"Recently?"

"No, years ago, when they were abroad together—and Mr Statham was still a poor man."

Charlie Rolfe was silent. He knew Adams; he knew, too, that evil was intended. He had warned old Sam Statham, but the latter had not heeded. Adams had had the audacity to approach him in confidence, believing that he might be bought over. When he had discovered that the millionaire's secretary was incorruptible, he openly declared his sinister intentions.

"I had no idea you were acquainted with Adams," he said, still puzzled to know who she was, and what was her motive.

"I happen to know certain details of the plot," she answered.

"And you will reveal them to me?" he asked in quick anxiety.

"Upon certain conditions."

"And what are they? I am all attention."

"The first is that you will not seek to learn the identity of the person who is associated with Mr Adams in the forthcoming exposure; and the second is that you say nothing to Mr Statham regarding our secret meeting."

"Why?" he asked, not quite understanding the reason of her last stipulation. "I thought you wished to warn Mr Statham?"

"No. I warn you. You can take measures of precaution, on Mr Statham's behalf without making explanation."

"Mr Statham has already seen John Adams and recognised him. He is already forewarned."

"And he has not taken any steps in self-defence?" she cried quickly.

"Why need he trouble?"

"Why, because that man Adams has sworn to hound him to self-destruction."

Rolfe shrugged his shoulders, and replied:

"Mr Statham has really no apprehension of any unpleasantness, Miss Lorena. It is true that in the old days the two men were friends, and, apparently, they quarrelled. Adams was lost for years to all who knew him, and now suddenly reappears to find his old acquaintance wealthy beyond the dreams of avarice, and seeks, as many more before him have done, to profit by his former friendship."

"Or enmity," added the girl, lowering her sunshade a little until for a moment it hid her features. "I do not think you realise the dastardly cunning of the plot in progress. It has not only as its object the ruin of the credit of the house of Statham Brothers, but the creation of a scandal which Mr Samuel Statham will not dare to face. He must either fly the country, or commit suicide."

"Well?"

"The latter is expected by the two men who have combined and are now perfecting their ingenious conspiracy. It is believed by them that he will take his own life."

Charlie Rolfe reflected for a moment. He recollected old Sam's terrible agitation on the day when he recognised John Adams leaning against the railings of the Park. Of late, the great financier had betrayed signs of unusual nervousness, and had complained several times of insomnia. To his secretary knowledge he had spent two nights that very week in walking the streets of London from midnight until dawn, ostensibly to do charitable actions to the homeless, but in reality because his mind was becoming unbalanced by the constant strain of not knowing from one moment to another when Adams would deal his staggering blow.

Had there been any question of blackmail, the aid of solicitors and of Scotland Yard could have been invoked. But there had been no threat beyond the statement made openly to Rolfe by the man who intended to encompass the ruin of the eccentric millionaire and philanthropist.

"I think, Miss Lorena, that we need have no fear of Mr Statham doing anything rash," he said. "But why is it hoped that he will prefer to take his life rather than face any exposure?"

"Because they will profit by his death—profit to an enormous degree."

"But how can Adams profit? He has had no dealings with Mr Statham of late."

"Not Adams, but his friend. The latter will become wealthy."

"And may I not know his name?"

"No. That is the stipulation which I make. For the present it is sufficient that you should be made aware of the broad lines of the plot, and that its main object is the death of Samuel Statham."

"And you wish me to tell him all this?"

"Certainly, only without explaining that I was your informant."

"Why do you wish to conceal the fact, Miss Lorena?" he asked. "Surely he would be only too delighted to be able to thank you for your warning?"

She shook her head, saying:

"If it were known that I had exposed their plans it would place me in peril. They are determined and relentless men, who would willingly sacrifice a woman in order to gain their ends, which in this case is a large fortune."

"And you will not tell me the name of Adams's associate in the matter?"

"No. I—I cannot do that. Please do not ask me," she answered hurriedly.

Rolfe was again silent for a few moments. At last he asked:

"Cannot you tell me something of the past relations between Adams and Statham? You seem to know all the details of the strange affair."

"Adams makes certain serious allegations which he can substantiate. There is a certain witness whom Mr Statham believes to be dead, but who is still alive, and is now in England."

"A witness—of what?" asked Rolfe quickly.

"Of the crime which Adams alleges."

"Crime—what crime?" ejaculated the young man in surprise, staring at his pretty companion.

"Some serious offence, but of what nature I am not permitted to explain to you."

"Why not, Miss Lorena? You must! Remember that Mr Statham is in ignorance of this—I mean that Adams intends to charge him with a crime. Surely the position is most serious! I imagined that Adams's charges were criticism of Mr Statham's methods of finance."

"Finance does not enter into it at all," said the girl. "The delegation is a secret crime by which the millionaire laid the foundation of his fortune; a crime committed abroad, and of which there are two witnesses still living, men who were, until a few weeks ago, believed to be dead.

"But you tell me that Adams's associate will, if Mr Statham commits suicide, profit to an enormous amount. Will you not explain? If this is so, why have they not attempted to levy blackmail? If the charge has foundation— which I do not for one moment believe—then surely Mr Statham would be prepared to make payment and hush up the affair? He would not be human if he refused."

"The pair are fully alive to the danger of any attempt to procure money by promise of secrecy," she replied. "They have already fully considered the matter, and arrived at the conclusion that to compel Mr Statham to take his own life is the wiser and easier course."

"You seem to be in their confidence, Miss Lorena?" he said, gazing at the pretty girl at his side.

"Yes, I am. That is why I am unable to reveal to you the name of Adams's companion," she replied. "All I can tell you is that the intention is to make against him a terrible charge of which they possess evidence which is, apparently, overwhelming."

"Then you know the charge it is intended to bring against him—eh?"

"Yes," was her prompt answer. "To me it seems outrageous, incomprehensible—and yet—"

"Well?"

"And yet, if it is really true, it would account to a very great degree for Mr Statham's eccentricity of which I've so often read in the papers. No one enters his house in Park Lane. Is not that so?"

"He is shy, and does not care for strangers," was Rolfe's response.

"But it said in the paper only a week ago that nobody has ever been upstairs in that house except himself. There is a door on the stairs, they say, which is always kept locked and bolted."

"And if that is so?"

"Well—have you ever been upstairs, Mr Rolfe. Tell me; I'm very anxious to know."

"I make no secret of it," was his reply, smiling the while. "I have never been upstairs. Entrance there is forbidden."

"Even to you—his confidential secretary?"

"Yes, even to me."

"And yet there are signs of the upstairs' rooms being occupied," she remarked. "I have seen lights there myself, as I've passed the house. I was along Park Lane late one evening last week."

"So you have been recently in London?"

"London is my home. I am only here on a visit," was her reply. "And ascertaining you were coming here, I resolved to see you."

"And has this serious allegation which Adams intends to bring any connection with the mystery concerning the mansion?"

"Yes. It has."

"In what way?"

She paused, as though uncertain whether or not to tell the truth.

"Because," she said at last, "because I firmly believe, from facts known to me, that confirmation of the truth of Adams's charge will be discovered beyond that locked door!"

Chapter Thirty Seven
Max Barclay is Inquisitive

"Miss Rolfe has left the firm's employ, sir."

"Left—left Cunnington's?" gasped Max Barclay, staring open-mouthed at Mr Warner, the buyer.

"Yes, sir. She left suddenly yesterday morning," repeated the dapper little man with the pen behind his ear.

"But this is most extraordinary—to leave at a moment's notice! I thought she was so very comfortable here. She always spoke so kindly of you, and for the consideration with which you always treated her."

"It was very kind of her, I'm sure," replied the buyer; "but it is the rule here—a moment's notice on either side."

"But why? Why has she left?"

Warner hesitated. He, of course, knew the truth, but he was not anxious to speak it.

"Some little misunderstanding, I think."

"With you?"

"Oh, dear no. She was called down to the counting-house yesterday morning, and she did not return."

"Then she's been discharged—eh?" asked Max in a hard voice.

"I believe so, sir. At least, it would appear so."

"And are they in the habit of discharging assistants in this manner—throwing them out of a home and out of employment at a moment's notice? Is Mr Cunnington himself aware of it?"

"It would be Mr Cunnington himself who discharged her," was the buyer's answer. "No other person has authority either to engage or discharge."

"But there must be a reason for her dismissal!" exclaimed Max.

"Certainly. But only Mr Cunnington knows that."

"Can I see him?"

"Well, at this hour he's generally very busy indeed; but if you go down to the counting-house in the next building, and ask for him, he may give you a moment."

"Thank you, Mr Warner," Barclay said, a little abruptly, and, turning on his heel, left the department.

"She hasn't told him evidently," remarked one girl-assistant to the other. "I'm sorry Rolfie's gone. She wasn't half a bad sort. She was old Warner's favourite, too, or her young gentleman would never have been allowed to talk to her in the shop. If you or I had had a young man to come and see us as she had, we'd have been fired out long ago."

"I wonder who her young man really is," remarked the second girl, watching him as he strode out, a lithe figure in a well-cut suit of grey tweeds.

"Well, he's a thorough gentleman, just like her brother," remarked her companion. "I saw him in his motor-boat up at Hampton the Sunday before last. He's completely gone on her. I wonder what'll happen now. I don't think much of the new girl; do you? Does her hair awfully badly." Unconscious of the criticism he had evoked, Max Barclay descended the stairs, passed through the long shops—crowded as they always were in the afternoon—into the adjoining building, and sought audience of the titular head of the great firm.

After waiting for some time in an outer office he was shown in. The moment he asked his question Mr Cunnington grasped the situation.

"I very much regret, sir, that it is not my habit to give information to a second party concerning the dismissal of any of my assistants. If the young lady applies for her character, she is perfectly entitled to have it."

"But I apply for her character," said Max promptly.

"You are not an employer, sir. She has not applied to you for a situation."

"No; but I may surely know the reason she has left your service?" Max pointed out. "Her brother, who is abroad just now, is my most intimate friend."

Mr Cunnington stroked his dark beard thoughtfully, but shook his head, saying:

"I much regret, Mr Barclay, that I am unable to give you the information you seek. Would it not be better to ask the young lady herself?"

"But she has left, and I have no idea of her address!" exclaimed Barclay. "Can you furnish me with it?"

The head of Cunnington's, Limited, took up the telephone receiver and asked for a certain Mr Hughes, of whom he made inquiry if Miss Rolfe had left her address.

There was a wait of a few moments, then Mr Cunnington turned and said:

"The young lady left no address. She was asked, but refused to give one."

Max's heart sank within him. She had been dismissed at an instant's notice, and was lost to him. He turned upon Mr Cunnington in quick anger and said:

"So I am to understand that you refuse me all information concerning her?"

"I merely adhere to my rule, sir. Any dismissal of my assistants is a matter between myself and the person dismissed. I am not called upon to give details or reasons to outsiders. I regret that I am very busy, and must wish you good afternoon."

Max Barclay bit his lip. He did not like the brisk, business-ike air of the man.

"I shall call upon Mr Statham, whom I happen to know," he said. "And I shall invoke his aid."

"You are perfectly at liberty to do just as you like, my dear sir. Even Mr Statham exercises no authority over the assistants in this establishment. It is my own department and I brook no interference."

Max did not reply, but left the office and strode out into Oxford Street, pushing past the crowd of women around the huge shop-windows admiring the feminine finery there displayed so temptingly.

Marion—his Marion—had disappeared. She had been dismissed—in disgrace evidently; probably for some petty fault or for breaking one of the hundred rules by which every assistant was bound. He had always heard Mr Cunnington spoken of as a most lenient, and even generous, employer, yet his treatment of Marion had been anything but just or humane.

When he thought of it his blood boiled. Charlie was away, he knew. He had telephoned to his rooms that very morning, but his man had replied that his master had left hurriedly for the Continent—for Paris, he thought.

At the corner of Bond Street he halted, and glanced at his watch. Should he try and find Charlie by telegraph or should he take the bull by the horns and go and see old Sam Statham. His well-beloved had disappeared. Would the old financier assist him to discover the truth?

He was well aware that for a comparative stranger to be deceived in that big house in Park Lane was exceptional. Old Levi had his orders, and few among the many callers ever placed their foot over the carefully-guarded threshold. Still, he resolved to make the attempt, and, with that object, jumped into a taxi-cab which happened at the moment to be passing.

Alighting at the house, he presented his card to old Levi, who opened the door, and asked the favour of a few moments' conversation with Mr Statham? The old servant scrutinised the card closely, and took stock of the visitor, who, noticing his hesitation, added: "Mr Statham will remember me, I believe."

Levi asked him into the hall, with a dissatisfied grunt, and disappeared, to return a few moments later, and usher the visitor into the presence of the millionaire.

Old Samuel, who had been dozing over a newspaper in the his easy-chair near the fireplace, rose, and, through his spectacles, regarded his visitor with some suspicion. The blinds were drawn, shading the room from the afternoon sun, therefore Max found the place was in comparative darkness after the glare outside.

In a few moments, however, when his eyes grew accustomed to the semi-darkness, he saw the old fellow wave his hand in the direction of a chair, saying:

"I'm very glad you called, Mr Barclay—very glad. Indeed, curiously enough, I intended to write to you only yesterday upon a business matter, but I was too busy."

Barclay seated himself, full of surprise that the great financier should wish to consult him upon any business matter.

"Well, Mr Statham," he said, "I may as well tell you at once that I am here to seek your kind assistance and help in a purely personal matter—a matter which closely concerns my own happiness."

Statham pricked up his ears. He knew what was coming. Marion Rolfe had told him of her visit there.

"Well?" he asked coldly, in a changed manner.

"You possibly are unaware that I am engaged to be married to Marion Rolfe, the sister of your secretary, a young lady in whom you were kind enough to take an interest am obtain for her a situation at Cunnington's."

The old man nodded, his countenance sphinx-like.

"The lady in question has been dismissed by Mr Cunnington at a moment's notice, and he refuses to tell me the reason of his very remarkable action. I want you to be good enough to obtain a response for me."

"And where is the young lady?" asked the wary Statham.

"Nobody knows. She would leave no address."

"Then you are unaware of her whereabouts?"

"She has disappeared."

"Extraordinary!" the old fellow remarked, reflecting deeply for a moment.

"Yes. I cannot imagine why, in the circumstances, she has not written to me," Max declared, the expression upon his face betraying his deep distress.

"It is certainly somewhat strange," the old man agreed. "Girls at Cunnington's are not often discharged in that manner. Cunnington himself is always most lenient. Have you seen him?"

"Yes; and he absolutely refuses any information."

"In that case, Mr Barclay, I don't see very well how I can assist you. The management and organisation of the concern are left to him, as managing director. I really cannot interfere."

"But was it not through you that Marion, without previous experience or apprenticeship, was engaged there?"

"Yes; I have some recollection of sending a line of recommendation to Cunnington," was the millionaire's response. "But, of course, my interest ended there. My secretary asked me to write the note, and I did so."

"Then you really cannot obtain for me the information I desire?"

"But why are you so inquisitive—eh?" snapped the old man. "Surely the lady will tell you the reason of her dismissal!"

"I don't know where she is."

"A fact which is—well—rather curious—shall we designate it?" the old man remarked meaningly.

"You mean to imply that her instant dismissal has cast a slur upon her character, and that she fears to meet me lest she be compelled to tell me the truth?" he said slowly as the suggestion dawned upon him. "Ah! I see. You refuse to help me, Mr Statham, because—because I love her."

And his face became pale, hard-set, and determined.

Chapter Thirty Eight
Friend or Foe?

The two men were silent for some moments. Statham was watching his visitor's face. To him it was, at least, satisfactory to know that Marion had disappeared, fearing to let her lover know the reason of her sudden dismissal lest he should misjudge her.

Truth to tell, he had anticipated that she would have gone straight to Barclay and told him the truth. Within himself he acknowledged that he had played the poor girl a scoundrelly trick, but consoled himself with the thought that when a man's life was at stake, as his was, any mode of escape became justifiable.

At last the old man stirred in his chair, and, turning to Max, said:

"Please understand plainly it is not because I refuse to help you, but because it is not within my province to dictate to Cunnington replies regarding his assistants."

"But you hold a controlling interest in the firm," declared the other.

"That may be so, but I have nothing to do with the details of organisation," he replied. "No, Mr Barclay, let us end this matter with an expression of my regret at being unable to assist you. Perhaps, however, I may be able to do so in another direction."

"In another direction!" he echoed. "How?"

"In a small matter of business."

Max Barclay was both surprised and interested. He knew quite well that Statham could if he wished, give him previous knowledge that would enable him to make a considerable coup. Ignorance of Marion's visit to the old man or the cause of her dismissal allowed him to regard the millionaire with feelings of friendliness, and to reflect that, after all, he had no power to dictate to Cunnington.

"You know, Mr Barclay," he said, "I frequently obtain confidential knowledge of what is transpiring in the world of finance. The other day it came to my ears, through a source it is unnecessary to mention, that the Adriatic railway concession has been placed before you."

Max opened his eyes. He believed that not a soul except the man who had joined him in partnership was aware of this. The information must have come from Constantinople, he thought.

"That is true," he admitted.

"A big thing!" remarked the old man in his croaking voice. "A very big thing indeed—means prosperity to the Balkan countries. But pardon me if I ask one or two questions. Do not think I have any intention of going behind your back, or attempting to upset your plans. I merely ask for information, because, as perhaps you know, there is but one man in London who could float such a thing, and it is myself."

"I know, Mr Statham, that we shall be compelled to come to you when we have the concession all in order."

"You will," he said with a smile. "But can you, without injury to yourself, tell me who is your associate in this business?"

"A Frenchman—Mr Jean Adam, of Constantinople." Statham's face never moved a muscle. Of this he was already quite well aware.

"An old friend of yours, I suppose?"

"Not—not exactly an old friend. I met him for the first time about a month or so ago," responded Max.

"And what do you know of him?"

"Nothing much except that I believe him to be a man of the highest integrity and the possessor of many friends interested in high finance."

"Oh! and what causes you to believe that?"

"Well, we first met in Paris, where, having mooted the idea of a partnership, he introduced me to several well-known people, among them Baron Tellier, who arranged the match monopoly of Turkey, and Herr Hengelmann, of Frankfort, whom, no doubt, you know as the concessionaire of the German railway from the Bosphorus to Bagdad."

The old man gave vent to a dissatisfied grant.

"Both men stand very high in the financial world, do they not?" Max asked.

"Well—they did," replied old Sam, smiling.

"Did? What, have they gone under?"

"No. Only Hengelmann has been in his coffin fully two years, and the Baron died at Nice last winter."

"What?" cried Max, starting forward.

"I repeat what I say, Mr Barclay. Your friend Adam has been indulging in a pretty fiction."

"Are you sure? Are you quite sure they are dead?"

"Most certainly. I was staying in the same hotel at Nice when the Baron died, and I followed him to the grave. He was a great friend of mine."

Max Barclay sat stunned. Until that moment he had believed in Jean Adam and his plausible tales, but he now saw how very cleverly he had been deceived and imposed upon.

"You're surprised," he laughed. "But you must remember that you can get a decent suit of gentlemanly clothes for five pounds, and visiting-cards are only two shillings a hundred. People so often overlook those two important facts in life. Thousands of men can put off their identity with their clothes."

"But Adam—do you happen to know him?" Max asked. "If you do, it will surely be a very friendly act to tell me the truth."

"Well," replied the elder man with some hesitancy, "I may as well tell you at once that the Sultan has never given any concession for the railway from Nisch to San Giovanni di Medua to cross Turkish territory—and will never give it. He fears Bulgaria and Servia too much, for he never knows what Power may be behind them. And, after all, who can blame him? Why should he open his gates to an enemy? Albania is always in unrest, for in the north the Christians predominate, and there is bound to be trouble ere long."

"Then you believe that the whole thing is a fiction?"

"Most certainly it is. If there was any idea of the Sultan giving an iradé, I should most certainly know of it. I have good agents in Constantinople. No. Take it from me that the concession will never be given. It is not to Turkey's interest to allow the development of Servia and Bulgaria, therefore your friend's pretty tale is all a fairy story."

"Then why is he pressing me to go out to Constantinople?" Max asked.

Statham shrugged his shoulders, indicative of ignorance.

"Perhaps he thinks you will plank down money?" he suggested.

"He wants nothing until I myself am satisfied with the *bonâ fides* of the business."

"Stuff on his part, most likely. He's a past-master of the art."

"How well do you know him?"

"Sufficiently well to have nothing to do with him."

"Then that accounts for his refusal to allow me to confide in you," said Barclay. "I see the reason now."

"Of course, act just as you think fit. Only recollect that what I've told you is bed-rock fact. The man who calls himself Adam is a person to be avoided."

"Have you had dealings with him?"

"Just once—and they had a very unpleasant result."

He reflected upon certain remarks and criticisms which the Frenchman had uttered concerning Statham and his normal methods. In the light of what he now knew, he saw that the two men were enemies. It seemed as though one man wished to tell him something, and yet was hesitant.

"Have you put any money into the scheme?" the millionaire asked.

"Not yet."

"Then don't. Tell him to take it somewhere else. Better still, tell him to bring it to me. You need not, however, say that it is I who warned you. Leave him in the dark in that direction. He's a clever fellow—extraordinarily clever. Who is with him now?"

"Well, he has a friend named Lyle—a mining engineer."

"Leonard Lyle—a hunchback?" asked Statham quickly.

The millionaire's countenance went a trifle paler, and about the corners of his thin lips was a hard expression. To him, the seriousness of the conspiracy was only too apparent.

Those two men intended that he should be driven to take his own life—to die an ignominious death.

"You've spoken to this man Lyle?" he asked in as steady a voice as he could.

"Once or twice. He seems to possess a very intimate knowledge of Servia, Bulgaria, and European Turkey. Is he an adventurer like Adam?"

"Not exactly," was the rather ambiguous reply. "But his association with Adam shows plainly that fraud is intended."

"But why does he want me to go post-haste out to Turkey?" queried Max, who had risen from his chair in the excitement of this sudden revelation which caused his brilliant scheme to vanish into thin air.

"To induce confidence, I expect he would have introduced you to some men wearing fezzes, and declared them to be Pashas high in favour at the Yildiz Kiosk. Then before you left Constantinople he would have held you to your bargain to put money into the thing. Oh! never fear, you would have fallen a victim in one way or another. So it's best that you should know the character of the two men with whom you are dealing. Take my advice; treat them with caution, but refuse to stir from London. They will, no doubt, use every persuasion to induce you to go, but your best course is to hear all their arguments, watch the gradual development of their scheme, and inform me of it. Will you do it?"

"Will my information assist you in any way, Mr Statham?"

"Yes, it will—very materially," the old man answered.

"I have revealed to you the truth, and I ask you, in return, to render me this little assistance. What I desire to know, is their movements daily, and how they intend to act."

"Towards whom?"

"Towards myself."

"Then they are associated against you, you believe?"

"I suspect them to be," the old man replied. "I know them to be my enemies. They are, like thousands of other men, jealous of my success, and believe they have a grievance against me—one that is entirely unfounded."

"And if I do this will you assist me to obtain knowledge of the reason why Marion Rolfe has been dismissed?" asked Max eagerly.

The old man hesitated, but only for a second. It was easy enough to give him a letter to Cunnington, and afterwards to telephone to Oxford Street instructions to the head of the firm to refuse a reply.

So, consenting, he took a sheet of note-paper, and scribbled a few lines of request to Mr Cunnington, which he handed to Max, saying:

"There, I hope that will have the desired effect, Mr Barclay. On your part, remember, you will keep in with Adam and Lyle, and give me all the information you can gather. I know how to repay a friendly service rendered to me, so you are, no doubt, well aware. You will be welcome here at any hour. I shall tell Levi to admit you."

"That's a bargain," the younger man asserted. "When will Rolfe return?"

"To-morrow, or next day. He's in Paris. Shall I tell him you wish to see him?"

"Please."

"But say nothing regarding Adam or his friend. Our compact is a strictly private one, remember."

And then Max, grasping the hands of the man whom he believed was his friend, placed the note in his pocket and went out into the blazing hot September afternoon.

As he disappeared along the pavement the old millionaire watched him unseen from behind the blind.

"To the friendship of that man—that man whom I have wronged—I shall owe my life," he murmured aloud.

And then, crossing to the telephone on his table, he asked for Mr Cunnington.

Chapter Thirty Nine
The City of Unrest

Ten days had passed since Charlie had met the mysterious Lorena in Paris.

To both Charlie and Max—though now separated by the breadth of Europe—they had been breathless, anxious, never-to-be-forgotten days.

The ominous words of Lorena ever recurred to him. Apparently the girl knew far more than she had told him, and her declaration that confirmation of Adams's charges would be found beyond that white-enamelled door in Park Lane gripped his senses. He could think of nothing else.

She had left him in the Rue de Rivoli, outside the Gardens, refusing her address or any further account of herself. She had warned him—that was, she said, all-sufficient.

He blamed himself a thousand times for not having followed her; for not having sought some further information concerning the peril of old Sam Statham.

Yet the afternoon following, just as he was about to drive from the Grand Hotel to the Gare du Nord, to return to London, one of the clerks from Old Broad Street had arrived, bearing a letter from the head of the firm, giving him instructions to proceed to Servia at once and transact certain business with the Government regarding certain copper concessions in the district of Kaopanik. The deal meant the introduction of a considerable amount of British capital into Servia, and had support from his Majesty King Peter downwards. Indeed, all were in favour save the Opposition in the Skuptchina, or Parliament, a set of unruly peasants who opposed every measure the Pashitch Government put forward.

The business brooked no delay. Therefore Charlie, that same night, entered the Orient express, that train of dusty *wagons-lit* which runs three times a week between Paris and Constantinople, and three days later arrived in Belgrade, the Servian capital.

He was no stranger in that rather pleasant town, perched high up at the junction of the Save with the broad Danube. The passport officer at Semlin station recognised him, and gave him a *visa* at once, and on alighting at Belgrade the little ferret-eyed man idling outside the station did not follow him, for he knew him by sight and was well aware that the Grand Hotel was his destination.

There are more spies in Belgrade than in any other city in Europe. So much foreign intrigue is ever in progress that the Servian authorities are compelled to support a whole army of secret agents to watch and report. Hence it is that the stranger, from the moment he sets foot in Belgrade to the moment he leaves it, is watched, and his every movement noted and reported. Yet all is so well managed that the foreigner is never aware of the close surveillance upon him, and Belgrade is as gay a town in the matter of entertaining and general freedom as, well, as any other you may choose to name.

During the days when, owing to the unfortunate events which terminated the reign of the half-imbecile King Alexander and the designing woman who became his Queen, when England had suspended diplomatic negotiations, the great stakes held in the country by Statham Brothers were in a somewhat precarious condition. For two years Servian finance had been in anything but a flourishing condition, but now, under the rule of King Peter, who had done his very utmost to reinstate his country in its former flourishing position, the confidence of Europe had been restored, and Statham Brothers were ready to make further investments.

In Charles Rolfe the great millionaire had the most perfect confidence. The letter he had sent him to Paris was clear and explicit in its instructions. If the concessions were confirmed by the Prime Minister Pashitch and the Council, a million dinars (or francs) were already deposited in the National Bank of Servia, and could be drawn at an hour's notice upon Charlie's signature.

So he drove to the Grand, the hotel with its great garish café, its restaurant where the sterlet is perhaps more delicious than at the Hermitage in Moscow, and its excellent Tzigane band. It was evening, so he ate a light meal, and, fagged out by the journey, retired early.

He tried to sleep, but could not. The noise and clatter of the café below, the weird strains of the gipsy music, the rattle of the cabs over the cobbles, all combined to prevent slumber.

And, over all, was the vivid recollection of that rather handsome girl who had called herself Lorena, and who had declared that the reason of Statham's peril lay behind the door which he always kept so carefully secured.

The hours passed slowly. He thought far more of Maud Petrovitch, and of what Lorena had told him, than of the business he had to transact on the morrow. He was there, in the city where Doctor Petrovitch had been worshipped almost as a demi-god, where the people cheered lustily as he drove out, and where he was called "The Servian Patriot." Where was the statesman now? What was the actual truth of that sadden disappearance?

Why had not Maud written? Sorely she might at least have trusted him with her secret!

The noise below had died away, and he knew that it must be two o'clock in the morning, the hour when the café closed. Presently there came a rap at his door, and the night-porter handed him a telegram. He tore it open mechanically, expecting it to be in cipher from old Sam, but instead saw the signature "Max."

Scanning it eagerly, he held his breath. The news it contained staggered him. It stated that his sister Marion had been discharged from Cunnington's, and her whereabouts were unknown.

"Have seen Statham, but cannot discover where your sister has gone. Can you suggest any friend she may have gone to visit? What shall I do? Am distracted. Wire immediately."

Marion left Cunnington's! Discharged, the telegram said. Was it possible, he thought, that old Sam would allow her discharge. He was certain he would not. He was his sister's friend, as he was his own.

Max's telegram added further to the burden of mystery upon him. What could it all mean?

Marion has evidently left Cunnington's and disappeared! He tried to think to whom she would go in her distress. There was her Aunt Anne at Wimborne, her cousin Lucy who had married the bank manager at Hereford, and there was her old schoolfellow Mary Craven who had only recently married Pelham, the manager of an insurance company in Moorgate Street.

Those three addresses he wrote on a telegraph form, urging Max to make inquiry and report progress. This he despatched, and again threw himself down, full of dark forebodings.

If Marion had really been discharged, she was in some disgrace. What could it possibly be? That it was something which she dared not face was proved by the fact that she had not confided in Max. She knew Maud's place of concealment, without a doubt; therefore, what more natural than she should have joined her?

The whole affair was a complete enigma, rendered the more tantalising by the distance which now separated him from London.

Next morning he rose, took his coffee, and went out along the broad central boulevard, gay and lively in the sunlight, thronged by well-dressed ladies and smart officers in uniforms on the Russian model—as bright and pleasant a scene as can be witnessed anywhere outside Paris. Up the hill, past the royal palace, he went. In the royal garden, separated from the roadway by high iron railings, the band of the Guards were playing, and over the palace floated the royal standard, showing that his Majesty was in residence.

Adjoining the palace was a large square castellated building, painted white, and into this he turned, saluted by the gendarmes on duty. Ascending a broad flight of steps, he passed through the swing doors, presented his card, and was shown into the large antechamber of the President of the Council of Ministers, the strongest man in Servia, Monsieur Nicholas Pashitch.

The long windows commanded a wide view of the tows and of the broad Danube shining in the morning sun, while upon the walls of the sombre apartment with its floor of polished oak and antique furniture covered with crimson plush, was a portrait of King Peter and several full length paintings of dead and gone statesmen.

"His Excellency is engaged for a few moments with the Turkish Minister," exclaimed a frock-coated secretary in French. "But he will give m'sieur audience almost immediately. His Excellency was going to Pirot, but has remained in order to see you. He received your telegram from Budapest."

And so Charlie Rolfe remained, gazing out of the window upon the quaint eastern town, watching the phantasmagoria of life up and down its principal thoroughfare. A company of infantry, headed by their band, marched past, hot and dusty, on their return from the early morning manoeuvres which the King had attended, as was his daily habit; and as it passed out of his sight the long doors opened, and he was ushered into the adjoining room, the private cabinet of his Excellency the Premier, an elderly, pleasant-faced old gentleman with a long grey beard, who rose from his big writing-table to greet his visitor. The meeting was a most cordial one, his Excellency inquiring after the health of his old personal friend Mr Statham.

Then, at the Prime Minister's invitation, Charlie seated himself, and explained the nature of his mission. Monsieur Pashitch heard him with interest to the end. Then he said: "Only yesterday his Majesty expressed to me his desire that we should attract British capital into Servia, therefore all that you tell me is most gratifying to us. Mr Statham, on his last visit here, had audience of his Majesty—on the occasion of the loan—and I think they found themselves perfectly in accord. The development of the Kaopanik has long been desired, and I will this afternoon inform his Majesty of your visit and your proposals."

Charlie then produced certain documents, reports of two celebrated mining engineers who had been sent out to Kaopanik by Statham Brothers, and these they discussed for a long time.

Presently Rolfe said:

"By the way, your Excellency, have you heard of late anything from Doctor Petrovitch?"

"Petrovitch!" exclaimed the old statesman, starting quickly. "Petrovitch? No!" he almost snapped.

"He has been living in England quite recently, but of late—well, of late I've lost sight of him. I know," he went on, "that you and he had some little difference of opinion upon the Customs war with Austria."

"Yes, we did," remarked the grey-bearded old gentleman, with a smile. "We differed upon one point. Afterwards, however, I found that my ideas were unsound, and I admitted it in the Skuptchina. I heard that Petrovitch was in London. The King invited him to come to Belgrade about six months ago, as he wished to consult him in private, but he declined the invitation."

"Why?"

"I think he feared on account of a political conspiracy which is known to have been formed against him. As you know, the Opposition are his bitter opponents."

"And they are opponents of his Majesty also," Rolfe remarked.

"Exactly—a fact which for the peace of Servia is most unfortunate."

"Then you have no idea where I could find the Doctor?"

"Not the least. But—" and he paused, thinking for a moment.

"Well?"

"If I remember aright my wife told me that she had met his daughter Maud at dinner at the British Legation one night recently."

"Then she's here—in Belgrade!" Rolfe cried.

"I'm not quite certain. I did not pay much attention to what she told me. I was preoccupied with other things. But I will ask her, and let you know. Or you might ask the wife of the British Minister. You know her, of course?"

"Yes," Rolfe answered, excitedly. "I will call upon her this afternoon. I'm sure I'm very much indebted to your Excellency for this information."

And his spirits rose again at the thought that his sweet-faced well-beloved was safe and well, and that, in all probability, she was actually in that city.

Chapter Forty
Gives a Clue

That afternoon, at as early an hour as he decently could, he called at the British Legation, the big white mansion in the centre of the town. Both Sir Charles Harrison, the Minister, and his charming wife were well-known to him, for more than once he had been invited to dine on previous visits to Belgrade.

The Minister was out, but Lady Harrison received him in the big drawing-room on the first floor, a handsome apartment filled with exquisite Japanese furniture and bric-à-brac, for, prior to his appointment to Belgrade, the Minister had been Secretary of the British Embassy in Tokio.

The first greetings over, Charlie explained the object of his call. Whereupon the Minister's wife replied:

"I think Mr Pashitch is mistaken, Mr Rolfe. I haven't seen Maud Petrovitch for quite a year. She was on a visit to her aunt, Madame Constantinovitch, about a year ago, and used to come here very often."

Charlie's hopes fell again.

"Perhaps the Minister-President has made a mistake. It may have been at some other house Madame Pashitch met the Doctor's daughter," he said.

"Well, if she were in Belgrade she surely would come to see me. All her friends come to me on Thursdays, as you know," replied the Minister's wife, as the man brought in tea — with lemon — in the Russian style.

He glanced around the handsome room, and recollected the brilliant receptions at which he had been present. The British Legation was one of the finest mansions in Belgrade, and Sir Charles gave weekly dinners to the diplomatic corps and his personal friends. He and his wife entertained largely, to keep up the prestige of Great Britain amid that seething area of intrigue, political conspiracy, and general unrest.

Within a small room off the drawing-room, which was Sir Charles' private den, many a diplomatic secret had been brewed, and many an important matter affecting the best interests of Servia had been decided.

Surely the post of Belgrade was one of the most difficult in the whole range of British diplomacy abroad.

Before Charlie rose to go Sir Charles entered, a middle-aged, merry, easy-going man, who greeted him cheerily, saying:—

"Hullo, Rolfe! Who'd have thought of seeing you here? and how is Mr Statham? When will he buy us all up to-day?"

Rolfe briefly explained the nature of his mission to the ex-President, and then, after a few minutes' chat, followed his host into the smaller room for a cigarette and chat. Eventually Rolfe, lying back in an easy-chair, said: "Do you know, Sir Charles, a very curious thing has happened recently in London?"

"Oh, I see by the papers that lots of curious things have happened," was the diplomat's reply, as he smiled upon his guest.

"Oh, yes; I know. But this is a serious matter. Doctor Petrovitch and his daughter Maud have disappeared."

Sir Charles raised his eyebrows, and was in a moment serious.

"Disappeared! There's been nothing about it in the papers."

"No; it is being kept dark. The police haven't been stirred about it. It was only a sudden removal from Cromwell Road, but both father, daughter, and household furniture disappeared."

"How? In what manner did the furniture disappear?"

Rolfe explained, while Sir Charles sat listening open-mouthed.

"Extraordinary!" he ejaculated, when the younger man concluded. "What can be the reason of it. Petrovitch is an old and dear friend of mine. Why, I knew him years ago when I was attaché here. He often wrote to me. The last letter I had was from London about four months ago."

"And he's my friend also."

"Yes; I know," was the other's reply. "It was whispered, Rolfe, that you were in love with the pretty Maud—eh?"

"I don't deny it?"

"Why should you, if you love her."

"But she's disappeared—without a word."

"And you are in search of her? Most natural. Well, I'll make inquiries and ascertain if she's been in Belgrade. I don't believe she has, or we should certainly have seen something of her. My wife is very fond of her, you know."

"I fear there's been foul play?" Rolfe remarked.

The Minister shrugged his shoulders.

"It's curious, to say the least, isn't it?" he observed. There, in confidence, Charlie told the Minister of Marion's friendship with Maud, of the strange and mysterious confession on the night of the disappearance, and her steadfast refusal to betray the girl's secret.

Sir Charles paused and reflected.

"Political intrigue is at the bottom of this—depend upon it, Rolfe," he said at last. "Petrovitch has enemies here, unscrupulous enemies, who would not hesitate to attempt his life. They fear that if he returns to power as the King had invited him, they will find themselves prisoners in the fortress—and that means death, as you know. When the Doctor acts, he acts boldly for the benefit of his country. He would make a clean sweep of his enemies once and for all."

"Then you think they've anticipated this, and killed him in secret?" cried Rolfe.

"It is, I fear, quite possible," was the diplomat's reply.

"What causes you to believe this?"

"I possess secret knowledge."

"Of a plot against him?"

"He was fully aware of it himself. That is why he lived in England," the Minister replied.

"But, surely, if he knew this, he might have taken steps for his self-protection!" Rolfe exclaimed. "The fact that his furniture was spirited away to some unknown place makes it almost appear as though he was in accord with the conspirators."

"No; I think not. The conspirators removed his furniture in order to prevent undue inquiries as to the Doctor's disappearance. The emptying of the house may have been one to make it appear to the police that the Doctor had suddenly removed—perhaps to avoid his creditors."

Rolfe shook his head. His opinion hardly coincided with that of the British diplomat. Besides, Max Barclay's story of having seen a man there closely resembling him wanted explanation. With what motive had an unknown man represented him on the night in question?

"Maud Petrovitch has never written to you?" asked Harrison.

"Not a line."

The Minister pursed his lips.

"Well," he said, "I'm perfectly sure if she's been in Belgrade she would certainly have come to see us. My wife used to have frequent letters from her in London."

"I have not told Lady Harrison the reason of my inquiry—or any of the facts," Rolfe said. "I thought I would leave it to you to tell her if you think proper. Up to the present, the Doctor's disappearance has been kept secret between my friend Max Barclay, who was the Doctor's most intimate chum in London, and myself."

"At present I shall not tell my wife," declared the diplomat. He was a man of secrets, and knew how to keep one. "Who is Max Barclay?" asked the Minister, after a pause. Rolfe explained, but said nothing regarding his engagement to his sister Marion. To it all Sir Charles listened attentively, without comment.

At last, after a long silence, he said:

"Well, look here, Rolfe. A sudden thought has occurred to me. I think it possible that to-morrow, in a certain quarter, I shall be able to make a confidential inquiry regarding the whereabouts of the Doctor. All that you've told me interests me exceedingly, because I have all along believed that very shortly Petrovitch was returning to power and join forces with Pashitch."

"But didn't they quarrel a short time ago?" Rolfe remarked.

"Oh, a mere trifle. It was nothing. The Austrian press made a great stir about it, as they always do. All news from Servia emanates from the factory across the river yonder, at Semlin. If the journalists dared to put foot on, Servian soil they'd soon find themselves under arrest, I can tell you. No, the broad lines of policy of both Petrovitch and Pashitch are identical. They intend to develop the country by the introduction of foreign capital. The king himself told me so at an audience I had a month ago. He then told me, in confidence, that he had invited the Doctor to return and rejoin the Ministry. That is why I firmly believe that the poor Doctor, one of the best and most straightforward statesmen in Europe, has fallen a victim to his enemies."

"Then you will set to work to discover what is known among the Opposition?" urged the young man.

"I promise you I will. But, of course, in strictest confidence," was the Minister's reply. "Petrovitch is my friend, as well as yours. I know only too well of the bitter enmity towards him in some quarters, especially among the partisans of the late king and a certain section of the Opposition in the Skuptchina. Mention of his name there causes cheers from the Government benches, but howls from the enemies of law and order. There was, some three years ago, a dastardly plot against his life, as you know."

"No, I don't know it. I have never heard about it," was Rolfe's reply.

"Ah! he never speaks about it, of course," Sir Charles said, reflectively. "While driving out at Topschieder with his little orphan niece, of whom he was very fond, a bomb was thrown at the carriage. The poor child was blown to atoms, the horses were maimed, the carriage smashed to matchwood, and the coachman so injure that he died within an hour. The Doctor alone escaped with nothing more serious than a cut across the cheek. But that terrible death of his dead sister's child was a terrible blow to him, and he has not been since in Belgrade. Because of that, I expect, he has hesitated to obey the king's command to return to office."

"Awful! I never knew of that. Maud has never told me," said Rolfe. "What blackguards to kill an innocent child! Was the man who threw the bomb caught?"

"Yes. And the conspiracy was revealed by me activity of the secret police. They made a report to the Minister of Justice, who showed it to me in confidence."

"Then you actually know who threw the explosive?"

"I know also who was responsible for the dastardly conspiracy—who aided and abetted it, and who furnished the assassins with money and promised a big reward if they encompassed the Doctor's death!" said the Minister, slowly and seriously.

"You do! Who?" cried Rolfe.

"It was someone well-known to you," was his reply. "The inquiries made by the Servian secret police led them far afield from Belgrade. They traced the conspiracy to its source—a source which would amaze you, as it would stagger the world. And if I am not much mistaken, Rolfe, this second plot has been formed and carried out by the same person whose first plot failed!"

"A person I know?" gasped the young man.

Chapter Forty One
The Gateway of the East

The diplomat would say nothing more. When pressed by Charlie Rolfe he said that it was a surmise. Until the truth was proved he refused to speak more plainly.

"You declare that the plot by which an innocent child died was formed by a friend of mine!" the younger man exclaimed.

"I tell you that such is my firm belief," Sir Charles repeated. "To-morrow I will endeavour to discover whether the same influence that caused the explosion of the bomb at Topschieder is responsible for the Doctor's disappearance."

"But cannot you be more explicit?" asked Rolfe. "Who is the assassin — the murderer of children?"

"At present I can say no more than what I have already told you," was the diplomat's grave response.

"You believe that the same motive has led to the Doctor's disappearance as was the cause of the bomb outrage at Topschieder?"

"I do."

"Then much depends upon the Doctor's death?"

"Very much. His enemies would reap a large profit."

"His enemies in the Skuptchina, you mean?"

"Those — and others."

"He had private enemies also — secret ones that were even more dangerous than the blatant political orators."

"Then private vengeance was the cause?"

"No — not exactly; at least, I think not," Sir Charles replied. "But please ask no more. I will tell you the truth when I have established it."

"I wish I could discover where Maud is. Surely it is strange that the Prime Minister's wife should have said she met her lately here, in Belgrade."

"Maud Petrovitch is not in Servia. I am certain of that point."

"Why?"

"Because her father would never allow her to return here after that tragedy at Topschieder."

"The assassin—the man who threw the bomb. Where is he?"

"In the fortress—condemned to a life sentence," the diplomat answered. "He was caught while running away from the scene—a raw peasant from Valjevo, hired evidently to hurl the bomb. He was subjected to a searching examination, but would never reveal by whom he was employed. He was tried and condemned to solitary confinement, which he now is undergoing. You know the horrors of the fortress here, on the Danube, with its subterranean cells—eh?"

"I've heard of them," responded the younger man. "But even that fate is too humane for a man who would deliberately kill an innocent child!"

"A life sentence in the fortress is scarcely humane," the British Minister remarked grimly. "No one has ever entered some of those underground dungeons built by the Turks centuries ago. Their horrors can only be surmised. To all outsiders, who have wished to inspect the place, the Minister of Justice has refused admission."

"Then the assassin has only received his deserts."

"The person who formed the plot and used the ignorant peasant as his cat's-paw should be there too—or even instead of him," declared Sir Charles angrily. "The peasant suffers, while the real culprit gets off scot-free and unknown."

"Then he is still unknown?" exclaimed Rolfe in surprise.

"Save to perhaps three persons, of whom I am one."

"And also the man who threw the bomb!"

"I have heard that the solitary confinement in a dark cell already worked its effect upon him. He is hopelessly insane."

Rolfe drew a long breath, and glanced around the cosy room with its long row of well-filled book-cases, its big writing-table, and its smaller tables filled with Japanese bric-à-brac, of which Sir Charles was an ardent collector.

In the silence that fell the footman tapped at the door and presented a card. Then Rolfe, declaring that he must go, rose, gripped the grey-haired Minister's hand, and extracting from him a promise to tell the truth as soon as he had established it, followed the smart English footman down the stairs.

That night, as he sat amid the clatter and music of the brilliantly lit Grand Café, he reflected deeply on all that had been told him, wondering who was the friend who had been responsible for the outrage, which had induced the Doctor to forsake his native land never to return. Servia was a country of intrigue and unrest, as is every young country. He looked around the tables at the gay crowd of smart officers with their ribbons and crosses upon their breasts and their well-dressed womenkind, and wondered whether any fresh conspiracy was in progress.

The rule of King Peter—maligned though that monarch had been—had brought beneficent reforms to Servia. And yet there was an opposition who never ceased to hurl hard epithets against him, and to charge him with taking part in a plot, of the true meaning of which he certainly had had no knowledge.

Belgrade is a city in which plots against the monarchy are hinted at and whispered in the corners of drawing-rooms, where diplomacy is a mass of intrigue, a city of spies and sycophants, of concession-hunters and political cliques. Gay, pleasant, and easy-going, with its fine boulevard, its pretty Kalamegdan Garden, and its spick-and-span new streets, it is different to any other capital of Europe; more full of tragedy, more full of plot and counter-plot.

Austria is there ever seeking by her swarm of secret agents to stir up strife and to organise demonstrations against the reigning dynasty. Germany is there seeking influence and making promises, while Bulgaria is ever watchful; Turkey is silent and spectral, and Great Britain looks on neutral, but noting every move of the deep diplomatic juggling of the Powers.

At night amid the clatter, the laughter, and the gipsy music of the Grand Café, with its billiard tables in the centre and its restaurant adjoining, the stranger would never dream of its close proximity to the tragedy of a throne. Just as the bright lights and calm, moonlit sea throw a glamour over that plague spot Monte Carlo, until the visitor believes that no evil can lurk in that terrestrial paradise, so in Belgrade is everything so pleasant, so happy, so careless that the stranger would never dream that the whole city sits ever upon the edge of a volcano, and that the red flag of revolt is ready at any, moment to be hoisted.

Charlie Rolfe knew Belgrade, and knew the tragedy that underlay its brightness. What greater tragedy could there be than the death of the innocent child blown to atoms by the bomb?

Who could be the culprit whom Sir Charles had told him was his "friend." He had known the Doctor well, but not intimately as Max Barclay had done. Curious that Max had told him nothing concerning that tragic incident which had caused the Servian statesman and patriot to turn his back upon his beloved country and live in studious seclusion in England. Max had told him many things, but had never mentioned that subject.

Was Max Barclay the "friend" to whom Sir Charles had referred. Was it really possible? He held his breath, contemplating the end of his half-smoked cigar and wondering.

It was a strange suspicion. Of late, ever since Max had charged him with having been present at Cromwell Road on the night of the disappearance, he had somehow held aloof from the man to whom Marion was so devoted.

And now? Even she had disappeared! What could it mean?

Did Max Barclay really know how and why Marion had disappeared, and for motives of his own was making a mystery?

The message from Barclay worried him. Marion was missing. Why had she left Cunnington's? She must have left of her own accord, he felt confident. She would never be discharged. Sam Statham would never, for a moment, allow that.

A tall man with a fair, pointed beard approached him, raised his hat, and gripped his hand. It was Drukovitch, the director of the National Theatre, and a friend of his. The new-comer seated himself at the table, and the waiter brought a tiny glass of "slivovitza," or plum gin, that liqueur so dear to the Servian palate. Drukovitch was one of the best-known and most popular men in Belgrade; a thorough-going cosmopolitan, and a man of the world. Sometimes he went to London, and whenever there Charlie entertained him at his club, or they went to the theatre and supped at the Savoy.

As they chatted, Rolfe explaining that he was in Servia upon financial matters as usual, Drukovitch nodded to the officers and civilians whom he knew, many of them famous for the part they had played in the recent *coup d'état*. Some of them, indeed, wore the white-enamelled cross, which decoration marked them as partisans of the dynasty of the Karageorge. And meanwhile the orchestra were playing the popular waltz from "The Merry Widow," the air haunting everybody and everyone.

That night there was a court hall at the Palace, and the forthcoming event was upon everyone's lips. There was seldom any entertainment at the New Konak, for his Majesty led a very quiet life, the almost ascetic life of a soldier—riding out at dawn, attending to duties of state during the day, and retiring early.

Perhaps the most maligned man in all Europe, King Peter of Servia was, nevertheless, known to those intimate around the throne to be a most conscientious ruler, fully aware of all his responsibilities, and striving ever to pacify the various political factions, sustaining the prestige of Servia abroad, and ameliorating the condition of his people at home.

The truth regarding King Peter had never been written. Of libels and vile calumnies there had been volumes, but no journalist had ever dared to put into print the real facts of King Peter's innocence of any connivance at the dastardly murder of Alexander and Draga.

Those who knew the real facts admired King Peter as a man and fearless patriot, but those who gathered their information from sensational newspapers and scurrilous books emanating from Austria believed every lie that the back-stairs scribes chose to write.

Drukovitch was one of the men who knew the truth, and many a time he had explained them to his friend, who, in turn, had told old Sam Statham, the hard-headed misanthrope whose prejudices were so strong, and yet the chords of whose heart-strings were so readily touched.

Sam had lent money to Servia—huge sums. And why? Because he knew his Majesty personally, and had heard from his own lips the story of his tragic difficulties and his high aspirations.

Once, indeed, in that silent study in Park Lane he had been reading a confidential report from Belgrade, predicting a black outlook, when he turned to his secretary and said:

"Rolfe. There will be trouble in Servia. But even though I may lose the million sterling I have loaned it will not trouble me. I have tried to assist an honest man who is at the same time a philanthropist and a king."

Charlie Rolfe recollected these words at that moment as he sat amid the noise and chatter of the café, where, above every other sound, rose the sweet, tuneful strains of the waltz that had within the past few weeks gripped all Europe.

There was something bizarre, something incongruous with it all.

He was thinking of his lost love—his sweet-faced Maud with the unruly wisp of hair straying across her white brow.

Where was she? Ay, where was she?

Chapter Forty Two
Advances a Theory

Next day, and the next, Charlie called upon the British Minister, but could obtain no further information.

Sir Charles had failed to establish his suspicion, and therefore declined to say anything further.

Rolfe, on his part, had learned from Drukovitch the full details of the dastardly attempt upon the Doctor's life at Topschieder, and how the little child had been blown to atoms. The escape of Petrovitch had been little short of miraculous, and it was now whispered that the conspiracy had no political significance, but was an act of private vengeance.

Whatever its motive might have been, it had had the desired effect of preventing the Doctor from returning to Servia.

In various quarters Rolfe made diligent inquiry, and established without a doubt that Maud Petrovitch had within the past ten days or so been in Belgrade.

A young officer of the King's guard, a Lieutenant Yankovitch, had seen her in the Zar Duschanowa Uliza. He described her as wearing a white serge gown and a big black hat. She was walking with a short, elderly, grey-haired woman, undoubtedly a foreigner—English or American. He was marching with his company, or would have stopped and spoken to her.

Another person discovered by Drukovitch was a domestic who had once been in the Doctor's service. She declared that early one morning when going from her home to the house in the Krunska where she was now employed, she met her young mistress Maud with the same elderly woman—a woman rather shabbily-dressed. The pair were passing the Russian Legation, and she stopped and spoke.

The young lady had told her that she was only on a flying visit to Belgrade, and that she was leaving again on the morrow. To the servant's inquiries regarding the Doctor his daughter was silent, as though she did not wish to mention her father.

According to the servant's description. Mademoiselle Maud looked very wan and pale, as though she had passed many sleepless nights full of anxiety and dread.

The Prime Minister's wife had no recollection of telling her husband about meeting the Doctor's daughter. Somebody else must have mentioned it to the grey-bearded statesman, who, full of the cares of office, had forgotten who it had been.

A third person who had seen Maud, however, was one of the agents of secret police on duty at the railway station. It was this man's work to watch arriving passengers, and detail agents to watch any suspected to be foreign spies. According to his report, made to the chief of police, Mademoiselle Petrovitch arrived in Belgrade late one night with an elderly Englishwoman and a tall, thin man, probably a German. They hired a cab and drove out to an address near the Botanical Gardens, on the opposite side of the city. Recognising who she was, he did not instruct an agent to follow her. The two ladies returned to the railway station four days later and left again by the Orient express for Budapest.

The officials of the international express, in passing through Servia, are compelled to furnish to the secret police the names and nationalities of all passengers travelling. When the train arrives in Belgrade the commissario is always handed the list, which is filed for reference. Upon the list on that particular day was shown the names of Mademoiselle Maud Pavlovitch, of Belgrade, and Mrs Wood, of London.

The girl had only slightly disguised her name.

These results of Charlie's inquiry showed quite plainly that his well-beloved was alive, and that she had been in Servia with some secret object. The police were unaware of the exact address near the Botanical Gardens where the couple stayed. It is only within their province to watch suspected foreigners. Of Servians they take no account.

Therefore, beyond the facts already stated, Rolfe could discover nothing.

Day after day he remained in Belgrade, sometimes spending the afternoon by going for a trip across the Danube to that dull and rather uninteresting frontier town of Hungary, Semlin, and always hoping to be able to discover something further—some clue to the strange disappearance of the Doctor, or the real reason why his Maud was so determined to hold aloof from him.

Thrice he received wild telegrams from Max Barclay, asking for information as to where he might best seek news of Marion. News of her? Her brother was just as staggered by her disappearance as was her lover.

He telegraphed that she might perhaps be at the house of an old servant of their fathers at Boston, in Lincolnshire. But next day came a report despatched from Boston that the good man and his wife had heard nothing of their late master's daughter.

Again to Bridlington he sent Max, to some friends there; but from that place came a similar response. Marion was, like Maud, in hiding! But why?

In the bright morning sunshine he strolled the streets, which were so full of quaint and interesting types. There in Belgrade, the gateway of the East, one saw the Servian peasant in his high boots, his white shirt worn outside his trousers, and his round, high cap of astrakhan. The better-class peasant wore his brown homespun, while the women with the gay coloured kerchiefs on their heads wore their heavy silver girdles and their ornaments reminiscent of the Turkish occupation. Big, burly men in scarlet waistbands and fur caps, women in pretty peasant costumes from the distant provinces, officers gay with ribbons and crosses, and ladies in gowns and hats that spoke mutely of Bond Street and the Rue de la Paix; all were seen in the ever moving panorama of that cosmopolitan little capital where East meets West.

The financial business which Charlie had come there to transact had already been concluded, to the mutual satisfaction of his Excellency the Prime Minister and of the grey-faced old misanthrope seated in the silent room in Park Lane. Many cables in cipher had been exchanged, and Charlie had placed his signature to half a dozen documents, which in due course would be countersigned with old Sam's scrawly calligraphy. The stake of Statham Brothers in Servia represented considerably over one million sterling, and nobody had been more conscious of old Sam's readiness to assist in the development of the country's rich resources than his Majesty the King.

Upon a side table in Statham's study in Park Lane was a big autographed portrait in a silver frame, which King Peter had given him at his last audience. Therefore it was with feelings of gratification that Charlie heard from the Minister-President's lips the verbal message which the King had sent—a message of thanks to Mr Rolfe for doing all that he had done to arrive at a satisfactory arrangement whereby with English capital Servia's wealth was to be exploited and work provided for her industrial population.

Though he knew that Maud Petrovitch was no longer in Belgrade, yet he still lingered on at the Grand Hotel amid all its clatter, its hustle, and its music. Truth to tell, he earnestly desired to obtain the truth from Sir Charles Harrison. For that dastardly attempt at Topschieder a friend of his was responsible!

It was the identity of the friend in question that he was deeply anxious to establish, so that in future he would know whom to doubt and whom to trust.

Was Max Barclay really his friend?

Hour upon hour he reflected upon that problem. He recollected incidents which, in his present state of mind, filled him with misgivings. Why had he openly charged him with having been present at the house in Cromwell Road after the disappearance of the Doctor and his daughter? Indeed, had he not practically charged him with opening the Doctor's safe and abstracting its contents? He had not made the charge directly, it was true, but his remarks had certainly been made in a spirit of antagonistic suspicion.

A long letter from Max explained the sudden disappearance of Marion from Cunnington's, and begged him to give all information regarding any likely quarter where the girl had sought refuge. It was now plain enough to Charlie that his sister had been discharged from the establishment in Oxford Street—and in disgrace! In what disgrace?

When he read the letter in his room at the hotel, he crushed it in his hand with an imprecation upon his lips. Cunnington should answer to him for this indignity. He would compel the fellow to tell him the truth. His sister's honour was at stake.

Disgraced by her sudden discharge, she had disappeared. She had, no doubt, been ashamed to face the man who loved her, ashamed, too, to write to her brother. Instead, she preferred to go away and efface herself, as, alas! so many London shop-girls have done before her.

Charlie Rolfe knew the cruelty practised by many a shop-keeper in London in discharging their female employées at a moment's notice. For a man it matters little. Perhaps, indeed, it is best for both parties. But for a helpless girl without friends, without money, and without home to be cast suddenly upon the great world of London, filled as it is with lures and temptations, is a grave sin which no tradesman ought to commit. And yet there are to-day in London and its suburbs hundreds of smug, top-hatted, frock-coated tradesmen, who, though pillars of their chapels and churches and stalking round the aisles with their plush collecting-bags on Sundays, will on six days in the week cast forth any poor girl in their employ without a grain of sympathy or compunction merely because she may break a rule, or even because she does not lie to customers sufficiently well to induce them to make purchases.

The general public are ignorant of the tyranny of shop-life in London. There have been strikes—strikes quickly suppressed because, by lifting his finger the employer is overwhelmed with assistants glad to live on a mere bread and butter wage—and those strikes have been treated humorously by the evening papers. Ah! the tragedy of it all.

Charles Rolfe, though secretary and trusted factotum of a millionaire, knew it all. His sister had been in a snug "billet," one from which he had fondly believed she could never have been dislodged.

But the hard, bitter truth was now apparent. Even his own brotherly protection had availed her nothing. She had been consigned to disgrace.

It was with such bitter thoughts he resolved to return to London. He went to the telegraph office and sent a long message to Sam Statham, explanatory of what had occurred, and beseeching his intervention with Cunnington.

Through the night he waited, but received no response.

Then he went round in the morning to bid Sir Charles adieu.

"Well, Rolfe!" exclaimed the representative of the British Government; "I'm sorry you're off so quickly. My wife was asking you to dine to-morrow night—usual weekly dinner, you know."

"And have you discovered nothing regarding Petrovitch?" asked Charlie quickly.

"Well," replied the diplomat, after a moment's hesitation, "to tell the truth, I have."

"You have!" gasped the young man eagerly. "What?" The other knit his brows, and was for a moment silent.

"Something—something!" he said, "that is astounding. I—I cannot give it credence. It is all too amazing—too tragic—too utterly incomprehensible."

Chapter Forty Three
The Lost Beloved

Weeks had dragged by. To Max Barclay they had been weeks of keen anxiety and unceasing search to discover traces of his lost beloved.

Once, and only once, had he seen Jean Adam, against whom Sam Statham had warned him. He had met the man of brilliant financial ideas by appointment at lunch at the Savoy, and had told him plainly that he had reconsidered the whole matter of the Turkish concession, and had decided to have nothing to do with it.

His excuse was lack of funds at that moment. To the old millionaire he owed a good deal for giving him the "tip" regarding the plausible Anglo-Frenchman. Adam, alias Adams, received Max's decision without the alteration of a muscle of his face. He was a perfect actor, and betrayed no sign of surprise or of chagrin.

"Well, my dear fellow," he remarked, raising his glass of Brauneberger and contemplating it before placing it to his lips; "you're losing the chance of a lifetime. If Baron Hirsch had been alive he wouldn't have allowed such a thing to slip. When old Statham knows of it he'll move heaven and earth to come in."

Max was silent. He did not allow his companion to know that Statham had been responsible for his refusal to join in the project.

"I'm sorry, too," he said. "But just now I'm rather pressed. I was hard hit last week over those Siberians."

"But the money required is a mere bagatelle. I have mine ready."

"I regret," answered Max, "but my decision is final."

"Very well, my dear fellow," replied Adam lightly. "I don't want to persuade you. There are a thousand men in the City who'll be ready to put up money to-morrow morning."

And the pair finished their luncheon and parted, Adam, of course, entirely unsuspicious of the part Statham had played in upsetting his deeply-laid plans.

To every address which Marion's brother had furnished he had gone at post-haste, only to draw blank every time. Charlie had, at Statham's instructions, gone first to Constantinople, then to Odessa and Batoum, after which he had returned direct to London.

In Odessa he had been met by a special messenger from the London office bearing a number of documents, and his business in that city had occupied him nearly a fortnight. Therefore it was early in October when, arriving by the evening train at Charing Cross from Paris, he took a cab straight to Park Lane.

In greeting him, old Sam was rather curious in his manner, he thought. There was a lack of cordiality. Usually, when he came off a long journey, the old fellow ordered Levi to bring the decanter of whisky and a syphon. But on this occasion the head of the great financial house merely sat in his chair at his desk and heard his secretary's report without even suggesting that he might be fagged by his rush across Europe.

Rolfe related, briefly and plainly, the various points upon which he had failed, and those upon which he had been successful. Some of his decisions had brought many thousands of pounds into the already overflowing coffers of Statham Brothers, and yet the old man made no sign. He heard all without any comment save now and then a grunt of satisfaction.

The younger man could not disguise from himself the fact that the millionaire was not himself. His face was paler and more transparent, while the green-shaded electric lamp shed upon it a hue that was unreal and ghastly. Old Levi, too, as he flitted in and out like a white-breasted shadow, seemed to regard him with unusual suspicion and distrust.

What could it all mean?

He looked from one to the other in puzzled surprise.

He was unaware that only on the previous night a thin, dark, bearded man had been ushered into that very room and had sat for two hours with the great financier. His countenance, his gestures, the cut of his clothes, all showed plainly that he was not English. Besides, the consultation was in French, a language which old Sam knew fairly well.

That man was a spy, and he was from Belgrade.

From the moment Charlie Rolfe had descended at the station to the moment he had left it, secret observation had been kept upon his movements. And to furnish the report to his master the spy had travelled from Servia to London. Samuel Statham trusted nobody. Even his most confidential assistant was spied upon, and his own reports compared with those of a spy's.

More than once, as Charlie Rolfe, all unconscious of the surveillance upon him, related what had occurred in King Peter's capital, the old man smiled—in disbelief. This the younger man could not understand. He was in ignorance of the great conspiracy in progress, or of the millionaire's ulterior motives. The old man's face was sphinx-like, as it ever was—a countenance in which no single trait was visible, neither was there human joy or human sympathy. It was the face of a statue—the face of a man whose greed and avarice had rendered him pitiless.

And yet, strangely enough, this very man was, to Charlie's knowledge, a philanthropist in secret, giving away thousands yearly to the deserving poor without any thought of laudatory comment of either press or public.

Samuel Statham was not well; of that Charlie felt assured. He noticed the slight trembling of the thin white hands, the fixed, anxious look in his eyes, the curl of the thin grey lips, all of which caused him anxiety. In his ignorance he had grown to be greatly fond of the eccentric old man who pulled so many of the financial wires of Europe and whose word could cause the stock markets to fluctuate. A scribbled word of his that night would be felt in Wall Street on the morrow, whilst the pulses of the Bourse of Berlin, Paris, and Vienna were ready at any moment to respond instantly to the transactions of Statham Brothers, often so gigantic as to cause a sensation.

Presently Sam Statham commenced his cross-questioning regarding the exact situation in Belgrade, the attitude of the Minister-President, and the strength of the Opposition in that wooden shed-like Parliament-house, the Skuptchina, of whom he had seen, and what information he had gathered regarding the tariff-war with Austria.

To all the questions Charlie replied in a manner which showed him to be perfectly alive to all the requirements of the firm. To those in Old Broad Street, City, secret information regarding the future policy of Servia means the gain or loss of many thousands, and though during his sojourn in the City of the White Fortress his mind had been so perturbed over his own private affairs, he had certainly not neglected those of the great firm who employed him.

The old man gave little sign of approbation, and after nearly an hour suddenly dismissed him abruptly, saying:

"Very well. You're tired, I expect. You'd better go to dinner. I'll see you in the morning."

"There's another matter I wanted to speak to you about," Charlie said, still remaining in his chair, watching the old fellow as he turned towards his desk and drew some papers on to his blotting-pad.

"Eh? What?" asked the old fellow sharply, turning again to the other.

"You did very well in Odessa. I was very pleased to receive that last cable from you. Souvaroff grew frightened evidently—afraid I should withdraw and let the whole business go into air." And he chuckled to himself in delight at how he had worsted a powerful Russian banker who was his enemy.

"It was not of that I wish to speak," remarked Rolfe quietly. "It was with regard to my sister Marion."

The old fellow started uneasily at his secretary's words. "Eh? Your sister?" he said. "What about her?"

"She's left Cunnington's," Charlie said. "According to what I hear, she's been discharged in some disgrace."

"Ah! yes," was the old man's response, as though recalling the fact. "I've heard so. Your friend Barclay came to see me, and told me some long story about her. I wrote to Cunnington, but I haven't seen any reply from him. It may have gone to the office."

"My sister has left Oxford Street—and hidden herself, in disgrace. We can't find her."

"Then if you can't find her, Rolfe, I don't see how I can assist you," remarked the elder man. "Girls entertain strange fancies, you know—especially the sentimental-minded. Been reading novels, perhaps—eh? Was she given to that?"

"The girls at Cunnington's have little time for reading," he said, piqued at Statham's careless manner. Hitherto he had believed that the old man was genuinely interested in her, but he now saw that her future was to him nothing. He was too much occupied in piling up wealth to trouble his head over a girl's distress, even though that girl might be the sister of the man who by his acute business foresight often won for him thousands in a single day.

Charlie rose, full of suppressed anger. He did not notice the look of anxiety and shame upon the old man's face, for his head was bowed beneath the lamplight as he pretended to fumble with his papers.

"Perhaps your sister was tired of the place—too much hard work. Thought to better herself."

"My sister was, like myself, much indebted to you, Mr Statham," was Rolfe's reply. "If she has been discharged in disgrace, it is, I feel confident, through no fault of her own. Therefore, I beg of you, to ask fit. Cunnington to make full inquiry."

"What is the use? It is Cunnington himself who engages the hands and discharges them," replied Statham evasively. "I can't interfere."

"But," Rolfe argued, "for the sake of my sister's good name you will surely do me this one small favour?"

"I have already seen Barclay, who says he's engaged to her. Call on him, and he'll explain what I have already said and the inquiry I have already made," replied the old man in growing impatience.

"But weeks have gone by, and you've received no reply from Cunnington. He does not usually treat you with such discourtesy."

"I can only think that he acted as his own judgment directed him," the millionaire replied. "You know how strict the rules are that govern shop-assistants, and I suppose he could not favour your sister any more than the others."

"Marion wanted no favours," he declared. "She never asked one of anybody at Oxford Street. She only desires justice and troth—and I mean to have them for her."

"Then go and see Cunnington for yourself," snapped the old man. "I've done all I can do. If your sister chooses to go away and hide herself, how can I help it?"

"But she was sent away?" cried Rolfe in anger. "Sent away in disgrace, and I intend to discover what charge there is against her—and the truth concerning it?"

"Dear me, Rolfe!" snapped the old man impatiently. "Do go home, for heaven's sake. You're tired and hungry—consequently out of temper."

"Yes," he cried, "I am out of temper because you refuse to render my sister justice! But she shall have it—she shall?"

And he stalked out of the room and closed the door noisily behind him.

Then, after the door had closed, old Sam raised his head, and his eyes followed the young man. In them was a look such as was seldom seen there—a look of double cunning which spoke mutely of false and double-dealing.

Chapter Forty Four
Tells of a Determination

Entering his chambers in Jermyn Street half an hour later, Rolfe was met by the faithful Green, to whom he gave orders to "ring up" Mr Barclay at Dover Street.

Then he went along to his room to wash and dress.

A few moments later Green came in, saying:

"Mr Barclay left town five days ago, sir. He's up at Kilmaronock."

His master made no reply for some moments. Then at last he said:

"Pack my suit-case, and 'phone to Euston to reserve me a seat to Perth on the ten-five to-morrow morning."

"Yes, sir."

"And to everybody except my sister, if she calls, you don't know where I've gone—you understand?"

"Perfectly, sir."

And the man set about packing up his master's traps.

"You may as well put in a dinner-coat Max may have friends," Rolfe said.

"Very well, sir."

His master dressed quickly and went alone to the club for a late dinner. Most of his friends were away shooting, therefore he idled alone for an hour over the paper and then returned to his chambers.

Next morning he scribbled a hasty note to Mr Statham, making an excuse for his sudden absence, and directly after ten was seated in the Scotch express travelling out of London.

At eight that evening he stepped out upon the big, dark station at Perth, sent a telegram to the Crown Inn at Kilmaronock village for a "machine," as a fly is called, and then took the slow branch line that runs by Crieff and skirts Loch Earn to the head of Glen Ogle, where lay the old castle and fine shooting of which Max Barclay was possessor.

A drive of three miles on the road beside Loch Voil brought him to the lodge-gates, and then another mile up through the park he came to the great portico of the castle.

It was nearly midnight. Lights were still in the billiard-room of the fine old castellated mansion, which Max's father had modernised and rendered so comfortable, and when Charlie rang, Burton, the butler, could not suppress an exclamation of surprise.

In a few moments, however, Charlie burst into the room where Max and five other men were playing "snooker" before retiring.

The host's surprise was great, but the visitor received a hearty welcome, and an hour later, when the guests had gone to their rooms, the two friends stood alone together in the long old-fashioned drawing-room which, without a woman's artistic hand to keep things in order, was rapidly going to decay.

A big wood fire blazed cheerfully in the wide old-fashioned grate, for October evenings in the Highlands are damp and chill, and as the two men stood before it they looked at one another, both hesitating to speak.

Across Charlie's mind flashed those suspicions which had oppressed him in Belgrade. Was the man before him his enemy or his friend?

"Well," he blurted forth, "I've come straight up to see you, Max. I only arrived home last night. I want to see you concerning Marion."

His companion's lips hardened.

"Marion!" he exclaimed. "I have done all I can. I've left no effort untried. I have sought the aid of the best confidential inquiry agency in London, and all to no avail. She's disappeared—as completely as Maud has done!"

"Yes, I know," replied her brother, thrusting his hands deep into the trousers-pockets of his blue serge travelling-suit. "I've seen Statham."

"And so have I. He wrote to Cunnington's, but the latter has not replied. I saw Cunnington myself."

"And what did he say?"

"The fellow refused to say anything," he replied in a hard tone.

Silence again fell between the pair.

The long, old-fashioned room, with its blue china, its chintz coverings, its grand piano, and its bowls of autumn roses, though full of quaint charm, was weird and unsuited to the home of a bachelor. Indeed, Kilmaronock was a white elephant to Max. He received a fair rental from the farms on the estate, but he never went near the place except for sport for six weeks or so each autumn. The old place possessed some bitter memories for him, for his mother had died there quite suddenly of heart disease on the night of a large dinner-party. He was only eighteen then, but he remembered it too well. It was that tragic memory which had caused him to abandon the place except when he invited a few of his friends to shoot over the estate.

"Let's go into my own room to talk," he suggested. "It's more cosy there." As a man hates all drawing-rooms, so did Max Barclay detest his. It was for him full of recollections of his dear dead mother.

And so they passed along the corridor to Max's own little den in the east wing of the house, a pleasant little room overlooking the deep shady glen from whence rose the constant music of the ever-rippling burn.

As Charlie sank into the big armchair near the fire Max pushed the cigar-box towards him. Then he seated himself, saying:

"Now, old fellow, what are we to do? Marion must be found."

"She must. But you've failed, you say?"

"Utterly," he sighed. "She was discharged from Cunnington's—disgraced!"

"Why?"

Max shrugged his shoulders. Both men knew well that the reason of the girl's disappearance was the shame of her dismissal. Both men knew also that by lifting his finger Sam Statham could have reinstated her—or could at least have had inquiry made as to the truth of what had really occurred.

But he had refused. Therefore both were indignant and angry. During the next half-hour they discussed the matter fully and seriously, and were agreed upon one main point, that Statham had acted against them both in refusing his aid to clear the unfortunate girl.

"Whatever fault she has committed," declared Max, "the truth should be told. I went to him acknowledging my love for her and beseeching his aid. And yet he has refused."

"Then let us combine, Max, in trying to discover the truth," her brother suggested. "Marion shall not be cast aside into oblivion by these drapery capitalists who gain fat profits upon the labour and lives of women."

"You may imperil your position with Statham if you act without discretion," remarked Max warningly.

"I shall do nothing without full consideration, depend upon it. Statham refused his assistance, therefore we must act for ourselves."

"How? Where shall we begin?" asked Max.

His friend raised his palms in a gesture of bewilderment.

"Look here, Charlie," said the other in a confidential tone. "Has it not occurred to you that there may be a method in old Statham's eccentricity regarding that house of his. Now tell me, what do you know of its interior? Let's be frank with each other. You have lost both your sister and the woman you adored, while I have lost Marion, my well-beloved. Let us act together. During these past weeks I've been thinking deeply regarding the mystery of that house in Park Lane."

"So have I, many times. I only know the ground floor and basement. I have never ascended the stairs, through that white-enamelled iron door concealed by the one of green baize."

"Where does old Levi sleep?"

"In a room at the back of the kitchen—when he sleeps at all. He's like a watch-dog, on the alert always for the slightest sound."

Max paused for a moment before making any further remark. Then he said in a quiet voice:

"There are some very queer stories afloat concerning that place, Charlie."

"I know. I've heard them—about mysterious people who enter there at night—and don't come forth again. But I don't believe them. Old Sam has earned a reputation for being eccentric, and his enemies have tacked on all sorts of sensational fictions."

"But I've heard lately from half a dozen sources most extraordinary stories. Up at the Moretouns' at Inversnaid the night before last, they were talking of it at dinner. They were unaware that I knew Statham."

"Just as the gossips are unaware that the persons who come and go so mysteriously at the Park-Lane mansion are secret agents of the great financier," Rolfe said. "Of course it would not do to say so openly, but that's who they are. The allegation that they don't come forth again is, I feel confident, mere embroidery to the tale."

"But," exclaimed Max with some hesitation, "has it not ever occurred to you somewhat curious that, so deeply involved in Servian finance, Statham has never sought to solve the mystery of the doctor's disappearance? Remember, they knew each other. The doctor, when he was in power at Belgrade, was probably the old man's cat's-paw. Is it not therefore surprising that he has never expressed a desire to seek out the truth?"

Rolfe held his breath as a new and terrible suspicion arose within him. He had never regarded the affair in that light. Was it possible that his master knew well all the circumstances which had led the doctor to disappear in that manner so extraordinary? Had he really had a hand in it?

Was he the "friend" of whom Sir Charles had spoken in Belgrade?

But no! He would not believe such a thing. Sam Statham was always honest in his dealings—or, at least, as honest as any millionaire can ever be. The man who habitually deals in colossal sums must now and then, of necessity ruin his opponents and wreck the homes of honest men. And strange it is that the world is ever ungrateful. If a very wealthy man gave every penny of his profits to the poor he would only be dubbed a fool or an idiot for his philanthropy.

He recollected that afternoon when, at work in old Sam's room, he had mentioned the doctor's sudden departure, and how deftly the old man had turned the conversation into a different channel.

Until two days ago he would hear no word nor believe any ill against the man who had befriended him. But the man's refusal to assist him to discover the truth concerning the charge against Marion or to order her to be reinstated had turned his heart.

He was now Sam Statham's enemy, as before he had been his friend.

The two men seated together discussed the matter carefully and seriously for the greater part of the night, and when they parted to go to their rooms they took each other's hands in solemn compact.

"We will investigate that house, Rolfe," Max declared; "and we'll lay bare the mystery it conceals!"

Chapter Forty Five
The Impending Blow

Four nights later Max and Charlie alighted from the Scotch express at Euston on their return to London to make investigation.

Next morning Rolfe went as usual to Park Lane, and spent some hours attending to the old man's correspondence. The excuse Charlie made for his absence was that he had been away in an endeavour to find his sister, whereat the millionaire merely grunted in dissatisfaction. Both Charlie and Max were full of sorrow and anxiety on Marion's behalf. What had befallen her they dreaded to guess. She had left Oxford Street, and from that moment had been swallowed in the bustling vortex of our great cruel London, the city where money alone is power and where gold can purchase everything, even to the death of one's enemy. Perhaps the poor girl had met with some charitable woman who had taken her in and given her shelter; but more probable, alas! she was wandering hungry and homeless, afraid to face the shame of the dastardly charge against her—the charge that to neither her brother nor her lover none would name.

That morning Charlie wrote on, mechanically, speaking little, with the old man seated near him sucking the stump of a cheap cigar. His mind was too full of the action he was about to execute—an action which in other circumstances would have indeed been culpable.

Both he and his friend had carefully considered all ways and means by which they might enter those premises. To get in would be difficult. Old Levi bolted the heavy front door each night at eleven, and then retired to his room in the basement, where he slept with one ear and his door open to catch the slightest sound.

And even though they obtained access to the hall and study there was the locked iron door at the head of the staircase—the door through which they must pass if their investigation of the house was to be made.

That morning he made excuse to leave the old man seated in his study, saying that he wanted to speak to Levi and give him a message for one of the clerks from Old Broad Street. Outside in the hall he sprang noiselessly up the stairs, and, pulling open the baize-covered door, swiftly examined the great iron fireproof door so carefully concealed and secured. His heart failed when he recognised the impossibility of passing beyond. The door was enamelled white like the panelling up the stairs, only over the small keyhole was a flap of shining brass bearing the name of a well-known safe-maker. At imminent peril of discovery by Levi, who often shuffled in noiseless slippers of felt, he lifted the flap and peered eagerly beyond. He could, however, see nothing. The hole did not penetrate the door.

Then, fearing that he might be discovered, he slipped downstairs again, and went to examine the front door. The bolts were long and heavy, and the chain was evidently in use every night.

In the kitchen he found Levi, preparing his master's frugal meal, which usually consisted of a small chop, a piece of stale bread, and one glass of light claret. His visit below gave him an opportunity of examining the fastenings of the windows. They were all patent ones, and, besides, the whole were protected from burglars by iron bars.

Patent fastenings were also upon the windows of the study, looking forth upon Park Lane, while often at night the heavy oaken shutters were closed and barred. He had never before noticed how every precaution had been taken to exclude the unwelcome intruders.

Through the whole morning his brain was actively at work to discover some means by which an entry might be effected, but there seemed none.

The secret, whatever it might be, was certainly well guarded.

He went across to the club to lunch, and returned again at three o'clock. About four he rose, asking old Sam, who was seated writing, for a document from the safe, the key of which was upon his watch-guard. The millionaire took out his watch and chain and handed them to his secretary, as he so often did, while the latter, crossing the room, opened the safe and fumbled about among some papers in one of the drawers.

Then he re-locked the safe, handed back the watch and chain, and re-seated himself at the table. Those few brief moments had been all-sufficient, for upon the bunch was the latch-key of the front door, an impression of which he had taken with the wax he had already prepared. The duplicate key could, he knew, be filed out of the handle of an old spoon, and such was his intention.

He had hoped to find upon the bunch the key to the iron door on the stairs, but it was not among them. He knew each key by sight. The old man evidently kept it in a safer place—some place where the hand of none other might be placed upon it.

Where did he keep it?

Its hiding-place must be somewhere handy, Charlie reflected, for at least half a dozen times a day the old man passed that iron barrier which shut off the upper part of the mansion. He wondered where he could find that key, but remained wondering.

That evening he took the impression of the latchkey to Dover Street, and with Max's help tried to fashion a key to that pattern, but though they tried for hours it was in vain. So they gave it up. Next day Max took train to Birmingham, and handed the impression to a locksmith he chanced to know. The latter, having looked at it, shook his head, and said:

"This impression is no use, sir. It's what they call a paracentric lock, and you must have impressions of both sides, as well as the exact width back and front before I can make you a duplicate."

The man showed how the impressions should be taken. Max, of course, concocting a story as to why it was wanted, and then back to London he travelled that same night to consult with his friend.

The outcome of this was that two days later complete impressions were taken of the small latchkey, and within three days came the duplicate by post.

Max bought two electric torches, two pairs of felt slippers, a piece of thin but very strong rope, screwdriver, chisel, and other implements, until he had a full burglar's equipment. The preparations were exciting during the next few days, yet when they came down to bed-rock fact there was that locked door which stood between them and the truth.

Charlie's object in obtaining a duplicate latchkey was to enter noiselessly one night shortly before eleven, and secrete, themselves somewhere until Levi bolted the door and retired. They must take their chance of making any discovery they could. Both were well aware of Levi's vigilance, and his quickness of hearing. Therefore they would be compelled to work without noise, and also to guard against any hidden electric burglar alarms which might be secreted in the sashes of windows or in lintels of doors.

Investigation by Charlie had not revealed the existence of any of these terrors to thieves; yet so many were the precautions against intruders that the least suspected contrivance for their detection was to be expected.

Nearly a fortnight passed before all arrangements were complete for the nocturnal tour of investigation. Daily Rolfe, though attentive to his duties as the old man's secretary, was always on the alert to discover the existence of that key to the iron door. By all manner of devices he endeavoured to compel Statham to unwittingly reveal its whereabouts. He made pretence of mistaking various keys to deed boxes and nests of drawers, in order that the old man should produce other keys. But he was too wary, and never once did he fall into the trap.

Yet often he left the study, passed up the stain, and through the door swiftly, until the younger man began to suspect that it might be opened by means of some secret spring.

Standing below, he could not obtain sight of the old fellow as he opened the door, and to follow him half-way up was too dangerous a proceeding. He had risked a good deal, but he dare not risk the old man's wrath in that.

Still that he passed the door quickly and without hindrance was plainly shown. He had a key secreted somewhere—a key which, when applied, turned quickly, with ease and without noise, to admit the owner of the great mansion to the apartments where his secret was so successfully hidden.

Sometimes he would descend pale, haggard, and agitated, his hand upon his heart, as though to recover his breath. At others he was flushed and angry, like a man who had a moment before taken part in a heated discussion which had ended in a serious difference.

Charlie watched all this, and wondered.

What secret could possibly be hidden in those upper storeys that were at times so brilliantly lit?

Each evening he called on Max at Dover Street, and with closed door, so that the man should not hear, they discussed the situation.

Of Jean Adam nothing further had been seen. Neither had the hunchback engineer, Leonard Lyle, been at all it evidence. Ever since Max had given the Frenchman his decision not to go to Constantinople Adam had held aloof from him. They had parted perfectly good friends, but Max could detect the bitter chagrin that his reply had caused.

One evening as the two sat together Charlie related his curious experience of the short, dark, good-looking girl who had met him in Paris and talked so strangely of Maud in the Tuileries Gardens.

Max sat smoking his cigar listening to every word.

"Curious—very curious!" he ejaculated. "Didn't she tall you her name?"

"She gave it as Lorena."

"Lorena!" gasped the other, starting up. "Lorena—why, it must have been Lorena Lyle—old Lyle's daughter?"

"His daughter! I never knew he had one."

"No; perhaps not. He doesn't often speak of her, I believe. I saw her once, not long ago."

"They have quarrelled—father and daughter!" exclaimed Rolfe. "And that accounts for her exposure of the plot against Statham to compel him to commit suicide rather than to face exposure. Remember, she would not betray who was Adam's associate in the matter. Because it is her own father, without a doubt."

"She alleged that Statham committed a secret crime, by which he laid the foundation of his great fortune," Max remembered. "And, further, that confirmation of the charge brought by Adam will be found beyond that locked door?"

"Yes," said his companion, in a hollow voice; "I see it all. The girl wishes to exclude her father from the business. Yet she knows more than she has told me."

"No doubt. She probably knew Maud also, for she has lived for years—indeed, nearly all her life—in Belgrade," Barclay remarked. "She quarrelled with her father, and went on the stage as a dancer in the Opera at Vienna. She is now in Paris in the same capacity. If I remember aright she was here at Covent Garden last season. They say she has great talent and that she's now being trained in Paris for the part of *première danseuse*."

"She alleged that there still live two witnesses of Statham's crime, whatever it was," Charlie went on.

"And they are probably Adam and her hunchback father—both men who have lived the life of the wilds beyond the fringe of civilisation—both men who are as unscrupulous as they are adventurous."

"But from all I knew of Lyle he was a most highly respectable person. In Belgrade they still speak of him with greatest respect."

"Leonard Lyle in Belgrade, my dear chap, may have been a very different person to Leonard Lyle in other countries, you know," was his friend's reply.

"But why has his daughter given me this warning, at the same time taking care to conceal her identity."

"She was a short, dark-haired girl, rather good-looking, except that her top teeth protruded a little; about nineteen or so—eh?"

"Exactly."

"And depend upon it that she has warned you at Maud's request, in order that you may be forearmed against the blow which the pair are going to strike."

"And which we—you and I, Max—are going to assist—eh?" added the other, grimly.

Chapter Forty Six
To Learn the Truth

The mystery by which old Sam Statham sometimes passed beyond that white-enamelled door was inexplicable.

Whenever he left the library to ascend the stairs, Charlie Rolfe stole quietly out behind him, and listened. Sometimes he distinctly heard the key in the lock; at others it sounded as though the closed door yielded to his touch and swung aside for him to pass beyond. It closed always with a thud, as though felt had been placed upon it to prevent any metallic clang.

While Charlie watched the great financier's every movement, Max was unceasing in his inquiries regarding Marion. Advertisements had Men published in the "personal" columns of various newspapers, and the private inquiry agents whose aid he had sought had been unremitting in their vigilance.

The whole affair from beginning to end now showed the existence of some powerful hand which had directed and rendered the mystery beyond solution. The strange re-appearance of Jean Adam and Leonard Lyle had been followed quickly by the extraordinary flight of Doctor Petrovitch and Maud. The latter had only an hour before she had disappeared into space made some remarkable confession to Marion—a confession which might or might not save Samuel Statham from an ignominious death.

But the girl had preserved the secret of the confession confided to her by her friend, and, preferring shame and misjudgment, she in turn had disappeared, whither no one knew.

The two men, brother and lover, who had now united their forces to solve the problem and at the same time ascertain for themselves what the secret of the house in Park Lane really was, were at their wits' ends. Their inquiries and their efforts always led them into a *cul-de-sac*. At every turn they seemed foiled and baffled. And was it surprising when it was considered the power of Samuel Statham and the means at his command for the preservation of a secret?

Charlie felt that he was being watched hourly by one or other of those spies who sometimes gave such valuable information to the head of the firm. Some of these secret agents of Statham he knew by sight, but there were others unseen and unknown.

Even though Max and his friend were able to enter unheard and secrete themselves before the place was locked up by old Levi, yet there was that white door barring their passage to the mystery beyond. Many times they discussed the possibilities, and each time hesitated. Charlie was sorely puzzled regarding the key of the iron door. Sometimes it was undoubtedly used, sometimes not.

At last one evening, after both men had dined at the St. James's, of which Max was a member, they resolved upon a bold move. Charlie suggested it, and the other was at once ready and eager.

So after Max had been round to his rooms to put on a suit of dark tweeds, he went to Charlie's chambers where the various implements were produced and laid upon the table. It was then nearly ten o'clock.

Rolfe, having sent Green to the other end of Jermyn Street out of the way, drew out the whisky decanter from the tantalus stand, poured out two "pegs" with soda, and drank:

"Success to the elucidation of old Statham's secret."

Then, carefully stowing the various articles in their pockets, they slipped down into the street and were out of sight before the inquisitive Green had returned.

Arrived in Park Lane, after a hasty walk, they strolled slowly along by the park railings past the house. All was in darkness save the hall, where the electric lamp showed above the fanlight. Old Sam was probably in his study, smoking his last cigar, for the shutters were that night closed, as they sometimes were. The shutters of the basement were also closed behind their iron bars, while at the upstairs windows all the blinds were carefully drawn.

Indeed, the exterior of the house presented nothing unusual. It was the same as any other mansion in Park Lane. Yet there were many who on going up and down the thoroughfare afoot or on the motor-'buses jerked their thumbs at it and whispered. The house had earned a reputation for mystery. Sam Statham was a mystery in himself, and of his house many weird things were alleged.

Thrice the pair passed and repassed. At the corner of Deanery Street stood a constable, and while he remained there it was injudicious to attempt an entry with a latchkey. So they strolled back in the direction of the fountain, conversing in undertones.

Max glanced at his watch, and found that it wanted a quarter to eleven. At last they crossed the road and passed the door. All seemed quiet. At that moment the only object in sight was a receding motor-'bus showing its red tail-light. Not a soul was on the pavement.

"All clear!" cried Charlie, scarce above a whisper, as he slipped up the two or three steps, followed by his companion.

That moment was an exciting one. Next second, however, the key was in the latch, and without a sound the wards of the lock were lifted.

In another moment the pair stood within the brightly-lit hall, and the door was closed noiselessly behind them.

Standing there, within a few yards of the door of the library, where from the smell of tobacco smoke it was evident that old Sam was taking his ease, they were in imminent risk of discovery. Besides, Levi had a habit of moving without sound in his old felt slippers, and might at any moment appear up the stairs from the lower regions.

Instinctively Charlie glanced upstairs towards the locked door. But next second he motioned his companion to follow, and stole on tiptoe over the thick Turkey carpets past the millionaire's door and on into a kind of small conservatory which lay behind the hall and was in darkness.

Though leading from the room behind the library, it was a fairly good spot as a place of hiding, yet so vigilant was old Levi that the chances were he would come in there poking about ere he retired to rest.

The two men stood together behind a bank of what had once been greenhouse plants, but all of them had died by neglect and want of water long ago. The range of pots and dried stalks still remained, forming an effectual barrier behind which they could conceal themselves.

Through the long French window of the room adjoining the light shone, and Charlie, slowly creeping forward, peered within.

Then he whispered to his friend, and both men bent to see what was transpiring.

The scene was unusual.

A full view of the library could be obtained from where they stood in the darkness. In the room two of the big armchairs had been pulled up, with a small coffee table between them. On one side was old Sam, lazily smoking one of his big cigars, while on the other was Levi, lying back, his legs stretched out, smoking with perfect equanimity and equally with his master. Upon the table was a decanter of whisky and two glasses, and, judging from the amused countenances of both men, Sam had been relating to Levi something which struck the other as humorous.

It was curious, to say the least, that Levi, the humble, even cringing, servant should place himself upon an equality with his master. That he was devoted to old Sam, Charlie knew well, but this friendship he had never suspected. There was a hidden reason for it all, without a doubt.

The two intruders watched with bated breath, neither daring to make a sound.

They saw Levi, his cigar stuck in the side of his mouth, lean back and thrust his hands deep into his trousers-pockets, uttering some words which they could not catch. His manner had changed, and so had Sam's. From gay the pair had suddenly grown grave. Upon the millionaire's brow was a dark shadow, such as Charlie, who knew him intimately in all his moods, had seldom seen there.

Levi was speaking quickly, his attitude changed, as though giving serious advice, to which his master listened with knit brows and deep attention. Then, with a suddenness that caused the two watchers to start, the electric bell at the hall-door sounded.

In an instant Levi tossed his cigar into the fire, whipped off his glass from the table, and in a single instant became the grave family servant again, as with a quick gesture of his hand he left the room to answer the summons at the door.

In a few moments he returned, closing the door quickly after him, so that whoever was in the hall could not overhear what was said.

Approaching his master he made some announcement in a whisper, whereat the millionaire clenched his fist, and struck violently in the air. Levi urged calmness; that was evident from his manner.

Then Sam, with a resigned air, shrugged his shoulders, paced the room in quick agitation, and turned upon his servant with his eyes flashing with anger.

Again Levi placed his thin hand on the old man's arm which calmed him into almost instant submission.

Then the grave-faced old servant went out, and an instant later ushered in a woman, all in black—a woman who, in instant, both Max and Charlie recognised.

They both stood watching, breathless—rooted to the spot.

The mystery, as they afterwards discovered, was even greater than they had ever anticipated.

It was beyond human credence.

Chapter Forty Seven
Contains More Mystery

The old-fashioned, ill-cut gown of black stuff and the rather unbecoming big black hat gave Sam's visitor an appearance of being older than she really was. A spotted veil concealed her features, but as she entered the room she raised it quickly.

The face revealed was the soft, sweet countenance of Maud Petrovitch.

Charlie gripped his companion's arm and gave vent to an exclamation of amazement as he stood peering forth open-mouthed.

As the girl entered the old man turned fiercely upon her and uttered some inquiry. What it was the watchers could not distinguish, for thick plate glass stood between the conservatory and the library. Yet whatever he said or however caustic and bitter his manner, the young girl stood defiant.

Her chin was raised, her eyes flashed upon him, and her gloved hand was outstretched in a gesture of calm denunciation as she replied with some words that caused the old fellow to draw back in surprise and confusion.

The door had closed, for Levi had left the pair together. Max wondered whether the old servant would now come and search the back premises prior to locking up. If so, they might easily be discovered. Those felt-soled boots of old Levi struck fear into their hearts. Charlie was, however, too occupied in watching the old man and the girl at that moment to think of any danger of detection.

His well-beloved stood pale, beautiful, and yet defiant before the man who a moment before had shaken his fist and clenched his teeth on hearing of her demand to see him. The words she had uttered had caused an instant change in his manner. His sudden anger had been succeeded by fear. Whatever she had said was evidently straight to the point.

For a moment he regarded her in silence, then over his grey face came a crafty smile as with mock courtesy he offered her a chair, still remaining standing himself.

She leaned her elbow on the arm of the chair, and, bending towards him, was speaking again, uttering slow, decisive words, each of which seemed to bite into his very soul. His countenance again changed; from mock humour it became hard, drawn, almost haggard.

Charlie, who knew the old man in every mood, had never witnessed such an expression upon his face. Beneath it all, however, he detected a look of unrelenting, almost fiendish revenge. He longed to rush forward and grasp his loved one in his arms, but Max, seeing his agitation, laid his hand firmly upon his shoulder.

"Let us watch in patience, Charlie," he urged. "We may learn something interesting."

Maud had altered but little since that afternoon when, in the haze of the red London sunset, Charlie had last walked with her in Nevern Square. She was, perhaps, a trifle pinched in the cheeks, but the sweet dimples were still there, and the little wisp of hair still strayed across her white brow. Her gown, however, seemed shabby and ill-fitting. Perhaps she had borrowed it in order to come there in garments by which she would not be recognised. For a young girl to make a visit at that late hour was, to say the least, somewhat unusual.

Both men standing in the shadow behind the thick glass longed to hear what the pair were saying. It was tantalising to be so near the disclosure of a secret—indeed, to have it enacted before one's eyes—and yet be debarred from learning the truth.

Max examined the door, hoping to open it ever so slightly, but to his chagrin he found it locked and bolted. Old Levi had already prepared to retire before they had made their surreptitious entrance there.

That he had at last found Maud again was to both a source of immense gratification. At last the truth of the doctor's strange disappearance would now be known. But what connection could old Statham have with the affair?

Charlie recollected what Sir Charles Harrison had told him in Belgrade— that the bomb outrage by which a poor innocent child had lost her life had been planned by one of his friends.

He had suspected Max. But in the light of Maud's secret visit to Statham, he now held the last-named in distinct suspicion. Was it part of the millionaire's cunning policy in Servia to rid the country of its greatest statesman?

No. That was impossible. The Doctor and Statham had been friends. When Petrovitch was in power they had worked hand-in-glove, with the result that the millionaire had lent money to the Servian Government upon very second-class security. Unrest in Servia would, Charlie was well aware, mean loss to Statham Brothers of perhaps a million sterling. It was therefore to the interest of the firm that the present Government should remain in power, and that the country should be allowed to develop and progress peacefully.

He tried to put behind him that increasing suspicion that Old Sam was the "friend" to whom the diplomat had so mysteriously referred.

And yet as he watched every movement, every gesture of the pair within that long room where the lights were so artistically shaded—the room wherein deals involving the loss or gain of hundreds of thousands of pounds were decided—he saw that the girl remained still defiant, and that the man stood vanquished by her slow, deliberate accusation.

Old Sam's bony fingers were twitching—a sign of suppressed wrath which his secretary knew well. He held his thin lower lip between his yellow teeth, and standing with his back to the fireplace, he now and then cast a supercilious smile upon the pretty girl who had come there in defiance of the convenances—in defiance, evidently, of his own imperious commands.

Samuel Statham at that moment was not the hard-faced old benefactor who haunted the seats in the park and gave so much money anonymously to the deserving among the "submerged tenth." He was a man fighting for his honour, his reputation, his gold—nay, his very life. He was a man whose keen wit was now pitted against that of a clear, level-headed girl—one who had right and justice on her side.

Was it possible, Charlie thought, that his well-beloved knew the old man's secret—that secret which, before he would face its exposure, he would prefer the grave itself?

He watched Maud and noted how balanced was her beautiful countenance, and yet how calm and how determined she was. When the old man spoke she listened with attention, but her replies, brief and pointed, were always made with a gesture and expression of triumph, as of one who knew the naked and astounding truth.

"What can it all mean?" whispered Max. "Why is she here? How tantalising it is that we cannot catch a single word she is uttering!"

"The door's bolted," Charlie said in a tone of chagrin. "We can only watch. See!—she's evidently telling him some home truths that are the reverse of palatable. He looks as though he could kill her!"

"He'd better not attempt it," remarked Max grimly, and they both stood again in silence, peering forward in breathless eagerness.

For fully ten minutes longer the old man and the young girl were in heated discussion. Sometimes Statham spoke quickly and angrily, with that caustic assertiveness that most people found so overbearing. Of a sudden both watchers were aware of a slow, stealthy movement behind them—a shuffling of feet it seemed.

It was old Levi, on his tour of inspection to reassure himself that all was secure. In an instant both intruders drew back into the deep shadow behind a high stand upon which stood choice plants in tiers, or rather the dried-up pots which had once contained them.

They were only just in time, for old Levi, peering forth into the semi-darkness as he stood in the doorway leading from the hall, searched around. Then, finding all quiet and detecting nobody, he closed the door and locked it.

They were thus locked out by both doors!

To re-enter the house would be difficult. It was a contingency for which they had not been prepared.

Still, they were too interested in watching the pair within to think much of the contretemps that had occurred. Old Levi had shuffled away, and was waiting, no doubt, to usher out the dainty little visitor before returning to the regions below.

Maud, however, showed no sign of haste to leave. Comfortably ensconced in her chair, with her veil thrown back, she sat facing him, and replying without hesitation to his allegations.

The sinister expression upon the old man's face told its own tale. His impatient bearing and quick gesture showed his eagerness to get rid of her. But she, on her part, seemed to have no intention of leaving just yet. She was speaking, her gloved finger raised to emphasise her words—hard words, which, from the expression upon her face seemed full of bitter sarcasm and reproach.

Of a sudden he turned upon the girl with a fierceness which took her by surprise. He uttered a few words, which she answered quickly. Then, striking his hands into the pockets of his trousers, he bent towards her with an evil grin upon his grey face and made some remarks which caused in her a quick change of attitude.

She rose from her chair, her face aflame with anger, and, taking a couple of paces towards him, replied with a vehemence which neither of the unseen onlookers suspected.

The battle of words continued. He was making some allegations, the truth of which she was denying. This girl, not yet out of her teens, was defiant of the man whose life had been one long struggle to grow rich, and whose gigantic wealth was now crushing the very soul from his body. Surely they were an incongruous pair. His defiance of her was only a half-hearted one. His sarcasm had irritated her, and now, alleging something, which was a lie, he had goaded her into all the fierce ebullition of anger which a woman, however calm and level-headed she may be, cannot at times restrain.

"I wonder what the old blackguard has said?" whispered Max to the man at his side.

"It seems as though he has made some charge against her."

"Or against her father," Max suggested.

"You suspected me of being privy to the Doctor's disappearance, Max," Charlie said, still in a whisper. "You said that you saw me at Cromwell Road that night. Are you still of that opinion?"

"No," responded his friend. "There was a plot—a cleverly devised plot. Someone went there dressed exactly like you."

"But you say you saw his face."

"So I did. And I could have sworn it was you."

"It is that conspiracy which we have to fathom," Charlie said. "At least, we have established the fact that Maud is alive. And having found Maud, we may also find Marion. Possibly she went to her into safe hiding from us."

"More than possible, I think."

But while they were whispering something occurred which made them both start. The girl, crimson with anger, suddenly dived her hand into her dress pocket, and, taking out a bundle of paper, flung it at the man before her.

They saw, to their amazement, that it was a bunch of crisp banknotes. She had cast it at his feet in open defiance.

Perhaps the money was the price of her silence—money he had sent to her or to her father to purchase secrecy!

The old man gave a glance at the notes crushed into a bundle and lying upon the carpet, and then, turning to her, snapped his bony finger and thumb in defiance, and laughed in her face—a grim, evil laugh, which Charlie knew from experience meant retaliation and bitter vengeance.

Chapter Forty Eight
Not Counting the Cost

The girl turned to leave, but the old man placed himself between her and the door.

She stamped her little foot angrily in command to be allowed to pass.

He saw her determination, and hesitated. Then he seemed to commence to argue, to place before her the probable result of her action in casting aside the money, but she would hear nothing. Her mind seemed fully made up. She had spoken her last word, and wished to leave him.

He saw in her decision an attitude antagonistic to himself. He was in deadly peril. Though his wealth could command all that was good and all that was bad, though it placed him above his fellow men and rendered him immune from much, yet it could not ensure her goodwill.

Both Max and Charlie realised plainly that Maud was in possession of some great secret, and that she had refused a bribe of silence. This man who had believed that his money could purchase anything had discovered, to his dismay, that it could not seal her lips. He saw himself facing an imminent peril, and was undecided how to act.

He argued. But she would not listen. He appealed. But she only smiled and shook her head.

Her mind was made up. She had decided to refuse the money. He picked it from the floor and handed it to her again, but she would not take it in her hand.

Then he crossed to his writing-table, took out his chequebook and scribbled a cheque—one for a large amount in all probability. Tearing it from its counterfoil, he gave it to her.

But with an expression of defiance she tore it into four and cast it upon the floor with a gesture of disgust. And in triumph, before he could prevent her, she opened the door, and disappeared from the room.

"We must follow her?" whispered Charlie eagerly.

"But, my dear fellow, we can't! We're locked in!"

Rolfe, realising the truth that they were prevented from overtaking his well-beloved, for whom they had been so long in active search, and that she must again dip from them into oblivion, gave vent to a forcible expression of despair.

"Let's remain here," urged Max. "We may learn something else."

"The old man will go to bed," was Charlie's response. "And we will follow and explore above."

"How?" asked Rolfe.

"That remains to be seen. We must, in this case, act discreetly, and trust to luck."

"But Maud? I must see her."

"That's impossible at present. You have seen her—that's enough for to-night. To-morrow we may discover something further—or even to-night."

Both men, scarce daring to breathe, were watching old Sam.

After the girl had gone, he placed his hand upon his heart, and, with face white and haggard, he sank into his writing-chair. He had collapsed as though he had received a sudden blow.

Levi entered hurriedly a few moments later, and, finding his master leaning forward upon his table muttering to himself, tried to rouse him.

A glance at his face showed that he had collapsed. Levi therefore rushed across the room, poured out some brandy from the tantalus, and compelled the old man to swallow it. This, after a few moments, revived him. The faithful servant, however, stood by in wonderment. He seemed puzzled as to what had occurred.

But the fragments of the torn cheque scattered upon the carpet showed defiance on the part of the visitor whom he had just shown out into the night.

Levi stooped as far as his rheumatism would allow, and slowly, very slowly, gathered up the torn pieces of paper and placed them in the basket, his eyes the whole time upon his master.

Straightening himself again, he spoke, making inquiry as to what had occurred. But his master, with a wave of his hand, commanded his silence. Then, sinking back in his chair, he remained, staring straight before him like a man in a dream. He seemed peering into the future—and he saw only exposure and ruin!

Hands and teeth were clenched, for he realised that he had taken a false step. He had misjudged his own power and influence. He had believed that a good and truthful woman could be purchased, as he might purchase any other thing or chattel.

She had cast his gold into his face. She had insulted him, for she had spoken a truth which he could not deny. Indeed, that slim, pale-faced girl, scarce more than a child, held over him power supreme—power for life, or for death.

The scene within that room was a strange one.

Old Levi, standing statuesque at his master's side, uttered some words. But the millionaire was silent. He only raised his grey head and sat staring at the great painting opposite—staring like a man peering into the grim unknown.

The door that divided the watchers from the watched prevented the words from being overheard. The thickness of its glass prevented the truth being known to the two men standing breathless behind it. Had it been ordinary glass they would no doubt have overheard the conversation between the old man and his fair visitor.

The anger of both men had been aroused by Statham's attitude towards the girl. Even Charlie, faithful and devoted as he had been to the millionaire, had now become fiercely antagonistic, for he had seen by the old man's countenance that some terrible revenge was intended upon the girl he loved so dearly.

Levi bent and placed his hand tenderly upon his master's shoulder.

But Statham shook him off, and, straightening himself, staggered to his feet and paced the room in a frenzy of despair.

Charlie recollected his agitation after the unexpected discovery of Jean Adam lounging outside the park railings. This repetition of his apprehension showed him to be in terror of exposure and denunciation.

Maud, so slim, sweet-faced, and innocent, had defied him. She held him, the man whose power in every European capital was recognised and feared, in the hollow of her hand.

Why? Ay, to that question there was no answer. They had witnessed the scene, but they had caught no sound of one single word.

At last Levi succeeded in calming his master. He mixed him another brandy and soda and handed it to him. The old man seized it with unsteady hand, and tossed it off at a single gulp.

Then he walked slowly from the room, followed by Levi.

An instant later the old servant turned the switch, and the room, and with it the neglected conservatory, were plunged in darkness.

The two intruders listened. Voices sounded, and then died away. A moment later they heard a thud, and knew that the old man had passed beyond the white-enamelled door and had closed it behind him.

For another few minutes they remained in silence, then Max whispered: "What shall we do?"

"We must get out of here," answered his friend promptly. "We're caught like a rat in a trap. To open either of the doors leading into the house is impossible. We must try and make our exit by the back," and, groping his way, he moved to the door, which opened on to a small, paved backyard.

But it had been secured. Levi, indeed, kept it always locked, and the key was not there.

"To break this open will create a noise, and arouse somebody," Max remarked.

"Well, we must get out at all hazards. We can't stay here till morning and court discovery," Rolfe argued. "If we only had a little light we might see what we're doing. By Jove! You've got a pocket-lamp, Max. Where is it?"

"Is it safe yet to show a light?" Barclay asked dubiously. "It may be seen from outside, you know!"

"It can't. There's a blank wall opposite."

"But will not the reflection be seen by Levi from below?" asked Max.

Rolfe saw that, after all, there was some danger of detection, and admitted it.

"Then let's wait a bit," his companion whispered. "By patience we may be able to escape without detection. Don't let us act indiscreetly."

So the pair, leaning against one of the stands of dead flowers, waited in silence, their ears strained to catch every sound. The moments seemed hours, until at last, all being quiet, Max, at his friend's suggestion pressed the electric button of the little hand-lamp and showed a light upon the door.

It was half of glass, with strong lock and double bolts. To escape meant to break away a hole large enough for a man's body to pass. Max suggested that they might find the key hanging somewhere upon a nail, as conservatory keys are often kept, in that manner. But though they searched the whole place, treading lightly as they went, they were unable to discover it.

"Levi keeps it upon his bunch, I expect," Charlie remarked. "I've never seen this door open in my life."

"That's why the flowers are all dead, perhaps," Max remarked grimly with a low laugh.

"Flowers! Old Sam declared that they were no use to him, therefore he forbade Levi to give them any water, and they all died. The old man isn't fond of flowers. Says they're only useful at weddings and funerals."

"There won't be many at his obsequies!" laughed Max beneath his breath, as he made another examination of the door.

Both agreed that to open it was impossible, while to break out the glass was far too risky a proceeding, for some of it must fall upon the paving outside.

Rain had begun to fall, pattering heavily upon the glass roof above; and as they were both searching about blindly for some other mode of egress Max suddenly exclaimed:

"Why, look here!" and pointed to a portion of the glass side of the conservatory which had opened outwardly upon a hinge, but which had been securely screwed up.

"Excellent!" cried Charlie, realising that an exit lay there, and, quickly drawing from his pocket a serviceable-looking screwdriver, set to work upon the screws.

They were long, and hard to withdraw, but ten minutes later all six of them were taken out, and, pushing back the movable frame upon its hinges, they found themselves outside in the narrow backyard.

Once free, Max turned his face upwards to the dark windows of the first floor of the mysterious mansion, saying: "We must get up there, Charlie, somehow or other. I'm not going from this place until I've learnt its secret."

"No," responded his friend. "Neither am I."

Chapter Forty Nine
What Lay behind the Door

Above the dome-shaped roof of the conservatory was a row of four long dark windows, and still above them two further storeys. On the second storey in the centre of the house was a high window covered with wire network, evidently a staircase window of stained glass.

The whole place was in darkness, as were the houses on either side, while at rear of them rose a blank wall, the back of one of the houses in Park Street. The only light showing was in the basement—a faint glimmer behind the green holland blinds, which showed the presence of Levi in the lower regions.

"He sleeps in the front," remarked Charlie. "I expect, however, he keeps this on all night."

"Where does old Sam sleep?"

"That I don't know. We'll have to discover."

The windows above the conservatory were their objective, but to ascend there was full of peril, for, even though they could climb up, one false step and they would come crashing through the glass roof. This would mean both serious personal injury as well as instant discovery.

In the whispered consultation that followed, both recognised the danger, but both were equally determined to risk it. They had plenty of time. The night was still young, therefore there was no need for haste.

They made careful examination as far as they could in the very faint light. Max was afraid to flash his electric lamp too often lest the attention of any neighbour might be attracted and an alarm of "burglars" given. Neither knew whether a servant might not be looking out upon the night. The house they desired to enter had earned a reputation as a house of mystery, therefore it was more than likely that some watchful eye of a curious neighbour, master or servant, was kept upon the rear of the premises.

At last, Max, who was the more athletic and nimble of the two, decided that the only way by which to reach the roof of the conservatory was by the spouting at the side. The ascent was a difficult one, but he resolved to attempt it.

Taking a small coil of thin but very strong rope which Charlie produced from the capacious pocket of the shooting-jacket he wore for that purpose, he mounted upon his friend's shoulders, and then climbed slowly up, with an agility which surprised his friend.

Once upon the roof he made fast the rope to one of the iron stays of the spouting, and let it down to Charlie, who a few moments later swarmed up it and stood on the edge of the glass roof beside his companion.

Their position there was one of greatest peril. They stood together upon the narrow edging of lead by which the glass roof was joined to the wall of the house. They moved slowly and gingerly, for it was quite uncertain whether it would bear their weight. Besides, there was nothing to grasp by which to relieve their weight, for above them rose the wall sheer to the ledges of the row of windows, too high for them to reach.

A step in the wrong direction, and down they must come with a crash into the neglected conservatory.

Max could hear his own heart beating. The risk was greater than he had ever anticipated. Yet so greatly was their curiosity now aroused that nothing could brook their attempt to learn the secret that dark mysterious house contained.

They stood together, not daring to move. At a short distance away was a thin iron support running into the wall—part of the framework of the roof—and towards that Max crept carefully, until at last he reached it and stood in a safer position.

The weight of both men caused the curved roof to give slightly, and more than once they heard sharp noises where the glass, fitting too tightly, cracked across by the undue pressure.

Neither spoke. Max was eagerly searching for some means by which to reach one of the windows above. In his ascent there he had torn his coat, and a great strip of it was hanging. He had left his hat below, and the light rain was falling upon his uncovered head.

Slowly he crept forward from iron to iron until he reached the opposite side of the big glass roof, and there found, as he had hoped, another iron rain-spout which led straight up past the end window, to the roof of the house.

Back he came to his companion in order to obtain the rope, and then, with it bulging in his pocket, he stole along and ascended the second pipe as he had done the first. This proceeding was, however, far more dangerous, for to fall with the glass beneath him meant almost certain death.

Charlie watched his form ascending in the darkness, scarce daring to breathe. Slowly he went up, until, on a level with the window, he halted. Around the ledge, six inches above, was an iron bar let into the wall in order to prevent flowerpots from being blown down upon the conservatory roof. This iron proved Max's salvation, for gripping it he steadied himself while he secured the rope to the spout as he had previously done on the first ascent.

Then, with a firm grip upon the strong bar, and his knee upon the stone ledge, he tried the window.

It was fastened. The green holland blind was drawn, but as far as he could ascertain the shutters were not closed.

From his pocket he drew a glazier's putty-knife, and, inserting it between the sashes, worked quietly until his heart gave a bound of satisfaction at feeling the latch slowly give.

A second later it went back with a sharp snap, and the window was free!

He lifted the sash, pushed the blind aside, and crept within.

Then leaning forth he whispered to Charlie to follow. Up the latter came by means of the rope as quickly as he was able, and a few moments later both men stood within the room.

By its sound, and by the fact that it was carpetless, they knew it was devoid of furniture. Max flashed on the light, and the truth was at once made plain. The apartment was square and of fair size, but within was not a single thing; was perfectly empty.

In a second a thought occurred to Charlie.

"If the door's locked on the outside we're done!" he gasped.

They both crossed to the door in an instant, and Max placed his hand upon it. The handle turned slowly, and the door yielded. By great good fortune it was not locked.

Creeping noiselessly outside, they found themselves upon a big square landing above half a dozen broad stairs. Below them was the white-enamelled iron door, which opened only to its owner and which no person had been known to pass.

The landing and stairs were thickly-carpeted, just as they were below the door. But about the place was the close musty smell of a house that for years had remained closed and neglected.

From the landing were three other doors beside the one at which they stood, all of them closed.

Charlie took his bearings, and, pointing to the door farthest away from them, whispered:

"That's the drawing-room, no doubt. And that's the door of the room adjoining. I expect it's a big room opening from back to front like all drawing-rooms in these houses."

"Awkward if it proves to be the old man's bedroom," Max replied, with a laugh.

"We must risk that. My own belief is that he sleeps up on the next floor. These are all reception-rooms, without a doubt," was Charlie's answer. It was strange, after all the time he had been in the old man's employ, that this should be the first occasion he should explore the house.

Those moments of pitch darkness were exciting ones.

They resolved to enter the door furthest away, the door which they believed led to the drawing-room, and together they moved noiselessly across with that purpose.

The key was in the lock. Without noise Max turned it, and slowly pushed open the door.

Both entered, holding their breath and fearing to make the slightest sound, for they knew not whether old Sam was asleep there.

For a full ten minutes they paused listening for sounds of breathing in the pitch darkness. But there were none, only the beating of their own hearts.

Then, with Charlie's whispered consent, Max pressed the button of the pocket-lamp, and it shed a streak of light across to the opposite wall of the big apartment.

What was revealed held them aghast and amazed.

"This is indeed strange?" gasped Charlie. "What can it be?"

Max was turning the light from side to side of the room, examining every corner.

What they saw had held them both speechless.

Charlie saw an electric switch near his hand, and touched it. In an instant the great room was flooded with light, revealing a scene, curious, unusual, extraordinary.

There was no thick carpet or upholstered furniture; no painted ceiling or pictures upon the walls; no cabinet or bric-à-brac, or grand piano, or palms, or anything connected with drawing-room furniture.

Instead, the two intruders found themselves inside a peasant's cottage in some far-off country—a house, it seemed, with quaint furniture painted and carved. Before them was an old-fashioned oak press, black with smoke and age, and along the wall a row of shining cooking utensils of copper. In the centre was a long old table, with big high-backed wooden chairs; at the side a high brick stove.

The men stepped within and gazed around, bewildered.

At one end was a small square window, where beyond lay a snow-clad scene, lit by the moon's rays—a cleverly contrived piece of scenery, showing the white road winding into the distance lined on each side by the dark forest of firs.

The scene was intended to be Russian, without a doubt, for over the stove a holy ikon hung against the wall, a small painted head surrounded by a square of highly burnished gold.

Every object was quaintly shaped and foreign. In one corner stood an old spinning-wheel with the flax upon it, while in another was an old-fashioned gun. A couple of wolves' skins were spread upon the floor, while upon the cleanly-scrubbed table showed a large brown stain—it might be of coffee, or it might be of blood!

The walls had been whitewashed, and across the ceiling, once gilt and adorned, no doubt, ran blackened beams in exact imitation, it seemed, of some house in the far east of Russia beyond the Volga.

Upon a side table lay a big, rather thin book, bearing upon its black, greasy cover the Imperial Russian arms—the double-headed eagle. Charlie opened it, and found it ruled like an attendance book, with careful entries in Russian in various hands. Neither could read the language, therefore it was to them unintelligible. By the stove was a low wooden settle, upon which lay a man's fur cap and big sheepskin winter coat, as though the owner of the place had just risen and left.

"What can this possibly mean?" asked Max, gazing around in sheer wonderment.

To this query, however, Charlie could venture no suggestion.

They stood amid surroundings that were to both a complete mystery.

Charlie touched the switch when, lo! the lights in the room were extinguished, and only a line of white brilliance as that of the full moon entering the window from the snow-covered land beyond, fell across the silent place full upon the table which bore that ugly dark brown stain.

Both men stood motionless and wondering, fascinated by the extraordinary and striking effect.

Was that stain shown so vividly beneath the white moonbeams actually the stain of blood?

Chapter Fifty
Face to Face

That a Park Lane drawing-room should be transformed into the interior of a log-built house of the Russian steppe was surely unsuspected by any of those who passed up and down that renowned thoroughfare every day.

The popular idea associated that long row of millionaires' houses facing Hyde Park with luxuriant saloons, priceless paintings, old Persian carpets, and exquisite furniture. Who would believe that behind those windows with their well-kept curtains, and *brisé-brisé* of silk and lace, was a room arranged with such care, with the snowy road and moonlight shown beyond the false window?

"With what object, I wonder, is all this?" asked Charlie, speaking in an undertone, as though to himself. There was something weird and uncanny about the scene with that white streak of brilliance falling like a bar across the place, an indescribable something which made it plain that all had been arranged with some evil design by the old man.

No second glance was needed to show that every bit of furniture, and every article in the place was genuine. They were no stage properties, but real things, brought from some far-distant spot in Eastern Russia. But with what motive?

Ay, that was the question!

They had turned, and were about to withdraw from the place, Max leading the way, when suddenly he halted, for his quick ears caught some sound. It was a curious, low, whirring noise, followed almost instantly by a swift swish close to him, so near, indeed, that it caused a current of air in his face as some object passed him from above.

At the same moment the noise of mechanism ceased.

For a few seconds both intruders hesitated.

Charlie asked breathlessly what it could be, whereupon his friend turned on the light, and the truth stood revealed.

By an ace he had escaped with his life!

At the door, in order to prevent the egress of any intruder, a cunning but dastardly mechanical device had been placed. A long iron lever, to which was attached a keen-edged Japanese cutlass, had come forth from its hiding-place in the lintel of the door, and, descending with terrific force, had only just escaped cutting Max down.

Both men saw the means by which old Statham guarded the secret of that room, and shuddered. To enter was easy, but it was intended that he who entered might not emerge alive.

Apparently one of the floor boards just within the door was loose, and, being trodden upon, the weight released the spring or mechanism, and the razor-edged cutlass shot forth with murderous force.

"By Jove!" gasped Charlie. "I had no idea the old man set traps for the unwary. We'd better be careful!"

"Yes. That was indeed a narrow escape!" whispered Max. "It would have been certain death. Let's get out of it."

The steel lever was down, the point of the cutlass touching the floor. Therefore they were both compelled to step over the death-trap in order to leave the remarkable apartment.

Then with careful hands Charlie tried the next door. It was locked.

Brief examination showed it to be the door of the back drawing-room, which had been thrown into the larger room with the mysterious purpose of constructing that striking rural interior.

So they crossed to the third door, on the opposite side of the landing, and, with greatest caution lest another pitfall should lurk there, opened it.

That night of investigation was full of surprises.

The instant Max flashed on his light the pair drew back with low exclamations of horror.

The small apartment was unfurnished. It contained only one object—gruesome and unexpected. In the centre of the place, upon the black trestles, stood a coffin of polished oak with shining electro handles and fittings.

The lid, they noticed, was screwed down. Was it possible that it contained an unburied corpse. Did that white-enamelled door upon the stairs conceal from the world the evidence of a crime?

For a moment both men stood in that bare, uncarpeted room, rooted to the spot.

The secret of Sam Statham stood revealed.

Then with a sudden effort Charlie crept forward, nearer the coffin, and read upon its plate the words, plainly engraved:

JEAN ADAM. AGED 49.

Then Adam had been entrapped there—and had lost his life!

Both men started as the tragic truth dawned upon them. Adam was old Sam's most bitter enemy. He was dead—in his coffin—yet the millionaire had, up to the present, been unable to dispose of the remains. There was no medical certificate, therefore burial was impossible.

The weird stories which both men had heard of nocturnal visitors to that house who had never been seen to emerge, and of long boxes like coffins which more than one person said they had seen being brought out and loaded upon four-wheeled cabs all now flashed across their minds.

Of a verity that house was a house of grim shadows, for murder was committed there. Men entered alive, and left it dead.

Max stood by the coffin of the man who had so cleverly sought to entice him away to Constantinople with stories of easily obtained wealth, and remained there breathless in wonder. He recollected Sam's words, and saw in them a bitter hatred of the Franco-English adventurer. Had he carried this hatred to the extreme limit—that of secret assassination?

Charlie, on his part, stood silent also. He knew well that upon the death of Adam depended the future prosperity of his master. He was well aware, alas! that Adam, having suddenly reappeared, had vowed a terrible and crushing vengeance upon the head of the great firm of Statham Brothers.

But old Sam, with his usual crafty forethought and innate cunning, had forestalled him. The adventurer had been done to death, and was already in his coffin!

In his cool audacity old Sam had actually prepared the lead-lined coffin with its plate ready inscribed!

Its secret arrival at night had evidently been witnessed, and had given rise to strange and embellished stories.

The last occasion Max had seen Adam was one night three weeks before when, dining with two other men in the gallery of the Trocadero Restaurant, he had seen him below seated with a rather young and good-looking lady in an evening-dress of black net. The pair were laughing together, and it struck him that the companion of the adventurer might be French. He had afterwards discovered that she was Lorena Lyle, daughter of the old hunchback engineer who was his partner in certain ventures.

"The girl who met me in Paris and gave me warning!" Rolfe exclaimed.

"Yes, the same. They dined together that night and hurried out to get to the theatre."

"And you've never seen him since?"

"No. Ten days ago, I wrote to the National Liberal Club giving him an appointment, but he never kept it."

"Because he was lying here, I suppose," remarked Charlie with bated breath, adding: "This, Max, is all utterly incomprehensible. How dare the old man do such a thing?"

"He's been driven into a corner, and as long as he preserves his secret he will still remain a power in the land."

"But his secret is out—we have laid it bare."

"At risk of our lives—eh?" remarked Max, shuddering again as he recollected his own narrow escape of a few minutes before.

They stood before the mortal remains of the man who had sworn vengeance upon Statham, neither of them speaking. Presently, however, Charlie proposed that they should make further investigation on the floor above.

Closing the door of the death-chamber, they stole noiselessly up the wide, thickly-carpeted staircase to the next landing, where four white doors opened. Which they should enter first they were undecided. They were faced by a serious problem. In either of those four chambers the old millionaire might be asleep. To enter might awaken him.

This they had no desire to do. They expected to be able to open the iron door from within and pass down the stairs into the hall, and so into the street without detection. That was their intention. To return by the way they had come would be impossible.

Together they consulted in low whispers, and, both agreed, Charlie very carefully turned the handle of the door nearest them. It yielded, and they crept forward and within. At first Max feared to show his light, yet as they found no carpet beneath their feet, and as they felt a vague sense of space in the darkness, he became bolder, and pressed the button of his little lamp.

It was, like the other apartments, entirely devoid of furniture! The upper part of those premises, believed by the world to be filled with costly furniture and magnificent antiques, seemed empty. Charlie was amazed. He had heard many romantic stories of why the old man never allowed a stranger to ascend the stairs, but he had never dreamed that the fine mansion was unfurnished.

The next room they examined was similar in character, rather larger, with two long windows overlooking the Park. They were, however, carefully curtained, and the blinds were down. Beyond a rusty old fender before the fireplace and a roll of old carpet in a corner, it, however, contained nothing.

They passed to the third apartment, likewise a front room, and Max slowly turned the door-handle. In the darkness they stepped within, and again finding it uncarpeted, he shone his light across the place.

Next instant the pair drew back, for sitting up upon a low, iron camp bedstead, glaring at them with eyes haggard and terrified, was old Sam Statham himself.

The room was bare save an old painted washstand and chest of drawers, dirty, uncarpeted, and neglected. The low, narrow bed was covered by an old blue and white counterpane, but its occupant sat glaring at the intruders, too terrified to speak.

In the darkness he probably could not recognise who it was. The electric light blinded him. Next second, however, he touched the switch near his hand, and the wretched room became illuminated, revealing the two intruders.

He tried to speak, but his lips refused to articulate. The old man's tongue clave to the roof of his mouth.

He knew that his carefully-guarded secret was out!

Chapter Fifty One
Describes Another Surprise

"To what, pray, do I owe this intrusion?" demanded the old man fiercely, rising from his bed, and standing erect and defiant before them.

"To your own guilt, Mr Statham," was Max Barclay's quiet but distinct response.

"My guilt?" gasped the old man. "Of what crime am I guilty?"

"That's best known to yourself," answered the younger man. "But I think, now that we've investigated your house and discovered your death-trap, we will bid you good-night."

"You've—you've found it—eh?" gasped the old fellow, pale as death.

"Yes; and, furthermore, we know how Maud Petrovitch had cast your money at your feet, and defied you."

"I—I must explain," he cried, as in frantic eagerness he put on his clothes. "Don't leave me. Come below, and—and'll tell you."

The pair remained in the wretchedly uncomfortable room, while the old man finished dressing. Then all three descended, the millionaire walking first. They passed the door of the room where stood the coffin, and by touching a spring the iron door opened, and they descended to the library.

The noise wakened old Levi, who appeared at the head of the back stairs, full of surprise.

A reassuring word from his master, however, caused him to at once retire again.

Within the library old Sam switched on the light, and invited both his unwelcome visitors to be seated. Then, standing before them, he said:

"I presume, gentlemen, that your curiosity led you to break into my house?"

Max Barclay nodded.

"I can understand you acting thus, sir; but I cannot understand Rolfe, who knows me so well and who has served me so faithfully."

"And, in return, how have I been served?" asked Charlie, bitterly. "My poor sister has been turned adrift, and you have refused to lift a finger to reinstate her."

"I admit that on the face of it, Rolfe, I have been hard and cruel," declared the old man. "But when you know the truth you will not, perhaps, think so unkindly of me as at this moment."

The old fellow was perfectly calm. All his fear had vanished, and he now stood his old and usual self, full of quiet assurance.

"Well," Rolfe said, "perhaps you will tell us the truth. Why, for instance, did Maud Petrovitch visit you to-night?"

"She came upon her own initiative. She wished to ask me a question."

"Which you refused to answer."

"It was not judicious for me to tell her what she desized to know—not at present, at least."

"But now that we are here together, in confidence you will, no doubt, allow us to know where she and her father are in hiding," Charlie asked, breathlessly.

"Certainly, if you will promise not to communicate with them or call upon them without my consent."

"We promise," declared Max.

"Then they are living in strictest seclusion at Fordham Cottage, Arundel, in Sussex."

"But you have quarrelled with Maud?" Charlie remarked, at the same time remembering that closed coffin in the room above.

"Upon one point only—a very small and unimportant one," responded the old man.

"Where is my sister?"

"Unfortunately, I have no knowledge of where she is at present."

"But you have just assured me that when I know the truth I shall not regard you so harshly," Rolfe exclaimed.

"And I repeat it," Statham said.

The old man's attitude amazed them both. He was perfectly calm and quite unperturbed by the grim discoveries they had made.

"You mean that you refuse to tell me anything concerning my sister?" Charlie asked, seriously.

"For the present—yes."

"Why not now? Why forbid us also from seeking the Doctor and his daughter?"

"For reasons of my own. I am expecting a visitor."

Max laughed sarcastically. The reason put forward seemed too absurd.

"Ah! you don't believe it!" cried the old fellow. "But you will see. Your curiosity has, no doubt, led you to misjudge me. It was only to have been expected. I ought to have guarded my secret better."

Neither man spoke. Both had their eyes fixed upon the grey face of the old millionaire before them. They recollected his despair before he had retired to rest, and remembered, too, the tender care of his faithful Levi.

The clock chimed the half-hour—half-past three in the morning.

The night had been fraught by so many surprises that neither Charlie nor his friend could believe in the grim reality of it all. They never suspected that that fine mansion was practically unfurnished, or that its millionaire owner practically lived the life of a pauper. Had not Charlie been well aware of his master's shrewdness in his business and clearness in his financial operations, he would have believed it all due to an unbalanced brain. But there was no madness in Samuel Statham. He was as sane as they were. All his eccentricity was evidently directed towards one purpose.

As he stood there he practically told them so.

"You misjudge me!" said he, his grey face relaxing in a smile. "You think me mad—eh? Well, you are not alone in that. A good many people believe the same of me. I am gratified to think they believe it. It is my intention that they should."

"But, Mr Statham, we have asked you a question to which you have refused to answer. We wish to know what has become of Marion Rolfe."

"You were engaged to her—eh? Yes, I know," responded the old man. "For that very reason I refuse to tell you. I can only reassure you, however, that you need experience no anxiety."

"But I do. I love her!"

"Then I am very sorry, your mind must still continue to be exercised. At present I cannot tell you anything."

"Why?"

"Have I not already told you? I am expecting a visitor."

It was all the satisfaction they could obtain.

Charlie longed for an opportunity to refer to the gruesome object in that locked room upstairs. The man who had so suddenly reappeared and sworn vengeance upon the great financier was dead—fallen a victim, no doubt, to the old man's clever cunning. He had, without doubt, been enticed there to his death. The secret reason of the white-enamelled door at the top of the stairs was now quite plain. In that house was a terrible death-trap, as deadly as it was unexpected.

They held knowledge of the truth. How would the old man act?

Contrary to their expectations, he remained quite indifferent. He even offered them a drink, which they refused.

His refusal to tell them anything regarding Marion and his treatment of Maud had incensed them, and they both were bitterly antagonistic towards him. He was, no doubt, playing a huge game of bluff. His disregard of their discoveries was in order to lessen their importance, and his story of a visitor told to gain time.

Probably he intended to make good his escape.

Both were expecting every moment that his coolness would break down, and that he would suggest that they kept silence as to what lay concealed on the floor above.

Indeed, they were not mistaken, for of a sudden he turned to them, and in rather strained voice said:

"Now, gentlemen, I admit that you have discovered my secret; that my position is—well—a disagreeable one, to say the least. Is there any real reason why you should divulge it—at least for the present?"

Charlie shrugged his shoulders, and Max at the same time realised that a deadly fear was creeping back upon the old man, whose enormous wealth had stifled all human feeling from his soul.

"I merely ask your indulgence," said the old man, in a low, eager tone.

"For how long?"

"For a day—maybe for a week—or perhaps a month. I cannot tell."

"That means that we preserve the secret indefinitely?"

"Until the arrival of my visitor."

"Ah! the visitor!" repeated Max, with a grin of disbelief. "When do you expect the visit?"

"I have expected it during many months," was the millionaire's brief reply.

"And you can tell us nothing more? Is not your story a somewhat lame one?"

"Very—I quite admit it. But I can only assure you of its truth."

"It is not often you speak the truth, Mr Statham, is it?" asked Max, pointedly.

"I suppose I am like many another man," was his reply. "I only speak it when obliged!"

As he uttered those words there sounded in the hall the loud electric bell of the front door. It was rung twice, whereupon old Sam drew himself up in an instant in an attitude of alertness.

"The visitor!" he gasped, raising his bony finger. "The long-expected caller!"

The two rings were evidently a pre-arranged signal.

They heard old Levi shuffling outside. The door opened, and he stood expectant, looking at his master, but uttering no word.

"Gentlemen," exclaimed old Sam. "If you will permit me, I will go and receive my visitor. May I ask you to remain here until I return to you—return to answer any inquiries you may be pleased to put to me?"

The old fellow was quite calm again. He seemed to have braced himself up to meet his visitor, whoever he or she might be. It was one of his secret agents, Charlie thought, without a doubt.

Both men consented, and old Sam withdrew with Levi.

"Please remain here. I ask you both to respect my wishes," he said, and going out, closed the door behind him.

The two men listened with strained ears.

They heard the sound of footsteps outside, but as far as they could distinguish, no word was spoken. Whether the mysterious visitor was male or female they could not ascertain.

For several moments they stood at the door, listening.

Then Max, unable to resist his own curiosity, opened the door slightly, and peered into the hall.

But only Levi was there, his back turned towards the door. His master and his visitor had ascended the stairs together, passing the iron door which now stood open for the first time.

Max beckoned Charlie, who, looking outside into the hall, saw Levi standing with both hands pressed to his brow in an attitude of wildest despair.

His agitation was evidently for his master's safety.

A visitor at a quarter to four in the morning was unusual, to say the least. Who could it be?

Levi turned, and as he did so Max closed the door noiselessly, for he did not wish the faithful old servant to discover him as an eavesdropper.

Fully ten minutes elapsed, when of a sudden the sharp crack of a pistol-shot echoed through the empty upstairs rooms.

It caused both men to start, so unexpected was it.

For a second they hesitated; then opening the door, they both dashed up the forbidden stain.

Chapter Fifty Two
Contains a Complete Revelation

A complete surprise awaited them.

The door of the small room on the first floor stood open, and within the light was switched on.

Upon the threshold they both paused, dumbfounded by the scene before them.

Just as they had left it, the coffin stood upon its trestles, but lying on the floor beside was the body of the man whose name it bore upon its plate—the man Jean Adam!

In his nerveless grasp was a big service revolver, while the small round hole in his white temple told its own tale—a tale of sudden denunciation and of suicide.

The dead man wore evening-dress. On his white shirt-front was an ugly crimson splash, while his fast-glazing eyes, still open, stared blankly into space. At the opposite wall, leaning against it for support, was old Sam Statham, his countenance blanched, his jaw set, unable to utter a word.

The sudden unexpectedness of the tragedy had appalled him. He stood speechless. He could only point to the inanimate form upon the floor.

Max lifted the body and sought eagerly for signs of life. There were, however, none. The bullet had penetrated his brain, causing instant death.

Sam Statham's enemy—the man whom they had presumed was already in his coffin was dead! Yet what was the meaning of it all? The whole affair was a complete enigma. Why had Jean Adam, the adventurer who had lived by his wits for years and the hero of a thousand thrilling adventures, taken his own life beside his own coffin?

Rolfe and Barclay turned away from the gruesome scene, and in silence descended the stairs, where, standing back in the shadow, trembling like an aspen, stood old Levi.

As they passed down, the servant entered the room to join his master, with whispered words of awe.

Then, at the millionaire's suggestion, when he descended to them five minutes later, Charlie went forth into Park Lane, and, walking hastily towards the fountain, found a constable, whom he informed of the tragedy.

As he went back to the house with the policeman at his side, he wondered whether, after all, he had not misjudged old Sam. In any case, there was a great and complete mystery which must now be elucidated.

Just outside the little old town of Arundel in rural Sussex at the top of the steep hill which leads on to the high road to Chichester, a road rendered dusty in summer and muddy in winter by the constant succession of motor cars which tear along it, stands Fordham Cottage, a small unpretentious redbrick house, surrounded by a pretty garden, and divided from the road by a high old wall clothed completely by ivy.

It was three o'clock in the afternoon.

Within the neat old-fashioned front parlour—for the owners of the house were two prim maiden ladies—stood Rolfe and Barclay, together with the grey-haired, grey-bearded man who, having rented the place furnished, was living there in complete seclusion—Doctor Michael Petrovitch.

They were in earnest conversation, but Charlie kept his eyes upon the window, as though in expectation of the arrival of someone. The autumn day was fine and dry, and Maud, returning from London by the first train, which had arrived at half-past six that morning, had, after luncheon, gone out upon her cycle as was her daily habit.

Her lover, anxious and impatient, scarcely heeded what the Doctor was explaining to Max.

For the past hour both men had been describing in brief what had occurred since the ex-Minister's disappearance from Cromwell Road, relating practically what has already been chronicled in the preceding chapters. They had told him of Adam's threats, of the warning given to Charlie by Lorena Lyle, of Adam's endeavour to entice Max to Constantinople and of Statham's evident terror of Adam's vengeance. To it all the grave grey-bearded statesman had listened attentively.

Only when they described their secret visit to the house in Park Lane, and the extraordinary discoveries they had made there, did their hearer evince surprise. Then, knitting his brows, he nodded as though he understood. And when they told him of Adam's suicide, he drew a deep breath of apparent relief.

"That man," he said, in a low, distinct voice, with scarce a trace of accent—"that man was my enemy, as well as Statham's. It was he who, in order to further his speculative financial schemes, paid an assassin to throw a bomb at my carriage—the bomb that killed the poor little child! He was an adventurer who had filched money from widows and orphans—a scoundrel, and an assassin. The assassin, when in the fortress at Belgrade, confessed to the identity of his employer. But in the meantime he disappeared—to South America, it is believed. Prior to the attempt upon me, Lyle, the mining engineer, was his cat's-paw, as he has ever since been—a good fellow at heart, but weak and at the same time adventurous. Once or twice they made big profits out of concessions for copper mining obtained from my predecessor in office. When Adam found that I refused to participate in business that was a fraud upon the public in Paris and London, he plotted to get rid of me. Fortunately he did not succeed; but when the truth was exposed to the Servian Government that he was the real assassin, certain valuable concessions were at once withdrawn from him, and he was thereby ruined. He vowed vengeance upon me, and also upon Statham—to whom the concessions had been transferred—a terrible vengeance. But soon afterwards he disappeared, and we heard, upon what seemed to be good authority, that he was dead. He had been shot in a drunken brawl in Caracas."

"And then he suddenly turned up again—eh?" Max remarked.

"Yes; and for that reason Mr Statham suggested that I and my daughter Maud should disappear to some place to which he could not trace us. Statham defied his threats, but at the same time thought that if we disappeared in such a manner that the police would not seek us, it would be a wise step. For that reason I arranged that the furniture, as well as ourselves, should disappear, in order to make it appear that we had suddenly removed, and also to prevent the police searching too inquisitively for 'missing persons.' Had they done this, our hiding-place would soon have been discovered. I disappeared more for Maud's sake, than for my own. I knew the desperate character of the man, and the mad vengeance within his villainous heart."

"But Statham also feared him," remarked Charlie, recollecting the occasion when his employer had betrayed such terror.

"Yes. The exact facts I do not know. He will tell you himself," answered the ex-Minister.

"Maud was in London last night, and called upon Statham," Max remarked.

"She called in secret lest she might be seen and followed by Adam," her father replied. "She went there to return to Statham a sum of money he had sent her."

"For what?"

"He wished to know the whereabouts of Lorena Lyle, who had been her schoolfellow in Belgrade. Statham, I fear, intended, in some way, to avenge himself upon Lyle—and on his daughter more especially—on account of his association with his enemy. The girl is in London, and he wished to know where she was living."

"And the money which she returned was given her in order, to induce her to divulge?"

The Doctor nodded in the affirmative, adding:

"You see that Statham, surrounded by unscrupulous enemies as he has been, was bound to act always for his own protection. He has been misjudged—by you—by everybody. I, who know him more intimately, perhaps, than anyone save his own brother Levi, assure you that it is so."

"His brother Levi!" cried Charlie.

"Of course, Levi, who poses as his servant, is his brother. They have been inseparable always, from the early days when Sam Statham was a mining prospector and concession-hunter—the days before fortune smiled upon the three Statham brothers, and they were able to open the doors of the offices in Old Broad Street. The romance of old Sam's life is the romance of the great firm."

"He treated my sister badly," declared Charlie. "For that I can never forgive him."

"No; there you are wrong. It is true that he would not allow her to be reinstated at Cunnington's, and, on the face of it, treated her unjustly. But he had a motive. True, she refused to betray to him something which my daughter had told her in confidence. For that refusal he allowed her to be dismissed from her situation; but on the following day he sent her down to me here to remain in concealment."

"Why?"

"Because of that man Adam. He had been attracted by her good looks, and had begun to pester her with his attentions. Statham knew this from the report of one who had watched her in secret. Therefore, by sending her here into hiding, he was acting in her best interests."

"Then she is here?" cried Max, anxiously, his face suddenly brightening.

"Yes. See! here she comes—with Maud!" and as both men turned quickly to the window they saw the two laughing girls, flushed by their ride, wheeling their cycles up the path from the road.

Next moment both men dashed outside, and both girls, utterly amazed and breathless, found themselves suddenly in the arms of their lovers.

The Doctor looked on, smiling, and in silence. He saw the lips of both girls covered with the hot fervent kisses of good and honest men. He heard their whispered words, and then he turned away.

Those long black days of suspicion and despair were at an end. The mystery of it all was now being rapidly solved, and both girls within that little parlour wept tears of joy upon the shoulders of the men whom they had chosen as their husbands.

The happiness of four young hearts was complete. The grim shadow had lifted, and upon them now fell at last the bright sunshine of life and of love.

The self-effacement of that little household was at an end. Freed from the bondage of silence, the truth was at last told. Maud, with her own lips, explained to Charlie the confession she had made to Marion on the night of their disappearance. She had told her how the man Adam, whom she had known in Belgrade, had followed her several times in the neighbourhood of Earl's Court, had spoken to her, and had declared his love for her. She never suspected that he had been her father's enemy—the man who had been the instigator of the dastardly outrage—until on the previous evening, her father had, in confidence, told her the truth, and added that, because of his re-appearance, they had to fly. She dared not tell him they had met, but she had made Marion her confidante. It was the story of the bomb outrage that had held Marion horrified.

Charlie, when he had listened open-mouthed to the explanation of his well-beloved, cried:

"The assassin! And he dared to speak to you of love!"

"He is dead, dearest," answered the girl, quietly stroking his hair from his brow. "Let us forgive him—and forget." For answer he took her again in his arms, and kissed her tenderly upon the lips.

Three days later.

The coroner's jury had returned a verdict of "suicide while of unsound mind," and the body of Jean Adam had, with the undertaker's assistance, been buried in Highgate Cemetery in the actual coffin which had been so long prepared for him. It was surely a weird revenge of old Sam's.

But the whole occurrence was a grim and terrible repayment of an old debt.

In the fading twilight of the wet and gloomy day on which the dead man's body was, without a single follower, committed to the grave, Rolfe and Barclay were seated with the millionaire in the familiar library in Park Lane.

Old Sam had been making explanations similar to those made by the Doctor down at Arundel. Suddenly he said, looking from one to the other:

"And now I have to apologise to you both. In arranging the disappearance of my dear friend the Doctor, I contrived to mislead you, in order to add mystery to the occurrence. I knew, Rolfe, you lost your train at Charing Cross that night; that you did not wish to be seen off by your sister Marion because you had—in my interests—quarrelled with Adam and had made murderous threats against him—perhaps unwisely. These threats, however, you believed Adam had told to Barclay, hence your fear of the last-named later on. I arranged that a man should be present at Cromwell Road in clothes resembling your own, that a garment should be placed in the house with a bloodstain upon it, and that the doctor's safe should be blown open as though thieves had visited the place after the removal of the furniture. I knew from the Doctor that you, Barclay, would go there that evening, and my object was to puzzle and mislead you, at the same time believing that, having suspicions of your friend Rolfe, you would not go to the police. Again, in order to test Rolfe's devotion to myself, I suggested that the honour of the woman he loved, if sacrificed, could save me. I made this suggestion in order to put Rolfe off the scent."

"Then it was all your own doing?" Max cried, in surprise.

"Entirely," was the old man's response. "In the interests of myself, as well as of both of you. Adam believed that you were aware of his secret intentions, therefore he was plotting to entice you to Turkey—a country where you might have disappeared with ease. That was undoubtedly his object."

For a few moments he paused; then, clearing his throat, the old man said, in a distinct voice:

"The other night you were no doubt both surprised to find my drawing-room transposed into the interior of a Russian house. Well, it was done with a distinct purpose—to defeat my enemy. He, with his friend and accomplice Lyle, had made a false charge against me—a charge supported by the perjured evidence of the hunchback—a charge of having in the old days, years ago, murdered a woman—the woman who was my wife."

A shadow of pain crossed the old man's brow at what seemed a bitter remembrance. Then, after a moment's pause, he went on:

"She was worthless! Ah! yes, I admit that. But I swear I am innocent of the charge they brought against me. She was killed in Caracas in a brutal manner, but by whom I could never discover. After her death I left South America. Adam and his friend dropped their foul charge against me, and I lost sight of them for years. Later on, I was prospecting in the Timan Mountains, in Northern Russia, within the Arctic Circle, a wild snow-covered country outside the edge of civilisation. Both gold and emeralds had been discovered along the Ishma Valley, and there had been a rush there. Among the many adventurous spirits attracted thither was Jean Adam, with his attendant *alter ego* Lyle. We met again. It was in winter, and we were in a state of semi-starvation, all three of us. Not a word was said regarding the charge they had made against me. Both were without means, and both down on their luck. For a fortnight we remained together, then, finding things hopeless resolved to struggle back to civilisation at the nearest little Russian village, a miserable little place called Ust Ussa, four hundred and fifty versts south. On the way we all three nearly succumbed to the intense cold and want of food. At last, however, late one night we came across a lonely house in a clearing in the pine forest on the outskirts of the village which was our goal. Sinking with fatigue, we begged shelter of the white-bearded old man who lived there. He took us in, gave us food, and allowed us to sleep. I was drowsy and slept heavily. It was late when I awoke—when I awoke to find lying beside the table opposite me the old man stone dead, stabbed to the heart! The place had been ransacked; the old man's hoard of money—for there are no banks there—had been found, and my two companions were missing. They had gone—no one knew whither! What could I do? To remain, would mean to be accused of the crime, and probably sent to Siberia. Well, I reflected for a moment. Then I took some food, stole out, and made my way again into the snow-covered wilderness. Ah! the recollection of it all is still upon me, though years have since elapsed."

"And then?" asked Max, when he found tongue.

"Since then I and my brothers Levi and Ben have abandoned the old life, but I have ever since been determined to avenge the brutal murder of that poor old peasant. I made a vow not to enjoy the luxuries which my money brought me until my conscience had been cleared and the assassin brought to justice. Hence, I have lived in the desolation attendant upon pauperism. I have been the Pauper of Park Lane. Seven years ago I sent an agent to the place, and purchased all the interior of the house. Then, when I came to live here, I had the drawing-room fitted as you see it, and have since awaited my opportunity. The other night, as you know, Jean Adam came to renew his false charge against me, and I took him upstairs and ushered him suddenly into the scene of his crime. Ah! his terror was horrible to witness: he trembled from head to foot. He saw the hangman's rope around his neck. Then I took him into the next room, and showed him in silence what I had prepared for him. He read his own name inscribed there, and with a curse upon his lips, drew his revolver and put an end to his life."

Both his hearers remained in silence. It had surely been a just vengeance—blood for blood!

A year has now passed.

Marion is now the wife of Max Barclay, and the pair spend the greater part of their time at the beautiful old castle Kilmaronock, up in Perthshire, for in her perfect happiness she prefers a healthy out-door life to that of London.

Rolfe, who is still confidential secretary to Mr Samuel Statham, has married Maud, and has abandoned his bachelor chambers in Jermyn Street for a pretty little house in Curzon Street, where he is quite near to the mansion in Park Lane.

Doctor Petrovitch has returned to Servia at the invitation of the King, and is expected every day to accept the portfolio of Prime Minister. Old Duncan Macgregor has been promoted to be general manager of the great Clyde and Motherwell Locomotive Works; while Levi acts as servant to his brother, their secret still being kept, and the position of Statham Brothers in the City is to-day higher than it has ever been.

As regards the Park Lane mansion, with the red-striped sun-blinds — the house you know well, without doubt — there is now no further mystery concerning it. The rumours regarding its beautiful interior, and the sounds of piano-playing were all of course, the outcome of gossip. The truth, however, is now common knowledge, and society during the past nine months or so has been amazed to see painters, decorators, and upholsterers so busily at work. It is evident that old Sam intends to entertain largely during this coming season.

The house is now exquisitely furnished from top to bottom. He no longer sleeps on his little camp bed, or dines off a chump chop cooked over a gas-stove by old Levi. The dark shadow has now been lifted from his life.

In fact, he no longer lives in the squalor of an empty house as "The Pauper of Park Lane."